Jodie Sinclair began writing after a long illness. She is married with two grown up children and a grandson. Her jobs have included debt collecting, psychiatric nursing, clerking for book-makers at various racecourses and working for tour operators. She now writes full time.

She has returned to live in Cornwall where she was born but also divides her time between Berkshire and Plymouth, where she and her husband also have other homes.

An avid reader herself, Jodie Sinclair also writes crime novels under another name.

Dangerous Games

Jodie Sinclair

PIATKUS

First published in Great Britain in 1997 by
Judy Piatkus (Publishers) Ltd of
5 Windmill Street, London W1

This edition published 1998

**The moral right of the author
has been asserted**

A catalogue record for this book
is available from the British Library

ISBN 0 7499 3034 8 (pbk)

Set in Times by
Intype, London Ltd

Printed and bound in Great Britain by
Mackays of Chatham PLC, Chatham, Kent

For Kate Brinton who, whilst at the *Slough Observer*, inspired this novel.

The author much appreciates the help given by
Val Bootle of the *Maidenhead Advertiser*
in her research for this novel.

Chapter 1

It was now or never; the culmination of a lifetime's ambition, or bitter disappointment. Kathryn tried not to think about it. Instead, she sat in the coffee shop of the Thames Riviera Hotel and observed the other customers. Some were guests staying at the hotel, alongside couples who were thirsty after walking and one or two, like herself, who were waiting for someone. It was 2.50 p.m. She took several deep breaths.

Between the wars, Maidenhead was *the* place to visit at weekends. The affluent would motor down from London in their crank-started, open-top cars and spend afternoons on the river before taking tea at the Thames Riviera.

It was different now. The affluent went elsewhere. Kathryn did not know whether this was because there was nothing left of the market town but office blocks, or if it had become that way because the wealthy had abandoned it for other pleasures.

The town had undoubtedly changed; the Hotel had not. The staff were polite and wore smiles as well as uniforms, and the waiters in the elegant dining room which over-looked the river were French and quietly efficient. The place retained an aura of gentility and style as if it were simply biding its time until the Twenties' flappers and those who were born to money – rather than those who had to earn it – returned.

Kathryn turned slightly in her seat, feeling her tension mounting. She did not want to be able to see the clock on the wall. The minute hand was laboriously advancing

1

towards the hour, but she knew that once three o'clock had come and gone, time would speed up again.

The irony of the situation struck her, and the waiter with the pony-tail and nice teeth caught her fleeting smile and grinned back as he passed her table with a loaded tray.

From where she sat she had an unimpeded view of the glass entrance doors through which Miss Megan Morris, bestselling but reclusive author, was supposed to appear miraculously. Kathryn's self-imposed mission, as a keen young reporter on the *Thames Valley Echo*, was to uncover the identity of the author – a feat no one else had ever managed to pull off. 'The scoop of the century', she thought feverishly to herself, and could scarcely believe that the other woman, whom she had approached via her London publisher, had contacted the paper to say that she would meet Kathryn here, *now* . . .

Kathryn looked up. The coffee shop was at the front of the Hotel, divided from the foyer by a wrought-iron balustrade. The glass doors were constantly opening and closing as the place filled up. It was ten past three and the tea in the pot had cooled. *Megan Morris wasn't coming.* She had known that, of course, even if she would not allow herself to admit it. The whole thing had simply been too good to be true.

The waiter was busy. He moved quickly to and fro with new orders or dirty crockery. Kathryn hoped to catch his eye the next time he returned from the kitchen. One more cup of tea and she'd go home to Alex, and the pain of his betrayal.

The glass doors swung open again. Several businessmen, loud with lunchtime beer, passed close by. Behind them was a woman. She had a good figure and reddish-brown hair. 'Graceful' was the word which Kathryn thought described her best. Her clothes seemed to flow with her movements as if they were an extension of her body. She hesitated, took a few steps across the chequered tile floor and stared straight at Kathryn. 'Do you mind if I join you?' she asked. 'I'm afraid there's nowhere else.'

'No. Please do.' It was twenty past three and for a split second she had harboured foolish hopes.

2

'I'm meeting a friend,' the woman explained. 'I thought at first you were her. Ridiculous really, I'm so short-sighted but too vain to wear my glasses unless I have to.' She signalled and caught the waiter's eye and ordered coffee.

'Madam?' The pony-tail swung as he turned to Kathryn.

'Yes. I'll have some more tea, please.' There was no hurry; she wasn't expected back at the office that afternoon and she had no article to write now. So much had already been written about Megan Morris, most of it speculative, some of it undoubtedly untrue, but the publishers remained silent. Nothing was ever acceded or repudiated. At some stage she would have to face the jibes of Keith and Dave, fellow reporters who shared her office, but not today.

'If you're expecting someone I can take my coffee through to the lounge.' The woman indicated the briefcase on the floor beside Kathryn's chair.

'I was. Sort of. They're obviously not coming.'

'I'm sorry. It's not very businesslike of them. Are you in selling, by any chance?'

'No. I'm a journalist. It happens occasionally.' Kathryn shrugged as if her disappointment was minimal.

'Really? Was it anybody famous?'

'Oh no, nothing like that.'

The woman glanced over her shoulder as she felt the draught from the opening doors. The glass reflected the weak April sun which was making a brief appearance between showers. Outside, traffic was queuing at the round-about on the bridge. The specious normality of other people's lives made Kathryn feel like crying.

'Looks as if I've been stood up, too. Unless my friend's been delayed somewhere.' The woman reached into her bag and pulled out a packet of cigarettes. 'Do you smoke? I believe it's an occupational hazard in journalism.' Kathryn shook her head. 'It must be an interesting job.'

'It is. I can't imagine doing anything else.'

'What's your name?'

'Kathryn Brooks.'

'Good heavens, you write that weekly column. It's contro-versial stuff for a local paper. I'm very pleased to meet you.'

3

She extended a hand across the stainless steel pots. Her grip was firm.

'And you are?' There was something odd about the woman, as if she was on edge. Perhaps it was a lover, not a friend, she had come to meet.

'Sorry, didn't I say? Jenny – Jenny Branagh.'

The slight hesitation indicated that Kathryn might be right. Jenny Branagh was wearing a wedding ring and, as Kathryn knew, adultery was not rare. The girl did not want to be a party to it. She drank one cup of the Earl Grey whilst they made a few remarks about the weather then went to the desk to pay her bill. 'Goodbye,' she said coolly on her way out.

She had parked at the back of the hotel, facing the Thames which was high with weeks of rain. An oily grey torrent turned into white spume as it gushed over the weir. Leaden clouds drifted nearer and a few spots of rain hit the windscreen. In the distance was a rainbow. By the time she had pulled out of the car park, large drops were hammering on the roof and a small cascade of water ran down the windows each time she braked.

Life goes on, she thought, heading towards Waitrose. They still had to eat. She extracted a trolley from the line outside the automatic doors and cursed life in general and herself. How stupid she had been to imagine Miss Morris would turn up to give an interview to a local paper! As the arrangement had been made by telephone it seemed likely that Keith or Dave or both were playing a cruel joke.

While selecting the items she needed, Kathryn thought of the most popular theories for the mystery surrounding the author's identity. Megan Morris was a recluse, some said, or she was so badly disfigured she would not appear in public. Others believed it was a clever form of hype which guaranteed column space. Bitterly, Kathryn decided she favoured the latter.

Clutching her bags she hurried back to the car. Backing out of her parking space she grazed the wing mirror of the vehicle beside her. She had to control her agitation if there was not to be another row with Alex.

Driving home along the A4 she was against the flow of

4

traffic which was pouring off the motorway. If she succeeded in obtaining a post with one of the nationals she, too, would have to commute. It was a disadvantage, but one she would readily accept. At the moment, their flat in Burnham was convenient for them both as Alex's boat-building company was situated on the Thames nearby.

Without taking off her raincoat Kathryn unpacked the shopping and filled the kettle. She kicked off her shoes and left them under the kitchen table. She had lost a couple of pounds recently; the shoes had become looser and rubbed her heels. Her body was firm and rounded, and although she had never given it much thought, she suddenly wanted to be thin like Rebecca, the girl with whom her husband Alex had recently had an affair.

Taking her coffee into the bedroom, Kathryn sat in front of the dressing-table and studied her face objectively. Nice eyes, brown with a slight upward slant, an average nose and well-defined mouth which she thought was too wide. The indentation in her chin added to her attractiveness and the angle of her jaw suggested determination, or what Alex called stubbornness. But Alex said a lot of things, some of them hurtful.

She took off her mac and flung it on the bed, not caring that it was damp. Her dark hair, parted on one side, was almost shoulder-length. She leaned forward, took it in both hands and twisted it behind her head. For no real reason, pinning it up made her feel better. She could do so now that the straggly ends from a too-short cut had grown out.

Kathryn went through to the lounge – a long, rectangular room with windows on two sides. It was always light in there, even in winter. A car pulled up outside the block of flats and its door slammed. She looked down. It wasn't Alex. Beneath her, shrubs gleamed wetly. Too late in the day the sun had reappeared and there was a warm glow on the horizon.

Jenny Branagh. Should the name mean something? Kathryn paced the length of the room. Or was her strangeness a sign of guilt? On the table next to the reading lamp was Megan Morris's latest novel which Kathryn had already read but now opened again to stop herself from thinking of the alternative – that the auburn-haired woman had been Miss Morris.

The dust-jacket was striking, completely subtle in muted shades of grey and blue. The blurb was on the front flap, and on the back one were some personal details. But there was no photograph; there never was.

Megan Morris is considered to be one of Britain's finest modern novelists, the text said. *She has ten books to her credit and two of them,* Homecoming *and* Aftermath, *have recently been adapted for television.*

A graduate of Oxford, Miss Morris initially worked in publishing before turning to full-time writing herself.
She works from her riverside home where the upkeep of her garden is her main hobby.

Megan Morris is a pseudonym.

Kathryn replaced the book on the table. It gave nothing away, not even the name of her college or the subject of her degree. The university would have no record of a student of that name and must already have been questioned extensively. Riverside home . . . Had Jenny Branagh arrived on foot? Kathryn thought so but put it down to wishful thinking because Alex was not yet home. There was something else, something the woman had said, but it was an indication of Kathryn's state of mind that she could not recall it.

'Oh, come on, Alex,' she muttered, unable to relax until she knew what sort of evening was in store. There were times when depression threatened and this was one of them. She accepted that she was not easy to live with, that she was single-minded when it came to work, but Alex had his faults. It was eight-thirty before he came home.

'You're late. Who was she this time?' The accusation was flung at him without thought and Kathryn hated herself for making it. So many of the things she came out with lately were said because she felt continually on the defensive.

'Please don't start, Kath, I've had a hard day.'

They studied each other, assessing how far they could go, what it would take to avert an argument and the hostile atmosphere which would follow. Alex sighed and sank into the settee. There were tired lines around his eyes and Kathryn sensed he had been nowhere other than his office.

Part of the problem was that Alex was not duplicitous and had therefore used her as his confessional when she could have coped better with doubt. The paradox was that he loved her but she could not bear it when he accused her of putting a distance between them, of driving him away because her job, her ambitions came before everything. She could not bear it because she suspected he was right. All she wanted was to return to the time when they had understood one another and made each other laugh. Alex did look haggard. He was in the process of finalising a big order. Perhaps the deal had fallen through.

Kathryn stood beside him, unsure how to form an apology but it was Alex who made the first move. He held out his hand and pulled her down beside him.

'I'm sorry,' she said. 'I had a bad day too.' At moments like this she thought they probably deserved each other.

'Ah, the famous Megan Morris. She didn't—' He stopped. It was clear that Kathryn had expected the woman to show up. She had ambitions he tried not to thwart, but seeking the identity of whoever was writing these best-selling books was only going to lead to disappointment and Alex could not bear to see any more unhappiness on his wife's face after what he had put her through. 'I should've rung,' he apologised. 'It was thoughtless of me. The damned specifications of that cruiser were wrong. Sometimes I wonder if it wouldn't be easier to do everything myself. Anyway, want to tell me what happened?'

Kathryn did so. Alex suppressed a smile; she wasn't going to let this go. Madness, maybe, but perhaps also a kind of therapy. Aware of how carefully he needed to tread he said none of the things which sprang to mind. Nor did he point out that if the national newspapers, with their vast resources, could not track her down, Kathryn's chances were less than nil.

Later, as they ate a meal in relative harmony, she reminded him she was going away the following week. 'I'm really looking forward to it – it's ages since I've had more than a day with Helena.'

'I hadn't forgotten.' But Alex was wondering whether her

pleasure was due more to the idea of being away from him for a week rather than the actual visit.

It took John Atherton almost a year to readjust to the British way of life. He had been absent for ten years and his outlook had changed. Around the time of his divorce, his teaching contract expired and he had not bothered to renew it. There were no regrets; there was nothing left in the States for him now.

As highly qualified as he was, he had been surprised to learn that lecturing posts back in Britain were hard to come by. He had finally been offered one at Cardiff University, one which he fully intended to be temporary, although he did not mention this at the interviews. To start with, he had rented a terraced house on a short tenancy, but rumours of the family money and his job in the States had already circulated and he found he was considered to be a glamorous figure amongst some of the more staid of his colleagues. He was back in the limelight and was enjoying it. On the spur of the moment he purchased an ugly Victorian dwelling which had caught his eye in an estate agent's window. It had what they called 'possibilities'. John knew that there was little chance of these possibilities becoming reality; the planning would take effort and he could not bear the disruption of workmen all over the house. Once he was settled in he hardly noticed the small inconveniences.

There was a vast bathroom, a fair-sized kitchen, four bedrooms, a dining room and what the estate agents described as a drawing room. All were in need of decoration. John could cope with that, but he had no intention of having a new bathroom suite or fitted cupboards in the kitchen. A sensible woman from the Welsh Language faculty recommended a man who was good but, more importantly, worked fast. With white and pastel shades of paint, one room at a time was transformed from dreary to airy. The same lady helped him choose curtains and bedding, for which service he showed his gratitude by presenting her with an enormous bouquet. The stammering thanks he received made him wonder if she had got the wrong impression. He avoided her for several days.

He planned to entertain, visualising like-minded people sharing good food and wine and conversation, but he had not yet worked out how the food was to appear. There was more to living alone than he had imagined. His student days did not count, he had never really been alone, there had always been someone to cater to his needs.

Towards the end of the first term he began to relax and to notice that during lectures and tutorials the students were quieter and more accepting than their American counterparts. His methods of tuition needed some modification – which John found a challenge. He had become stale over the past couple of years. But he was still lacking a social life.

He advertised for someone to do his cleaning. Luck was with him: a capable woman called Sheila Roberts said she could both clean and cook. John invited a small group of students to dinner. They would be grateful for a free meal and couldn't afford to be fussy, and he would be able to test the veracity of Sheila's claim. He was not disappointed.

Over Christmas he received several invitations to parties and one for lunch on the twenty-fifth which turned out to be dull. It was a family occasion, the house full of children and the drinks in short supply, but it got him through a period when he might have lapsed into self-pity.

One freezing January evening when he had been back at work for several days, John was having a drink with a colleague who politely asked if he had settled in. It came as a shock to realise that the answer was yes and that he no longer felt he wanted to move on. He liked the university and the city. He also liked the interest he aroused amongst staff and students. It was a pity his parents showed so little. Being unsure of his welcome he had written to inform them of his plans. The reply from his mother contained the usual pleasantries about his health and his employment, but they were formally phrased. She might have been writing to a maiden aunt. After he had thought about it John's aggrievement evaporated. They no longer had anything in common. The Athertons were proud, and their son's lack of communication over the past decade rankled and they wanted him to know that. The final paragraph made it quite clear. *'We wish you all the best for the future. Love, Mother.'* There was no mention of a visit.

He had not expected the fatted calf but he sensed he was no longer regarded as part of the family. Charles had always been the favourite, of course. He had wisely married a girl from the same background who regularly took the children to see their grandparents. John knew that his cynicism was a mask for his envy. Charles was happy and he was not and he did not know why that should be. His own life was virtually a cliché – public school, Oxford, a prestigious job, money, health and, judging from the attention he still received from women, his good looks had not totally faded. He lacked for nothing except whatever it took to dispel the dissatisfaction which accompanied almost everything he did. There was more time to ruminate now that Angela was not around to organise his life. He had never had to fight for anything yet; on the other hand, his need to be liked had turned him into a caricature. He suspected he was still trying to win his parents' approval but with the contrariness of his nature refused to play the dutiful son.

The bitter frosts of winter were behind him and, as spring flowers blossomed so did John's social life, thanks to the advent of Sheila. He was a natural host and was not afraid to mix students with staff or the staid with the charismatic. His invitations were returned and he met people unconnected with the university. But still there was something missing. It was the element of danger. Yes, he could cause outrage amongst his colleagues and flirt with professors' wives, but the feeling of living on a knife's edge had deserted him. Stagnation was leading to boredom and he knew that he would soon have to remedy that, as he had done in his Oxford days.

Danger and Oxford. The words were synonymous. It was a long time since he had thought of those times. He poured another drink and indulged himself.

There had been five of them, a closely-knit group, impenetrable until they had allowed Jenny admission; Jenny, so like Sarah to look at but so different in other ways. With youthful optimism they had believed they were bound together for ever, but their shared knowledge had later severed the bonds.

It was at Oxford that he had learned to use his wit and his looks to draw people to him, to manipulate them. It was a game he played to amuse himself. But for this he despised both the people involved *and* himself, yet was incapable of dropping the act. It was useless to expect to be liked now for what he was because he no longer knew himself.

Oxford seemed light years away and a time best forgotten, but since his return John had felt an urge to renew contact. It would be entertaining, and dangerous, for the group to get together again.

The Easter break was approaching, and as there were no signs of reconciliation as far as his parents were concerned, he would be at a loss. Suddenly he grinned. Why not? he thought. Why not go to London and look the old crowd up? It would be interesting and amusing to see how they had fared, to see if the past had left any scars.

It still seemed like a good idea in the morning although his drink-induced plans frequently appeared insane in the light of day. In the large bathroom with its black and white tiled floor and clawed enamel bath with which he would not part, he inspected his tongue in the mirror. Angela had objected to the amount he drank but Angela was no longer around to curb him. He could smell his own breath. It was rancid. He cleaned his teeth and swilled undiluted mouthwash around his gums, the strong mint taste a welcome relief from stale whisky.

How would his old friends receive him? And did he care? ' "They will more easily fall victim to a big lie than a small one",' he told his reflection as he roughly quoted Hitler and lathered his face with shaving foam. Some of the bristles were ginger, he noticed. Strange, as his hair was dark. He had lost his train of thought. What had Hitler to do with anything? He ought to cut down on the drinking. Ah yes, the big lie, the one they had all fallen for at the time: the police, the press, everyone. As a group they had stuck together. They had concocted a story, an alibi, and no one had suspected a thing. That was seventeen years ago, and in all that time he had heard from no one except Laura who had written once or twice in the early days. Then came that final postcard with its innocuous picture of the Changing of the Guard sent to him in America. '*I know, John*' had been the cryptic message above the scrawl of her signature. It had been posted in London, at Paddington, but there had been no address to which to write back.

John shivered, his bare feet cold on the stone tiles. He rinsed his face and dried it, wondering why lectures were ever scheduled for nine o'clock when no one was at their best, least of all himself, and many of the students opted to stay in bed rather than attend. He dressed and combed his hair which was wiry and thick and longer than he used to wear it, then set off on foot to the campus which was only a short distance from where he lived.

Laura Tennyson strolled home along the tow-path, stopping to watch the boats in the lock. She had no coat which was silly because more rain had been forecast. As the dark clouds banked up over the Thames, she hastened her footsteps. Intermittent drops spotted the tarmac before falling faster. In the few minutes it took her to reach her house, her hair and shoulders were saturated. She let herself in and closed the door, leaning back against the smooth wood. There was the smell of the furniture polish which her cleaner Peggy had used earlier. 'What have I done?' she whispered to the empty house. 'What on earth have I done?'

Shaking and weak-kneed she went to the kitchen and filled the kettle before deciding she needed a proper drink. There was tonic water in the fridge which she added to a measure of gin. She draped her sodden jacket over the back of a chair and pulled on a cardigan which hung inside the laundry-room door. Carefully she carried her drink across the wood-block hall and into the lounge.

The house was far too big for one person but that did not bother Laura. She required space, physically as well as mentally, to combat the claustrophobia of her fears.

The lounge ran the depth of the house and had once been two rooms. There was a telephone on the table near the tall windows at the back which opened onto the garden. Twice she picked up the receiver before she was able to dial her publisher's number. 'Giles,' she said, 'I think I've done something incredibly stupid.' It was his private line, only to be used in an emergency.

'Don't tell me you went, Laura. Surely you didn't speak to that girl?'

'Yes. Not an interview, nothing like that. We just chatted. It's all right, she doesn't have a clue who I am.' There was a disbelieving grunt followed by silence. Laura took a deep breath. 'It wasn't that. You see, the thing is, I told her my name was Jenny Branagh. It was the first thing which came into my head.' It was a name which was always in her head. Giles did not know that, but there were a lot of other things Giles did not know. Laura listened to the continued silence at the end of the line.

'You realise what you may have done,' Giles finally said, speaking slowly as if he were dealing with an idiot. 'My God, Laura, that was a reporter, not some gullible woman out for afternoon tea!'

'Yes, but it's only a local paper. And she won't seriously have been expecting me.' Laura had rung him for reassurance but found she was having to defend herself. She did not believe what she had just said any more than Giles did.

'You told me she was good. If so, then she'll have her suspicions.'

Kathryn Brooks *was* good, Laura knew that. She was better than good and would go a long way.

'What did you talk about?'

'Her job. The weather. She didn't stay long and I'd invented a friend.'

'You're unreal, Laura. Why did you go through with it? I didn't think for one moment you meant it when you said you would go ahead and arrange it.'

'What *did* you think?'

'At worst that you'd developed a warped sense of humour. I was crazy to go along with it. And why, when you've got more imagination than anyone I know, call yourself Jenny Branagh?'

'Oh, forget it, Giles. I'm sorry I rang. Take my word for

13

it, she doesn't suspect a thing. Anyway, nothing's going to happen – you're overreacting.'

'If you're so sure of that, why ring me at all? Why try to convince me you're so bloody unconcerned? Christ, woman, think of the possible consequences!'

'For an atheist you mention the Almighty rather a lot.' Laura slammed the phone down, hoping she had damaged his ear-drum. It was herself she was angry with rather than Giles, and she was more worried than she had allowed him to believe.

A long bath and a second drink failed to calm her. She tried to take refuge from her fears in the usual way, by working, but for once it failed to provide a distraction. No amount of analysis brought her any nearer to discovering her reasons for deciding to respond to Kathryn Brooks in the first place, let alone turn up. Although her identity would remain a secret, Giles always informed her of requests for interviews. Laura admired Kathryn Brooks's writing but it was not curiosity which had taken her to the Thames Riviera. A small rebellion after all the years of secrecy? Surely not, it was far too risky. Perhaps she had been trying to prove that her disguise was impregnable and that she was finally safe.

When her writing career began, it had not seemed possible she would become such a success – therefore the lack of biographical material was irrelevant. No one, not even Giles, knew how she had come by her pseudonym. But her intentions had backfired. The mystery surrounding her had added to public interest instead of shielding her from it.

At ten-thirty she swallowed a sleeping tablet and read until the words began to blur. She slept, shallowly and restlessly until the old nightmare returned. With a sweating palm she reached for the cord which hung over the head-board and flooded the room with light. Whatever she might have set in motion she would have to face alone.

Kathryn fixed a smile on her face and sailed past Keith and Dave who sat smirking at their own desks. She would not give them the satisfaction of discussing her abortive rendez-vous, especially as she had convinced herself that they had set it up. She busied herself with telephone and keyboard and tried to ignore their presence. Her weekly column ready for the editor, she closeted herself with him for twenty minutes and went over what needed doing in her absence. Kathryn was in dire need of a holiday but there was not long to go now before her week off. Keith had agreed to cover any assignments and she had meticulously typed up a list of day-to-day tasks.

It was mid-afternoon before she remembered that she had meant to look up the name Jenny Branagh in their records, just in case the woman was someone she ought to know about. It took her until almost seven o'clock to work back over the previous five years, but the name did not appear. She locked up and left the office.

Like so many dismal days in early spring, the weather cleared up towards evening. The pavements were dry and daffodils swayed on the verges in the slipstream of traffic. She had missed the rush-hour. She wondered if the hesitation had been merely a valuable second or so for the woman to come up with a different name – a likely explanation if she was married and meeting a man. There was something else stirring at the edges of her memory but she was too tired to dredge it up.

For two months she had been building up a file on Megan Morris. The thinness of the folder in which she kept the information attested to the success of the author's ingenuity in retaining her anonymity. Most of the cuttings referred to her work.

'Hi, I was just about to ring you at the office.' Alex looked up from the paper he was reading.

'Sorry. I got tied up.'

He stared at the space where she had briefly stood and wondered why she looked so cheerful. Following her to the kitchen he said, 'The deal's finally gone through. We signed the papers today. No, don't open that.' He took the bottle of wine from her hand. 'I thought we might go out to celebrate.'

By mutual consent their joint outings had been less frequent since the Rebecca episode. There was too much

15

tension to allow for easy conversation. Kathryn nodded. 'Yes, that'll be nice. I'll go and change.'

'I'll book somewhere and order a taxi. How long will you be?'

'Ten minutes.' In the bedroom she decided to please Alex by wearing his favourite green dress and putting her hair up.

Alex appreciated the gesture. 'Very nice,' he approved. Occasionally he worried about the seven years' difference in their ages, but only because he had achieved what he wanted from life and Kathryn was still on the ladder. He was thirty-six. His family had emigrated to Australia when he was eleven but he had always known he would return to England one day. It did not happen until he had qualified as an architect, which had seemed the right thing to do even if his existence centred around water. Once back in England, he had found it easy to diversify into boat-building and then, when he had some money behind him, he set up on his own. By the time he met Kathryn he was making a profit and was buying the flat. She had come to the opening of the boat-yard he now owned, larger than the first and in a better position. The paper had carried an article and photographs and her by-line. Having found out her name he rang her and she accepted his invitation to dinner in a manner which amused him. 'Yes' was what she had said; no coyness, no flattery, just a single word which told him a lot. She still had so much ahead of her and he sometimes feared she was determined to overtake him.

'Okay, let's go.' He took her hand, and as they went downstairs to the waiting taxi, each of them was prepared to call a truce.

Laura watched the rain as it swept in bursts against the sloping window of the attic room. She pressed her head against a pane, grateful for its coolness. Words had not come easily that day and the sense of what she had written was disjointed. It was not a problem; it happened sometimes, often after a particularly good spell when her mind demanded a rest.

The attic had been converted into a study which was

reached by a wooden staircase that could be folded flush to the ceiling when not in use. The room contained an L-shaped desk from which she could look out over the river as she worked, shelves of reference books, stationery and a telephone. No one but Laura had entered it since the conversion was completed and if Peggy, who came in two mornings a week to clean, ever wondered what the brass ring attached to the pine boards of the ceiling was for, she never asked. The long, hooked pole to lower the stairs was kept out of sight on Peggy's days.

Laura liked order. Her working hours had a pattern. Whilst Peggy was there Laura met acquaintances for coffee or shopping or lunch, never disillusioning them that she was anything other than a divorcee with enough funds to make life comfortable.

Her breath misted the glass and her blurred outline was reflected as the night began to close in. The rain showed no sign of abating but she did not mind, she liked it. During summer showers when the windows were open she would listen to the hiss of car tyres and the rhythmic tattoo on the glass roof of the porch.

Her eyes felt gritty. The attic was full of smoke. For some reason it accumulated there more than anywhere else in the house, hanging in a bluish film under the eaves. She had not been out that day and was in need of a walk. Downstairs she pulled on a belted raincoat and tucked her hair under a matching gaberdine fisherman's hat and went out into the darkness.

On the opposite side of the road she stood and watched the dim outlines of rowing boats as they bobbed on their moorings in the currents. She heard the call of a moorhen and the gurgling of water in a drain, loud enough to mask the sounds of the river. Breathing deeply, oblivious to the sporadic oncoming headlights, she began to walk.

Water dripped off her hat but she was dry inside the mac as she continued along the tow-path in the direction of Cookham. Laura would not walk as far as that at night because the pavement petered out and there were sharp bends where she would be invisible to drivers. An elderly man, walking his dog, approached her. He raised his trilby and said good evening. Laura responded, smiling at his old-fashioned courtesy and thought how little it took to please her when she managed to forget her fears.

Turning back she realised that she was hungry and that she would be able to sleep without resorting to a pill. It was a good sign.

Chapter 2

Kathryn had often made the journey to Witney to see
Helena, but because she was going to stay for a week and
was in a holiday mood the route seemed strangely unfamiliar. Helena's house lay north of the town at the end of a
lane leading off from a B-road. There was little traffic over
the last few miles but Kathryn signalled automatically
before swinging into the drive.

The wooden gate stood open, as it had done for years,
one end rotten and sagging into the undergrowth. The same
potholes remained unrepaired and retained an inch of
muddy water. She slowed, changing gear to negotiate them,
as she passed through an avenue of rhododendron bushes
so tall they cut out the light. Ahead, in a clearing, stood the
house. It was built of honey-coloured Cotswold stone and
sprawled like a two-storey ranch. She could not have borne
it if anything had changed.

They had heard the car. The arched timber door was
flung open and the dog bounded out followed by Amy, the
most excitable of the children, then Helena.

Kathryn switched off the ignition and immediately
became aware of the peacefulness of her surroundings. Only
then did she realise the stress which she had been under,
and tears filled her eyes.

'Kathryn! Kathryn!' Amy was banging impatiently on the
window. Kathryn sniffed and squeezed her eyelids between
thumb and forefinger before getting out of the car and
stepping into the chaotic reality of Helena's life.

Ben tumbled over the front step and began to cry. Helena

yanked him to his feet by the back of his jumper, kissed the top of his head then held out her arms to her friend who promptly burst into tears on her shoulder.

From the doorway Clara, who was almost fourteen and considered herself to be more sophisticated than her parents and their contemporaries, watched the scene with detachment. But when Ben tugged at the hem of her denim skirt, demanding attention, she picked him up and made a fuss of him and suddenly became a child again herself.

'That bad?' Helena held Kathryn at arm's length and studied her face with concern.

'No. It was just seeing you again.'

Helena laughed and Kathryn, realising how it had sounded, couldn't help but smile. 'I think you need a drink. Gerald brought some decent stuff back from his last trip. Inside, you lot.' The children obeyed, even Amy who had been circling the adults, arms outstretched in imitation of a plane.

The house was very old but it was uncertain just when it dated back to. None of it was on the same level. There were steps up and down on both floors and a hazardous drop of six inches into one of the guest-rooms. The family negotiated them without thinking.

'Amy, please be quiet. Clara, be a love and sort them out, will you?'

Clara nodded and gave Kathryn a shy smile, desperate to be noticed by the woman whom she most wished to emulate. Her mother didn't count, of course, because at the moment she was viewed as nothing more than an obstacle to anything and everything Clara wanted to do.

Kathryn returned the smile. 'Go on,' she said, 'your mum and I want to catch up on the gossip. I've got you a present, though. You can have it when I've unpacked.'

Clara was pleased and led the younger children away. Helena uncorked the wine and handed Kathryn a glass. 'Now, tell me, is it still Alex?'

'No, it's definitely over. The affair, I mean. It's me.'

'Reaction. You'll get over it.' Helena paused and looked at her friend over the rim of her glass. 'If you want to, that is.'

It was shrewd observations such as this that made Kathryn appreciate Helena's friendship. It really was that simple. Alex had made his confession although he had offered no excuses for himself or Rebecca. Only later did he explain that he had felt shut out, ignored and irrelevant as Kathryn accepted every assignment that came her way. Between times she was also preparing her CV and making tentative enquiries about other jobs. In the evenings she would come home late and too tired to cook or to eat what Alex had prepared. At night she fell asleep at once and in the mornings there was no time to make love because she did not want to be late for work. By the time she realised which particular treadmill she was on, it was too late. Helena's remark was pertinent in that there was a masochistic pleasure in feeling wronged.

'Well?' Helena was waiting for an answer, her head tilted to one side.

'I want things to be as they were.' Kathryn sipped the wine. It was red; rich and smooth and, she suspected, too potent to be drunk on an empty stomach.

'Then you're wasting your time. It's happened, Kath – you either have to accept it or get out. It isn't fair on you or Alex otherwise.'

Helena sat down and threw her long hair back over her shoulders. It was thick and wavy and very fair, but rough-textured – the sort of hair that did not shine. There was a lot of it for such a small person. She had had three children and never dieted but still wore a size 8, mostly dressing in jeans or leggings. Nervous energy kept her that size.

Kathryn had not expected sympathy, nor did she want it. Even during that tearful telephone conversation when Helena learned what had happened she had made it clear she was not taking sides. Helena understood what she was going through but was aware that Kathryn's single-mindedness could be a stumbling-block in any relationship.

'You're right, but I wish I could be more like you.'

'Me?' Helena grinned in surprise.

'You always seem to cope.'

'I don't, not really. I just ignore what I can't change. Oh no, I'd better go and see what's happened now. God help us if Social Services ever decide to pay us a visit. That child's covered in bruises.' A hefty thump had been followed by Ben's wails. He was at the stage where his brain worked faster than his limbs could receive its messages and his lack of co-ordination caused numerous minor accidents.

Kathryn watched Helena's slender figure disappear along the corridor. Despite their dissimilarities their friendship had survived for over ten years, through crises and childbirth and Kathryn's marriage. When they first caught one another's eyes, laughing during a lecture, there had only been Clara, and Kathryn was still single. They were at Reading University; Helena lived near there at the time. She had looked no older than the other students; it was her air of confidence and of being in control of her life that had given her away. Kathryn admired her for the ease with which she combined running a home, bringing up a child and studying for a degree in English, and yet still managed to remain unflappable. 'I wanted my chance and I wasn't going to miss it,' she had once admitted. Helena had, after all, forgone a university place earlier in order to marry and travel with Gerald. Doggedness was the one characteristic Helena and Kathryn shared. Helena had wanted Gerald and his children but she also wanted a degree. She attained all three, though not necessarily in the same order as other people. And Helena had succeeded in keeping them all.

Alex had vaguely mentioned children but seemed to be leaving the decision to Kathryn. She had postponed making it because she was afraid she would be diminished in some way and lose out on the career ladder. Even with Helena as an example her fears remained. She was very much a modern woman but felt the choices available to her created as many problems as they solved. When she became a mother she would be a different sort of parent from her own.

Helena's voice could be heard as she spoke soothing words to Ben. 'Nothing serious,' she said when she returned to the kitchen. They sat at the table, a large, solid piece of furniture which would not have looked out of place in a monastery. 'You're not pregnant, are you?'

Kathryn almost spilled her wine. They were very close,

22

but surely not so close as to have become telepathic. 'No. Why?'

'The tears. And you've lost weight. I did in the early weeks with all three.'

'A baby's the last thing I need at the moment.'

I'm not so sure, Helena thought, but wisely did not say so. 'Do you want to unpack? Gerald'll be here soon. I've done a casserole for tonight but we'll eat out tomorrow. I've organised a baby-sitter. I thought we could go into Oxford.'

'Sounds good to me. In fact, I was thinking of spending a day there, if that's all right.'

'Whatever you like. You're here to relax.'

Kathryn picked up her hold-all and went along the corridor, mounting two steps before coming to the main flight of stairs which led to the room she always used when she stayed.

Despite the money that Gerald and Helena made between them, it was typical that they spent little on the house. It was clean and redecorated at regular intervals, but they otherwise left things as they were, preferring to use their earnings for entertainment and travelling and eating out. Yet each room had an individuality that was hard to define because although things often didn't match, they seemed to go together. The nicest feature was that all the rooms on the first floor had a clear view over open countryside.

Kathryn hung up the few clothes she had brought. Life was informal here. Oxford, she thought, was no distance. It wasn't terribly far from Burnham either, but now she was away from home the possibilities seemed more real. One visit, she promised herself, then she would give it up.

The window was open wide and rattled on the metal latch. There were no traffic sounds, only country noises. Birds were noisily roosting and cows, which were no more than dots in the distance, lowed, impatient to be milked, the sound carrying across the valley in the direction of the breeze. Then a car engine, changing gear as it wound through the lanes, sounded closer. Below she heard the children, excited because they knew it was their father. They were able to reach out to him, to show him how much he was loved and needed without losing their own identities. If only she could do the same with Alex. Maybe because he was older she found it hard to accept that he, too, needed his ego boosted occasionally.

Fudge, the young Labrador christened by Clara, joined the welcome party by barking. The last dog had had to be put down. She was elderly and had suffered from a complaint common to the breed. 'Her back legs collapsed,' Amy had informed her over the telephone a month or so ago, trying to be adult, but crying anyway.

Kathryn unzipped the side compartment of her bag and produced the presents for the children. Helena's and Gerald's would take the form of an evening out. She had taken the precaution of booking theatre seats on a credit card after making sure they had no alternative plans for the following Friday. Afterwards she would buy them a meal at the Randolph Hotel. Their lives were as unscheduled as her own but they still managed to make time for each other.

Gerald's job as a wildlife cameraman took him all over the world. He was part of a team which produced television programmes and although he had no need to be, he was extremely knowledgeable about the subjects he filmed. Whenever possible Helena accompanied him, but her fares were at their own expense. Having become pregnant for the second time a year after receiving her degree, Helena had had little chance to put it to any use so attempted to write children's books. Her lack of success in getting anything published did not deter her and even now she was modest about her achievements. 'I can't really claim the credit,' she had pointed out fairly. 'That's down to the illustrator.' The illustrations were the main feature of the series; Helena simply added the appropriate words to form a simple story. Kathryn smiled as she wondered if her friend did anything in the accepted order.

The family was assembled in the kitchen but Fudge, having been fed, was in his basket in the scullery which now housed the washing machine and drier and a deep freeze. 'Aha, here's my favourite journalist.' Gerald gave Kathryn a squeeze and kissed her on both cheeks. 'Um, a little peaky, but she'll do.' Aware of the situation between Kathryn and Alex he said nothing, knowing it was his wife in whom she would confide. Beneath the loose pinafore and T-shirt there was less flesh. Gerald did not think it suited her.

'You look well,' she told him. It was true. He was just over six feet and gangly, his arms and legs taking up more space than seemed natural and, when he sat, his children were forever tripping over his feet. A lock of soft, straight hair fell across his brow and he wore thick framed glasses. It was a strange existence, Kathryn thought, one or both of them being away for a week or two at a time, then periods when Gerald commuted to the studios in London. Between assignments he would be at home. Constant readjustments were necessary whilst Kathryn was unable to come to terms with only one.

'What's this? You haven't brought work with you, surely?' Helena picked up the stiff buff envelope folder on the table beside the presents.

'Not exactly. I wanted your opinion on something.'

Helena glanced at Gerald over her head. They had discussed Kathryn's visit and agreed that what she required was a complete break. They could not recall when she had last had a real holiday. They both hoped that after this one, their friend would return to Alex ready to start again.

'Is this the reason for your sudden desire to spend a day in Oxford?' Kathryn had been there many times.

'Sort of. Now, this is for you, Ben.' She handed him a small package, suddenly defensive about her project. Ben ripped the paper off, his teeth gritted purposefully as he struggled with the sellotape.

'Finger-paints. Thank you *so* much, Kathryn,' Helena said with a mock-grimace.

Amy, at an age where such things were desirable, screamed dramatically when she saw the bubble-wrapped kit of plastic beads with which she could make her own jewellery. She ran around the kitchen noisily, her face red, until Helena grabbed her arm and told her to calm down or she would be sent to bed. Maybe because she was the middle child, she felt the need to draw attention to herself – even though all three were treated with the same mixture

25

of tolerance and discipline. Paradoxically, the child who most resembled her mother physically was the least like her temperamentally. Clara and Ben were more like Gerald.

Clara waited expectantly whilst trying not to appear too eager. She prayed that Kathryn had not let her down by buying something too babyish. 'Thank you,' she said when she was handed the square, squashy parcel. She opened it carefully. Inside was a taupe-coloured top which had decorative buttons down the front and was loose around the bottom as if it had been badly washed. 'Oh, it's brilliant! Thanks!' Clara's eyes were shining. It was exactly what everyone else was wearing. She was about to kiss Kathryn then thought better of it. 'I'll go and try it on.'

Amy had taken herself off elsewhere to make a necklace. 'Shall we have a pre-dinner drink?'

Gerald lowered his head and smiled at Helena over the top of his glasses. 'Seems to me you've already had one. However, I shall do the honours. Ben, don't do that.' At three years old the little boy seemed to have learned that the best way to gain attention was not in the manner of his sisters – Amy's loud theatricals, Clara's hurt silences – but by reverting to babyhood. Having pulverised several slices of banana he proceeded to push the sludge through the gaps in his teeth and let it ooze down his chin, his expression deadpan. When Gerald picked up the dishcloth to wipe his face he smiled beatifically, his brown eyes innocent.

While Helena put him to bed and supervised Amy's washing and undressing, Gerald and Kathryn set the table. Over the meal they discussed Gerald's next job – filming a feature on the life-cycle of snakes. Snakes held no fear for any of them but Amy, who reappeared in her nightdress, necklace and clip-on earrings on the pretext of wanting a glass of water, squirmed and pulled faces and said she would have nightmares. 'Bed!' Helena said sternly, ignoring the performance.

The discussion on snakes led Kathryn to tell them about the tuatara, a peculiar dried reptile that had been a present to Alex from one of his friends. The reptilian creature stood on a shelf in their lounge, and Kathryn enjoyed looking at it. So did Alex. *Alex*. She hadn't phoned him to say that she had arrived safely. Helena guessed her thoughts and suggested she did so right away. 'Use the other phone, the one in the lounge,' she added tactfully. Kathryn might feel uneasy with all of them listening.

She returned within minutes. 'There's no reply,' she said bleakly. Helena began to clear the table, all too aware of the implications.

Clara disappeared to her room to read, still wearing the new top. Once the dishwasher was loaded, the two women went into the larger room at the back of the house because it faced west and retained the warmth from the last of the sun. 'Are we allowed to know what's in that folder?' Helena asked as she poured coffee.

'Yes, but you'll probably think I'm crazy.'

Helena, kneeling by the low table which held the tray, flung back her hair and arched an eyebrow. 'I've always *known* you were crazy. Come on then, tell us.' She almost disappeared as she took her coffee and sank into one of the deep armchairs. Gerald took a corner of the sofa and crossed his long legs, one ankle circling.

'I rang Megan Morris's publishers, you see, and hard as it is to believe, she agreed to meet me.'

'*What*?' Helena leaned forward in disbelief. 'Are you saying you've met her?'

'No, that's just the point. She didn't show up. Not that I expected her to – I thought Dave and Keith had set me up.'

'And now?'

'And now I'm not so sure. They haven't said a word about it, and they would have done, if they'd been behind it.' Kathryn paused and chewed her lip. 'It was strange. Someone did turn up, you see. A woman in her mid- to late-thirties, I'd guess, and very attractive. She made a beeline for me. Well, to be fair, there wasn't anywhere else to sit. It was just that there was something odd about her, as if she was afraid, or maybe guilty.'

Gerald was staring at her. 'Kathryn, are you saying that you're really trying to find this woman? You do realise that you haven't got a hope in hell.' His wife's assessment of crazy fell a little short of the mark. Had Alex reduced her to this?

27

Kathryn shrugged. 'It's worth a try.' She had hoped her friends would share her enthusiasm.

'Isn't Oxford where she was supposed to have been educated?' Helena began to understand. 'Mind you, it doesn't necessarily mean it's true.'

'I know. Anyway I just thought, as I'm here, it was worth investigating.'

'I might come with you.'

'Great. We can have lunch or something if we make it a day when Ben's not at playgroup.'

'I'd prefer to make it a day when he was,' Helena admitted candidly. 'I'll get someone to have him for an hour or so after they finish.'

Kathryn went to bed early. She was more tired than she had realised and she fell into a deep sleep without dwelling on the fact that although she had not tried to reach Alex again that evening, neither had he telephoned her.

She woke to the muffled sounds of music coming from Clara's room. It was nine-fifteen, the latest she had lain in for as long as she could remember, or as long as she wished to remember. Those Sunday mornings in bed with Alex were a thing of the past.

The sun was shining, which was a good omen. The weekend would be devoted to her friends but on Monday she was going to Oxford.

It wasn't until the Sunday evening that Kathryn mentioned the name Jenny Branagh. The children were all in bed, bathed and ready for school in the morning, and Gerald was spending the night in their London flat prior to a breakfast meeting.

'Can I see?' Helena nodded towards the folder which was on the floor beside Kathryn. 'You don't seem to have got very far.' She examined the cuttings and the few notes that Kathryn had made. 'Jenny Branagh – was she the woman who sat with you? You don't really think it was Megan Morris, do you?'

'I don't know what to think.'

'That's no answer for a journalist, especially one as good as you.' But Kathryn's secretive smile gave her friend all the answer she needed. There would be no stopping her now.

Giles expressed no surprise when Laura asked if he would read through her latest chapter. She experienced fleeting moments of insecurity and he had come to recognise the pattern. Several weeks, or even months of excellent writing would be followed by a hiatus. No amount of explanation could convince Laura that all that was happening was that her imagination required a break. Only he understood how hard she worked. What he did on those occasions was to treat her to a decent lunch, tell her the chapter was brilliant, suggest she take herself out somewhere nice for the day and leave it at that. So far it had worked. There was always the danger of becoming too complaisant, however, for there might come a time when Laura truly did dry up.

'It's good,' he told her, genuinely puzzled because it was better than usual. At other times, after a rest, Laura would recognise any weaknesses herself and correct them. 'Aren't you pleased with it?'

'Yes. In a way. I just had the feeling that I'd somehow altered the style.'

'No. Leave it just as it is.' He pushed the typed sheets back into their plastic cover and handed them to Laura. 'Come on, let's go and eat.'

They were sitting in the car outside Alfonso's, a small restaurant in Cookham Rise where, they both suspected, they were taken for a married couple. Their conversation flowed naturally and they never discussed business in public. The collection and delivery of all that pertained to Megan Morris's work was conducted on neutral territory. Contracts, manuscripts, royalty statements and fan mail were sealed in envelopes and exchanged in Giles's car. Laura could not afford to be seen with him in London, he was too well-known a figure in the literary world for someone not to put two and two together. They always met in Berkshire although Giles rarely went to the house.

'Ah, Mrs Tennyson, it's good to see you again.' Alfonso kissed her on both cheeks then shook Giles's hand. 'And you, sir.' He was unsure how to address him. The bill was always paid in cash, unusual in a world of credit cards. Alfonso did not know that this was a precaution in case anyone recognised his name.

They were shown to a table near the window. Laura got out her cigarettes and placed her large handbag which contained the thirty pages of her manuscript under the table beneath the floor-length pink cloth. She lit a cigarette just as Maria, Alfonso's wife, deposited a plate of hors d'oeuvres between them. Laura watched with amusement as Giles devoured the whorls of bread lined with smoked salmon and cream cheese.

Through the filmy white curtain they saw cars coming and going as people pulled in to make use of the small parade of shops. Inside, it was quiet. Muted conversation and the clink of glasses and cutlery were the only sounds. The aroma of expensive cigars reached them from a table where three businessmen had finished eating and had lit up.

Laura studied Giles as she sipped a Punt E mes, preferring its medicinal flavour to the more traditional sherry. He has, she thought, vulpine appeal. His hair was greying rapidly and was almost white, but there was plenty of it. His deep-set blue eyes and strong nose made women look twice. Yes, women, she realised – not girls, who would not appreciate the humour and intelligence which showed in his face or his air of quiet self-control.

'Champagne?'

'What? Oh, sorry, no, I'd prefer wine.'

'Ah, yes. I'd forgotten.' Giles's smile was gentle. But he hadn't forgotten, not really. There were few things concerning Laura he did not remember. And Laura had been so very sick that freezing afternoon in the cemetery. It had been John's idea, as most things were. A picnic, in January, in a graveyard. Typical madness, but they had gone along with it. They always did. John had provided the booze, a bottle of champagne apiece. There were six of them because Jenny was one of the group by then. Laura hardly seemed to have altered; in Oxford she had simply been a younger version of the woman she now was, far more beautiful than Jenny and Sarah with their long blonde hair and skinny figures. He sighed. There were so many regrets. In those days she had eyes for no one but John, who treated her badly although she would never admit it. How much better life would have been if it had been Giles whom she had loved. And how much pain would have been avoided . . .

Something rich and pungent was being prepared in the kitchen, pheasant, maybe – it had the tangy smell of game. There was no temperamental crashing of pans, everything here worked smoothly. They ordered their meals. Giles was having guinea fowl in a plum sauce, while Laura opted for grilled fish with a side salad. She rarely ate much at lunch-time as most of the day she was sitting. She eschewed formal exercise and sport but made up for it by walking. It was also a form of relaxation. Every evening, whatever the weather, she set off from the house and covered three or four miles comfortably. It also gave her a chance to escape from her characters or, conversely, sort out flaws in a plot.

Giles asked for the wine to be served right away as they were only having one course. He tasted the Chablis and nodded his approval. 'Laura, what made you do it?' he asked once Alfonso had filled their glasses and moved away. 'You know what I'm talking about.'

Laura fiddled with the pink linen serviette, folding it into different shapes. It had been too much to hope that Giles would not bring the subject up. 'I don't know. And it's no good interrogating me because I can't work it out myself. Call it middle-aged madness if you like. It won't happen again.' Colour spread across her cheekbones.

Giles placed a hand on hers, pressing firmly. She stopped fiddling. 'Interrogate you? Do I do that?'

'No. Not really.'

He still loved her. He always had done. In his mind he enacted his favourite scene, himself and Laura, alone somewhere, a hotel maybe. He would unclasp her silky red hair and bury his face in it, holding her closely, soothing away some of the tension with which she always seemed to be filled. He wanted to take care of her, make everything all right. The dream went no further than that. It was boyish in its simplicity; Laura would probably laugh in his face if he told her. She had done a more than adequate job of taking care of herself.

Laura steered the conversation away from her act of folly and they set about the business of eating. Most of the wine had already been drunk but she would refuse a second bottle if it was offered. Giles had to drive back to London and although she enjoyed a drink in the evenings it affected her more in the day and she did not want to have to consume the lion's share. Placing her knife and fork neatly together Laura sat back and lit a cigarette. Giles had given up smoking years ago.

'No, nothing else, thanks. I'm full, but coffee would be lovely.'

When they had drunk it, Giles insisted on driving her part of the way back although she wanted to walk. 'This'll do,' Laura said when they reached the river. He pulled in and she got out of the car.

Giles leaned across the passenger seat. She looked wonderful with her face flushed from the wine and a strand of hair escaping from its clasp. Her loose trousers and silk shirt were topped with a long jacket. 'How long before I can expect the finished typescript?' he asked for no other reason than to detain her a few more seconds.

'Not long. Six weeks maybe.' She waved as he pulled out and saw his arm emerge from the driver's window before he rounded the bend and disappeared from sight.

Having been out to lunch Laura felt vaguely disorientated and tried to decide whether it was worth attempting any work that afternoon. Giles often had that effect on her. He had remarried a few years ago but they did not discuss his second wife. All she had managed to find out was that her name was Ingrid and that she was something in computers, a world which was alien to Laura. Her books were bashed out on an electronic typewriter, although she had been toying with the idea of getting a word-processor.

She began to walk briskly. She was sluggish after the food and wine and it was chilly whenever a cloud passed in front of the sun. She was still trying to form a picture of Ingrid as she carried on walking past her house towards Maidenhead. Seeing the sign for the Thames Riviera brought Kathryn Brooks to mind. What had the girl made of their brief acquaintanceship? Laura felt she had not liked her much.

At least, so far, there had been no repercussions and she had managed to gloss over her error of judgment as far as Giles was concerned. There was something about Kathryn which reminded her of herself at that age. She had put her at about twenty-six or -seven. It was a shame she could not get to know her better. Her talent was obvious and she possessed a deceptive air of innocence and the sort of looks which, although they could not be described as pretty, were more potent than the girl seemed to realise.

The river was still high but not like it had been three weeks previously, when it had flooded the road, which had been closed to traffic. Thankfully it had not reached her house. Running water was a palliative to Laura. She leaned against the rail and watched it now, greenish today, with discs of gold skimming the surface when the sun shone on the ripples. Some mallards were busily feeding, their white rumps stuck saucily in the air as they paddled their webbed feet just below the surface. They amused her and sometimes she would throw them bread in order to watch their noisy squabbling. Her relationship with them was perfect. She could observe them from a distance or ignore them if she chose.

There were few people in Laura Tennyson's life and she had never owned a pet. Since her own divorce, some twelve years previously, she had never felt the need to remarry. Perhaps I'm selfish, she thought. She preferred her own company to that of any living thing. Why she had married in the first place remained a mystery and, in retrospect, she wondered if she had really loved John all those years ago. She suspected her feelings had more to do with hero-worship and infatuation. He was the best-looking, the most intelligent, at least according to John, and he was certainly the wealthiest of her contemporaries. There had also been the element of flattery because he had selected her with whom to share his bed. Had she really been so shallow as to value those dubious attributes? It had taken a good many years before she was able to see him for what he was.

Laura buttoned her jacket against a chill which was not entirely due to the breeze. The last contact she had had with John had been the postcard she sent after he had gone to America. She had deliberately withheld her address but it would have been interesting to know what he had made of it. '*I know*' she had written, but even now she was not entirely sure that she did. Strange how meeting Kathryn Brooks had brought it all back with such clarity. Kathryn Brooks, she thought as two swans, their necks gracefully bent, lowered their heads towards the same piece of bread. Behind her a mother was handing her small son broken crusts which he only succeeded in throwing a short distance as he was restrained by her firm hand on his reins. Kathryn Brooks, she decided, was, like herself, an observer rather than a participator. In which case, she wondered, just how much had she observed?

John Atherton was too experienced to need to do a great deal of preparation for the following semester but he decided to get whatever was necessary out of the way before leaving for London. It did not deter him that he had lost touch with his friends; he did not dream that they might not be pleased to see him.

There was one more lecture before he was free – another early one as it happened, which meant roughly a fifty per cent turn out. Little Tina Parry would be there; she never missed an opportunity to gaze at him with doe-eyed reverence, trembling every time he went near her. He had better watch his step; she was already choosing to misconstrue their necessary conversations. He had been through it all before, it was not unusual, but he rarely bothered to take advantage of it. He preferred his meat more mature, as he liked to remind himself. The young were strong but in Tina's case some discretion was required as he recognised the type. He did not relish a half-hearted suicide attempt, which had happened when a colleague in the States had seduced a student then dumped her. The girl had harboured romantic visions of her tutor rushing to her bedside with a proposal of marriage.

An unopened letter from Angela lay on the dining-room table. It had arrived yesterday, along with some unsolicited circulars which made up the bulk of his mail. With the usual platitudes of an amicable divorce they had promised to keep in touch, but Angela had meant it. She wrote at regular intervals to keep him up to date with family news. John was not a good correspondent and rarely replied. He felt mean; her family had been good to him and had opened all the right doors, but the truth was he no longer had anything to say.

Slitting open the envelope with his thumbnail he went out to the kitchen. The place was already beginning to feel like home. When he was in the city centre he bought odd bits, not with any theme in mind, but things which caught his eye. He boiled the kettle and made tea which he laced with Scotch before sitting down to read the letter.

Johnny, Angela's military brother, had been promoted again. *Johnny.* Already he found it hard to picture his namesake and even Angela, so blonde and beautiful and aptly named, was fading into insignificance. He stared at the horse chestnut, whose boughs hung over the garden fence. Its pink candles would soon be visible. I'm a bastard, he thought, knowing he had not shown the gratitude due to her parents, nor to his ex-wife either. She had tried desperately to become the perfect college wife: she had invited students to the house, attended all the functions and supported him in all he did, yet she had failed because she was uncomfortable with teenagers and her efforts came across as patronising.

'Credit where it's due,' he informed the whisky bottle. 'We both tried.' It was something to drink to. He did so, slopping an inch or so more into his tea cup.

In the morning the familiar feeling of self-loathing and disgust made him angry. He ran the shower fully and had to admit that the Americans understood plumbing. Their showers hissed forcefully, hard enough to hurt the top of your head, and sprayed from all angles, sobering you up in minutes.

'Oh, for God's sake, Tina, even you can grasp a concept that basic,' he snapped towards the end of the lecture. The girl flinched but, thankfully, did not cry as she had done on one other occasion. John did not apologise because he knew it was what she was waiting for and that she would take it as a sign of encouragement. He left her sitting staring dumbly at the floor.

After a faculty meeting he left the campus. In two days' time, maybe three, he would leave for London. Tonight there was a dinner to attend and he had been invited to a drinks party on Saturday. In between he would go over the syllabus.

From home he rang the station. There was an hourly train service to London. It was the first time in his adult life he had been without a car but he lived so near the university it would have been ridiculous to drive to work and, having found he could get to most places in the city by public transport it hardly seemed worth buying one. Awkward places could be reached by taxi. And he did not have to worry about his whisky consumption. He changed into his evening suit and fastened his bow tie, cursing until it looked right, then dialled Directory Enquiries and got the number for several hotels. He made a reservation at the first one which had a room in order to ensure he did not change his mind about going to London.

The school bus collected Clara and Amy from the end of the drive. They were looking forward to breaking up for Easter at the end of the week. Living where they did, the girls' social lives needed organising with care. Helena took her turn ferrying other people's children along with her own if they stayed on for after-school activities. Ben she delivered and collected twice a week from the playgroup he attended in Witney.

'That's that,' she said when she returned to the car. Kathryn had watched Ben's sturdy figure run ahead of his mother without hesitation. 'Carol's going to keep him until we get back so there's no rush.' But Kathryn knew that Helena would want to be back before the school bus deposited her daughters. 'Do you want me to come with you?' Helena was referring to the discussion they had had the previous night. Kathryn was going to try the university only because it seemed the logical place to start, but she was going to have to base her questions on a hypothesis.

'No, you go and do your shopping. We'll meet at, what – twelve?'

They agreed on a wine bar which had recently opened and which served a good selection of salads. 'You don't need to lose any more weight, Kath, you're fine as you are,' Helena had said after Kathryn suggested the venue.

Kathryn made no comment. She had her own views on that subject. Helena drove to a car park and fed the meter then set off to buy a couple of lightweight, creaseproof dresses for her next trip with Gerald.

Kathryn stopped a group of students who were heatedly discussing something and asked the way to the administration offices. There was something about Oxford that made it like no other place. Admittedly it had its rougher parts and, like everywhere else, not every small business was able to survive, but there was an atmosphere of generations of learning which seemed to have permeated the stones. Perhaps it was because the university and the students dominated the city, unlike Reading where they were an adjunct. The students did not look any different, yet they were, perhaps because they considered themselves to be the elite. It would, Kathryn thought, be the sort of place which moulded someone with Megan Morris's intelligence and ability.

'It certainly makes a change,' a smart, grey-haired woman in administration told her when Kathryn had made her request. 'Over the years, we've been inundated with requests for details about Megan Morris. My view, for what it's worth, is that she wasn't a student here at all. Anyway, with regard now to Jenny, or Jennifer Branagh. Somewhere between the middle and late 1970s, you said?'

Kathryn had produced her press card and explained that she only wanted verification of the dates Jenny Branagh had attended the university. She was unable to give any information as to subjects or which college. The woman had been wearing a wedding ring, but so what? It might be for protection, it might be that she was divorced and had reverted to her maiden name, but the more Kathryn thought about it, the more certain she became that the name ought to mean something.

'I'm so sorry, there's absolutely no record of anyone with that name during the 1970s.'

Kathryn had wasted most of the morning but at least the woman had taken her request seriously. She could have been turned away at the door and she would never have known. She hoped she did not sound as dejected as she felt as she thanked her and left.

For the half-hour that remained until she was due to meet Helena, Kathryn strolled around the college buildings. Even to her they seemed awe-inspiring, so much a part of history that it was no wonder tourists flocked to see them. At twenty-eight her own student days seemed a long time ago and watching the undergraduates made her feel old. They had everything ahead of them. She sat on a low wall. To her right was a mixed group but they all exuded confidence. She might, she thought, be looking at a future Prime Minister, a Nobel Prize-winner or a serial killer, but she wondered how many would have to settle for a down-to-earth job, a family and a mortgage.

Recognising the incipient black cloud of depression which hovered over her even though the sun was shining, she got up and walked briskly to the meeting place. 'It was coincidence, that's all,' she muttered to herself, then blushed as two men in suits turned to stare at her. Further on, a man about her own age was inadequately strumming a guitar. He swore crudely when she did not drop any coins into the scarf he had laid out on the ground. Kathryn ignored him.

Either Jenny Branagh had not attended the university or Kathryn had wildly misjudged her age – yet she had had Oxford written all over her. But she had to accept she was being simplistic in pinning all her hopes on the theory that Jenny Branagh and Megan Morris were one and the same person.

The wine bar was already crowded. The two women settled for a glass of house white each and a salad. Helena asked what they should do with the afternoon. 'I don't mind, as long as I'm back by four,' she added.

'Would you mind a quick visit to the library?'

'No. Any particular one?'

38

'The central public lending library. Do you know where it is?'

Helena did and they set off as soon as they had eaten because it was too congested to remain at their table in comfort. In the quiet calmness of the building Kathryn asked where she might find the electoral roll.

'I said you were mad,' Helena whispered. 'It'll take for ever. Why don't you just look up the name in the telephone directory?'

She could do that at home – Slough or Maidenhead central libraries would have a complete set – but for some reason she imagined if she flicked through the list the name would jump out at her. It didn't. Helena was right but Kathryn was still coming to terms with her disappointment, unable to see that, realistically, she could not have hoped to discover anything.

Behind her someone coughed in the way that people in libraries do. It was a sort of apologetic clearing of the throat. She turned around, ready to leave. The page of someone's newspaper rustled. It was a copy of the Oxford *Star*. She suddenly grinned. 'You're right,' she said to Helena, 'it's a waste of time. Let's go.' She had promised herself one visit but now she had another idea.

They returned to the car and Helena negotiated the traffic with its predominance of bicycles until they reached the drabber outskirts of the city. Here were parades of shops which might have been situated anywhere. There were shabby newsagents outside which stood boards holding sheets of white paper with headlines written in felt-tipped pens, sub-Post-Offices, old-fashioned hairdressers and miniature supermarkets. The houses grew smaller and meaner and finally the city came to an end.

When they returned, Helena's house was unnaturally quiet. Even Fudge's welcome was no more than a wagging tail as he sniffed their ankles. Kathryn put the kettle on while Helena rang Carol to say she could bring Ben back as soon as she liked. 'I'll have Jason one day next week,' she promised.

At six Kathryn rang Alex. There was the faint hum of the television in the background. Presumably he was alone.

She must, she thought, start trusting him again, if she was to stop torturing herself. It was the second time they had spoken since her departure; both conversations had been strained but she managed to refrain from asking him where he had been on Friday when she rang.

'Take care,' Alex concluded. But not, Kathryn noticed, that he loved or missed her.

David Shawcross was stunned. The receiver knocked against the side of his face when he heard John Atherton's voice. He had had no idea he was back in the country, and he had hoped never to hear from him again. Those days were over, the fear and the nightmares were finally fading. Oxford was a thing of the past. 'Yes, all right,' he said, his voice a croak. Too shaken to do otherwise, he had agreed to a meeting.

'Why now?' he enquired of the bookshelves. He was in the habit of speaking aloud, especially when he was at home. His cat, his only companion for five years, was the recipient of many of his private thoughts. It was as well the cat could not speak. David suspected he was classed as mildly eccentric but it did not bother him. What did was the fact that John had made contact. It could only mean trouble. It always had.

David did not want to remember those days, nor his part in it. He feared he was susceptible, that he could be drawn in again and he knew he was capable of dreadful acts. Confusion filled his brain and he wondered how it was possible for terror and curiosity to be combined. He did not want to see John but he knew that he would.

In those days he had felt a part of life – more than that, he'd felt *alive*. Later, after leaving Oxford and meeting Nicola he had hoped that he had become a full member of the human race. He had a business and a girlfriend to whom he finally became engaged. Nicola, so shy, so self-effacing, so very much like himself, had changed overnight. One day she abruptly announced that the engagement was off, she had found someone else and was going to get married in two months' time. David had felt mortified but not bitter. He always expected that sort of thing to happen to him. He had seen her only once since that day and he had hardly recognised her. Gone was the perpetual student image; she had become what he supposed would be described as trendy. His vocabulary was wide-ranging, but when it came to idiom he was stuck firmly in the 1970s – perhaps because it was a period when he felt he truly existed.

Nowadays he often found himself observing his actions as if he were two people, one of them an interested bystander. He did so then as he went about the shop tidying shelves and making lists, outwardly methodical, inwardly in turmoil.

Strange he should suddenly think of Nicola, his ex-fiancée who was now married with a child. But of course, it was hearing from John which had reminded him of her.

For no more than a second, David had been tempted to invite John to the flat, but then he'd decided against it, for two reasons. Firstly, the place was shabby and he did not want John to think less of him. Having it decorated was something he kept postponing although he didn't know why this should be. Secondly, he knew from experience that there was the danger of John outstaying his welcome. He might need a bed and David was out of practice at being sociable.

And *he*, too, was shabby, he realised, catching sight of himself in the small mirror over the sink at the back of the shop. Stoop-shouldered, underweight, his thinning hair in need of a cut and his grey eyes, almost colourless behind the lenses of his glasses, were lacklustre. How strange he had never noticed before, but that one brief telephone call from John had alerted him to these things. 'Ah, well,' he said as he pulled the blinds down over the windows to protect the stock before locking up.

Of all the crowd it was David whom John had thought he would find most easily. He had always been the most placid and the least adventuresome of them despite, or maybe because of, the year-long trip he had made to India before taking up his university place. Good old David, still plodding away in the shop where he sold specialised books. At least he sounded as if he was doing well. John had been there once, just before he left for the States. To him the stock was of little interest to average human beings, unless you counted the second-hand paperbacks David put out to entice the less esoteric customers into the shop.

He drank little over the day, not wishing to turn up halfcut. The pub where they were to meet, John noticed, was more convenient for David than for himself, but that was hardly surprising. David was a territorial creature.

'John, it's good to see you again.' David shook his hand. They had arrived together.

'And you. Business as good as ever?'

'Better than I hoped. You haven't acquired the accent.'

'No, I made damn sure I didn't. A bit of English charm goes a long way over there.'

'Yes, I can imagine.'

John could not decide whether the comment was prompted by envy or sarcasm. David should be flattered. It had taken John a while to dredge up the name of his bookshop because his home number was unlisted. It was obvious he was expected to buy the first round. He did so and they took their drinks to a table. John would have preferred to remain at the bar; it was less intimate somehow.

It was strange being back in London but nothing seemed to have changed much. David's shop was in Charing Cross, the bar in which they were seated was close by. It was the usual West End pub with lots of Victoriana. Of them all, John had been most keen to see Laura, but he couldn't get a number for her under the name of Tennyson and he did not know if she had married. If Giles was still in publishing he would be easy to find, even if he had moved to another firm. It was a small world and someone would know where he was. And Jenny? John grinned. Anything could have happened to *that* one. Which only left Sarah. The smile faded. Sarah was dead. It no longer seemed such a good idea to try to look up the others. Seventeen years was a very long time, and it was at least ten since he had last set eyes on any of them.

Back then they had had their futures ahead of them, except Sarah; hers had been cut short . . .

David was toying with his glass. It was clear he had no idea how to further the conversation. John downed half of his drink before sitting back and crossing his legs. He never seemed ill at ease, wherever he was. David studied him. It was just like old times; no question who was in the driving seat.

He listened as John regaled him with anecdotes and stories of his life in America. It would not have suited David. He had been stunned when he had recognised Atherton immediately; apart from one or two grey hairs and a few extra pounds around the middle, he might have seen him yesterday. Watching him, he surmised that John still took the bulk of his calorific intake in the form of alcohol – then asked himself why he was being so mean-minded on what, under other circumstances, should have been an enjoyable reunion.

'Shall I get us another?' John stood and reached for David's glass, pausing a second. So David wasn't going to offer to buy it. John shrugged mentally and went to the bar where he downed a surreptitious whisky while he waited for the fresh pints to be pulled.

From where he sat David heard the familiar bellow of laughter. He was still the same old John, able to strike up a conversation with a total stranger in a minute and to be sharing a joke almost at once. He had always envied him this ability, but not the laugh. It was too ostentatious, too clearly heard, as if he was trying to draw attention to himself.

When John returned to the table he raised his glass and said, 'Cheers!' rather pointedly but David seemed not to notice. 'Well, you've heard my side, for what it's worth, now tell me what's been happening to you. It's twelve years or more since we last saw each other; it doesn't seem credible.'

'There isn't much to tell.'

'The same old modest Dave, I see. Come off it, man, there must be something. You don't spend your whole life in the shop!' Only then did John recall his final visit to those premises when he called in to say goodbye. David had been boring then, he seemed more so now and he queried his motives for wishing to repeat the experience. Was it simply to satisfy himself that now he was back, none of them intended to break their silence? Or was it more than that? Was he hoping to discover that he hadn't lost whatever it was that had drawn them all to him in the first place? Was he, he wondered, that egotistical?

David smiled wryly. 'You're wrong. There really isn't a lot to say, not unless you count having a minor royal as one of my customers. Are you back for good?' He wanted to change the subject. He couldn't bear John to know what a parochial existence he led.

'Yes. I've got a post in Cardiff. It's a great city, suits me down to the ground. Big fish in a small pool syndrome,' he added with a touch of self-mockery.

'Are you married?'

'I was. An American girl, Angela. It's a shame it all went wrong; she was a stunner. We're divorced, that was one of the reasons I decided not to renew my contract. It might have been awkward moving in the same circles even though there were no hard feelings on either side. How about you?'

'No. But nearly once.'

'Really? Will you tell me about it, or is it too painful?' John angled his body on the narrow bench-seat in order to see David's face. There had not been any girls at Oxford although it was clear he had had a soft spot for Laura. David had been too intense, too intent upon his studies to seem to have the time, and he had always needed the most persuasion to join them on their jaunts – not that there was any question about his sexuality. John sometimes suspected he might be asexual but he had also been aware of depths in David which the rest of them did not possess. He had been grimly determined to do well but he had also had a peculiar sensitivity to other people's feelings at a time when everyone else was busily being selfish and hedonistic, all too aware of the short years of freedom before they had to join the real world. David, he considered, might almost have been born an adult. But he had added a dimension to their group and his presence usually prevented things from becoming too anarchistic. Except that once.

David sipped his beer. 'No,' he shook his head. 'It's not at all painful now.'

'What went wrong?'

'She found someone better.'

44

'Bad luck.' John realised that time had not corrupted him; he was still as honest and straightforward as when they had first met. He stared into the bottom of his glass feeling slightly ashamed of himself and, for once, unable to think of anything to say. Another drink might help – alcohol usually loosened his tongue.

'My shout.' David jerked to his feet. How rude he must have appeared, allowing John to buy both lots of drinks. But he would make this the last one then go home.

'Did you have any children?' he asked when their glasses were replenished. Three pints were his limit, he would not allow John to talk him into a fourth.

'No. Angela wanted to wait. So did I. Just as well, as it turned out in the end.' So they were both childless. John wondered about the others. They had all envisaged wonderfully satisfying careers and brilliant marriages which would produce children who would change the future of the world. How egocentric and how very wrong they had been. 'Do you ever hear from the rest of the crowd?' He hoped the question sounded off-hand.

'No. I believe Laura moved out of London years ago. Giles is still here, of course. I don't think he'd be happy anywhere other than in the metropolis, but I only know that because of what I've read in the papers. They say he's got one of the best lists of authors in Britain, not to mention Megan Morris. Have you heard of her?' David wasn't sure if her work was popular overseas.

'Megan Morris? My God, yes. Trust Giles. He always was a go-getter.' John knew of the author by reputation but hadn't read her books. His reading lately consisted of anything which was in direct contrast to the literature he discussed with his students. 'She's very highly rated, isn't she?'

'She is. I've read a couple myself, just to see if the critics were to be believed.'

'Oh, don't be so bloody prissy, Dave. Even you must have accepted that women are as capable as men of writing decently.'

David felt the colour flood his face. John had misinterpreted his meaning but there was still no need to be rude.

45

And he hated being called Dave. John was the only person he knew who had not respected his desire to be called by his given name. 'I wasn't being prissy,' he said quietly. 'It's just that I refuse to be influenced by hype, whatever the sex of the author, or by someone else's personal judgment of a writer.'

John's hand, holding his glass, stopped halfway to his mouth. It shook as he began to laugh. 'Good for you,' he said, unsure if he was more surprised at hearing such a positive opinion or at David's having stood up to him.

David was angry, had felt vaguely angry all evening. He almost snatched John's glass from him as he muttered that he would get them a refill. Too bad about his earlier decision not to drink more than three pints. Acid gnawed at his stomach and he chewed a couple of chalky tablets as he waited to be served then elbowed his way back through the rapidly filling bar to where John sat.

They pondered over what might have become of Jenny and Laura, but neither of them mentioned Sarah's name.

Indigestion held marginally at bay, David followed John out of the pub into the street. Darkness had fallen. The pavements were crowded and impatient taxis tooted as they queued around Piccadilly Circus. Faces took on strange hues under the changing neon lights. David wondered what on earth had prompted him to agree to eat with John.

John was wondering why he had issued the invitation.

Chapter 3

'Damn her!' Alex swore after learning that Kathryn had gone out quite early in the morning and hadn't yet returned. It was now after 6 p.m. She had claimed to be looking forward so much to seeing Helena, yet she seemed to be spending most of the time alone! Or perhaps she wasn't alone . . .

Alex ran a hand through his thick hair. It was an uncharitable thought; Kathryn was not like that. But neither had he been until Rebecca came along, just when he was at his lowest ebb. Too late he knew he should have fought the temptation but, unusually, he had been wondering what the point of it all was. He worked hard, enjoying it, true, although it was all for Kathryn. His reward had been an intensification of her own efforts, and what he took to be her turning aside from him. He had felt lonely, which was strange when he valued his own company.

Today, the weather had been pleasantly mild and Alex had opened one of the windows when he returned from the boat-yard. Outside he heard wood-pigeons calling and a conversation taking place between two other residents from the flats. With a glass of beer in his hand he stood and surveyed the spacious lounge, part of his and Kathryn's home. Floor-to-ceiling shelves held their books, Kathryn's more well-thumbed than his. There was a sofa and three armchairs, each with its own small table at the side. A long shelf over the stone surround of the fireplace had a porcelain vase at each end; heirlooms from one of his great-aunts. There was a carriage clock and a glass vase containing tulips whose petals had started to drop. In the middle was the tuatara, still lifelike although it was stuffed. It reminded him of Kathryn. 'My Tuatara Woman', he called her, because he recognised and admired her ability to see things which others did not. The tuatara had a third eye in the centre of its head just as Kath, in her own way, had an extra eye. He wished she knew what he felt for her, but understood what he had put her through. The telephone interrupted his thoughts.

'Alex? I've just got back. Helena said you rang.'

'Where have you been?' Relief at hearing her voice made him sound accusatory.

'Out.' Kathryn was puzzled by his tone and vaguely annoyed. He did not usually question her movements and he was hardly in a position to start doing so.

'I see. You disappear for a week, ostensibly to see your friends, and all you can say is "out".'

'Alex, I don't know what's bothering you but I can't see much point in continuing this conversation. I'll give you a ring tomorrow.'

'Oh, Kathryn, take no notice. I'm sorry. I'm missing you, that's all.'

There were a couple of seconds of silence. She could picture him, standing beside the table, one hand raking through his hair in a gesture that was so familiar to her. Had it occurred to him how much she had missed *him* when Rebecca was on the scene? 'Okay. I'll speak to you soon.'

'Shit,' he said aloud after she had hung up. Kathryn had given no indication that she was missing him. He went to change into a suit before driving into Windsor where he was taking prospective clients to dinner, over which he hoped to conclude another deal.

'Problems?'

'No, just Alex's foul temper. Can I do anything to help?'

'You can wash the salad if you really want to be useful, or you can cast your eyes over this.' Helena slid some sheets of paper across the table towards her. 'The pictures are in the folder. Tell me what you think.'

Kathryn removed them and read what Helena had

48

written to accompany them. 'It's great. I don't know how you do it.' Writing for children was so different from what she did. 'Don't you like it?'

Helena nodded and her pale hair, tied back when she cooked, bounced between her shoulder-blades. 'I just wanted a second opinion.'

It hadn't taken long to read as her current project was for the very young. Kathryn got out a chopping board and a knife then stood, frowning. 'It's awfully quiet.'

'I was just thinking the same myself. I'd better see what they're up to.' Clara had gone to stay with a schoolfriend in Oxford, Amy and Ben were in the playroom at the end of the passage. When Helena returned to say there was nothing ominous going on, the children were simply painting, Kathryn was staring out of the window at the expanse of countryside which dropped away from the back of the house.

'Helena, would you mind if I spent one more morning in Oxford?'

'Of course not, it's your holiday. Anyway, I've got quite a few things to sort out because I'm spending a couple of days away with Gerald soon, and Joanna's coming to stay to look after my shower.' Joanna was nineteen and lived in Witney. Between jobs she was grateful for the extra income.

'How do you come to terms with it all so easily?' Kathryn asked, once Amy and Ben were in bed and they had sat down to their meal. 'Don't you ever feel you're between two stools?'

'No. The children know they're loved and it does them no harm being with other people sometimes. Like tonight. God knows what Clara and Michelle will get up to, but if I allow her to stay with a friend, then I have to accept that that friend's parents will take responsibility. It's a school night, I can't see them being given permission to roam the streets. And you see, Kath, one day they'll be gone and if I don't invest time in Gerald now, it might be too late then.'

'But what about your career?'

'I suppose it's on hold for the moment, until Ben's older.'

'I meant your writing.'

Helena laughed. 'Do you think of it like that? Strange, I

49

don't. It's just something to occupy me for the time being. It's still the question of babies, isn't it? I don't know what you're so afraid of; they needn't alter your life drastically, not after the first few months anyway.' Helena decided not to mention Megan Morris or what Kathryn intended doing in Oxford because she feared the quest was becoming a bit of an obsession. They had finished their steak and began clearing the table. 'No, leave that – Mrs Potter's coming in tomorrow.' Kathryn had got out a cloth to wipe the surfaces.

'There, that's what I mean.' She smiled and looked more relaxed than when she had first arrived. 'If I had a cleaning lady, I'd be tidying up before she came.'

It was, Kathryn suspected, a complete waste of time but she could not get Jenny Branagh out of her mind. Once she had parked the car she followed the directions Helena had given her to the offices of the Oxford *Star*. Inside the building she asked if she could look through the archives.

'When for?' A young man had been summoned by the receptionist to help her.

'Roughly 1972 to 1980.'

'They're on microfiche. Know how to work it?'

'Yes, thanks.'

He took her to where they were housed and left her to it. With a practised eye she assimilated the format of the paper, learning which parts she could safely ignore. She avoided everything but news and local interest stories, but ploughing through so many copies was tedious and she began to lose concentration.

'Anything you want copying?' The young man poked his head around the door.

'No, nothing, thank you.' Kathryn was disheartened, which was ridiculous because she had not been expecting to find anything. There was no mention of Jenny Branagh, and Megan Morris's first novel had not been published until 1986. She might as well give up and admit defeat. Because he had been pleasant and helpful she chatted to the young man, telling him she was also a journalist and asking if he enjoyed his job and what his ambitions were.

'I love it, but I'm not certain about the future. I haven't

got my feet under the table here yet, but I have a feeling it's where I want to be. I suppose that makes me unambitious. At least I spent three years away when I was at college.'

Kathryn thought he hardly seemed old enough to have left school.

'I've lived here since I was four, went to school here and—'

'School – of course! Please don't think me rude,' she interrupted, 'but would it be all right if I had another quick look?'

'Of course. Carry on.'

School. It was a feeble hope but one she could not overlook. Jenny Branagh had not been to Oxford University but she might have lived here. Or Megan Morris might have done. It was still at the back of her mind that they could be one and the same person.

The task was far easier this time because there were only two newspapers to go through for each year, the two that published school examination results. 'Excuse me, could you do me a couple of copies of this, please?' Kathryn blushed as heads were raised from desks to stare in her direction. In her excitement she had spoken louder than she intended. Fumbling for coins to pay for the copies, she then dropped her purse and had to bend down to retrieve its contents. She hurried to the exit and went to find the car.

There were few students about as the Easter vacation had already started and their absence had created a different atmosphere in the city centre. She ran across the road in front of a slow-moving bus as her pay-and-display ticket was about to expire. Driving back to Helena's she did not allow herself to think it might be coincidence.

'You're all flushed. Did you find something?' Helena had Ben on one hip. She had just collected him from his playgroup and there was a fresh bump on his head.

'I'll tell you later. See to Ben first.'

'I'm going to put him down for a nap. I thought we'd go for a walk when he wakes. The woods are lovely at this time of year and we'll be back before the school bus. Make yourself a coffee, I shan't be a moment.'

Kathryn did so but was too excited to eat more than half the ham salad roll which constituted their lunch.

'Out with it then.' Helena flung her hair back with spread fingers.

'Read that.' Kathryn held the photocopy under her nose.

'All of it?' The print was tiny and covered the page.

'No, no, just that bit.' She squinted at the upside-down writing and found the relevant place. 'Look, there.'

'Calm down, Kath. Yes,' Helena continued slowly, 'I see what you mean.'

'And please don't tell me it mightn't be the same person. Besides, it fits my theory.'

'I didn't know you had one. But look, Kath, I think you're going to be in for one hell of a disappointment. You said she was wearing a wedding ring. Branagh's got to be her married name. The one here's a schoolgirl and you've only got the initial J.'

'Yes, but don't you see, the woman I met was the right age to have taken her O-levels in 1974 and the name's not that common. And she turned up when I was supposed to be meeting Megan Morris and made a point of speaking to me. Miss Morris was supposed to have been to Oxford and now it seems this woman went to school here. There must be a connection.'

Helena gave a deep sigh. 'I can't see it myself, but if it makes you happy . . .' She shrugged; it was gesture of resignation.

'You've got to admit it's possible, though.'

'It's possible, but there are an awful lot of *ifs*. Aren't you going to eat that?'

'No, I'm sorry, I can't. There's one other thing.' Kathryn paused. When she continued her voice was more subdued. 'The woman calling herself Branagh, she was well-dressed and spoke nicely and I got the impression that she'd had a good education. It doesn't tie in.' The J. Branagh mentioned in the Oxford *Star* had passed only two O-levels, both with low grades. She might have sat for others but the failures were not published.

'People change,' Helena told her, going along with it.

52

'Perhaps she was a late developer. Let's have another coffee then I'll wake Ben.'

Ben was crotchety but soon cheered up when Fudge licked his face and nudged him with his cold nose. The four of them left by the back door and headed down the gentle slope towards the woods.

The rough ground was unsuitable for the pushchair which Ben had almost outgrown. Helena kept a tight hold of his hand to prevent him tripping over the gnarled tree roots which bisected their path. Fudge ran on ahead, sniffing at rabbit holes and returning at intervals to make sure he had not been abandoned. Steam rose from the damp grass as the sun warmed up.

Ben was tiring. They sat on a log and let him play about with leaves and twigs as they discussed their futures. Helena admitted she had always wanted to write a novel.

'Me, too,' Kathryn told her as she removed her cream linen jacket. 'It's just a case of getting started, really.'

'Oh, I shall wait. It'll be something to look forward to when the children are off my hands. There's nothing to stop you, though, even if you get another job.'

Helena was so confident but Kathryn knew that if she attempted it she would not be satisfied unless her work was comparable with that of someone like Megan Morris.

'We'd better make tracks.' Helena picked Ben up. There was mud on his hands and bits of dried leaves sticking to his jumper. She ignored his protests and continued chatting to Kathryn. 'Only two more days and the holidays begin. Amy's got a friend coming for a week and—'

'Two days?' Kathryn, jacket hooked over her shoulder stood still.

'What's the matter?'

'Oh, Helena, you'll hate me for this but I've got something else to do in Oxford.'

Helena did not answer and Kathryn wondered if she had offended her. It couldn't be helped. Their friendship had survived many things; it would surely survive this. Tomorrow was Thursday. Kathryn vowed that the remaining three days would be devoted to her friends. Gerald was returning that evening and there was the theatre trip to look forward to on Friday. They walked in silence, both in jeans and T-shirts, two attractive women deep in their own thoughts. Helena's were concentrated upon what she had come to call Kathryn's mission and the reasons for it. She could not bear to think of her parting from Alex. Alex was strong and steady and adored her, and although she accepted the Rebecca thing should not have happened, Helena had a strong suspicion that Alex was more sinned against than sinning.

Kathryn, too, was thinking along similar lines, although Alex did not come into it. It was twenty-two years since J. Branagh had sat those exams and the likelihood of anyone remembering the girl or knowing what had become of her were extremely remote. But she had to find out.

After his meeting with John, David Shawcross lay in bed, his hands behind his head, and tried to analyse his feelings. Right up to the last minute, he had been determined not to turn up but the old pull still worked. Besides, John knew where the shop was; it would have been embarrassing if he'd come to find out what had happened. Anger, he thought, had been his predominant feeling. Anger – edged with fear. The effort to act normally, to make small talk and polite conversation had been enormous. Desperately he had tried to keep off the subject of the past and to make light of it as John had done.

Outwardly it had been a pleasant social meeting but David had sensed an underlying current. There was, he was certain, unfinished business and, knowing John, it would be to do with their Oxford days. What other conceivable reason was there for meeting?

John's abrasiveness and self-confidence had reminded him of his own fallibility when it came to character assessment. Look how wrong he had been about Nicola. But it was more than that; he was annoyed with himself for the feeble way in which he had gone along with John's plans without question and had drunk more than he was used to or wanted. He was, it seemed, still incapable of saying no to the man. What if more was asked of him? Was he strong enough to refuse?

From their conversation he gathered that John's life had not turned out to be as charmed as he had expected, but he still appeared untroubled. If he were more egocentric, more selfish, David thought, his own life would be happier.

But I am happy, he decided, sitting up and reaching for the light cord above him because he knew that sleep would elude him. I have my books. He loved them for their feel and their smell as well as for their contents. And there was Kitty and the flat. Contented perhaps, was a better word. Contented but far from blissful.

He sighed. It was useless to deny it. He had fallen for the old charisma and had found himself warming to John despite his efforts to remain aloof. No explanation had been offered as to why he had sought David out; he had nothing to offer other than his silence. Seventeen years ago he had given his word, they all had, and he did not intend breaking it.

He got out of bed, his thin ankles showing beneath the striped pyjamas, and went to the bathroom where he uncapped a bottle of antacid tablets. He no longer kept them by the bed because he feared he was becoming addicted to them.

They had eaten in a steak-house because it had been late by that time and David had been unable to suggest a decent restaurant. He had been relieved when John had said he didn't fancy an Indian or Chinese because he would be suffering even more now. He cursed mildly as he knocked his hip against the basin, knowing that there had been nothing to stop him advocating Italian food if John had wanted something spicy. There were enough dishes with herbs and garlic and he could have settled for some bland pasta.

He realised how long it was since he had had a proper night out, but he did not want any more like that one.

Back in bed he reached for one of the numerous volumes which surrounded him and read until the early hours. When he slept he dreamed of Sarah but he kept confusing her with Jenny.

Kathryn made several telephone calls before she left the

house. Helena had gone into Witney to post her manuscript and to buy fresh vegetables. Ben was with her and the girls were at school. Kathryn felt a pang of guilt. She ought to have offered to have Ben to give Helena a break.

The school J. Branagh had attended was no longer in existence. It had been swallowed up by a comprehensive but it was easy to find and Kathryn parked in one of the spaces reserved for staff. The buildings sprawled in the manner of all such local authority schools and she arrived just as the mid-morning break started. Pupils streamed out of the doors to enjoy a few minutes of sunshine, and although they were clad in regulation clothes they wore them in such differing ways that it was hard to see that they comprised a uniform.

As Kathryn had anticipated, the relevant headmistress had retired, and there were only a couple of members of staff who remained from the original school.

The corridors were busy and she had to make her way through throngs of adolescents and teachers who were too busy with end-of-term activities to pay her much attention. Kathryn had decided that her approach would be along the lines of writing an article about retired teachers.

One of the secretaries directed her to the headmistress's office. Miss Jefferson was expecting her.

'Come in and have a seat,' the woman called out. 'You're just in time for coffee.'

Kathryn had not expected her welcome to be so cordial, but Mary Jefferson was beginning to relax, counting the hours until the term was over. Coffee was poured and pleasantries about the weather were exchanged. 'I was hoping you might be able to tell me where I can find Mrs Robertson,' Kathryn began.

'Glynis? That's her.' Mary Jefferson stood and pointed to one of the portraits on the wall behind her. It was dated 1978 and showed a woman in her middle years. She was strong-featured with a hint of a smile, and handsome rather than attractive. 'I don't know, I'm afraid, and if we still have a record of her address it's probably out of date. Ah, just a minute, Peter Evans might know.' Her smile suggested a soft spot for the man. 'He'll be in the staffroom. I'll show you where it is.'

Peter Evans was not far from retirement himself and looked older than his years. He was oblivious to the frenetic activity elsewhere in the school and sat in a shabby armchair gazing out across the playing-fields. In his hand was a pipe which he studied lovingly. 'It's not allowed any more,' he said sadly after Kathryn introduced herself. 'Bad influence on the children and all that. Ridiculous. Most of them could teach me a thing or two. Now, what can I do for you?'

Kathryn was transported back to her own schooldays as she explained. The room smelled of tea and books and chalk and another indefinable ingredient which was always present in schools.

'Dear Glynis, one of the best. Did you know the name means pure and good? She *was* good.' There was humour in his eyes and Kathryn wondered if there had been more to their relationship than that of teaching colleagues, even though Peter Evans was some years her junior. 'After her husband died she went to live with a daughter, in Cowley of all places. She sold up the house, she said it held too many memories. She has what I believe they call a granny flat, but spends a lot of time travelling. That was always her intention once she retired and I suppose, however grim the daughter is, Glynis doesn't have to worry about leaving her house empty.'

'Do you keep in touch?'

'Yes. Infrequently these days, however. You know what it's like, one's good intentions get lost along the wayside.'

Kathryn sensed the man's respect for Mrs Robertson and doubted he would give her address to a stranger. She was right but he said he would ring her up and see if she was willing to speak to Kathryn. 'If she's at home, that is,' he added.

Kathryn waited while he made the call. 'I can't thank you enough,' she said when she learned that Glynis Robertson was not only at home but was prepared to see her that same afternoon.

Peter Evans escorted her part of the way along the corridor, books under his arm as he made his way to a class.

He wondered what this Mrs Brooks was up to; her gratitude was out of proportion to her request.

Kathryn had an hour or so to kill and decided she ought to telephone Helena to let her know roughly what time to expect her. If she was hungry she could have bought herself some lunch, but her appetite had diminished lately. For several minutes Kathryn sat in the car and watched the red-faced girls on the hockey-field. The grass was lush after all the rain but there were bare patches around the goalmouths. A man on a miniature tractor towed a roller over an adjacent field. Kathryn opened the window and breathed in the fragrance of crushed grass.

She drove towards the city centre and found a space where she could park for twenty minutes. After letting Helena know of her movements her elation dissolved. Her ridiculous quest was upsetting her husband and antagonising her friend. Helena had made no comment but her tone was cool.

Glynis Robertson's residence was not at all what Kathryn had expected for a retired headmistress. The address turned out to be that of a bungalow with an extension added at the back – presumably the granny flat. If the lady in question still travelled a lot, Kathryn thought she could safely assume she had not lost the use of her faculties.

She parked and locked the car and approached the front door, unsure where she ought to knock. Without warning an elderly woman appeared from around the side. 'I was watching for you, I have a separate entrance. My daughter's out at work all day so we won't be disturbed.'

Inside, everything was neat although there was a strong smell of cat. Mrs Robertson, head on one side, smiled. 'You've noticed.'

'I'm sorry?'

'Cats. Not mine, I hasten to add. They're my daughter's. She has five of them. Sometimes they get in here and make a nuisance of themselves. They used to sleep in here until it was converted for me.' She shrugged. 'I can't really complain. She lost a child some years back and they seem to have taken her place.'

'I'm sorry.'

'I always thought it was meant to be. She wouldn't have made a good mother.'

Kathryn was taken aback. She had not expected such forthrightness on a first meeting.

'Would you like some tea? Let's go through to the kitchen, it's sunnier there.'

While the tea was being made Kathryn stood in the open doorway and studied the garden. It was medium-sized and a small portion had been fenced off. 'That's my bit. I sit out there in my deck-chair in the summer. The fence doesn't keep the cats out but it discourages them. Peter said you're writing some sort of article?'

'Yes.' She hesitated then decided nothing but the truth would satisfy her hostess. 'I'm trying to follow up the history of one of your ex-pupils. Unfortunately it was a long time ago so I don't suppose you'll remember her. She would have attended the school somewhere between 1969 and 1974, before it became the Comprehensive. Her name was Jennifer Branagh.' Kathryn waited as Mrs Robertson spooned sugar into her tea. If there was no Jennifer Branagh or Mrs Robertson could not remember her, it was over.

'As it happens I do remember her.' Kathryn held her breath. 'For the simple reason she wasted every opportunity given to her. I don't mind when they're not well-equipped in the brains department, I don't mind when they do their best. But that one . . .' she shook her head. 'Well, girls like that infuriate me.'

Glynis Robertson was taller than she had appeared in her photograph and her hair was grey now but she still gave the impression she would be more than capable of controlling an unruly class. Why she had chosen to throw in her lot with her daughter was an enigma, and Kathryn wondered if she was really happy there.

'Funny, really,' she continued. 'You're from the press and it was Jennifer who was responsible for bringing them to my door once before. To the school, to be more accurate.'

'I hope I haven't brought back bad memories.'

There was a deep sigh. 'No. It was drugs. The problem was rife at the time. I daresay it still is. Their use had been increasing since the sixties, but not amongst schoolchildren, and, of course, at that time, we weren't trained to recognise the signs until it was too late. Several pupils were suspended – "excluded" they call it now. Heaven only knows why they keep messing around with the language. If there's a stigma attached to a word its replacement will acquire it anyway. Oh dear, I hope I haven't offended you. You're not into all this political correctness nonsense, are you?'

Kathryn grinned. 'No. Only equality.'

'Now that's a different matter. More tea?' Glynis Robertson was assessing her visitor. She thought she had an attractive face, a determined manner and a pretty smile, one that she suspected did not operate as frequently as it should. There was a wistfulness about the eyes. 'What was I saying? Yes, Jennifer. Nothing was ever proved but I always suspected she was the ringleader although she got off lightest. It was the usual story: the parents weren't interested and she was allowed to run wild with her elder brothers. It's the waste that saddens me. She had her fair share of intelligence – with a bit of encouragement she could have done well.'

'Could have? Do you know what happened to her?'

'No, I've no idea.'

A fair share of intelligence, Mrs Robertson had said. Had someone succeeded where she had failed, or was this a different Jennifer Branagh? Mrs Robertson was staring sadly into her cup.

'I hope I haven't upset you,' Kathryn said gently.

'Not at all.' And then, as if she had read Kathryn's mind, the older woman added, 'I was just wondering if it was me who failed. Why, exactly, do you want to find her?'

'I'm putting a piece together about girls who were teenagers during that decade.'

'And you'd like to find that good can come of bad?' The teasing tone was reminiscent of Peter Evans and Kathryn understood why they should have got on so well. 'I think you'll be disappointed. No, don't go yet. I enjoy company. I'll make some more tea.'

Kathryn did not refuse the offer but bit her lip as she realised how late it was getting. She could not blame Helena if she was angry.

Whilst the kettle boiled Glynis Robertson left the room and returned with a small box. 'I thought you might like to look at these. I don't know if it'll be of any help.' Inside the box were some yellowed newspaper cuttings and others that were more recent. 'Ignore these. Here.' She handed Kathryn a small one from the Oxford *Star*; it referred to several teenagers who had been charged with possessing drugs. Kathryn was puzzled as Jennifer was not one of them.

'She was a juvenile,' Mrs Robertson explained, 'and therefore dealt with separately.'

It did not help Kathryn but she thanked her just the same.

'But if you want to find her I thought you'd need an address from which to begin. Of course, you don't know. This one, Martin Bush, he was Jennifer's half-brother, or was it stepbrother? It was a bit of a mixed-up family. Anyway, he lived with them at this address.'

Kathryn made a note of it. From what she could recall, it was an area in the suburbs of Oxford. 'I really must go. I'm staying with a friend and I haven't seen much of her.'

'I enjoyed talking to you. If you do succeed in finding her, let me know, I'd be interested.' She walked with Kathryn to the car and waved as she drove away. For some reason, Mrs Robertson suspected she had not been told the whole truth.

Laura Tennyson watched a broadening band of pale blue sky. The rain had stopped – cleansing rain which had washed the streets of grime, freshened the plants and left her skin and hair feeling soft after she had walked in it. Rain, too, had washed away Sarah's blood. Nature had seen to the rest. By the time the body had been found there was nothing more than bones with which to identify her. It had not been easy, despite the distinctive ring she wore and the presence of her handbag.

She put the past to the back of her mind and concentrated on work. It was going well at the moment and she did not want to lose the thread. Peggy had been in that morning so she had not begun until after one and therefore intended continuing until about eight. Earlier, on the spur of the moment, she had taken herself to Reading and purchased a new outfit; a skirt and jacket in a coppery-coloured silk. The jacket was long and flowing, a style she most favoured and, feeling reckless, she had gone on to buy underwear and some chunky gold costume jewellery to go with it. She could, after all, afford it. Under the dressing-room lights the combination of the suit and her tawny hair had seemed autumnal and she was pleased with her purchases. Laura decided to keep the outfit to wear to the theatre in Windsor. Eileen Sprague had asked her to accompany her there. Eileen was several years her senior and widowed, but neither fact prevented her from enjoying life to the full. Laura suspected the only reason she had been offered the ticket was that Eileen had not found a man to partner her. She was so full of fun and, at times, so outrageous, that Laura could not help liking her.

It had been what Laura called one of her treat days, a day when she bought something to wear and something special to eat. There had also been that irresistible new biography of the Brontë family which would be added to her collection of biographies once she had read it. Treat days were usually reserved for the completion of a novel or to cure the blues. This one, she thought, had just been for the hell of it. Laura thought it ironical that she found the lives of authors more fascinating than the novels they had written. At least no one would ever be able to write *her* biography!

She returned to the desk and rattled off a few more paragraphs. It was easier now that she was on the third draft – more a case of tidying up than writing. Her concentration was just returning when she heard a click and a bleep as the answering machine picked up a message. She did not answer the phone when she was working and only returned calls when she had finished. For some reason she had forgotten to turn down the sound and therefore heard Giles's voice as clearly as if he was in the room. 'Are you there, Laura? I need to talk to you. It's quite important. You can reach me at home later.' Before she could get to the telephone to field the call he had hung up.

It was a little after six. Giles rarely left the office before then, not that she contacted him there unless it was an emergency, and only then on his private line. She was in possession of his home number but had had no occasion to use it and therefore had to look it up. Distracted by his serious tone she switched off the typewriter and went downstairs, taking some pages with her to check them for errors. She sat with a glass of wine beside her until she thought Giles had had time to reach home then she dialled his number.

'Gut evening.' The accent was distinctly guttural. It was the first time Laura had heard Ingrid's voice. Naturally she was aware that she was foreign, but it still gave her a jolt. Surely Giles, the epitome of Englishness, had not fallen for a stereotypical Scandinavian blonde? No, she was more than likely an intense Teutonic of average looks who would not cause a stir.

'Hello, may I speak to Giles, please?'

'Who is this calling?'

Laura bit back a retort. Giles was not in his office, he did not need protection from an unwanted caller and the number was unlisted; he would not have given it to someone he did not wish to use it. 'He left a message for me to contact him. It sounded urgent.' Laura was smugly gratified that she had avoided giving her name, then wondered why she had wanted to put the woman down. Maybe it was Giles's fault. They had always been close, sharing confidences since their university days, but Ingrid he refused to discuss.

'It is some woman,' she heard quite distinctly, as she was meant to do, while she waited for Giles to come to the phone.

'I wouldn't have troubled you at home, only . . .'

'Yes, yes, that's fine. Look, I had a call today. John Atherton's back from the States and he wants to meet me for a drink.'

'Oh, God.' Weak-kneed, Laura carried the telephone to the nearest armchair, dragging the long extension lead behind her. John. Myriad thoughts flashed through her mind.

'He was asking about you. Well, about all of us really.'

'What did you tell him?' Laura heard the rising note of panic in her voice and lit a cigarette with a shaking hand.

'Nothing. You know me better than that.'

'And are you going to see him?'

'Yes. He'd have thought it odd if I'd refused. He's already seen David. I think he just wants to check the position.'

'The position, as you succinctly put it, can hardly have altered, and he damned well knows that.'

'Look, you haven't done anything I don't know about, have you?'

'What on earth are you talking about?'

'I don't know. It's just this, coming so soon after that business with Kathryn Brooks.'

'Oh, don't be such an ass, Giles. You can't imagine that girl has anything to do with John's appearance.'

'No, not really. And he did mention that his contract had expired.'

'There you are then. He's just looking up old friends. You worry too much, you'll give yourself an ulcer. Get Ingrid to pour you a large drink and stroke your troubled brow.' She had not meant to sound cynical but she was as worried as Giles was.

'Ingrid?' Giles sounded as though the idea was preposterous.

Laura was amused. 'Well, just remember Montaigne.' She quoted in French before hanging up.

'Fame and tranquillity can never be bedfellows', was the translation. It was John who had made it their motto in the days when they all envisaged achieving notability.

Two things struck Laura simultaneously as she took the manuscript back to the attic. Giles had not once used her name during the conversation. And she had not thought of their games for a very long time. One mention of John Atherton's name had been enough to bring all the quotations rushing back.

Montaigne may have penned the original words, John may have adopted them for their own use, but it was Laura who had to live by them.

Kathryn made her peace with Helena, who was not as

annoyed as she had sounded over the telephone. She handed her two bunches of irises which was a feeble token but they were accepted with pleasure.

'Again?' Helena was incredulous when Kathryn said she needed another hour or so in Oxford. Her eyes widened and the flecks of pigmentation which made them so unusual were clearly visible. 'All right. Then why don't you make it in the afternoon and we can all meet up for the theatre? That way we can have the morning together – Ben'll be at his playgroup.'

Kathryn hugged her. 'Thank you.'

'For what?'

'For being my friend. And for being so understanding.'

Kathryn had put on a dress to visit the school. Now she went upstairs to change. The light in her bedroom was almost orange as the sun began to set. Her skin smelled of it, warm and pleasant and reminiscent of summer. She hung up the dress and slipped into jeans and a shirt, one of Alex's which was too big but went well worn over the jeans with a waistcoat. Alex. What was he doing right now? With an almost physical sensation she realised she was missing him but there was no answer when she rang her home number.

It was noisy downstairs as the whole family was assembled. Amy was on Gerald's knee, twiddling his hair between her none-too-clean fingers. Helena, as unruffled as ever, was pouring drinks; Clara was given a sherry glass of wine. 'Not in?'

'No. I know he had several meetings to attend.' Kathryn busied herself by cutting up Ben's bread and butter. Alex had informed her of his plans for the week but she had not listened. She hadn't listened to a lot of things but Rebecca, presumably, had. Kathryn began to see the root of the problem.

Chapter 4

John Atherton had not missed the hesitancy in Giles's voice and he smiled to himself. Surely his old friend was not still afraid of the past – or maybe even of John himself? He had been in London for four days. His hotel was more than comfortable and there was plenty to do, but the city was beginning to bore him. This was odd when he had left Cardiff in search of excitement.

His university city was on a smaller, more manageable scale; unlike the West End, there were locals and regulars in the central pubs. John particularly liked the area around The Hayes and St Mary Street, where many of the pubs sold Brains Bitter and had retained their character, making no concessions to youth. According to his female colleagues, there was more than enough choice in the various shopping arcades, but this aspect did not interest him. The whole place had changed since his visits as a young man. Queen Street had been pedestrianised, a modern phenomenon with which he did not agree. Such places became eerie and impersonal at night. He preferred a mixture of traffic and people. Cardiff Bay, however, was being revitalised and the National Stadium upgraded to host the Rugby Union World Cup in 1999.

He strolled along the Embankment adversely comparing the Thames with the Taff and wondered what was happening to him. Travel and change were losing their appeal and he found himself wishing he was in Bute Gardens or walking past the cricket ground alongside the river which led to the woods. Woods used by people jogging or

66

exercising their dogs ... such different woods from the one where they used to go.

In retrospect, John realised it would have been better for his health to have forgotten all about contacting the old crowd and instead to have gone further north, to the Lakes, maybe, where he could walk and enjoy good food which was not overpriced and regain some semblance of physical fitness. It wasn't too late to do so, but he was feeling the need for companionship. His problem was that he had not had a woman for a long time. A brief fling would suit him nicely. If he did move on, he might find a solitary female to share his walks and his bed.

Despite his diffidence, Giles had been more accommodating than David and had offered to meet John at his hotel. He glanced at his watch. It was still too soon to return because he knew he would end up in the bar. Leaning against the stone parapet he watched the busy river traffic. Already a few pleasure-boats were sedately ploughing through the steely water, expectant gulls bobbing in their wake.

At five-thirty he turned back. Having managed to cross several sets of traffic lights without mishap he finally hailed a taxi which then took ten minutes to negotiate the first hundred yards. By the time he got to the hotel there was only ten minutes in which to splash his face with water and change his clothes. Even so he was nursing a Scotch when Giles arrived a few minutes late.

Giles was as tall and distinguished as John had remembered him. The mane of hair, almost white now, shocked him until he recalled that Giles had already been greying at university. He stood up to greet him. They shook hands: Giles rather formally, John with one arm possessively around the other man's shoulders.

'Hello, there,' John said heartily. 'It's great to see you again. You're looking well. Oh, and I hear you're a bit of a star in the publishing world.'

'The authors are the stars, old boy, temperament and all,' Giles replied, ignoring John's initial enthusiastic greeting. He had no idea why he had agreed to come. Long ago he had decided he wanted nothing to do with anyone from the

67

past, apart from Laura. In addition, he was suspicious of John's motive. There had to be one, there always was. 'Are we staying here or shall we find a decent hostelry?' he enquired. 'One with real ale?'

'I know a place up the road.' John downed his drink in one. He was pleased that, like himself, Giles had not lost the taste for beer that was cask-conditioned. Hotel bars were for gin and tonics or cocktails. They strolled around the corner. The sky was overcast and murky, and grit was disturbed by passing cars.

Giles surreptitiously watched his old friend. By the look of him, John had continued to live a vaguely debauched existence – the telltale signs were there. Yet it suited him in a way; he had grown into his looks and he still radiated confidence. There was only the faintest hint of flesh around his middle, even after sixteen or seventeen years. They had not seen each other since Oxford. Whilst Giles had gone straight into publishing, John, uncertain what he wanted of his future, had spent time on a post-grad, course. Giles had learned this from Laura, with whom he had never lost touch. It was she who later informed him that John had taken a post in America – news which had filled Giles with relief.

'Are you back for good?' he asked now, as they left Hyde Park behind them and strolled past Arabic restaurants and banks until they came to the Edgware Road and the pub John had mentioned.

'Yes. Ten years was enough.' He had not been mistaken, Giles was definitely cool.

The pub door was wedged open and the feeble sunshine made rainbows on the polished wood of the tables where it shone through the stained glass in the lower half of the windows. It was a typical Victorian pub with brass fittings and plenty of crimson plush, although none of these features was original. Commuters, briefcases at their feet, propped up the bar or sat at tables, their ties loosened as they read the *Evening Standard* and relaxed for half an hour to avoid the rush before their homeward journey. Giles paid for the drinks but remained standing at the bar as he did not intend staying long.

'I take it it's true, what David told me about your being Megan Morris's publisher?'

'It is. But that's one lady I make a point of never discussing.' Giles frowned. He was still trying to work out what had induced Laura to go to the Thames Riviera that day. Yes, she had agreed to the meeting with Kathryn Brooks ... but at the time he had only thought she was being uncharacteristically cruel.

'Why all the secrecy?'

Giles shrugged. 'That's the way the lady wants it.'

'But surely people have tried to find out who she is?'

'You wouldn't believe just how many, but we've got a water-tight system.' He tried not to think of Kathryn Brooks.

John was studying him with the half-quizzical, half-amused expression he remembered of old. 'Is it anyone I know?'

Giles was pleased he hadn't taken a mouthful of his beer or he might have choked. He laughed uncertainly. 'No, of course not. What on earth made you ask?'

'Oh, nothing in particular. Except the blurb claims she was at Oxford.'

'Ah, I see.' Giles relaxed against the bar, unaware that the elbow of his jacket was in a small pool of beer. 'That was my idea. The biog's a fiction, a safeguard. I know Oxford and I thought it would be easier to field any questions if I used a familiar place. It's that simple. You must have read her to know that.'

'Not yet. I picked up a copy of one of her novels after David mentioned it.'

'You'll enjoy it, whichever one it is.' Giles wondered if there was any way in which John would recognise Laura's style. He used to read her essays and make his own brand of vicious criticism. Because he had believed himself to be better than the rest of them, he had underrated Laura's abilities. His ego would probably preclude him from guessing that it was she who had later become so successful. Giles had never been completely certain why she wanted to remain anonymous, but he respected her wishes and had no intention of discussing her further with John, who was in the process of lighting a cigarette.

'You didn't give up then?' Giles had done so at the same time as Laura but she had only lasted a couple of weeks before she started smoking again.

'No. Only during lectures.'

'You ought to give it a try. It can't be doing you much good, the way you go at it.'

' "More people are flattered into virtue than bullied out of vice".'

'I apologise.' Giles managed a weak smile. He knew he had sounded pompous. 'Surtees, wasn't it?'

'Correct.' John laughed as he slapped the other man on the back, and suddenly the ice was broken. All restraint on Giles's part dissipated as they discussed their old word-games. They used to try to find an appropriate quotation for any given situation, and spent hours searching for something relevant and trying to catch each other out. Once they had maintained a conversation for over two minutes using nothing else.

'So you've achieved professional eminence,' John said finally. 'Now, tell me: how're things on the home front?'

'I'm married – to a German lady called Ingrid. She's rather beautiful and extremely bright. No children, though. How about you?'

'Divorced. No kids either.' He spoke of his life in the States. 'It's very different and I'm glad I went. However, I'm also glad to be back. I hadn't realised how many things I missed. And now I'm looking forward to settling down to a life of academic pursuits and becoming a crusty old professor whom the students will adore and christen with an appropriate nickname. I might even remarry. I shall find myself a nice little Welsh girl who will cook and clean for me and entertain me late into the night with intelligent discourse before I take her to bed.'

Giles found himself laughing again. 'Good God, man, you don't want much.'

'Only what every man wants but is afraid to admit for fear of being labelled sexist.'

'Do such creatures exist – women like that?'

'Not on the other side of the Pond, that's for sure. Tell me about Ingrid, she sounds fascinating.'

'She does things with computers, but don't ask me what exactly because I don't fully understand the jargon, and she's got more hobbies than anyone I've ever met. There's just one downfall. She can't cook. And that's putting it kindly. And she's got a son, Paul.' It was added as an afterthought, as if the boy barely existed.

'Oh? Is that a problem?'

'Not really. He's away at school during term-time and he seems to prefer spending most of his holidays elsewhere. That's the one thing which puzzles me about Ingrid.' Giles was warming to his theme, not realising how quickly his intention of keeping the meeting short and businesslike had evaporated. John was the last person he would have imagined confiding in. 'She was a single mother but she planned the baby. At the time she meant never to marry. She picked a man whose genes, combined with her own, would theoretically produce a perfect specimen.'

'My God, that's a bit cold-blooded, isn't it?'

'Nor did she inform the father. She wanted to bring the child up herself. You know, I think despite everything she was insecure; she wanted something all of her very own to show for her life. What puzzles me is why she sent the boy away to school.'

'Perhaps the experiment went wrong.'

Giles had not viewed it in this light but he could not credit Ingrid with such heartlessness; she had only wanted what she considered the best for Paul. There was nothing wrong with the boy. He was bright and polite and kept out of trouble, but Giles had never been able to form a bond with him. He lacked experience with children and Paul had been eleven, not an easy age, when he married Ingrid. That was six years ago and Paul was almost a man now. Giles hoped their relationship would improve with time.

'Don't you find it odd, that the three males of our crowd are without children? How did the female side fare, I wonder? I don't suppose you ever hear from Jenny or Laura?' John recalled the cryptic postcard.

'No, not a word in all these years.' Giles felt uncomfortable. He neither wished to discuss Laura nor to have to lie. 'I imagine Jenny stayed in Oxford and, awful as it sounds, she wasn't exactly the sort of friend one needed at the start of a career.'

John, who was more liberal than Giles, had to agree. 'I expect they've made up for us and are bogged down with children and the PTA and domesticity. All that intelligence wasted.'

Giles smiled into his beer. He could never have thought of Laura in that way. 'Perhaps. Fancy another?'

'It's my shout.'

Giles glanced at the large clock behind the bar. He had told Ingrid he would not be late, that he was only meeting John out of politeness because he was certain they would no longer have anything in common. The past, he assumed, would be a taboo subject yet they had touched upon it quite naturally, without embarrassment or pain, and the verbal sparring had returned spontaneously. At least he had the consolation that whatever Ingrid had prepared to eat, the outcome would not be worsened by his tardiness. He admired her for her perseverence, and her other attributes far outweighed her culinary disasters. She was outspoken, perspicacious and refused to settle for soft options. Theoretically she was more beautiful than Laura, with the palest hair and the body of a woman half her age. He loved her but not in the way in which he loved Laura – in whose presence he felt bewitched.

It was after ten before Giles made his way to the nearest tube station. The air was cool with a hint of rain, which was welcome to his flushed face. He was, he realised, a little drunk.

'I've apologised, Alex, I can't do more than that.' Kathryn was becoming exasperated by his persistent questions as to how she spent every minute of her time.

'It's always the same! You get an idea in your head and you won't let it go. Surely it isn't asking too much for you to ring me once in a while?'

'I've just done so, if you recall. I'll have to go now, I'm meeting Helena and Gerald in a few minutes.' Kathryn had called from a public telephone box and was sorry now that she'd bothered. Alex had not shown the slightest interest in

72

what she had managed to find out. 'Look,' she hesitated, half-fearful of the answer, 'are you coping all right? It's only for another couple of days.'

'I won't starve, if that's what you mean.' It was Alex's turn to pause. 'But hurry home, Kath. I really miss your bum.'

'You what?' She laughed, despite her annoyance, peculiarly pleased at the bizarre compliment.

'In bed. When I turn over, it isn't there to cuddle into.'

'Well, I'll be back on Sunday.' Her dark hair swung forward as she replaced the receiver. She tucked it behind her ears and smoothed down the pale blue short-sleeved dress she had bought that afternoon and decided to wear for their evening out. The sales assistant had cut off the tags and given her a carrier bag for her skirt and blouse.

Kathryn walked the short distance to the Randolph Hotel where she was meeting Helena and Gerald for a pre-theatre cocktail. She was the first to arrive and ordered her drink which the barman brought to her table on a tray. She had not, she realised, missed Alex, not in the way he seemed to be missing her. He concentrated upon her absence, while she spent her time looking forward to seeing him again. Unaccountably, she worried more about what he might be doing when she was with him, than when she had no chance of knowing.

She looked up. A uniformed porter stood next to her table. 'Mrs Brooks?' She nodded. 'A message for you.' He handed her a small piece of paper. Helena had rung to say the baby-sitter had arrived late but they were on their way.

'Thank you.' Kathryn sank back into the chair and thought about the events of the day.

With the much-studied street map Helena had provided, Kathryn had driven to the outskirts of Oxford to the address given in the cutting Glynis Robertson had shown her. The street was long and narrow and lined with cars because there were no parking restrictions. The houses were brick-built and cramped and grubby, a side of Oxford unknown to tourists. Although the sky was cloudless, the sun did not seem to penetrate the street and there was an unpleasant smell of stale grease which came from the fish and chip shop on the corner.

The newspaper cutting had not stated a number and Kathryn had been extremely doubtful if anyone called Branagh still lived in the area. She had had no option but to knock on doors. The first two yielded no response and at the third, a frail man bent over a stick shut the door in her face before she had a chance to say anything. She eventually found herself confronting a pimply youth who jerked his thumb towards the end of the road. 'Yeah, I know her,' he said. 'Number nine.' He stared expectantly for a couple of seconds as though he might be rewarded for this information, then shut the door before Kathryn had a chance to thank him. She was scarcely able to believe what she had heard.

Saliva dried in her mouth as she knocked at the door of number nine. They were still there, or someone by that name was. She hadn't been able to understand it as there was no Branagh listed in the telephone directory, and the operator had told her it was neither a new nor unlisted number.

When the door was answered she thought there must have been a mistake. A woman, head cocked to one side, regarded her through a cloud of smoke. With her elbow cupped in her right hand, a cigarette held between two fingers of her left hand, close to her mouth as if to save time between drags, her eyes narrowed suspiciously when Kathryn said who she was. A quarter of an inch of ash had fallen to the floor when she was finally invited inside.

Mrs Branagh wore a wedding ring and seemed about the right age to be Jennifer's mother but, like the house, she reeked of stale tobacco and from what Kathryn had been able to see of the place, every penny must have been spent on cigarettes. The stair carpet was threadbare and greasy and the wallpaper discoloured.

'What're you raking up now, duck?' Mrs Branagh asked as she showed her into the front room. 'Whatever it is I daresay you could do with a cup of tea.'

Kathryn was unsure whether she would be able to drink

anything produced under such conditions but she needed a few minutes' breathing space. 'I'd love one. Thank you.'

The front room was dingy due to lack of sunlight and the presence of a yellowish net curtain. The room was relatively tidy but in need of a clean. Old newspapers were heaped on a 1950s-style coffee table, on top of which was an over-flowing ashtray. The grate held a brown banana skin and screwed-up cigarette packets. It had, she had decided, been a wild-goose chase. This woman could not possibly have had anything to do with the elegant Ms Branagh in the Thames Riviera.

'Here we are, dear, push that lot on the floor.'

Kathryn was surprised when the tea was served in a pot with milk and sugar in their respective containers. She watched the tea being poured, trying hard not to stare at Mrs Branagh's purplish-red hair and her brightly coloured, too tight clothes.

'It's a long time since we've had a reporter round here. They soon lose interest once another tragedy comes along.'

'I wouldn't have come unannounced, Mrs Branagh, but I couldn't find a telephone number.' Kathryn wanted to get off on the right note.

The response was friendly enough. 'Sylvie, dear. Everyone calls me Sylvie. And it's not surprising, the phone was cut off years ago. There's a box on the corner if I need it.'

'You said tragedy?' Kathryn had decided to be polite, drink her tea and leave as quickly as she was able.

'You don't know? My son got himself killed in a motor-bike accident. He always did go too fast. Mind you, that was some years ago now.'

'I'm sorry.'

'Why? Wasn't your fault. It wasn't Dean you wanted to speak to, was it?'

Kathryn explained as best she could that she was trying to follow up people who were teenagers in the 1970s. 'I expect you know the type of thing – what they're doing twenty years on.'

Mrs Branagh's raucous laughter filled the room. 'I can't

75

help you there. I've been taken for younger than my years, but not that young.'

Kathryn doubted it, but smiled. 'I was speaking to a Mrs Robertson, who used to be a headmistress. She's getting old so she may have been mistaken, but she led me to believe that you once had a daughter at her school.' Kathryn mentally crossed her fingers. There was no question of Glynis Robertson's memory being faulty.

Sylvie lit another cigarette and sucked at it without replying. Kathryn waited.

'Yes. Jennifer did go to her school. She was trouble, that girl. She gave us all a bad name, getting into drugs like that. She was suspended but went back to do her exams. I don't know why she bothered, she had no chance of catching up. I told her she'd be better off getting a job right away, but that one had ideas above her station. She soon learned when she got her results. Moved out, she did, and got a job as a waitress.'

'Here in Oxford?'

'Where else? I never did find out where she was living. Then Dean told me she'd got a new set of friends. We weren't good enough any more.'

'Do you keep in touch now?'

'Be a bit difficult, duck. She buggered off years ago. I've not heard a word from her since.'

Kathryn placed her cup and saucer on the tray and stood up to leave. All her hopes had been dashed.

'In that case I won't take up any more of your time. Thank you for talking to me. And for the tea.'

'Oh, don't look so upset, dear, she isn't worth the effort. If you ask me, you'd be better off talking to some of her posh friends – they'll have done all right for themselves.'

By that time they had reached the front door. 'Her friends? I thought you didn't know them.'

'I didn't. Not personally, like. But they were all from the university.'

Kathryn felt like hugging Sylvie Branagh. It was a connection, however tenuous. 'Oxford University?'

'Yes.' Sylvie studied her as if she wasn't very bright. 'As I said, Dean kept me informed. One of them was called

Giles. It always sticks in my mind because I can't imagine any mother calling a poor innocent baby that. Mickey took it badly when she got mixed up with that lot. He thought they'd get married; he blamed the students for taking Jenny away from him. I told him straight, he was better off without her.'

'Mickey?' Kathryn had begun scribbling furiously.

'Jenny's ex-boyfriend. He's still around, living with some girl. Living off her, more like. Still, it's none of my business. He'll be in if you want to speak to him, glued to the television, no doubt.'

'I might.' Kathryn's reply had been vaguely noncommittal. She wrote down the address and left. Mrs Branagh, she considered as she followed the directions given, probably had reason to overindulge in cigarettes: one son dead, one daughter missing and, she had learned at the last minute, a husband who had run off with a younger woman. Only later did Kathryn realise that she had not thought of Alex in connection with this piece of news. Perhaps she was starting to forgive him.

'Kathryn, I'm so sorry. Have you been here long?'

'Not very. And you're not as late as I expected. What happened?'

'Joanna's car wouldn't start so I had to go and fetch her,' Gerald explained as he bent to kiss her cheek. 'You look rather glam.'

'So do both of you.' The annoying thing was that Helena always did, no matter what she wore. Tonight the masses of hair were piled up and she wore a dress which was neither green nor blue but changed colour as she moved. Unusually her heels were high. Helena caught her glance.

'Oh, don't worry, I shall probably slip them off in the theatre. Have we got time for a drink?'

Gerald said they had and ordered a round. 'It's all right.' He forestalled Kathryn's protests. 'We came by cab and I've already spoken to Reception. As we're eating here later you can leave your car overnight.' The play, they knew from the reviews, only lasted an hour and a half which they had all agreed was perfect as they would not have to rush over the meal. It was one of those quirky productions which was unlikely to make it to the West End.

'Out with it, I can see you're bursting,' Helena said whilst Gerald was talking to the barman.

Kathryn gave her a brief resumé of her conversation with Sylvie Branagh. 'I did go to see him, Michael Jarvis, but I'll tell you about that tomorrow. This is my treat and I'm not going to spoil it by talking shop.'

'Is that why you changed? The new dress?' Helena fingered it. 'It's lovely and soft.'

'Partly. I felt I needed a bath when I left Mrs Branagh. I was going to buy something new anyway. My clothes don't seem to fit properly.'

'That's because you've lost weight. I'm not sure that it suits you, Kath.'

'That's ironical, coming from you.' But Helena was naturally tiny and could eat whatever she wanted. 'Hey, look at the time. We'd better drink up.'

Kathryn felt proud to be with her friends. Gerald looked elegant and intelligent behind his thick-rimmed glasses and the play was a success, likewise the meal. 'You do realise what this means,' Kathryn commented as they waited for the taxi to drive them back to Witney. 'I'll have to come in tomorrow to pick up the car.'

'We're all coming in,' Gerald reassured her. 'Some shopping and lunch on me. Joanna's staying overnight and has agreed to have the children for the day. Clara's made her own arrangements.'

Kathryn was exhausted. She lay in the comfort of her bed with a slight breeze from the window ruffling the curtains. There was a safety lock which meant it could be left open an inch. Deciding it wasn't quite warm enough to leave it open, she got out of bed to close it and, in doing so, knocked her file to the floor. She switched on the bedside light and found she was no longer tired. Taking out the pages of notes she had made, she reread them.

Michael, or Mickey Jarvis, lived only a few streets away from Sylvie Branagh. The house was similar but in a better condition. From outside she could hear a television blaring away. Her first impression was that he had the build of a manual labourer until she saw that some of the muscle had run to fat. His reception was less than welcoming.

'Sylvie sent me,' Kathryn explained, hoping that the two were on speaking terms. 'I'm doing a feature about teenagers in the 1970s.'

'For the telly?' Michael stood in the doorway, filling the space, and it seemed unlikely that Kathryn would be invited in. She had taken a chance and said it was possible.

'How much do I get?'

It took almost ten minutes to negotiate with him. Eventually Kathryn offered ten pounds of her own money for what she described as the initial interview. If Alex or Helena had seen her, she thought, they would have been sending for the men in white coats.

Lying under the lightness and warmth of Helena's duvet, Kathryn read the transcript of the interview and tried to decipher what it was about Michael Jarvis that she did not like. He was gruff and not very articulate, but she had dealt with far worse than that in the course of her job, and he had not objected to her taking their conversation down in shorthand.

Quickly she had run through his schooling and his apprenticeship in the building trade. 'I was in work for a long time, then my boss went bust. I got the odd job here and there but things weren't good. They're still not. At least Maggie's in work.'

'Maggie?'

'My girlfriend.'

Kathryn had taken the opportunity to introduce Jenny. 'Have you been together long? I mean, is she a long-standing girlfriend?'

When Michael grinned she had seen his appeal. 'No. There've been more than a few. I thought I was going to get married once, but it didn't work out.'

'Jennifer Branagh?'

'Yes.'

Kathryn looked up from her notes, unable to define the expression which had crossed his face when he answered. Pain? Anger? She instinctively knew that he did not want to talk about her. She persisted anyway. 'What went wrong?'

79

Michael Jarvis may have been large and fleshy, but his face was pinched and there were furrows across his forehead which she thought him too young to have earned. 'Everything. She got in with people from the University, she became moody. At first I thought it was just her. Later I realised she was on drugs. I loved that girl, I really did. They took her away from me. Anyway . . . I thought it was me you wanted to talk about?'

She reassured him. 'Yes, I do. But anything from that period of your life might be relevant. Past events often shape the future. Don't worry, I shan't use any material without your permission.'

'You're bloody right about the past. My life would've been a lot different if Jenny had stayed with me. She got taken in by that crowd, she even ended up looking like one of them. I hated them.' Kathryn wondered if he spent a great deal of time brooding over what might have been. One thing was certain, he had never forgotten Jennifer Branagh.

Outside her bedroom door she heard muffled footsteps and, a couple of minutes later, the lavatory cistern refilling. Helena or Gerald must also be restless. They had an ensuite bathroom, but whoever was up presumably did not want to wake the other. The footsteps neared then faded, followed by a creak of the stairs. Someone was going to make tea. Kathryn decided to join them.

She got up and put on the navy satin robe Alex had bought for her previous birthday. It felt chilly against her skin. In bare feet she crossed the thick pile carpet and opened her door as quietly as she could. It still creaked.

It was dark until she had reached the bottom of the stairs and made her way along the narrow corridor, then a wedge of light from the kitchen guided her.

'Helena?' She was sitting at the table, her head in her hands. Behind her the kettle began to boil. 'Helena, what is it?'

'I don't know, Kathryn. I can't think what's the matter with me. I've been so worried about you and Alex – I couldn't bear it if you split up. It makes me think how illusive it all is and if I'm doing the right thing.'

'No, stay there, I'll make the tea.' Kathryn needed those seconds to absorb what Helena had said. She had always been the one she looked to when she had a problem, the one stable influence in her life, someone who was fun yet sensible and coped, someone she would like to emulate. How thoughtless and naive she had been not to see that she was also human.

'I don't want to split up with Alex,' she said quietly. 'It's just been a difficult time. We'll be all right, I promise.'

'But if you did split up, you're a free agent, and you've got your work.'

'Is there anything wrong between you and Gerald?'

'No, it's just seeing how positive you are about your life makes me question if *I'm* doing the right thing. Everything seems such a muddle. Am I being fair to the children, do you think?'

'Oh Helena, you know you are. You only have to look at them. They're healthy and happy and well-balanced, and they love you both.'

The other woman smiled wanly. 'I know. Even Clara isn't too much of a handful and I know what some of her friends' parents have to go through. Take no notice, it's all down to hormones. God, you always did make disgusting tea.' Helena stood and took her mug to the sink where she emptied half the contents and added hot water from the kettle. 'Do you want to talk about your day? It'll divert me from my moping.'

'Sure? Okay, then. I went to see Jenny's ex-boyfriend, as you know. However, I'm coming around to your way of thinking that it's all just a coincidence. Unless she's changed drastically, the woman I met would not have gone out with someone like Michael Jarvis.'

'Was he that bad?'

'No. It's just that they're worlds apart.'

'So what happened?'

'Jenny became involved with a group of students, got into drugs and, according to both Michael and her mother, simply upped and left without warning. He tried to find her but couldn't. He said he thought she might have gone to London – she'd talked about it. And then he dropped his bombshell.' Kathryn sipped her tea. It was unsweetened and very dark, the way both she and Alex liked it.

'Well, go on.' Helena no longer looked miserable; she was genuinely interested.

'He mentioned the names of several of the students; they used to go into the café where Jenny worked, that's how she got to know them. Anyway, he obviously assumed I knew more than I did because he said, and these are his words, "And there was that little tart, Sarah Milton, who managed to get herself murdered".'

'Murdered? What on earth are you getting into, Kath?'

She shook her head and hitched her hair back again. It was at the length where the ends tickled her mouth. 'I don't know, but as they say, the plot is definitely thickening. I've lost track, though, because Megan Morris doesn't come into any of this.'

'What are you going to do now?'

'I'm not sure, except I might try to contact these old friends of Jenny's. Don't worry, I shan't get into any trouble, it's just to satisfy my own curiosity. You see, again according to Michael, there were six of them. Jenny Branagh disappeared, yet someone of that name introduces herself to me, and this Sarah Milton was murdered.'

'Did you get the other names?'

'Sort of. One of them was called Giles. Sylvie Branagh remembered the name, so did Michael, but not the surname. Two others were called John Atherton and Laura Something, but he said he wasn't sure he ever knew the name of the other boy. All he could remember was that he was what he called a boring bastard.'

'He seems to have remembered quite a lot.'

'Yes. I had the impression that he's never got over losing Jenny – he was very intense about her.'

'Do you think it's wise, trying to find them? After all this time they won't thank you for raking up the past, especially if one of their friends was killed.'

'I'm not sure about wise, but I have to do it.'

'Yes, that's typical. Hey, look at the time, we ought to try to get some sleep. You know what Gerald is like, up before the dawn chorus. At least we don't seem to have disturbed anybody. Did you hear Joanna snoring?' They giggled as they went upstairs and listened outside her room. 'Adenoids, poor thing,' Helena whispered before they parted.

The following morning, feeling reckless, Kathryn spent more than she intended. Helena decided she needed one more dress because she didn't want to let Gerald down on their next trip. To Kathryn's surprise Gerald accompanied them throughout their shopping – something Alex would not have dreamed of doing.

The streets were busy but in a different way from when the students were in residence. The pedestrians were house-wives and schoolchildren carrying plastic bags of groceries and jeans rather than armfuls of books, and yet the ancient buildings still dominated.

They found a pub which was not too busy and had a bar snack. Their purchases stowed in the boot of the car, they walked off lunch in the Parks where, in a week or two, there would be cricket matches.

'It's your last night, Kathryn. Is there anything in particular you'd like to do?' Gerald's expression was serious. He was a considerate man and treated friends as if they were precious.

'No, unless you've anything in mind.'

'Why don't we just stay in and drink some wine and play Scrabble or something. We can't impose on Joanna any longer, even though she likes the money.' Helena's suggestion was agreed upon.

It felt to Kathryn that she had been away a long time, but when the morning came it seemed as if she had not seen much of Helena and she was sorry to be leaving. They had eaten late so did not bother with breakfast, apart from some toast.

The whole family was assembled to wave her goodbye under another deceptively cloudless sky. The breeze was cold. Fudge ran after the car, barking, as she slowly made her way down the drive. On the back seat was the folder, thicker now, containing all her notes. Kathryn concentrated on these rather than the reception she might get from Alex.

She was determined to make a go of things and hoped he would reciprocate.

The flats looked the same, neat and white, freshly painted the previous summer, and the spring flowers in the raised beds were fully open. For some reason she had expected things to have changed in her absence.

Alex's car was in its usual place and the lounge window was open a fraction. He came into the hall when he heard her key in the lock. 'You're back then,' were his unenthusiastic words of greeting. 'Did you have a good time?'

'It was great. And you?' There were dark smudges under his eyes and he was dressed in lightweight trousers and the shirt she had bought for him, for no reason other than she thought it would suit him. Kathryn wanted to take him in her arms and tell him she had missed him but she held back, afraid of his reaction. Or am I still punishing him? she asked herself.

'You look well. A bit thinner too.'

'I feel it. I'll just go and unpack.' She walked through to the bedroom, unable to cope with the stilted phrases more suitable to acquaintances than husband and wife. The bed, she noticed, had been made. Alex, too, was making an effort.

'I thought we'd go out to lunch,' she called. 'Somewhere on the river maybe, before it's inundated with tourists.'

'I'd like that.' He had followed her into the bedroom and sat on the edge of the bed. His hand came into contact with her folder. 'I thought a week with Helena would have got this nonsense about Megan Morris out of your head.'

Kathryn's stomach contracted. This was not the welcome she had been hoping for and her disappointment was bitter. Why did he have to treat her as if she was either a child or stupid? She desperately wanted things to get back to normal but was not sure how to go about it.

'I found out quite a lot actually.' She kept her voice low and calm.

'In that case perhaps we should eat at the Thames Riviera. You might see your friend again.'

It was too much. 'Oh, Alex, why're you being so hateful?' The idea of spending Sunday lunchtime in a restaurant with

84

him was suddenly unappealing. They needed to talk, to get everything out into the open, not sit in strained silence, their food untasted.

She was bending over, folding a couple of jumpers into a drawer when she felt the hot tears threatening. At the same time, knowing he had gone too far, Alex laid a hand on her shoulder. She felt its warmth through her shirt. 'Forgive me, Kath. I've been so worried.'

'Worried? Is something wrong?'

'Worried about you. All week I had this awful feeling you might not come back, and it would have been my fault. I deserve it. And when you didn't phone . . .' The sentence trailed off.

'But I did!' Obviously not often enough. She bit her tongue, as a retaliatory comment about Rebecca would have had disastrous results. Alex was doing his best to apologise.

'Please let me off the hook,' he implored. 'I made a mistake, a bloody stupid one at that, and maybe I shouldn't have told you, but I couldn't live with it, having that secret between us. Please don't shut me out again.'

'I don't.' Her body felt rigid. If he was going to blame her, it was all pointless.

'I know you don't mean to, but you don't see things the way I do. Your work always comes first.'

'So does yours.' But that was unfair, and untrue. Alex put in a lot of hours but he tried to fit them around their joint lives.

'It's not just that, you're so obsessive at times. Can't you see you're doing it again, with this Megan Morris thing? You don't seem to have any time to listen to me. We haven't really talked about it, but that was the reason I was drawn to Rebecca.'

Alex was saying something else but now, as he had just reproached her, she wasn't listening. *Rebecca*. Before he had always called her Becky. Now Kathryn knew it was really over.

'We could have gone together, to Helena and Gerald's. If you'd asked I would have taken the week off.'

'What about your meetings?'

'I'd have cancelled them, Kath, which is a damned sight

more than you would have done. God, can't you see I need you with me, on my side? That's all I've ever wanted. Perhaps the age gap is too much after all,' he finished sadly.

'No, it isn't that.' Kathryn's face, reflected in the dressing-table mirror, was full of misery. It was not only Alex she had treated cavalierly, she had done much the same to Helena.

'Come on, let's go out. I don't mind where.'

Alex took his car and drove them to Cookham. Neither of them was hungry but they went into the Royal Exchange and had a couple of drinks, moving away from the bar as they did not want their conversation to be overheard.

'I'm sorry, too, Alex. I'm really trying to forget it happened.'

He laid a hand over hers. There was some oil under his thumbnail which, strangely, filled her with tenderness. She had to stop punishing him or she would lose him altogether.

Laura was spending Easter in Shropshire. She packed the few clothes she would require and the Brontë biography which she had hardly started, and set off on Good Friday morning hoping she had missed the general exodus.

Marcia Tennyson's house was virtually isolated but, like her daughter, she enjoyed walking to such an extent that she considered five miles a day to be nothing and was consequently extremely fit. She was also an excellent cook with a larger appetite than Laura. She dished up simple but wholesome food, enough to ensure that Laura joined her on her walks. Now she waited impatiently for her to arrive.

When Laura pulled up, Marcia was standing in the doorway, having heard the car from some distance away in the unbroken silence. Even the birds were mute. 'You look marvellous!' she said, hugging her daughter. 'Come on in. It's a shame about the weather, it was lovely earlier.'

Low cloud hung over the rolling hills and there was mist in the valleys. The thick-walled cottage had no neighbours but Marcia did not believe in roughing it. There was oil-fired central heating, plenty of hot water and an efficient shower as well as a bath. The kitchen had been modernised although the original flagstones remained. The rest of the cottage was carpeted and there was a television set and CD-player in the lounge, upon which Marcia played the Mozart operas she loved but which were not inflicted upon Laura, who preferred jazz and blues.

'Coffee or a drink? A drink, I think. It's not often I have someone to share one with. You go and take your things upstairs.'

Laura did so. Her hold-all contained casual trousers, boots, two shirts and a couple of warm jumpers. At the last minute she had packed a long-sleeved olive dress with a gold belt in case she could persuade Marcia to allow her to buy them a meal in Shrewsbury.

She was closer to Marcia than anyone. Giles would have been mortified if he knew that Laura's mother had been entrusted with more of her secrets than he was. It was to Shropshire that Laura had fled after her divorce, not expecting sympathy, only common sense and a comfortable bed, both of which had been provided. And years ago, at the time of Sarah's disappearance, it was Marcia who listened without comment until Laura was able to discuss matters rationally.

Laura had not brought any work with her. Whenever she went away she had a complete break – besides, Marcia refused to read anything of hers until it was in print. 'It's something I really look forward to,' she had once explained. But Laura did not take proper holidays, preferring to spend a few days with her mother or treat herself to a weekend in a decent hotel somewhere in the UK. She was reluctant to leave the sanctuary of her home for long.

She gazed at the unspoilt view for several minutes then went back downstairs. 'Ah, there you are. Here, whisky and soda.' Marcia winked. 'Well, why not? The sun's over the yard-arm somewhere or other.'

Laura accepted the heavy crystal glass. At home she drank gin and tonic but at her mother's the whisky tasted nicer somehow. Marcia fumbled in a kitchen drawer for a packet of cigarettes. She smoked four or five each day, unlike Laura who got through at least one pack, sometimes two. 'I miss you, you know. I can't tell you how much I enjoy your visits.'

'I miss you too. I don't know why you won't come and live with me. There's more than enough room.'

Marcia leaned over the back of the solid wooden chair. 'I could say the same of you. There are three bedrooms here, and the box-room you could use to write in. But it wouldn't work, you know; our lives are so different and we'd probably get on each other's nerves in the end.'

She was right, of course, as she so often was. Physically they were alike, the same build and the same lustrous hair, although Marcia's was beginning to fade. Both were slender but full-breasted and wide-hipped – what Giles always referred to as 'a proper figure'. Their dress was where they differed most. Laura was never less than elegant, while Marcia's tastes verged on the outlandish. She threw on whatever was suitable for the weather regardless of fashion or colour and often without any sense of co-ordination. The pale blue and white shirt she wore with the Black Watch tartan trousers was incongruous and Laura suspected that the beige and brown cardigan had once belonged to Marcia's husband – a man upon whom she had doted, but who died of cancer three years after their marriage. Laura barely remembered him. Of her own father she knew nothing, other than that he had been in the Services and spent a wild weekend with her mother, during the course of which she had become pregnant.

Marcia had always been quite open about it and admitted she had never had so much fun. She seemed not to care about being an unmarried mother in the fifties when such things were considered shocking. She had already qualified as a teacher and once Laura was at school, her hours had fitted in quite well. She was, Laura thought, a comforting figure as she stood, hands thrust deep into the pockets of the shapeless garment and discussed what they would be having to eat. 'But first, come and see what I've done to the garden. The damp is a bit chilling so you'll be ready for a second drink when you come in.'

'Honestly, you don't change. Any excuse, it seems to me.'

But Marcia was smiling. It wasn't an excuse, it was a celebration because her daughter was there.

The improvements had encroached beyond the garden,

which was unfenced, and onto ground which did not belong with the house but was commonland. There were no formal flowerbeds but a multitude of trees and shrubs and climbing plants intertwined. These were interspersed with thistles which would later flower, and clumps of weeds and nettles. 'For the wildlife, especially the butterflies,' Marcia informed her.

Laura was shivering by the time they returned to the warmth of the kitchen. They had another drink to accompany the ham and tomato sandwiches. The mist had finally settled into a fine drizzle but the room was cheerful with its assortment of red and blue crockery which was not merely decorative but in everyday use.

'Tell me about the book,' Marcia said eventually.

'It's going well,' Laura answered, as she caught a wayward slice of tomato which was escaping from between the chunks of granary bread. 'I can't explain it, but this one's sort of writing itself.'

'What's it about?'

'Oh no, it'll spoil it for you.'

'I doubt that, my darling. Nothing spoils my enjoyment of your books. I'm so proud of you.'

'All right then, it's about choices several women have to make. What it boils down to is the way in which their decisions affect their lives. And that's all I'm telling you.'

'I can see I'll have to wait. Let's just shove the plates in the sink and we'll have a stroll.'

Laura was starting to relax and felt reluctant to leave the house, which was filled with the tempting smells of beef and herbs slowly cooking in a pan. By the time they ate, the strands of meat would fall apart. But if she didn't accompany Marcia, Laura knew the danger of having another drink and feeling too sluggish to eat later. They put on outdoor clothes and Marcia exchanged a pair of moccasins for boots which had seen better days.

'What else have you been up to, apart from rearranging the surrounding countryside?' They walked quite briskly, side by side when the path was wide enough.

'I've been making a note of birds and their nesting sites, just for my own interest. I didn't realise there was so much enjoyment to be had. Daphne from the village shop got me on to it. I'd no idea she was so knowledgeable, especially considering she spends most of her time behind the counter. But you know I've always preferred autumn and spring; there isn't much time for things in the summer and the winters can be pretty bleak.' During July and August Marcia took in paying guests – hikers and walkers mostly. She did not need the money but liked the company of younger people. Usually they stayed only one or two nights but many returned the following year, delighted with the complete lack of formality, the plentiful food and Marcia's own brand of eccentricity.

'That colour rather suits you.'

Laura glanced down at the mustard wool jacket she had been persuaded to borrow because Marcia believed in wrapping up well. The buttons were enormous and were clearly not the originals.

They trudged back across several fields, the damp grass staining their boots and wetting the hems of their trousers. As they reached the cottage, a few rays of watery sun appeared like fingers over the distant hills and they could just make out a rainbow. Woodsmoke from one of the farms hung in the air, redolent of autumn rather than spring. From behind a hedge came a continuous bleating of sheep and their lambs. Laura tried to concentrate as Marcia pointed out and named wild flowers, but lethargy was sweeping over her as she temporarily left her anonymous life behind.

Later they ate a leisurely meal and sipped red wine and talked until nearly midnight. Laura fell into bed and in the morning could not recall when she had last enjoyed eight hours of uninterrupted sleep.

The clouds had disappeared and the fields were verdant. From a distance, the sheep were as white as the few remaining tendrils of cirrus which drifted across the sky. Close to, of course, they looked filthy. For some inexplicable reason, as she gazed over the gentle English landscape, Laura began to cry.

The long Easter weekend was approaching and by Wednesday lunchtime Kathryn felt she had not been to Oxford at all. Keith had covered for her during her absence, but there was a busy time ahead. Over the holiday she would be covering for someone else, a fact which had not gone down well with Alex, although she had given him plenty of warning. Usually her work consisted of features and her column, but she was required to cover a couple of outdoor events. At least Alex would be at the boat-yard for some of the time because everyone was clamouring for their cruisers and smaller craft to be ready for Easter.

It was not until Wednesday afternoon that her feet seemed to be on the ground again and she was able to contact the Oxford *Star*. Having explained who she was, she asked to be put through to the editor.

'All I can tell you,' she said when she had made her initial request, 'is that her name was Sarah Milton and she was at the University. It would have been 1978 or 1979.'

'No problem – the story would've made the front page. I don't remember it myself because I wasn't here then. I'll dig it up and send you copies. It won't be until after the break though.'

Kathryn thanked him, grateful that he could be bothered to go to the trouble but he said he was pleased to help a fellow journalist. Surely she herself would have noticed the article during her research, especially if it concerned a student? But she had been looking for two other names. There hadn't been much time to think about what Helena had said on the subject of Jenny Branagh, either. 'If she commented about enjoying your work, it's more than likely she's local,' was the suggestion she had made, but the electoral roll would have to wait.

Having made do with some fruit and two cups of black coffee for lunch, she glanced out of the window, decided it would be wise to take a jacket, and told Keith she would be away for about an hour and a half. He raised a hand in acknowledgement but did not take his eyes off his computer screen.

The offices had been completely refurbished in March and still retained their new smell – a combination of paint and carpet and the rough hessian with which the lower half of the walls had been covered. Both she and Keith, who commanded the most by-lines, had been able to choose their own chairs. Kathryn's was more traditional in that it was black leather, high-backed and, most importantly, comfortable.

The man she was due to see at two-thirty was a local poet who had finally succeeded in getting a slim book of verse published. It was a double achievement because poetry was difficult to sell and he was an octogenarian who had not put pen to paper until he was into his late seventies. Kathryn had read as many of the poems as she was able, during her brief lunch-break. They were evocative if a little bland but had the advantage of being intelligible. The last poet she had interviewed had been a fierce feminist who dressed to create an impression, spoke in a way to make even more of one – if it could be argued that a plethora of four-letter words was the way in which to make an impact – and wrote free verse which was incomprehensible even after the symbolism and purported meaning had been laboriously explained. Kathryn had later read a lauditory review in one of the Sunday heavies and cynically wondered if it had been written tongue in cheek. What, after all, did artistic integrity mean?

Archibald Potts took an age to answer the door but she had been expecting this. Physically he was infirm, being afflicted with many of the inconveniences of old age, but nature had recompensed him, for his mind remained agile. 'Come in, dear, it's all nice and tidy. They send someone round twice a day to organise me. The one who came this morning has left a tea tray out.'

Kathryn followed his slow progress into the main living area as he manoeuvred his walking frame painfully. 'Would you like me to make you some tea now?' she asked. Seeing what an effort it had been for him to come to the door she thought he might need time to recover. He said it was very kind of her to offer.

The spotless kitchen reminded her it was time to do some spring cleaning of her own. She and Alex often talked about getting someone in once or twice a week but the inconvenience of housework was outweighed by their joint preference for privacy.

'Have you actually read any of them?' Mr Potts indicated a copy of his book which sat proudly on the table beside him.

'Some, not all.'

'That's honest of you. Now, be even more candid and give me your opinion.'

'I enjoyed them. They're easy to follow and they're rather soothing.'

'Ah, good. I didn't set out to be a literary genius and I cannot see any point in being deliberately abstruse.' As he talked Kathryn realised there would be a decent article if she quoted some of his strongly-held opinions. 'I don't like modern art either,' he later told her. 'I can never understand what it's supposed to represent. The Emperor's New Clothes syndrome, I believe they call it. I like your column, by the way. I've always enjoyed people who aren't afraid to speak their mind. Listen to me, taking up all your time. But have a biscuit, won't you? I've never met anyone who can resist chocolate digestives.'

'No, just tea's fine, thank you.'

'Dieting, I suppose.' He appraised her without embarrassment. Not pretty, not really beautiful, he decided, but open-faced and attractive with clearly-defined features and a wide smile – looks which underlined her character. A stunner, he thought, when she was dressed up for an evening out. 'I don't know what's wrong with young women today, but I do hope no one's suggested you aren't delightful exactly as you are.' There was a flicker of flirtatiousness in the rheumy eyes and Kathryn grinned. 'I shan't mind what you write about me. I enjoy what I write and I hope it will give pleasure to others. And,' he added with another twinkle, 'it keeps me off the streets.'

Having ascertained that Archibald Potts gained his inspiration from the view through the plate-glass window which made up one wall of the bungalow's living area and overlooked the medium-sized garden, Kathryn washed up the tea things and said she had to go. He insisted upon seeing her to the door.

The breeze had dropped but there was a scattering of blossom on the pavement. With the sun warming the top of her head she walked to where she had left the car. Several children were playing in the cul-de-sac, huddled beneath a tree, apparantly involved in some mysterious ritual. They whispered and giggled but did not look up as she passed them. The car smelled of the apples she had bought the previous day and forgotten to take home. She took one from the bag and bit into it, holding it awkwardly in her left hand as she changed gear. The visit had uplifted her spirits. If Archibald Potts could be so grateful and so enthusiastic about life, when he could barely move and had only his home-help and the blackbirds for company, then how much more did she have to appreciate? Thank you, Mr Potts, she thought. You were well worth the trip.

Ideas were buzzing around in her head as she made her way back to the office. There was plenty of material from which to work but it would need careful condensing for the finished piece. At her desk she hooked her hair back, tapped her teeth with the end of a pen and began to construct it mentally. For the moment Jennifer Branagh and Megan Morris were forgotten.

Chapter 5

David Shawcross locked the shop door on Saturday evening, half-dreading the two empty days ahead of him. Had he thought it worthwhile to open on the Monday morning he would have done so, but there would be too few people around, only tourists, who would be doing the sights. Good Friday had passed easily enough as he had spent the day going through the stock-lists for ordering purposes. He had also gone through the files relating to his credit customers and typed up any outstanding invoices. To say that his life had stagnated would be an understatement but David seemed afraid – or unable – to do anything about it. Dealing with customers was second nature and involved no effort because they spoke of things which interested him, books and authors, but since his engagement had ended he had allowed his social life to grind to a halt. The thought of joining clubs or societies for the main purpose of meeting new people was repugnant to him.

Only the previous week his mother, noticing the state of his bitten fingernails, had had the temerity to suggest he was neurotic and that he was wasting his life. She also pointed out, not for the first time, that he ought to make an effort to find himself a girlfriend, if not a wife. 'Perhaps you ought to go and see someone,' she had concluded.

Until that point David had not really been listening. He had sat through an abysmal Sunday lunch at his parents' home in Brighton whilst their friends droned on about the successes of their adult children which, in his opinion, seemed merely to amount to how much wealth they had accumulated. The lone female, invited to make up the numbers, he had managed to ignore; a woman in her early thirties who remained single for reasons David thought only too obvious. He knew he was not a great catch himself but Charlotte possessed the long-faced, horsey features of her class and a laugh that could have outmatched a hyena. Fortunately she spent the whole lunchtime flirting with her other neighbour at the table in order, David assumed, to make him jealous. He had simply let her get on with it and concentrated on the food which was never less than excellent at home.

'Such as?' he had asked, not understanding what his mother was talking about. At least he was grateful that her carping had not taken place whilst the other guests were present.

'I don't know – a counsellor or something. They've got them for everything these days, I believe. Honestly, David, all that education wasted and not even a family to show for it. I find it overwhelmingly embarrassing, having to tell people that my son works in a shop.'

It was not true. For a start it was his own business and he was doing well, but his mother certainly said no such thing. She made comments along the lines of his dealing in antique and specialist books, which was the truth. And she often boasted about his expertise. 'Oh, in London, of course. He's terriby busy and there's so much to do in town that we don't see him very often,' he had overheard her say once.

As he made his way back to his flat through streets busy with people laden with exclusive carriers, and the theatre matinée audiences who were retiring to pubs and restaurants, David considered the possibility of his hating his mother. There was, he realised, something he shared with John Atherton: they were both the least-favoured son, although David was older than his brother, Andrew. Andrew had married young and his wife had rapidly produced two girls.

It was ironical that Andrew lived in the stockbroker belt in a large house he could barely afford, yet was respected for this. David owned his flat outright and had three times the disposable income of his brother but, strangely, in a family where money was the measure of success, this counted for little.

He did not really know his father. Their conversations were superficial and awkward. Cyril Shawcross was a nondescript character, content to let his wife take control, but even he had expressed disappointment that David was not yet married.

The weather was typical of a Bank Holiday weekend. Intermittent sunshine was interspersed with brief showers and a chill wind which sent litter scurrying in his wake. He buttoned his checked jacket, saddened to think that his parents understood nothing about him – that their son's absorption in books gave him pleasure and that he was a man content with very little. He was the antithesis of John, who craved much and usually got it; his magnetism was responsible for that. David toyed with the idea of ringing John to see if he fancied another drink, surprised that the idea had even occurred to him. He did not want to become involved in any way; the reverse, in fact. He wanted to forget. But he knew, without a word having been said, that he was being drawn into something. In that case, he thought, the sooner he knew what it was the better. And it might, to use one of his mother's latest words, be *therapeutic*.

There were times when he longed to break out of the respectable mould he had cast for himself, when he was tempted to shock them all, to nonchalantly reveal in front of his parents' friends that he had been involved in the murder of a pretty female student – one whose killer had never been found. How differently they would see him then – if, he added silently, they believed him. His mother would be convinced he was mad.

On Easter Sunday Alex got up first, very quietly so as not to wake Kathryn. He stood watching her sleeping for several minutes. Against the white broderie anglaise pillowcase her dark hair was almost black, and the smudges beneath her eyes caused by sleepless nights had faded. Her visit to Helena had done her good. He felt a sudden sense of helplessness. If only he could have reached out, stroked her hair until she woke and said the words which would transport them back to the days before Rebecca. But there were no such words and he had to face a long haul back to normality, with effort needed on both sides. Breakfast in bed for his wife was a start.

He halved two grapefruits and squeezed the juice and used the percolator to make coffee. In two glass bowls he arranged sliced fruit and topped it with thick Greek yogurt. Neither of them ate much in the mornings. Alex wished Kathryn would eat more; he preferred her with a little more flesh, but any criticism at the moment would not be wise.

His side of the bed was still warm when he got back in, but his bare feet were cold and Kathryn woke when they made contact with her ankles. She rolled onto her back, opened her eyes and smiled at him. The smile faded as unwelcome thoughts filled her mind. Her face was faintly flushed with sleep and gave her an air of innocence which disguised the stubborn streak which had prevented her throwing Alex out because she would never give up on anything unless a situation was proved to be beyond repair.

'I thought I could smell coffee.' She sat up and adjusted the thin straps of her satin nightdress. There were several in a drawer, bought to make her more attractive to Alex, the soft cotton T-shirts relegated to a charity shop. Kathryn did not know that her purchases were unnecessary, that Alex just wanted her to be close to him and, besides, although she wore them for him, she had been unable to let him touch her for some time.

Alex steadied the tray as she moved then bent to kiss her cheek but only succeeded in getting a mouthful of hair as she turned her head. 'The weather doesn't look too bad, shall we go out somewhere for the day?' He had drawn the curtains and weak sunshine enhanced the whites and yellows of the room. The fickle onset of spring had temporarily returned. 'Can you think of something you'd like to do?'

Kathryn shook her head, her mouth full of fruit. They drank the coffee and Alex placed the tray on the floor before turning and caressing the back of her neck. He felt her muscles ease under his fingers. 'I can think of one thing we can do.' He kissed her, tasting pears in her mouth. Momentarily she had stiffened before returning the kiss. It was going to be all right.

The next day, Bank Holiday Monday, was hectic as Kathryn had two events to cover – a gymkhana and a fête. They were the sort of jobs she had cut her teeth on. Not wishing to spoil the mood of Sunday, Alex accompanied her and in the evening they tried a new Thai restaurant.

Over the meal Kathryn told him what she had found out in Oxford. It was the first time the subject had been mentioned since her return. 'I'm waiting to hear from the editor of the Oxford *Star*. After that,' she shrugged, 'well, I'll just take it from there. And if Helena's right and Jennifer Branagh is local, it shouldn't be too hard to find her. Just to satisfy my own curiosity,' she added as she caught Alex's unguarded frown.

He made a noncommittal comment and changed the subject. At least it would not entail her traipsing all over the country.

The editor had kept his word, and a week after her conversation with him, a large brown envelope was dropped on her desk along with her other mail. It was, as she had requested, marked *Private and Confidential*. She did not want any of the other reporters asking questions. Kathryn placed it, unopened, in the large shoulder-bag which sometimes doubled as a briefcase.

The Bank Holiday pieces were ready early because they had been easy to write, but a bit more work was required on the article about Archibald Potts. When she was satisfied that she had depicted him as the intelligent and humorous man that he was, she took the lot to the editor. It was quiet in the office, Keith was out on an assignment and Dave was nowhere to be seen. The sports correspondent was sitting on her desk, catching up on the gossip when Alex rang to say he would be late that evening. 'Someone's kicking up a fuss, they want their boat yesterday.'

Kathryn's fellow reporter commented upon how thoughtful Alex was as he left to attend the semi-final of some sporting event she had already forgotten about. She

sighed. He did not know the reason for Alex's recent solici-
tousness; no one did locally as Helena and Gerald were the
only people she had told.

When she got home Kathryn decided a salad with something grilled would suffice for their meal as she was unsure
just how late Alex would be. The preparations done, she
made a large mug of coffee and took it into the lounge. The
tuatara's glittering eyes seemed to watch her. It had become
a talisman, something from which she did not want to be
parted and, of course, it reminded her of Alex. Sometimes
she patted it on its scaly head as if it were alive.

Slipping off her shoes she sank into an armchair and
retrieved the envelope from her bag, looking quickly
through the photocopied pages of newsprint about the dead
girl, Sarah Milton. She had to force herself to read them
carefully.

An hour later, when she almost knew the articles by
heart, Alex arrived. 'You'll strain your eyes.' He switched
on the table lamps. Outside, the dusk had deepened and
the sky was a pale mauve. 'Have you eaten?'

'No. I was waiting for you.'

Alex went to wash his hands then joined her in the
kitchen. As meat sizzled under the grill she told him about
Sarah Milton. 'Michael Jarvis was right. She *was* murdered.'

'Um. In which case, if Megan Morris really was at Oxford
she might have known her, which would be a good reason
to remain anonymous. No offence, but you know what it's
like; you only have to be in the vicinity of something nasty
and the tabloids will turn it into a sleaze story.'

'I don't . . .'

Alex held up both hands to ward off her protests. 'Don't
be touchy. I wasn't referring to you. You're so bloody objective when it comes to work but you always seem to turn
everything I say into a personal criticism. Sorry, the lecture's
over. I just wish you'd give me the benefit of the doubt
occasionally.'

Kathryn's shoulders sagged. Alex was right. It was just
that she was expecting him to behave perfectly whilst she
could say what she wanted. It was no good trying to change
him, to turn him into a yes man, he was far too independent

and too strong, and she didn't want him any other way. 'Okay. But what if there *is* something nasty to find? Sarah Milton disappeared back in 1978, but her body wasn't found for years. And she was supposed to have been a friend of Jennifer Branagh.'

'No!' Alex stated vehemently. 'No more, Kath. You don't know what you might be getting into.'

She stared at him thoughtfully. It wasn't his actual words but the meaning behind them she was considering. He cared about her safety but, more than that, he seemed to be implying that if there was something to unearth, she was capable of doing so. However, it was as if she was being led away from, rather than *towards* uncovering the identity of Megan Morris – and she needed to remind herself there was nothing to connect the woman with Oxford other than one short sentence in the back of her books, a sentence which might not bear any semblance to the truth. The question that nagged at her was why Megan Morris had agreed to meet her? But Jenny Branagh had turned up, or someone calling herself by that name, and a Jenny Branagh really had existed in Oxford.

'Look, Alex, I'm not interested in solving the murder,' she said slowly 'I'm not that unrealistic. I just want to find out a bit more about these people.'

There was disappointment in his face, but resignation too. He had known it was useless to try to dissuade her. If he stood in her way now he might alienate her further and he could not afford to do that.

After the meal he dried the dishes and they both watched an hour of television.

Sleep was impossible. Without switching on a light, Kathryn pulled on her robe and left the bedroom, closing the door quietly behind her. Outside she listened. Alex continued breathing evenly.

In the kitchen she spread the notes from her folder over the table, shook the kettle to make sure there was enough water in it for a drink, then depressed the switch. In the stillness of the night every noise sounded unnaturally loud. Somewhere down the street a car door slammed and she heard voices, a man and a woman bickering. The voices receded and stopped altogether. Kathryn glanced at the clock. One-thirty. Late-night revellers who would be tired in the morning as she would be herself.

The boiling water seemed like a roar until the automatic switch clicked off. Beneath her the chair creaked.

The editor of the *Star* had certainly done his homework. Items were clipped together in chronological order. There was an explanatory note with a message of good luck. He had, he stated, initially been searching for a report of the murder. It had taken some time to connect the *disappearance* of Sarah Milton with later reports of her body being discovered.

The first article was sketchy and only indicated that a twenty-year-old student had been reported as missing. There was no photograph. The second, dated a little later, said the girl's parents had travelled to Oxford and both they and the police were appealing for information concerning her whereabouts. From her own university days Kathryn was aware that these investigations would not have taken place for some time. The girl was of age and students did go missing for a variety of reasons. It was only after Sarah had not turned up for a promised visit to her family that the police had started to take the matter seriously. By the time the search was really under way, it was early August – not the ideal time as her peers had gone home for the long vacation.

Then came nothing – or nothing the editor had thought worth forwarding, anyway – until 1985. This time Sarah's name was in large print on the front page.

The remains of a body found in a wooded area several miles outside Oxford are believed to be those of the missing student Sarah Milton, who was last seen in June 1978. At the time it was believed that the pressure of forthcoming examinations was the reason for her absence, the paper stated. *A police spokesman explained that although the body had lain there for some time, it was impossible to estimate the date of death until extensive forensic tests had been completed. No details have been released as to the possible cause of death*. Some family details followed and a blurred picture which could have been of any student of roughly the same age. Her hair was long and loose and she was smiling. The photograph, which stopped at the waist, suggested she was wearing some sort of kaftan.

The final photocopied sheet, dated a week or so later, said that the police were tracing and questioning friends and acquaintances who had been at Oxford at the same time. A herculean task, Kathryn imagined. Some would be abroad, others would have married and changed their names.

Her tea had gone cold. She made another pot and started again, in case she had missed any of the names mentioned by Michael Jarvis. She hadn't. Finally, realising she was uncomfortable, perched on the edge of the chair, its wooden lip cutting into her thighs, she got up and put everything away, sliding the folder into the drawer of one of the oak units they had had installed the previous year. It slid shut smoothly and noiselessly.

She crept along the hall on tiptoes which accentuated the slenderness of her calves. Alex stirred and muttered but did not wake and she got back into bed beside him; without thinking, she automatically moved into the curve of his back.

When she woke the room was flooded with daylight and the flat was quiet. Alex had already left, presumably to oversee the last of the work to the boat. It was still only eight o'clock, but it was a lovely morning.

Over coffee and toast, Kathryn thought about what she had read. A positive identification had finally been made. The hand-bag and Sarah's distinctive ring which had been found with the body, were not proof enough that it was actually hers. The editor's note had ended with the suggestion that if she required more information, she might try Inspector Forbes who was still with the Thames Valley Police. He had been on the case as a young sergeant. Kathryn doubted that he would enlighten her further, especially as the case had not been officially closed, but it was still worth a try. She felt strangely sluggish, and stayed under the shower for longer than usual, letting the water run over her slimmed-down body and her jutting hipbones.

Having dressed, she dried her hair and tied it back with a scarf then applied make-up. In a short-sleeved summer suit she looked sophisticated as well as professional, and was ready to face the world.

Laura had extended her stay for a couple more days. She was in need of the rest.

'You're pale. Didn't you sleep well?' Marcia eyed her over the bread she was slicing for breakfast. She had already walked to the village and back and left her daughter to lie in.

'Ghosts,' was the enigmatic reply.

Marcia did not demand an explanation. She cut another slice from the crusty white loaf which fell to bits because it was so fresh. 'Toast, or a bacon sandwich? I can do the full works if you want but I know you don't usually bother in the mornings.'

'Just toast. And coffee. I'll make it, I'm gasping. Too much red wine, I suspect. You're a bad influence, you know.'

'Be thankful I didn't subject you to my home-made plonk – you'd really be suffering now.'

'Thanks for small mercies. I don't know how you can be bothered, all that fruit-gathering and fiddling about, especially as it's so cheap in the supermarkets now.' But Marcia in a supermarket was not something easily envisaged, although she did take the car on a fortnightly expedition and stock up on the heavy items which she could not lug back from the village. On those occasions she would also treat herself to something exotic from the nearby delicatessen. Marcia had told her that now there were so many cookery programmes on the television, the village store carried a wider selection of ingredients, including fennel and olives and juniper berries. 'Betty tells me there's always a run on something after a Delia Smith or that man – what's his name? – who drinks like a fish. Last week it was redcurrant jelly.' Apart from the trips into Shrewsbury, the rusting Escort estate which lived in the three-sided shelter of the old wood-store was rarely used.

'I meant to ask if you'd heard from Giles lately.'

'Um.' Laura nodded. She had just bitten into the hot

104

toast and butter. 'Quite recently, in fact. I wanted him to cast his eyes over the latest chapter. He looks remarkably well. Ingrid must be good for him.'

'Ingrid, indeed. I can't understand the man. Still, he's always been a faithful servant to you.'

'I know. He's kind and decent.' Laura stopped. She recalled how he had looked after her in Oxford that fateful summer. 'Mind you, he has the other editors eating out of his hand.'

'Giles always had a knack of putting people over a barrel. He's got you to threaten them with. But don't forget, Laura, he's got you in the same position.'

'Maybe, but he'd never do anything about it.' This was not wishful thinking, it was true.

Laura was gazing vacantly at some vegetables on the chopping board. Next to them was a long-bladed sharp knife, and suddenly all she beheld was Sarah's body and the blood, the result of a game gone badly wrong. Once they were back on their staircase it was Giles who had taken Laura to his rooms. She should not have been there but Giles, always a gentleman, had slept on his shabby settee. At the time Laura was confused. In her naivety she had imagined spending the rest of her life with John but he seemed to be losing interest, making excuses as to why he could not see her. Even the knowledge of her grandmother's inheritance made no impression and, in retrospect, Laura saw that she had been prepared to use that as the bait by which to hook him. What a fool she had been. During that period the pattern of her life was disrupted: she loved John, who no longer cared, and Giles loved Laura. At least she had the consolation that she had never encouraged him.

John had always been their accepted leader. He had a natural ability to take control of any situation. On the night when the game went wrong, as soon as it was obvious that things had gone too far, John had immediately known what they had to do. Seventeen years had passed but none of them were safe. They never would be.

It was difficult to pinpoint where the blame lay. Perhaps the fault was with all of them. Sarah and Jenny, aping each other and dressing alike. Sarah was wild but it was Jenny who had introduced them to drugs. On that fatal night they had also been drinking heavily.

At last Laura had come to see that John had used her. They no longer indulged in their games and each had tried to settle down to their final year, although none of them did as well as had been predicted. David had a viva for a 'first' but he had gone to pieces. Laura and Giles only got seconds. John, who had thrown himself into work at the last minutes, had achieved what they had all hoped for. Either he had successfully banished the events of the previous summer, or he had no conscience. They saw less of him and the disintegration of the group began. This did not prevent them from adhering to the alibi which John had concocted, and no one had discovered their secret place. The police investigations seemed to lose impetus and as the weeks turned into months they had begun to believe that Sarah's body might not be found.

Laura knew she would never again experience the heights and depths of the emotions of that era, but what she had was enough. And there was Marcia. If worry did not hang so heavily over her, she thought life could be wonderful.

The final year had come to an end. Laura saw more and more of Giles although their relationship remained platonic. By that time someone else was occupying Sarah's rooms.

'Laura? I said, more coffee?'

'Yes. Yes, I'd love some.'

'Ghosts again?'

Laura smiled. She was not being fair to her mother. 'They've gone now.'

'Good. I thought we might venture as far as Shrewsbury. I could do with some new shoes and your taste's so much better than mine.'

Laura reached up and squeezed her shoulder. She saw the distracting device for what it was. Marcia would not care what the shoes looked like as long as they were comfortable and made to last. 'Why don't we leave it until this afternoon, then we can have an early evening drink and I'll treat us to a meal. Oh, I'd forgotten.'

Marcia followed the direction of her glance. 'The veg will

keep for another time. I'll put it in the slow cooker with some meat and we can have it tomorrow. Now, you go and have an hour with your book and I'll finish up out here.' An evening out might be just what Laura needed but Marcia, too, was haunted by the past.

'There was a phone call for you,' Dave said when Kathryn returned from doing some photocopying.

'Oh?' She placed the copies on her desk. 'Well, who was it?' She glanced up, irritated, when he did not expound. Leaning against the cold radiator with his arms folded, he was leering. It made him look evil. He was lean and fit and always had the latest haircut; Keith told her that the girls in the clubs and discos flocked around him. Kathryn couldn't see why. He was vain and sarcastic. Perhaps to young girls he came across as sophisticated, a man of the world.

'He didn't say.'

'Oh, for Christ's sake, Dave.'

'Got a bloke on the side, have you?'

Dave mistook the flush which spread over her cheek-bones as embarrassment. He did not know her situation or how much the comment had hurt. Kathryn was furious, not embarrassed, but she did not want to create an atmosphere in the office. 'Sorry,' he said when she did not respond. 'All I can tell you was it came through the switchboard and that a man asked for you. I said you'd be back later.' He paused. 'He asked for your home number and address.'

'What? You didn't give it to him!'

'Of course not.'

'Was that it?'

'Yes. Perhaps he'll ring back later.' Dave sat down and began to tap away at his keyboard. He hadn't meant to upset Kathryn. 'By the way, he didn't have a local accent. Wasn't a Londoner either.'

Kathryn nodded. Everything seemed so normal; Dave, opposite her, a constant thorn in her side, the car park visible from the open window, the sounds of other staff at work and their voices in the corridor now and then, yet she sensed something was wrong – that events were closing in . . . and the first chill of fear made her shiver.

John Atherton was beginning to suspect that his presence in London had not been received with as much enthusiasm as he had hoped for. David had been offhand and Giles cool, although he had mellowed towards the end of the evening they had spent together. They both knew where he was staying but neither had telephoned to suggest a second meeting. He was well aware of the adage of not being able to turn back the clock, but it was more than that; it was as if they wished to forget they had spent any time together at all.

The visit had not been fortuitous and John had lost interest in pursuing Laura. She was, as Giles suggested, more than likely married with teenage children, and he saw enough of those in term-time. Until 1982 Laura had kept in touch by letter. She hadn't mentioned anyone special and he flattered himself into thinking he might have spoiled her for other men. He did regret that he would not be able to ascertain what she had meant by that final postcard.

Vaguely dispirited, John decided to call it a day and return to Cardiff. Travelling north no longer appealed to him. At least at home he knew enough casual acquaintances with whom to share a drink and plenty of landlords who appreciated his custom.

As he threw his possessions into a travelling bag he mulled over the idea of contacting Tina Parry. Unlike many of the students she was a local girl, from Caerphilly. It would be simple enough to talk someone into giving him her address or her number. No, he thought, as he held the bag and pulled the zip sharply across. It wasn't worth the risk. But he knew he would go mad if he didn't have a woman soon.

He went downstairs and asked for his account, grimacing when he saw how much he had run up on his bar bill. He slid a credit card onto the reception desk and sighed, exasperated at his own weakness. When the redhead in the smart uniform checked his signature and smiled, he nearly changed his mind about staying.

A cab deposited him at Paddington and the indicator board told him there was a Cardiff train in twenty-five minutes. Automatically heading across the wide concourse towards the bar, he manoeuvred his way around individuals and groups of youths with baggage at their feet and a party of pensioners who were queuing obediently behind a board marked as their meeting point. Businessmen, and those who lived in the city, showed no signs of indecision but scurried towards the tube station entrances at speeds which suggested they were uncomfortable above ground and couldn't wait to be swallowed into the bowels of the earth. You're welcome to it, Giles, John thought as he reached the dim sanctuary of the bar and ordered his first drink of the day.

On the train he found a seat in the carriage next to the buffet before realising he was unable to smoke. He walked down the length of the train, cursing the railways and their employees until he reached carriage B, the only smoking compartment left. It was almost as far from the buffet as it was possible to be. Once the train was moving though, his mood improved.

At Reading a female boarded the train. 'Is anyone sitting there?' she asked, indicating the two seats on the opposite side of his table.

He ignored the stupidity of the question and shook his head, smiling. The journey might be more pleasant than he had anticipated. The woman was about thirty. She had an interesting, rather than beautiful face, and a superb body. And she was alone. 'A fellow inhaler,' he commented. 'Not many of us about these days.'

'No.' She ignored the gold lighter which he produced, a legacy from the days of Angela, and lit her cigarette using a disposable one before placing an inflexible briefcase on the table between them. She raised the lid and rustled some papers. The body language was unmistakable and John felt rebuffed. She had obviously chosen to sit near him only because she wanted a table seat.

'Travelling far?' he asked when the briefcase had been removed to the seat beside her. He flipped open the lid of the ashtray in the arm of his own seat with more force than he intended. It clattered back on the rebound.

The woman frowned. 'Cardiff.'

'You're on the right train then.' His bruised ego caused him to be facetious.

109

'Quite.' She uncapped a biro and began studying her papers.

Just as in the old days, John would not be defeated and he felt there was some amusement to be gained from the situation. 'I take it you'd rather not talk.'

The look he received suggested she would rather he hadn't been born. 'Look, I'm married. I'm going away on business and I have work to do before I get there. This was the only table not taken and I need the space to complete my notes. And would you mind moving your leg.'

Ten out of ten for assertiveness, he thought. He had stretched out his leg, allowing his knee to rest gently against hers. He could feel her warmth through his trousers but he did as she had requested. As she started to write, her hair fell over her face and he saw what had attracted him: she reminded him of Laura.

Memories flooded back. *Laura*. How unfair he had been to her. He closed his eyes and let his thoughts take over. How many hours had Laura spent in his rooms, naked and supple and compliant? Adoration shone from her face. He had used her, just as he had used many females, but he was young then; he had no excuse now. To his credit, he had not used Angela; what he had felt for her was, he supposed, the nearest he would ever come to love. At Oxford it had seemed as if they swapped partners as often as they changed their clothes, but there was always an element of bragging. And Sarah? Had he used her? No, if anything it was the other way around. He was sorry she was dead but felt no real remorse. It was often at her instigation that they carried things too far.

'Pardon?' He opened his eyes. The table was clear and the woman was leaning forward expectantly.

'I asked if you wanted anything from the buffet. I'm going to get a drink.'

'I, uh, yes. Why not?' John had a bottle of wine and a plastic beaker in his bag, the bottle uncorked and resealed, in anticipation of the journey. 'Here, let me. What would you like?' He stood before she was able to do so.

'A vodka and tomato juice, please. No ice.' She fumbled

110

in her bag for her purse but John was already halfway down the carriage.

Things are looking up, he thought, as he lurched down the train, grabbing at the knobs on alternate seats to prevent himself being thrown into the laps of seated passengers. Only when he was on his feet did he become aware of the speed at which they were travelling. He whistled gaily, hoping his luck was about to change.

Kathryn dialled the number for the police station from which she had discovered Inspector Forbes operated, only to learn that he was not on duty. She did not leave a message other than to say she would ring back the following day.

As far as Keith and Dave were concerned, her non-existent interview with Megan Morris was a thing of the past, but she had still waited until she had the office to herself because she did not want them to guess she had not given up.

Alex was taking her out that night, a small celebration to mark the completion of yet another job. It was probably as well that there would be no new information to occupy her. She decided to wear the blue dress she had bought in Oxford.

Back at the flat she bathed and washed her hair then stood in front of the mirror, satisfied with what she saw. The dress was flattering, cut away at the shoulders and flaring gently, but she had also had to buy a strapless bra to wear under it because her breasts were too visible through the thin material. She put her purse, keys, lipstick and a tissue into the small bag she kept for the evenings and was dabbing perfume on her wrists when the telephone rang.

'Kath? It's me. Something's cropped up, and I'm going to be a bit late. One of the wynches is buggered and we've managed to damage an engine. I'll—'

'It's all right, Alex, it's nothing I'm not used to.' With quiet deliberation she replaced the receiver. She felt sick. Wasn't that the excuse the first time she had become aware he was seeing Rebecca?

Pacing the long length of the lounge she fought back

111

tears and eventually her misery was replaced by anger. She had made such an effort for him and there was nothing worse than being at a loose end after getting all dressed up to go out. Taking a deep breath, she rang for a taxi and waited outside in the balmy evening air for it to arrive so she would not hear the telephone if Alex tried to contact her again. It was now too late to ask Annie or one of her other friends if they wanted to go out.

'Drop me in East Street, please,' she told the driver. She would go to the Portland Arms, a pub she knew Alex frequented. Feeling bitter, and childish, she was aware that word would get back to him that she had been there alone. She knew several of the regulars and would go out of her way to show she was enjoying herself. It was petty and stupid, but so what?

The driver took the A4 approach to Maidenhead bridge. Still fuming, Kathryn gave no thought to Jenny Branagh as they crossed the roundabout by the Thames Riviera. At the next roundabout the driver waited for a car from the opposite direction to make a right-hand turn. Kathryn glanced out of the window, only half-noticing the gleaming executive model on her left. The taxi moved off and she jerked around in her seat. Sitting behind the wheel of the car they were rapidly leaving behind was a woman with flowing auburn hair, the woman who had introduced herself as Jenny Branagh.

It was too late to ask the driver to change direction; the other car was already heading away from them and there was no knowing which road it would take at the roundabout.

'You all right, love?' The driver caught her eye in the rearview mirror. He had heard her gasp.

'Yes, fine, thanks.'

Within minutes she was paying her fare. If only she had not been so furious with Alex, she might have been able to make a note of the registration number. But she would waste no time now in checking the electoral roll.

Only when she was seated at the bar of the Portland Arms did the irony strike her. If she had not been so annoyed with Alex she would not have seen Jenny Branagh at all.

After two glasses of dry white wine Kathryn began to feel slightly ridiculous. Her anger had evaporated and she wondered what she was doing and why. These were silly games to play and, in the end, they upset only herself. She used the pay-phone to order a cab home. When they reached the walled-off space in front of the flats her stomach churned. Alex was back, his car was there.

He flung open the door before she had her key in the lock. 'Where the hell have you been? I rang back almost immediately. I only said I'd be a bit late, I wasn't going to let you down, Kath. I was just waiting for Pete to turn up.' He hadn't been given a chance to explain properly. Alex rubbed his brow as if he was very tired. 'What's happening, Kath? We can't go on like this.'

'I'm sorry.' The apology, through gritted teeth, did not sound like one. Alex had managed to put her in the wrong again. He had done his best and, in her absence, had got ready to go out. He looked very handsome and very vulnerable. 'I was so fed up. I just wanted us to have a good night out.'

'That's fine, I can understand that. But just think what it would've been like had it been the other way around. Oh, Christ.' He sank into a chair. 'I can't just walk away from problems which occur with the business and I'm trying so hard, can't you see that? I even bought you some flowers. Please try to meet me halfway.'

Surely she had done so, and more. She stood staring at him mutely. There seemed to be nothing more to say. After his confession she had continued to look after the house and to share his bed, although the sexual side of their marriage had only recently been re-established. But these were not the things to which Alex was referring and she knew it.

Alex reached out a hand. 'Please stop chastising me for every minor misdemeanour.'

'I don't.' She ignored the suffering in his face.

'You are, Kath. Like tonight. The moment I tell you I'm going to be late you're out of the door as if you're trying to show me it doesn't matter whether I'm here or not, your life is going to carry on the way you want it. Every time

I'm not home on the dot you make a point of being late yourself the next night, and I'm not honoured with an explanation.'

Kathryn had no defence. It was no way in which to conduct a marriage, yet she could not bring herself to move closer to him, to touch him and let him know that it would be all right. Once more she heard herself speaking as though she was being controlled by outside forces. 'Perhaps we'd better call it a day then.'

'What are you saying?' Alex paled.

'Perhaps it would have been more sensible to have done so at the time. It wasn't me that was unfaithful, Alex, it was you. You're right, we can't go on as we are.'

'You mean it, don't you.' It was a statement, spoken quietly and with sadness.

'Yes.' Kathryn exhaled deeply as though she had been holding her breath and tried to unclench her fists which were held rigidly at her sides.

Alex stood up slowly, like an old man. 'Then it's a pity you didn't say so at the time. It would have saved us both a lot of heartache.' He left the room, closing the door quietly behind him.

Kathryn froze, unable to believe what she had done. 'Alex!' But it was too late. She heard the front door and the sound of his footsteps as he ran down the stairs.

There were no tears, nothing but a cold blankness in the knowledge that she had driven him away, possibly back to Rebecca. In a trancelike state she moved to the kitchen and poured a glass of wine from a bottle already open. She did not want it but could think of nothing else to do. There was no point in waiting for Alex to crawl back, begging forgiveness. He had apologised and attempted to make amends, and she would have respected him less if he had tried to debase himself.

As she turned to replace the wine bottle in the fridge she noticed the flowers. Red roses, a symbol of love. They were up to their necks in water in the washing-up bowl in the sink. Attached to the sellophane in which they were still wrapped, the bottom of which had carefully been removed

114

by Alex, was a card. Kathryn opened the tiny envelope. *For my Tuatara Woman, the woman I love*, it said.

And then she did cry.

Chapter 6

David was tired and grubby. All day he had been up and down the wooden library steps which could be wheeled along in order to get at the top shelves where he kept the stock which was less in demand. An inventory and some rearrangement had been long overdue and he used his pent-up energy to begin the arduous task. His nostrils felt dry and full of dust, and there was a mustiness in the air after so much disturbance. His neck ached and his shirt stuck to his back. It was time to call it a day.

When he got home he was too exhausted to bath immediately. He flopped into a chair and decided that later, clean and shaven, it would be nice to have a couple of pints of beer. He reached across for the telephone book and found the number of John's hotel. Mr Atherton, he was told, had already left. David sighed. It was another example of the result of his habit of procrastination.

Kitty jumped onto his knees, purring loudly. He stroked her. Initially he had toyed with the idea of giving her a grand name, something with literary allusions. In the end, deciding it might be rather pretentious, he had gone to the other extreme and stuck with Kitty. She had followed him in off the street one night and although he had advertised and put a notice in the local newsagent's window, no one had claimed her. His bitten nails caught in her fur.

'What do you think we should do?' he said aloud, another of his habits which served to confirm his mother's opinion that he was on the verge of madness. His customers thought he was mildly eccentric, not that he cared. 'Who is there who would understand? I wish there was someone I could talk to, and I don't mean a counsellor.' The crease across Kitty's forehead deepened as her green eyes narrowed. 'No offence meant,' David added, lifting her up on a level with his own face where he could feel, as well as hear, her purrs. Then, in one fluid movement she slunk to the floor and disappeared between the narrow gap between door and jamb. Food, apparently, took priority over love.

From the kitchen came plaintive mewing. David levered himself from his chair and crossed the mozaic tiled hallway. From the fridge he took half a can of cat food and removed the plastic film covering it. He disliked the fishy smell of the brand but it was Kitty's favourite. He spooned the remains into a bowl and stood watching her eat.

So John had gone, still pleasing himself where his movements were concerned, just as he had always done. David recalled the times when he thought nothing of interrupting his study, when he would walk into his rooms without knocking and chivvy him until he agreed to whatever scheme John had in mind. His concentration broken, David would lay down his pen and, cursing silently, go along with whatever he wanted. Afterwards he would curse even harder. Tired and drunk he wished he had the power to resist. He would still not allow himself to admit that he had been flattered, that he secretly enjoyed belonging to that small, elite circle of the beautiful and intelligent, although why he was included in the first place was a mystery. He had the brains but not the looks or the charisma of the others.

He wondered if there really had been an ulterior motive in John looking him up, but if there was it eluded him because nothing out of the ordinary had been mentioned. However, John's Machiavellian mind was unchartered territory.

When they had finally left Oxford for good David had known that there would be no further communication between them. Their very closeness had caused a tragedy and he suspected the others would want to forget they had ever known one another. Sarah's death would be filed away for ever. Of course, both Giles and Laura, out of politeness, had promised to keep in touch, but nothing had transpired and he doubted if he would have replied had they done so. David knew their transient friendships were not built on respect and liking but something else, something more sinister. There would be no reunions for them. Except now. It worried him.

He winced as he chewed too hard at a piece of loose skin at the side of his thumb. A spot of blood appeared and formed a bead. He wiped it on his trouser leg, uncaring of his clothes or the state his hands were in.

Kitty had returned to her favourite armchair. David ran a bath, adding several handfuls of the salts he kept in a jar on the wide ledge. Steam filled the air and clouded the window. He couldn't wait to get into the water. His clothes he discarded into the laundry basket. The trousers were washable and would be seen to by his cleaning lady. The jacket lay on the floor; it would have to go to the dry cleaner's.

Sinking into the scented water he felt it get to work on his tired muscles. John's reappearance hung over him much in the way a forthcoming appointment with the dentist did. Both were irrational fears, except in the case of the dentist there was a demarcation line, drawn neatly at the end of the appointment, or the treatment if any was necessary. In John's case he realised it might hang over him for ever. Perhaps Giles could enlighten him. John would not have come to London without getting in touch with him. Giles would have a shock, hearing from two of them within a matter of days.

Dried and dressed in pyjamas and a striped towelling robe, David realised that there would probably be more than one G. Harris listed and, anyway, being Megan Morris's publisher, it was unlikely his number would be in the phone book. There was also the possibility that Giles commuted from somewhere outside the Greater London area.

However, the name of the publishers would be on the book jacket. It was somewhere around. He tried the bedroom, a high-ceilinged, spacious room, large enough to have once housed a four-poster and its accompanying furniture. His own bed was a queen-sized divan with a solid pine headboard which would have been swamped by the space, except for the shelves which extended from it. On these, and elsewhere, was an assortment of books, hard and soft covers, piled haphazardly. The collection had grown, and when shelf-space ran out they were heaped on the floor. Amongst them he found *Homecoming*, the publisher's name clearly printed on the spine and elsewhere.

The number was listed. David noted it down and decided he would ring Giles in the office now the interminable Easter break was over.

The week dragged to an end. On Friday Kathryn shopped in her lunch hour, buying enough food for two people even though she had not heard from Alex. In her usual way she refused to let her personal life interfere with work. It had not been easy but she had always been able to compartmentalise her life. And that, she suspected, was part of the problem.

There was a small room with a single divan at the boatyard. Alex must be sleeping there, or at one of the local hotels. No other explanation was palatable. He bought me flowers, she thought, as she unloaded the trolley and fruit and vegetables, coffee and bread made their jerky progress along the conveyor belt towards the cashier. She rubbed a plastic carrier between thumb and forefinger to open it and bit her lip. Why couldn't she be more like Helena, able to take things in her stride, to look to the future instead of dwelling on the past?

Struggling back laden to the car she saw the lines of washing strung on pulleys at the back of a row of terraced houses. There were small items, children's clothes, and she wondered if having a child would have made any difference.

Trying to forget the weekend which loomed ahead of her she decided to continue with her search. She had not yet rung Inspector Forbes; because of Alex her enquiries had temporarily taken second place. But she was not going to give up. Alex would not be allowed to reduce her to the kind of woman who sat at home weeping and waiting.

Back at the office she reached out for the telephone, startled as it rang before she could touch it.

'Kathryn Brooks?'

'Yes, speaking.' She waited. It wasn't a voice she recognised and it sounded muffled. 'Hello?' There was a click and the line was disconnected. The events of the past couple of days had made her forget that other telephone call, the one Dave had told her about. She swore. Her chin rose. Here was another man trying to disrupt her life. Alone or not she would not let them get to her. She dialled the Oxford number.

Inspector Forbes had a deep voice and a reassuring manner and sounded as if he had nothing better to do than chat with Kathryn.

'No, it's not really the Miltons themselves I'm interested in,' she concluded, 'but people Sarah knew at university.'

'You're not an amateur detective, by any chance, Mrs Brooks?'

The wry way in which he said it suggested he was amused. 'No. I didn't know of Sarah Milton's existence until long after I'd started this,' she hesitated, seeking the appropriate word, 'project.' Having explained what she was trying to do, but omitting any mention of Megan Morris, she listened to the silence and began to think they'd been cut off.

'I wonder if you would do me the favour of allowing me to buy you a drink.'

'I, well, yes. When?' She was taken by surprise.

'Tonight? Or one day next week if it's more convenient.'

'Tonight would be fine. But where?'

Inspector Forbes gave the matter some thought. 'I have to be in London tomorrow for a conference. If you can recommend somewhere to stay I can drive over to Maidenhead and meet you there and go on in the morning.'

They arranged to meet at Bolter's Lock and Kathryn agreed to find him somewhere to stay before he arrived at seven-thirty. When she hung up she began to have second thoughts. Did Inspector Forbes have ulterior motives for making the arrangement? She would go anyway; there was nothing to stay at home for.

On her way to the car she glanced casually around. Apart from other staff on the paper there was no one else in the

120

car park. The two peculiar telephone calls had made her edgy but she would not allow them to intimidate her.

Once home, she unpacked the shopping, changed and brushed her hair. She put on the dress she had bought to go out with Alex, then questioned her motives for doing so. As she drove back from Burnham towards Maidenhead she suddenly realised she had no idea how she and Inspector Forbes were meant to recognise one another.

He did not look like a policeman. The man who stood at the bar was of medium height and a little on the plump side. Soft brown curls framed a bald pate and he was wearing brown cord trousers and an open-necked shirt. He had spotted her immediately, perhaps because she was the only female to enter alone. 'Mrs Brooks?' His hand was warm and dry, his grip firm. 'What can I get you?'

'Gin and slimline tonic, please. It's all right, I shall only have the one.'

His laugh was as deep as his voice. 'That's one disadvantage of the job. Everybody becomes defensive when they know what I do. I don't doubt that you're a responsible citizen. Now, shall we sit outside, do you think?'

It was just about warm enough to do so. They took their drinks to the wooden balcony which hung over the lock and from where they could see one of the weirs. 'I wasn't sure you'd come. A married woman: an invitation from a strange man. You are still married?'

'Yes.' Kathryn did not elaborate. 'If I can't be safe with a police escort, what chance does anyone have?'

'Now, this project of yours. Want to tell me more about it?'

For fifteen minutes Kathryn thought of nothing but what she hoped to achieve. Her enthusiasm lit up her face and Inspector Forbes thought how attractive she was. As she leaned forward, he saw the smooth roundness of her breasts beneath the cut-away dress and, for a brief second, wished that neither of them was married.

'I looked up the case again, in case there was anything of use to you, but really, there's nothing I can tell you that you won't have read in the papers.'

'And no one's ever been arrested?'

'No. We had our theories, but theories alone are not enough. And there was the added complication of the time element.' He held up a hand, as if to ward off criticism. 'That's not as weak an excuse as it seems. Even in a recent murder, the more days that pass the harder it is to make an arrest. Initially we didn't take a great deal of notice of her disappearance because the consensus among her friends was that the strain of the forthcoming exams had taken their toll. However, we did make a search of the area – the usual places, squats and outbuildings and the woods – because we knew that kids and students went out there to do drugs. Only when her parents became frantic did we take things a stage further. Believe it or not, there's little we can do if someone who's healthy and of age has a mind to take off without letting anyone know. In this case, if it was exam nerves there was the possibility of an overdose. Her friends were questioned but weren't much help.' Inspector Forbes hesitated. Kathryn sensed that he had his own ideas about Sarah's friends. 'And then, six and a half years later, the body turns up. It was a mammoth task trying to trace those who had known Sarah all those years ago but we considered ourselves to be reasonably successful. Once we'd got over the problem of identification, that is.'

'So all the students were interrogated?'

He smiled at her amazement and tried to avert his eyes as she crossed her slender legs. 'No. And I think the word you're looking for is interviewed.'

'Yes. Sorry.'

'Some had been questioned back in 1978, soon after she went missing, and again in 1985. Likewise family and friends from her home town, but by then many had forgotten her.'

'I have the names of some of the students I believe were her contemporaries at Oxford. Would you be able to confirm the surname of one of them?'

Inspector Forbes shook his head. 'I'm not free to discuss possible witnesses.'

Kathryn almost mentioned the telephone calls but thought better of it. The Inspector would think her over-sensitive or hysterical, trying to create drama where there was none. He offered to replenish their glasses and refused Kathryn's offer to pay.

'Do you intend contacting her parents?' he asked when he came back with the drinks, just tonic for Kathryn this time. The breeze had freshened and ripples rose on the surface of the Thames. They sat contemplating the craft queuing to go into the lock and the people on board, pulling on jerseys and jackets. 'Why do they do that, I wonder?' Inspector Forbes nodded in the direction of a man in a blazer and a captain's peaked cap on his head. 'Do you suppose it makes them feel important?'

Kathryn had often wondered why herself but was thinking of his previous question. 'Sarah's parents? It hadn't crossed my mind actually. It wouldn't be right – it would be too painful for them.' Yet she thought they would be able to help her as far as their daughter's friends were concerned. They might even know something about Megan Morris.

'I'm not so sure.' He deliberated for a moment. 'Look, you may be aware that we've now got a policy on following up crime as far as keeping the victim's relatives informed. We let them know when we've apprehended someone, when they're going to trial, and what the outcome is. In the Miltons' case there's been nothing to tell them since 1985, but I keep in touch once or twice a year, just to let them know that Sarah hasn't been forgotten. They lived through six years of not knowing if she was dead or alive, and they've had to suffer a further eleven knowing that her killer is free. I think they might welcome some fresh interest. It would show them people still care.'

It was Kathryn's turn for silence. Events were escalating rapidly. It would be interesting to speak to the Miltons, but cruel to raise their hopes because they would undoubtedly believe she was working on their behalf. 'Can you give me their telephone number?' she heard herself asking.

'No, that's not on. You can imagine how much they were bothered by the press. What I can do is speak to Mrs Milton and see if she's willing to get in touch with you herself.'

'Thank you.' She got a card out of her bag and wrote her home number on the back of it. 'You can give her either or both of these.' Kathryn realised it meant Inspector Forbes also had her home number, but he was not the sort of man to abuse it.

'Now, if you'd like to tell me where you've arranged for me to stay, I'll let you get back to your husband.'

She did so, giving him clear directions. A room had been booked at one of the pubs. The journey from Oxford to London did not merit expenses for overnight accommodation and Forbes would be footing the bill himself. He had explained over the telephone that his wife was visiting her mother and that he would not be going out of his way by coming to Maidenhead because a night away from home would do him good. He did not proffer an invitation for dinner, for which Kathryn was glad. She needed time to think.

'I'll contact Mrs Milton this evening. She doesn't go out at night very often.' He extended his hand. 'It was a pleasure meeting you, and an added pleasure to be seen in such a public place with such an attractive young lady.'

'Thank you. And thank you for all you've told me.' The compliment, given so naturally, restored some of her self-esteem.

They walked through the main body of the bar together and down the stairs out into the darkening evening. Fairy lights were strung around the building and one or two shouts from the river could be heard, but the lock was empty now. People were packing up to go home.

In the car park some yards away and across the road, they said their goodnights. Inspector Forbes thoughtfully waited until Kathryn was behind the wheel. Just as she turned the key in the ignition he said, 'Oh, it might be more tactful to let Mrs Milton mention the baby.' He raised his hand in salute and was striding rapidly towards his own car before Kathryn absorbed what he had said.

The *baby*? She stared at the bushes in front of her. They were black except where the headlights gave them back a greenness. Had he really said that? Of course, a child might be a motive for wanting someone dead. Now she could not ask the Inspector because he had already done her as much of a favour as she could expect.

She drove home slowly, unaware of the car behind her which was making no effort to overtake.

Immediately she was indoors she threw on all the lights and grabbed her file from the drawer. Scanning every news-paper cutting again she knew she had been right. There was no mention of a baby! Perhaps there was an article in the Oxford *Star* that the editor had missed, or maybe the police had kept it quiet for reasons of their own. Then why had she been told now? Surely it wasn't carelessness on the part of Forbes?

Kathryn suddenly wanted another drink, badly. With shaking hands she opened a bottle of wine, unable to under-stand if she was anxious or excited or simply missing Alex. One thing was certain; if the Miltons did contact her, she would not hesitate to go and see them, no matter where they lived.

The switchboard put the call through. 'Giles, is that you?'

Giles swallowed hard, his throat hurting because his mouth was dry. 'Yes. It's been a long time.' He waited. He hadn't wanted to take the call but this was David's third attempt to contact him and he knew he would persevere until he succeeded. Coming on top of John's visit it was too much to cope with. He had been right, they were being inexplicably drawn together, however unwillingly. He wondered what it would lead to this time, and if they would be lucky enough to get away with it.

David wished he had not made the call. Giles's tone was unfriendly, aggressive almost, but the receptionist had given his name. If Giles was so reluctant to speak to him he could have made an excuse. 'I saw John Atherton. He's back from the States. Has he been in touch with you?'

'Yes. We met for a drink. He said he'd seen you.' Giles began to relax. It appeared that David was merely curious, as he had been.

'Do you think we could meet? I understand how busy you must be but, well . . .' The sentence trailed off.

Giles did not want to meet him; he wanted nothing to do with any of them, but David might start talking about things better left unsaid over an open line. 'All right. Hold on.' He flipped over the pages of his diary thinking the sooner the better. After that he would sever all contact. David had always been tenacious; if Giles refused a meeting, he would not put it past him to turn up at the office. But surely they were safe now? No one, not even someone as egocentric as John, would be foolish enough to risk everything now. If he did, he would take them all with him. They were all successful in their own right, although none of the others knew of Laura's achievements and it was her, above all, he was considering. To his credit the sentiment was genuine. He cared for her, not for her reputation or his own as her publisher. The real worry was David's anxiety. He had never coped well with stress; the lead up to his finals and his viva had proved that. Giles would reassure him. 'I'm free on Wednesday, would that suit you? We could have a couple of drinks and a bite to eat, maybe? On me,' he added hastily, unsure of David's financial position. Did he still run that second-hand bookshop?

'Wednesday's fine.'

They arranged to meet at six by the exit barrier of Covent Garden tube. As there was only one it would be impossible to miss each other and it was handy for them both.

Wednesday suited Giles because Ingrid was teaching some course or other and would be away. He strolled over to the window and looked down on the heads of passing pedestrians. On the opposite side of the road were numerous bistros and wine bars and already, optimistically, tables and chairs had been set out on the pavement where one or two customers were taking advantage of the sunshine, despite the fact that the brightly-striped awnings which gave the street a Continental appearance deflected most of the heat. It was hardly surprising that there was a foreign feel to the area, as most of the restaurants were run by Italians and Chinese and Cypriots. In less than an hour he would be patronising one of them, lunching in a wine bar with a new writer who showed great promise. He was keeping his fingers crossed because the man was bringing the manuscript of his second novel with him, and they often did not live up to the first one.

Giles could justify his salary and his expenses on Megan

Morris's work alone, but his pragmatic nature refused to allow him to take anything for granted. If Laura dried up or simply decided to stop writing, he needed other authors to fall back on and he always encouraged new writers.

The telephone interrupted his ruminations. It was his direct line so he answered it on the second ring.

'Giles,' Ingrid said without preamble. 'Can you get some cheeses? I have not the time.'

'Of course.'

'Thank you. I see you later, darling.'

He felt himself grinning foolishly. Ingrid's voice always did that to him, and the way she spoke, as if they were in the same room and simply continuing a conversation in progress. From her few words he was supposed to remember that they were having people to dinner. Dear Ingrid, who sounded far bossier than she was because of her guttural accent and the way in which she constructed her sentences. Ingrid, who had always known exactly what she wanted out of life and set about getting it, even down to the child, Paul. Ingrid, who for some inexplicable reason had fallen in love with him. He had done nothing to charm her, it was she who had made the first move. On the second night of their meeting when they were both staying in a large hotel in Liverpool, both attending different conferences, he had taken her to bed and they had not looked back. He loved her, but not in the way he loved Laura.

He was glad of the reminder about the dinner that night because he would limit what he ate at lunch. It was one of life's mysteries why none of their friends was put off by Ingrid's cooking although, whenever possible, he persuaded her to hire caterers. Her looks and her personality must be compensation enough. Giles wrote himself a note. There was a delicatessen a few doors away. He must not forget the cheeses; at least they would be edible.

John Atherton completed the journey to Cardiff having forked out for a miniature vodka, a can of tomato juice and his own drink at the cost of over six pounds, and had received nothing in return, not even some polite small talk. His female travelling companion had offered him her share of the cost but he refused it, expecting her to agree to his suggestion of another drink once they reached their destination. Bluntly she had told him it was impossible; her offer to fetch him something from the buffet car was not a pick-up line. She had then taken a paperback from her briefcase and read until the train pulled into Cardiff Central. When they alighted she barely smiled and walked briskly ahead of him to the line of waiting taxis. John took the one behind hers and went straight home.

He had always kept his options open, even during his marriage, but he had lost some of the impetus which had driven him, making him desire change of people or places once they had become too familiar. He opened the door of his house to the now-customary smells of furniture polish, disinfectant and freesias, the legacy of one of Sheila Roberts's days. Her husband grew the flowers in his greenhouse.

His footsteps echoed in the high wide hall as he crossed the black and white tiled floor. The light on the answering machine was flashing, three times in succession. He played the messages. A tutor inviting him to a cocktail party, the female colleague who had helped him choose his soft furnishings wondering if he'd like to accompany her to the New Theatre as she happened to have a spare ticket for *That Good Night*, a play by N.J. Crisp. Oh yes? he thought cynically. Women always claimed they had been given or somehow acquired a spare ticket when they wanted to invite you out. 'Why can't they bloody well admit they've bought them?' he asked the empty house. 'It would be far more flattering.' Fortunately the date she had in mind had already passed. The third call was a reminder that the Dean was hosting a get-together during the last afternoon of the break. John knew he would have to attend.

The post was even less interesting. There were four letters in the wire box attached to the door. A bill, two circulars and a letter addressed to the previous occupants. He chucked the last three into the freshly lined bin in the kitchen as he had no forwarding address. The bill he opened and stuck on a prong on his desk.

He took his bag upstairs and unpacked. There were clean

white sheets on the bed and more freesias on the mantel-piece in his bedroom. The smell was cloying but Sheila only wanted to please. He grinned at himself in the mirror. Plump and pretty, he had not been able to resist making advances. In her lilting voice she had scolded him as if he were a child, not ten years her senior. He was glad; he would have hated to lose her now.

Downstairs again, he did not have the slightest hesitation in reaching for the bottle of Scotch from the cupboard next to the sink. The woman on the train had reminded him of Laura; he began thinking about the others, especially Sarah. Sarah had possessed a zest for living he doubted he would ever see equalled. Ironic that it should be her life that was snuffed out. Her metamorphosis had been staggering. She had arrived at Oxford a mousy little thing he would not have glanced at twice but, it seemed to him, her personality had grown in direct proportion to her hair which, by the end of the first year, was halfway down her back. Sarah, he recalled, had had a complete disregard for danger.

John slugged another couple of inches into a glass. The hunger he had felt on the train had disappeared but Sheila had probably put something in the fridge for later.

So much had happened since Oxford; his post-grad course, an unsettled time at a redbrick university then the chance to go to the States. And Angela. Before her, there had been numerous women and he had astonished himself by remaining faithful to her. In retrospect he saw there were few opportunities to be otherwise. They lived in a small community which mostly revolved around the univer-sity and Angela organised most of his spare time. To give her her due, she had always been sexually accommodating. Tina Parry came into his mind. Long of limb, young and innocent and smelling so clean. How very much he would enjoy a tumble with her ... He raised his glass to the thought.

' "My only books were women's looks, and folly's all they've taught me".' He said the words aloud and grinned. Not quite true in his case, but near enough. Laura would have been able to say immediately whose words they were, but John had to stop and think. Finally he came up with

Thomas Moore, the Irish poet, pleased that there were still a few brain cells intact.

He knew the root of his present problem. He needed sex. Not love or romance or even companionship – he had given up on those. A woman in his bed, or anywhere for that matter, would help obliterate the memories of Laura and Sarah. It was his own fault. He would not have thought about them if he had not been stupid enough to look up David and Giles. For so long he had sublimated the knowledge of the group's existence. Murderers all, perhaps, but nobody knew for certain, not even Laura, no matter what she had meant by her final postcard.

The whisky bottle, nearly half-full, was now empty. He threw it in the bin on top of the envelopes and pulled out another. He bought them by the caseload at an off-licence where he had a monthly account. First he needed to pee. He used the downstairs cloakroom. As he washed his hands in the tiny guest sink he caught sight of his face in the mirror above it. Apart from a faint flush across his cheekbones and a slight bleariness in his eyes, there were no signs that he had been drinking and he still considered himself to be handsome. He smoothed down his thick hair which curled just over the collar of his shirt. He was broad-shouldered and solid, and dark hairs sprouted from the open neck of his denim shirt. 'You'll do,' he told himself, then dried his hands.

Later, he opened the French windows and sat facing the garden which was becoming overgrown. He would have to do something about that, in the form of getting a gardener. For some reason he was shaking but he wasn't cold, nor was it the effects of the alcohol. He was thinking he might be wrong, that the past might yet come back to haunt them.

Tina Parry, or any other woman would have to wait. There was some serious drinking to be done before he could face the future.

When he woke it was after midnight and he was very cold. The heavy damask curtains flapped in the breeze and there were rustlings at the end of the garden. Night sounds, different from the ones he was used to, nothing like the clink of glasses and the conversation of bars, getting louder as the evening progressed. No groups of youths swaggering and yelling, no police sirens. He felt strangely at peace and realised what he had been missing.

He closed the windows and drew the curtains then took himself to bed.

When he awoke for the second time it was broad daylight, after eleven. He closed his eyes again, sickened with self-disgust. His hangover was tremendous. It had to stop.

Just carry on as normal, Kathryn told herself when she woke to an empty bed on Saturday morning. Go through the motions and he'll walk in the door at any moment.

She drank coffee and had a shower, changed the sheets and put them in the washing machine then got out the hoover. Life with Alex was not, nor ever could be, what her parents would describe as settled, by which they meant routine and boring. But that was part of his attraction. Her own job entailed unsociable hours occasionally and they both preferred to live without making too many plans. One thing she had let slip was her friends. It was ages since she had invited anyone for a meal or gone out for the evening with a girlfriend. Part of the trouble was that she did not feel able to carry on as though everything was all right between her and Alex, but neither did she want to confide in anyone.

Duster and polish in hand she took all the books down from the shelves and cleaned them. Everything back in its place, she dusted the shelf which held the tuatara, patted its head then turned her attention to the windowsill. Alex's flowers, in a cut-glass vase, stood there like an accusation. They were blood-red and thornless, stark against the white paint, and nothing like the blowsy ones which grew in her parents' garden and whose petals littered the lawn. These uniform blooms had been greenhouse-grown, forced into submission in much the same way as she tried to treat Alex. Except he wasn't having it. The buds were still tight and would remain perfect for several days, but they would not open and flower properly, only turn purple and dry. There was a lesson to be learned, Kathryn thought, as she compared them with her marriage. She fiddled with the ring on

131

her left hand. It was loose, she was in danger of losing it. And more.

For several seconds she was tempted to drive down to the boat-yard to see if Alex was there and to have it out with him, no matter what the consequences. Pride prevented her from doing so, and the thought that he might not be there. Willing herself not to dwell on the problem, she prepared lamb kebabs for later, enough for two; they would not be wasted, she could eat the rest tomorrow. She had found the mundane chores enjoyable. It was a nice feeling to walk through the spotless flat and know there was a meal ready for the evening. The question now was what to do with the afternoon.

Collecting together a book, sunglasses and a towel, Kathryn was just on her way out of the flat to sit on the lawn at the back of the building and soak up some sun when the telephone rang. Please let it be Alex, she thought as she ran to take the call before the answering machine clicked into life. For some obscure reason, just as she lifted the receiver, she remembered she still had not checked the register of electors, but it was too late now, the library was shut on Saturday afternoons.

'Mrs Brooks?' The voice was female and unfamiliar. For one awful moment Kathryn thought it might be Rebecca ringing to say Alex had moved in with her. 'I'm Harriet Milton, Sarah's mother.'

Kathryn inhaled sharply. Inspector Forbes had wasted no time. 'Thank you for contacting me. I wasn't sure that you would.'

'Well, I wasn't sure whether to, it being the weekend, but I thought if I didn't do it right away I might change my mind. It's such a relief, to know that people are still interested. Gary Forbes gave me a rough idea of what you're doing.'

Gary Forbes. So he had not exaggerated when he said he kept in touch, not if they were on first-name terms. No doubt, after all those years, some sort of relationship had been formed. Kathryn sensed it had taken courage on Mrs Milton's part to pick up the telephone. 'I don't want to disappoint you, Mrs Milton, but what I'm working on is only indirectly connected with your daughter.' She paused. 'Would it be possible to come and see you some time?'

'Of course. I'd like to meet you. We live in Gloucestershire now, not all that far from Cheltenham. I can pick you up at the station if you don't want to drive.'

'There's no need. It'll have to be a weekend though.'

'Yes.' Kathryn waited and was astonished to hear her say, 'I suppose tomorrow's out of the question?'

Tomorrow. What if Alex returned and she was out? No, she couldn't sit around waiting for something which might or might not occur.

'Or even today if you like.'

Kathryn made a quick calculation. Cheltenham was roughly seventy, seventy-five miles away. She could be there by two and it solved the problem of how she was to spend her time.

'Today suits me better actually.'

'That's wonderful. I'll do us a late lunch. Oh, what about your husband? Won't he mind?'

'He's away at the moment.' Kathryn said it with finality. It was true, and as she had no idea just where he was, there was nothing to stop her leaving immediately. She wrote down the directions, put the towel back in the airing cupboard and changed out of jeans into a dress. Her hair tied back in a matching scarf and her sunglasses perched on her nose she looked confident and self-assured and received an appreciative whistle from a youth on a bike as she strode to the car. It had been in the sun all morning and the steering-wheel was warm beneath her hands. She wound down the window and felt the breeze blowing loose ends of her hair across her neck as she drove. Feeling calm and relaxed, if not quite happy, she turned on the radio and headed towards High Wycombe and the M40 which would take her to Oxford. From there she would join the A40. Oxford: she had not expected to be heading in that direction again quite so soon.

Although Laura enjoyed cooking, lunch parties were not a form of entertainment she particularly relished. There was always a sense of anti-climax once the guests had departed, unlike the evenings when she could go straight to bed. They had to be borne, though, because it was a recognised ritual amongst her acquaintances and occasionally she had to repay the hospitality. Eileen Sprague, the Merry Widow as she thought of her, would be coming because Laura was in debt for the theatre ticket. Her next-door neighbours, Pam and Joss Fuller, were always good company, and she had included, for Eileen's benefit, Pierre Masters who considered himself intriguing and a ladies' man (even if no one else did) on the feeble excuse that his mother was French. Laura thought him a pompous fool. Giles was the fourth man. He rarely visited the house although it was doubtful he would have been recognised, but as Ingrid was still away he could spare a Saturday afternoon and there was no one else Laura could think of inviting as her partner.

Peggy's offer of assistance had been declined. The fewer people who met Giles the better. Laura had kept the meal simple. Parma ham with chicory which had marinaded overnight, and a veal-based casserole, light enough for the warmer weather. She cared nothing for other people's sensibilities although she accepted her own perverseness. Egg scares, beef panics, animal rights groups ... none of it phased her; she would continue to eat what she had always eaten. It was the same with the occasional IRA bombings in London; they did not deter her from using the Tube or from theatre trips. Giles often said she was too stubborn for her own good.

There was an hour to go before the guests were due to arrive. Laura hoped that a dessert of fresh fruit or cheese did not seem parsimonious, but she did not like puddings and Giles had been warned to watch his cholesterol levels so she didn't see why she should bother.

Laura went to the kitchen and poured a glass of chilled wine, toasted herself and grinned. Of course, she always made sure there was enough alcohol flowing that no one would be too bothered by the end of the meal. Joss Fuller certainly wouldn't notice – he could be guaranteed to make serious inroads into the wine – and Eileen would be too busy playing footsie with Pierre who would take it as his right even though she was some years his senior.

What a cynic I've become, she thought as she laid the dining-room table. It was a pleasant room but one not often in use. Laura's solitary meals were taken at the kitchen table or up in the attic or, occasionally, on a tray in front of the television. At least she knew Giles would be appreciative; he loved her cooking. Perhaps the lovely Ingrid fed him a diet of sauerkraut and sausage and potato salad. Now, now, she told herself, don't be bitchy. And what had suddenly made her assume Ingrid was lovely?

She stood back to admire the table. Shining cutlery and glasses on a white linen cloth, white napkins and a bowl of white rosebuds; it looked cool and rather chic without having caused her any work. Satisfied there was nothing left to do, she carried her drink outside and sat on a bench and lit a cigarette. The attic stairs had been folded up and there were no signs of her writing anywhere about the house, not even a copy of one of her books. Those, too, were kept in her study. 'How the hell do I end this novel?' It had been preying on her mind. It seemed that, like the women about whom she was writing, she was unable to make a decision. There were several possible alternatives ... She had spoken aloud. The Fullers' cat, prowling amongst the bluebells, turned his head and glared. She had disturbed the bird he was stalking. Probably a blackbird, Laura thought. One was nesting in the hedge.

The doorbell rang. She had almost forgotten she was expecting guests. Giles was the first to arrive. He kissed her on both cheeks. 'I came by train so I'm a bit early. I take it I'm the first?' He handed her a bunch of rather tatty flowers which he had purchased from a street vendor as an afterthought and which had become crushed during the journey, but the bottle of wine he produced was expensive, one of her favourites. She thanked him and put the flowers in a vase where they looked even worse.

Giles wore a suit. He had always dressed formally. Laura had chosen the skirt of the outfit she had bought to go to the theatre with Eileen but instead of the jacket, wore a pale silk blouse.

Giles had followed her to the kitchen where she poured him some wine. It was a room he felt comfortable in, modern and well-equipped, but functional. Unlike Ingrid's kitchen there were no bunches of herbs and no old-fashioned gadgets which were ornamental rather than useful.

'What's up?' Laura was regarding him, hands on hips.

'I was thinking about your kitchen actually.' He smiled ruefully. 'But apart from that, I don't like the way things keep cropping up.'

'What things?'

'Please don't take this the wrong way, Laura, but it makes me nervous the way both John and David suddenly appeared on the scene so quickly after your encounter with that Brooks girl.'

'David? Good heavens. You didn't say anything before. Anyway, why the melodrama? Think about it logically. John looks you both up, it follows naturally that David's going to do the same. Perhaps he just wanted to know there weren't going to be any problems. And you do both work in London; it's not as if he had to make a special journey.' But Laura refilled her glass. Giles was right, it *was* uncanny.

'Coincidence, I know. But John always was the catalyst.'

'For what? Dammit. Leave it now, Giles.' The doorbell had rung again.

'I don't think David's completely sane,' he said as Laura removed her apron.

'Really? But don't forget " . . . one half of the nation is mad – and the other not very sound". And that includes you. Smollett,' she added swiftly, in case he had forgotten.

She introduced Giles to Eileen and left them in the lounge whilst she went to answer the door once more. Joss and Pam and Pierre had arrived simultaneously and the serious business of eating and drinking began. If asked, Giles was going to pose as the managing director of a typesetting company, about which he knew enough to be able to discuss it. It was, he thought, not a subject in which anyone would show much interest.

When the others had left and Laura was loading the dishwasher, Giles told her about his meeting with David.

'You know how it is when you don't see someone for years. It's always awkward to begin with – all those remarks about looking well and how's business. He told me he was a bachelor. David always did have a quaint turn of phrase, haven't heard that expression for a long time. Anyway, he spent a great deal of the time chewing at his bloody finger-nails. It was irritating.'

'Get on with it, Giles. What did he want?' Laura felt the beginnings of a headache and was longing to have the house to herself again.

'I'm not really sure. I think he wanted me to tell him that there was nothing sinister in John's coming to London. I suppose David's life is so uncomplicated he sees ulterior motives where there are none. He's let himself go – David, that is. It doesn't take much effort to get a decent haircut, and he's sort of stooped, yet he said the shop's doing well and he owns his flat outright.'

'So what else did you talk about?'

'John mostly. David suggested he might be lonely.'

Laura made a sound not unlike a snort. 'Not that man. He'll have surrounded himself with another coterie by now.'

'I said it was best to forget it – that it was all in the past.' Giles folded his arms and rubbed his chin. 'Strange, that. It must be John's influence. Before lunch you quoted at me, just like in the old days. David did the same.'

'Oh?' Laura sounded nonchalant but she knew what was happening. John Atherton's influence was reasserting itself. 'Which quote?'

'He said "Those who cannot remember the past are con-demned to repeat it".'

'George Santayana.' Laura could not help herself. She had fallen into the old habit at once. 'But how about "The past is a foreign country: they do things differently there" ?'

Giles frowned. 'I'm never sure if they mean the same thing or not. No,' he shook his head. 'Tell me.'

'It's from *The Go-Between*. L.P. Hartley.'

'Of course.'

They stared at each other in silence. 'Oh, Giles,' Laura finally said before sinking into a chair.

'I know. We can't forget the past. Not us. Not ever. I'd better go now, Laura. Thanks for the lunch, it was terrific.'

Laura nodded but she did not get up to show him to the

door. She wished she was still in Shropshire with Marcia where there was some respite from her thoughts.

The shop door stood open but David closed it if he needed to go out to the back because without the warning of the bell, anyone could walk in and help themselves.

He was still trying to work out what had got into him. He had told Giles that he was glad he had lost touch with the group, that, deep down, he felt that during their Oxford years they were dysfunctional, dragging each other down instead of celebrating and sharing their youth. Yet they had each supplied something the others lacked. But David was honest enough to admit, although only to himself, that he was still dysfunctional. Parents, school, John and the crowd and even his customers dictated the course of his life. He had allowed others to mould him, and it was time he re-shaped himself. Look how he had spent the evening with John, drinking as much as John wanted, eating where John chose . . . still the immature schoolboy eager to please his hero. But John was *not* a hero. And while we're at it, he thought, as he unpacked a box the postman had delivered, what about Nicola? She had left him because he was weak, because, to please her, he had let her make all the decisions and really, now he thought about it, she had probably got bored with walking all over him.

Seated with Giles in an average London pub he had suddenly realised that the past was just that and it must not interfere with his future. He cringed as he thought of how he had treated Giles.

With blinding clarity he had known that the long-ago night would always remain a mystery. Guilty or not, he would never know what had happened, and it didn't seem to matter any more. He really had nothing to lose. He had laughed, he couldn't help it, and when Giles had said, 'What's up, old boy?' he had laughed harder, drawing attention to them both. 'Old boy.' How patronising.

Wiping his eyes he had stood, avoiding Giles's horrified expression in case he became hysterical. 'It was nice seeing you again, but I must be off. And, as far as I'm concerned, John Atherton can do the other thing.'

He had noticed nothing and no one as he walked home. He knew that Giles thought he'd finally cracked and maybe he had, but John was just a man, in as much danger as the rest of them – except David no longer cared. ' "And those, who have much to hope for and nothing to lose, will always be more dangerous, more or less," ' he remembered thinking as he turned the corner to his flat, then cursed himself for his Pavlovian response to thoughts of a man he had already decided to forget. But Edmund Burk who had penned those words in a letter, had hit the nail on the head.

One of his regular customers came in. David pushed his glasses higher up his nose, fixed a smile on his face and hoped the package he was in the process of opening contained the book for which the man had come.

Chapter 7

That Saturday lunchtime it seemed as if spring had been by-passed. A winter of freezing fog, followed by weeks of rain had given way to unseasonal warmth. It was hard to recall that only a short while ago she had been numb with cold if she was outdoors for more than a few minutes.

Kathryn's mood had lifted but whether it was due to the sunshine or being away from the flat, she wasn't sure. There was also an element of anticipation in meeting Mrs Milton.

As she drove she came to the conclusion that trying to change Alex was a mug's game and he, in turn, had not been able to alter her. Both possessing strength of character, there were bound to be disagreements but she had to ask herself why, if she loved him, did she wish to humiliate him? The only honest answer was revenge for what she felt was her own humiliation.

The radio was churning out pop music and although she preferred classical she did not change the station because the tunes were bouncy and she knew that whatever happened she was going to be all right. 'The Tuatara Woman', Alex called her, and that was what she intended being today. With surprise she noticed a signpost which told her there were only ten more miles to Cheltenham.

The directions she had been given were perfectly clear but the unmarked turning was concealed and she had to drive on until she found a gateway to reverse into before going back. She was still earlier than she had expected to be.

The house was isolated, more so than Helena's, but not

at all similar. Standing open was a brand-new gate of reddish wood which opened onto a cobbled yard edged with tubs and terracotta pots containing healthy-looking seedlings. They had recently been planted, to judge from the small mounds of fresh compost beneath them. In a month or so they would produce a riot of colour but for the moment they fitted in with the general air of starkness which the sunshine did not alleviate. The building itself was a barn, the brickwork cleaned up, the woodwork new. It had obviously only just been converted. Kathryn got out of the car into an eerie silence; not even a farm dog barked. Once the house had weathered and mellowed into its surroundings it would be idyllic, but it would take a long time. A movement caught her eye. Mrs Milton was emerging from the stable door.

'Hello, you made good time.' She extended a thin hand. Her skin was dry and stretched across the bones which emphasised the veins.

'Yes. Your directions were perfect.' Kathryn smiled at her warm welcome. Not content with shaking hands, Mrs Milton had taken Kathryn's in both of hers and there was a mixture of pleasure and relief in her expression.

'Come on in.'

She did not close the front door and although it was a warm day Kathryn suspected it was more to do with the strong smell of wood and varnish. There was no entrance hall, they stepped straight into the living area which was spacious and cool and airy but would cost a fortune to heat in winter. The floor was constructed of plain boards which sanding and polishing had rendered the colour of syrup. There were a couple of striped cotton rugs in the same muted purples and greens as the other soft furnishings, which gave the place a Scandinavian feel. It was a lovely room but had not yet acquired that elusive quality which would have made it a home.

Mrs Milton had promised a late lunch and must have worked quickly. Set out on a pine table were dips and crudités, cold meats and cheeses, bread and fruit.

Faintly discernible was the fragrance of pot pourri, the same mixture as had been in her honeymoon hotel room.

141

Just as she thought she was strong again, without warning, tears pricked her eyes and began to fall. Alex had come here to haunt her.

'Mrs Brooks?' Mrs Milton was staring at her with horror. 'Whatever is it?'

'I'm so sorry. I feel so stupid. It's nothing, just a row with my husband.' Before she could apologise further she found herself on a squashy sofa with a bunch of tissues in her hand and, from apparently out of thin air, a small glass of brandy in her hand. The situation was ridiculous. Kathryn had expected to be handing out sympathy to her hostess! Seeing the funny side of it she blew her nose and smiled.

'Go on, drink it, you'll feel better,' Mrs Milton said.

Kathryn felt the burning sensation of the alcohol as it travelled to her stomach and colour returned to her cheeks. She realised two things simultaneously; Mrs Milton was a very nice woman whereas she, Kathryn, no longer was.

'You shouldn't have come, not if you've got problems. I could have seen you another time.'

'I wanted to come. I'm fine now. Really.'

The two women appraised one another, each a little startled by their unorthodox introduction. Mrs Milton was model-thin and flat-chested, but more as if the years had worn her away rather than naturally or by design. Yet her face was gentle and her eyes were soft and kind. Kathryn had expected only bitterness. Her trousers were smart, pleated at the waist, which helped to disguise the narrowness of her hips. Tucked into them was a surprisingly youthful T-shirt depicting a cartoon character. Her hair, as dark as Kathryn's, was wiry and cropped short with one or two silvery threads. Her skin was smooth olive, the kind that tanned easily, and barely lined. She was one of those women who made Kathryn feel she had met her somewhere before. If Mrs Milton had survived so much suffering without rancour it should be easy for Kathryn. At least Alex was alive.

Kathryn handed back the dimpled glass which had contained the brandy. 'Thank you. Goodness knows what you must think of me. I don't usually arrive at strangers' houses and burst into tears.'

'Think nothing of it. And perhaps it was because I *am* a stranger. It's often easier to let go with people you don't know.' She was speaking from experience. 'Now, shall we talk or would you rather eat first? Everything's cold so it doesn't matter either way.' She shrugged apologetically. 'I'm afraid I don't do a lot of cooking these days. I've become extremely lazy and say a nightly thank you for the existence of good old Marks and Spencer.'

Her honesty made Kathryn like her further. 'We might make a start before we eat.' She had not got over her embarrassment at her tears and was not yet hungry. She withdrew a notepad and pen from her bag. 'Do you mind if I make notes?'

'Not at all.'

'As I said on the phone, I started out following up some students who were at Oxford in the 1970s. When I began I had no idea about your daughter; you must understand that it was pure chance I found out that Sarah was one of them and that she had been . . .' Kathryn stopped and chewed the end of her pen, unsure what pain she might be causing and how much Mrs Milton would be able to take.

Mrs Milton leaned across from where she sat on a sofa at right angles to Kathryn's and touched her arm. Gently she said, 'It's quite all right to talk about Sarah and to use words like "killed" and "murdered" in connection with her name. Repetition, and time, desensitise you – condition you not to flinch.' She smiled to soften any harshness in what she had said.

Kathryn nodded. 'I was amazed you agreed to speak to me, especially as it's not a story about Sarah herself. Perhaps it might be easier if you just tell me all about it, Mrs Milton.'

'Oh, please. Let's not be so formal. Call me Harriet. And may I call you Kathryn? Good. And, yes, you made it quite clear on the telephone what you were after but it doesn't make any difference. You have to understand that any mention of her is welcome. Although it's seventeen years since she first disappeared, deep down I'm sure that there's someone out there who knows something, and I don't just mean whoever killed her. Things like that don't happen in isolation, there has to be a chain of events leading up to

143

them. My worst nightmare is that he or she will never be caught and, unfortunately, with each year that passes that probability becomes more and more likely. Whatever you print will be a reminder, and if I can't have justice, then the least I can hope for is for the culprit to keep being reminded so that he might suffer, even if it's only because of the fear of getting caught. Does that sound vindictive?'

'Not in the least.'

Harriet Milton noticed that Kathryn had not yet written anything. Now that the brandy had taken effect she thought how attractive she was, but in a different way from Sarah, whose blonde prettiness had increased as she grew older. Kathryn was almost Latin-looking with her brown eyes and wide smile.

Kathryn was tapping her teeth with the biro. She had not planned the interview because there had not been time, and formalised questions were not always the way to unearth small, but important snippets of information. She decided to let Harriet carry on talking. 'Do you think you could tell me about Sarah? What she was like, what she enjoyed, anything you think is relevant. That way I can get a better picture of her.'

'I'd love to. It's a long time since I've been able to talk about her freely. It's an indulgence friends will only put up with for a certain period before they decide it's time you pulled yourself together and got on with life. Kathryn, shall we have some wine? I've already opened a bottle and the food will soak it up. You won't be rushing off, will you?'

Kathryn suspected she was trying hard to keep the pleading note out of her voice. Harriet struck her as a very lonely woman. 'No, I've nothing to rush back to.' And if Alex did return it would do him good to wonder where she was. Even as she thought this, Kathryn suddenly understood what she was doing – still punishing him – and knew it was where she was going wrong.

The wine was red, too heavy for a hot afternoon but Kathryn thought it would not hurt if she sipped it slowly. Once Harriet was seated, her thin legs crossed, she began to talk again. 'Sarah was an only child but Jim and I took great care to avoid all the pitfalls – you know, not to spoil her, not to overcompensate the other way with strictness. I'd always hoped for three or four babies, enough to fill a place like this.' She waved a hand to indicate the large room. 'We've only been here two months. Ironic, isn't it, moving to a larger property when we were already rattling around in the one we had.' She sighed. 'I can't complain. Earning money and spending it seems to be Jim's way of coping. Anyway, back to Sarah. She was above average at school but even so she worked hard. We were so proud of her when she passed all her O-levels and said she wanted to stay on. We wouldn't have forced her to – couldn't really, I suppose. Anyway, once she was in the sixth form she really came into her own; she blossomed, became more confident. She still sat up in her room night after night studying, she was so damned determined to get to Oxford, but it paid off; she succeeded. We lived in Kent then, but not long after she took up her place we moved to London. Oh, not for Sarah's sake, but because of Jim's business. He was utterly fed up with commuting.' Harriet paused. 'Kathryn, do you mind if I smoke?'

'Good heavens, of course not.' She was taken aback at the question. It was Harriet's house and had the situation been reversed, Kathryn knew she would not have asked anyone permission to do anything she pleased in her own home. However, if she was desperate for a cigarette it might explain the vague restlessness she had been displaying. She waited, anxious for more insight into Sarah Milton's character.

'She was an extremely determined young lady. Do you know, it's quite hard to describe her now. After so long I feel I'm in danger of attributing qualities to her which she did not possess, but as far as I know she didn't have any serious faults.'

As far as I know. A telling statement. Kathryn guessed that Harriet was implying she might have done, which would explain the reason for her death. As she listened it occurred to Kathryn that this was the first time she had interviewed the next-of-kin of a murder victim yet, strangely, it felt more like talking to a friend. One thing puzzled her. Where was Jim Milton? She felt unable to ask.

'Sarah was not a girl to follow the crowd and she always thought about things before taking any action. When she was very young she was introspective, but that changed as she grew up. We were so lucky, our friends' children caused all sorts of problems. And she was tidy, another bonus, I can assure you. I always got the impression she preferred the company of a few close confidants rather than mixing in crowds. Don't get me wrong, she was sociable, but not gregarious. And I know it sounds dreadful, but the girls she did bring home were the sort we'd have chosen for her ourselves if such a thing were possible. That was at school, though – we rarely saw any of her Oxford pals. I always wonder if it would have made a difference if we had.'

Harriet shrugged but seemed not to notice as ash from her cigarette rolled down her arm and sprinkled over the cushion beside her. Her face was animated, as if talking about Sarah had brought her briefly back to life.

'Boys didn't feature much, not when she was still at home. She mentioned one or two in her letters from Oxford but I got the impression they were more friends than boyfriends. And much as we loved her we were rather pleased that she didn't come rushing home every weekend. London was no distance but we felt to have done so would have defeated the whole object of university.' The animation faded. The voice lowered. 'She was nineteen. One year, that's all she had as an adult.'

'I'm sorry.' It was an inadequate comment but there was nothing Kathryn could say to put the clock back.

Harriet drained her glass. Maybe the remedy for her pain came from a bottle. But Kathryn then noticed that her own glass was empty. Both were refilled without comment.

'Where was I?' Harriet lit another cigarette. 'A negative point is that Sarah was no good at coping with failure – it's the only fault I can recall. It must sound as if I'm seeing the past through the proverbial rose-tinted, but it's true. However, she was so bloody determined to succeed at everything she attempted that she rarely put herself in that position. When she was seven she wanted piano lessons, I suspect it was only because all her friends were having them, but it was a waste of time. She wasn't in the least

146

musically inclined and her tutor suggested our money would be better spent elsewhere. She went on and on about it. "Why can't I get it right?" she kept asking. Later, when she took her driving test, she didn't sleep the night before it and she was as white as a sheet until she came home to tell us she'd passed first time . . .'

There was a long pause. Harriet inhaled deeply and blew smoke towards the ceiling. It seemed as if she had forgotten Kathryn was present. She stubbed out the cigarette.

'At first,' she continued quietly, 'when she didn't come home that weekend, we thought she must be ill – summer 'flu or something. I rang up but no one seemed to know where she was. I then convinced myself she'd gone off somewhere for the weekend and had forgotten she was supposed to be coming home. She only did so once each term and we'd made the arrangement some weeks before. Then, when she didn't telephone on the Monday evening, I knew without question something was wrong. We made a real fuss by contacting the police but they didn't think they could do much. Exams were looming and we wondered if perhaps after all she couldn't keep up. As I said, she hated failure. I was sure she wouldn't run away from a problem but I had to convince myself that's what she'd done. Only when she didn't come home for the summer did everyone really start to take notice. I got the impression people's efforts to find her had been half-hearted until that point.

'Years later, when they found her body we thought we were right, that the pressure had been too much and she had committed suicide.'

'How did you know she hadn't?'

Harriet lit another cigarette. 'Suicides don't usually stab themselves to death. The post mortem, if you can call it that, was quite conclusive. There were marks, I can't remember the terminology now, but they could tell where a knife had entered her body between her ribs. Several times.' There was a short pause. 'From the back.'

It was stated with equanimity but Kathryn sensed the anger behind the words. 'What about her friends, couldn't they help?'

'No. It seems she didn't have that many and they didn't

realise she was missing for a couple of days. They reported it, too, as soon as they knew.'

'Can you remember any of them? Anyone she was particularly close to? You see, it could be someone I'm already following up.' Kathryn hastily covered herself. The only information in her possession was that which Michael Jarvis had provided, and as he had not been a student himself it might well be inaccurate.

'Yes. I met one or two of them. Jim and I went to Oxford just as soon as we knew something was wrong. Poor things, the police really put them through it. There was Giles, Giles Harris, John Atherton, a girl called Jenny, but if my memory serves me right she wasn't a student. I saw a picture of her once, she looked a lot like Sarah.'

'Jenny Branagh?' It had to be.

Harriet shook her head. 'I'm sorry, I couldn't tell you.'

'Anyone else?'

'Yes, another girl – Laura Something or other. I believe she was due to come into some money. Sarah wrote to me along those lines. I'm sure too that she had a poet's name. Browning? No – Tennyson, that was it. And there was one other lad called David. He was very quiet and I don't think I ever did know his surname.'

The same names then that Michael had come up with. And that was strange. Why should someone with no connection with the university, apart from a girlfriend who waited at tables on the students, have such vivid recall of the names of people who had left seventeen years previously? Was he that obsessed with Jenny Branagh? The answer had to be yes. It no longer mattered that Inspector Forbes had not been able to supply her with full names, she now knew five of them. If she could find only one of them it would not be hard to get the sixth. She ran through the connections, however tenuous. Megan Morris's book jackets claimed she was an Oxford graduate, Jenny Branagh lived and worked in the same city and someone turned up at the Thames Riviera using the name of a girl who had befriended the murdered Sarah Milton. It was too much to believe that this was a series of coincidences.

'Would it be too painful to tell me what happened once

people began to take an interest in her disappearance?' she asked.

'No, not now. It seems like a lifetime ago. The press published details not long after the police search. You see, they knew that there had been parties in the surrounding areas, in the woods mostly, and they were trying to clamp down on drugs. It was one of the most obvious places to start looking. In fact, it was the first place they looked. They didn't put it in so many words but I think they thought she might have been out there and accidentally or deliberately taken an overdose. I didn't know, and I still don't, if she ever did use drugs. Perhaps it's just as well, I'm not sure how I'd have coped.'

By the number of cigarettes Harriet was getting through Kathryn realised the interview was more harrowing than she would have her believe.

'The police were very good, they kept us informed.' She laughed, but it was mirthless. 'Not that there was anything to tell us. Not for six years. I don't know how we survived but we did. Everyone was very good and tried in all sorts of ways to help, even down to bringing us meals we could heat up. It was the waiting: it was a killer. Sometimes a day seemed to last a week and then a week would fly by. Hope kept us going – no news is good news and all those ridiculous things you think to try to convince yourself the worst hasn't happened. Christmas came, then Easter, Sarah's birthday, then another Christmas.' She stopped. Kathryn could only imagine a fraction of what it must have felt like to have waited for six years only to be told your daughter had been dead all the time. It put Alex's absence of a couple of days into perspective. For a split second Kathryn panicked, thinking something might have happened to him but good sense told her that he carried his wallet with credit cards and identification and her own name as next-of-kin.

'We weren't even allowed to identify her, not that we could have done, not then.' Harriet folded her legs beneath her and leaned her head against the back of the sofa. She seemed exhausted. 'I would have felt better if I could have seen her . . . what was left of her. Can you understand that?' The grey eyes glittered but Harriet did not cry. She had done her weeping years ago. 'But it was a relief in a way. It meant Sarah wasn't out there alone and afraid or suffering or confused. She had been at peace longer than we had.'

'Yes.' It was an odd sort of comfort but Kathryn thought she understood. She wasn't prepared for the next words.

'But when they told us she was pregnant I believed it couldn't be Sarah.'

Was Harriet still deluding herself? No one, no matter how clear the evidence, wants to believe their child is dead and, presumably, as she had not seen a body, she was able to convince herself it was a terrible mistake and that Sarah would one day miraculously walk through the door. Kathryn realised her mistake. Harriet was not stupid nor did she seem prone to make-believe and she had moved house. If she harboured any suspicions that Sarah was still alive she would not have done so, because the girl would not have known where to find her.

'Why do you say that?'

'Because I didn't think she would have been so careless. You see, before she went to Oxford I took her to our GP to make sure she was prescribed contraceptives. Sarah informed me she had no intention of forming a sexual relationship, but I warned her there would be parties and she wasn't used to a lot of drink. She was very reluctant to see the doctor, but in the end she gave in. If she had been pregnant I'm sure she would've told me.' But Harriet did not sound as certain as she meant to. 'Later going through her things, I found the pills. She hadn't been taking them regularly'.

'If Sarah was terrified of failure, perhaps that's why she went missing initially. She might have considered becoming pregnant as a failure and thought she was letting you down.'

Kathryn's supposition was ignored because the wine bottle was empty and Harriet had gone to fetch a replacement. As she returned she glanced at the plain-faced, pine-framed clock on the wall. 'Good Lord, it's after three. You must be starving. We'd better eat.'

Kathryn closed her notebook. It was the perfect time for a break and it had not been very tactful to suggest to the mother of a murdered daughter that perhaps she had not known her as well as she thought she had done. There was little more she could learn about Sarah Milton but after they had eaten she would try to discover something about her friends.

'Now please don't be polite, just help yourself to whatever you want. I do hope you've got a good appetite, as I rather think I've overdone things. I don't really eat a lot myself these days. Still, what's left will keep me going for a while.'

'No, not for me, thanks.' Kathryn placed a hand over her glass as Harriet tilted the bottle towards it.

'Of course, you're driving. How thoughtless of me.' She stood, still holding the bottle and chewed the side of her mouth as if coming to some sort of decision. 'Look, you might think this a strange offer considering we've only known each other a couple of hours, but if you want to let your hair down you're more than welcome to a bed for the night. It might help you sort out your troubles and, to be honest, I could do with a bit of company.'

'Won't your husband mind?'

'Jim?' Harriet's laugh was cynical. 'He won't even know. We have what I believe is commonly known as a marriage of convenience these days. Convenient for him, that is. He has a flat in London and an obliging female companion. Forgive me, you don't want to hear this when you've got enough on your own plate.' Harriet's face softened. 'I don't blame him too much. The constant strain drove us apart and, at first, I refused to accept the truth of Sarah's death. I didn't see that Jim needed comfort as much as I did. I've learned since that a tremendously high proportion of marriages split up after something like that. And, on paper, we're still together. Jim mostly comes home at weekends.'

Harriet Milton had made an enormous compromise to save her marriage. It fascinated Kathryn and she wanted to hear more. 'I *will* have that glass of wine, please.' She had made her choice; she would not be driving home that day. Immediately she was more relaxed and they chatted about ordinary things as they ate. Sarah Milton was beginning to come alive for Kathryn but her dying had led to her parents' estrangement.

'It became an obsession,' Harriet was saying, 'this

151

conviction that Sarah was alive. I shut Jim out completely – no wonder he turned to someone else.'

Obsession. There was that word again. Mrs Robertson, Jenny's ex-headmistress, had used it about her daughter, now Harriet was admitting to it. It was uncanny. Despite thirty odd years' difference in their ages, she and Harriet had a lot in common. Alex had accused her of being obsessive, of shutting him out. She had better take heed. Harriet Milton had already given her a lot to think about.

John Atherton soon forgot about his trip to London once the new term was about to start. He wanted to acquaint himself with his timetable and ensure his lectures were properly prepared before the Dean's get-together.

He called into his office to collect a few bits and pieces and saw that a note had been placed on his desk. Giles had rung with a message to say he wanted to speak to him. There was a number where he could be contacted. The secretary had been extra-efficient, or Giles had made it seem urgent because, later, John discovered there was also a note in his pigeon-hole.

He cursed and screwed the scrap of paper into a ball and aimed it at the bin. He wished he had not made contact.

From a filing cabinet he took a folder which contained notes he had made in the States. Amongst them were one or two anecdotes. He believed that the best way of gaining, then keeping the attention of the students, was to make them laugh now and again.

As he left the office he noticed the crumpled paper which had fallen short of the bin. He bent down to retrieve it, roughly flattening it before placing it in his wallet. As he straightened up, a dull ache started in his temples. It was an old, familiar feeling which began when the effects of the previous day's drinking started to wear off and his body falsely suggested it was time for a hair of the dog. He felt faint and had to sit down as the blood rushed from his head. Sweat beaded his brow. He wiped it with the back of his hand. Soon, very soon, he would have to start limiting himself. He knew he had started drinking to forget, but that was seventeen years ago, even though the others had always

152

thought him over-indulgent. It wasn't true – he had enjoyed being able to provide them with champagne. It had been a sort of repayment for their company, for their making him what he was – outgoing, popular and easier with himself after the loneliness of home. But in the end it had all backfired.

Feeling marginally better he headed for the nearest pub, pleased that the law had changed during his absence from the UK and that he could get a drink at any time of the day. It was preferable to solitary drinking at home. Only one though, he promised himself. It wouldn't do to turn up at the Dean's half-cut.

Giles's message forgotten, he left the building and strolled down in the direction of the castle to one of his favourite drinking establishments.

He stuck to his promise then went to the Gents to wash his hands and splash his face with cold water. As he combed his hair he noted the greyness of his skin. The Dean, he decided, was going to be amazed at his abstemiousness.

Laura began to relax as she sat with a cup of black coffee listening to the dishwasher making soothing liquid noises. She was able to view the lunch-party with objectivity now that she was alone. It had been amusing watching Eileen Sprague batting her eyelashes at Pierre like someone out of a 1920s film. His ego had lapped it up and she could picture what they were doing at that precise moment. Pierre had offered Eileen a lift home although she only lived a short distance away.

Pam and Joss, comfortable in each other's presence, were always a pleasure to entertain. They exhibited none of the behaviour she had observed in other long-standing couples. They did not try to outdo one another in relating witty anecdotes, nor did they interrupt when one of them was speaking. So often she had heard one or other partner butt in and finish a story; usually, she admitted, the male was the culprit. Better still, Pam and Joss did not make jokes at the other one's expense. Would they be hurt or flattered if they knew she had based two of the characters in her latest novel upon them? Laura smiled. Chances are they would not recognise themselves – people rarely did. But perhaps they had never read a Megan Morris.

Giles had seemed concerned about David Shawcross but he had always been a little neurotic. If David was a candidate for a breakdown of some description, it would have happened years ago. Even if she was wrong, he was no real danger; anything he said now would be construed as confusion about a traumatic past event. And weren't they all a little crazy? There were still nights when Laura couldn't bear to close her eyes in case the nightmare returned.

There was a little more tidying to be done. Laura crossed the hall, her heels echoing on the wood blocks. So recently occupied, the empty dining room suddenly accentuated her aloneness. She sat at the table as lethargy filled her. Not lonely, she thought, I've never been lonely. That was partly because her own company held no fears but also because Marcia was always there, in the background mostly, but always within reach. Absentmindedly she drew the side of her palm over the linen tablecloth, sweeping the crumbs of broken bread rolls towards her. The idea of falling into bed and staying there until the morning crossed her mind. How nice to forget about Giles and John and Sarah and the other thing which worried her to such an extent that she would not allow it room in her mind; the mistake she may have made.

Laura stood. The crumbs she had been idly gathering had fallen into her lap and now dropped to the floor. Vacuuming them up would provide some necessary action and it was hardly fair to leave them for Peggy on Monday. The large house took a lot of effort to keep spotless. Fighting an inexplicable desire to confide in someone, preferably a stranger, even someone like Kathryn Brooks who, she was sure, could take anything in her stride, she retraced her steps to the kitchen and out to the laundry room where the cleaning things were kept. She knew that the appeal of the confessional was becoming stronger all the time and that turning up at the Thames Riviera had been the first step in admitting that she was not inviolate, that life would be sweeter if the secret was out in the open, whatever the consequences. But there was one thing which stopped her, which would always stop her from discussing it, and it was not what she stood to lose. She would continue to protect the person she thought might be guilty until the end of her days.

Saturday afternoon proved to be busier than most and David was satisfied with the takings as he checked the till roll and removed the cash and cheques from the drawer. These, along with credit-card slips, he locked in the safe. He had had two enquiries concerning rare books and knew it would be a challenge to find them for his potential customers. He had quietly made a name for himself in the business and no longer had to travel to sales or house auctions. Dealers and individuals now came to him. He was respected for his integrity and therefore people were willing to give him contact names if they were unable to help. His complete lack of pressurising techniques and cut-throat dealing was anathema to many who knew him, yet it guaranteed their loyalty.

Only when he had pulled down the grills over the windows and locked up did he think about the effects of his meeting with Giles. It had, he concluded, started something in him spinning off-axis, although he wasn't sure what it was.

The air in the street was heavy with diesel fumes which had amassed between the buildings in the heat of the day and, as he crossed Leicester Square, the smell of fried onions was overwhelming. None of this bothered David, for he was at home in the city, the parks satisfying his occasional need for grass and trees. He did not question why this might be so. One day his parents would die and although he suspected the bulk of their estate would go to his brother and his family, it worried him to think there was a chance he might inherit their house. He could not live there under any circumstances, not with the woods so very near. Besides, he had convinced himself he possessed everything he wanted.

The flat was less than thirty yards away. David paused, causing a man to swerve to avoid bumping into him. He smiled. He was going to walk back to the pub around the corner and buy himself a drink. It was, after all, Saturday night.

One drink sufficed. The place was packed and hot and smoky, and he thought most of the customers did not look old enough to drink. A crowd of girls giggled and shrieked and he suspected they had been there most of the afternoon. His double whisky seemed to have little taste, and although he drank it without ice the glass was warm and wet, straight from the dishwashing machine. It was a start, this break in routine, but he did not want to stay there any longer.

Once he was indoors he fed Kitty who was put out by the lack of fuss she received. He inhaled deeply then went to the telephone and dialled his parents' number. 'Hello, Mother. It's me, David.' Kitty jumped onto the table. He picked her up in his free hand and nestled her under his chin. Too many times she had been responsible for treading on the telephone and disconnecting the line.

'Hello, dear. We were just talking about you. What time are you coming tomorrow? We've invited Patricia Gifford as well as the Crawleys. You remember Pat, don't you? She's still recovering from an horrendous divorce and we thought . . .'

'You thought you'd pair her off with me. Two losers together.'

'Really, David. What a thing to say. You haven't been drinking, have you?'

Either his mother was more astute than he had given her credit for, or she could not believe he would speak to her in that way unless he had been drinking. Although a double Scotch hardly amounted to what she meant by *drinking*. 'No, but it's true, isn't it? That is what you thought.'

'I was thinking of *you*, David. If you won't make the effort to find a nice girl, at least I can try.'

'I do not consider Patricia as either a girl or particularly nice and the truth is, I always felt sorry for her husband. If you insist upon taking every lame duck under your wing, that's your prerogative. However, the reason I'm ringing is to say that I can't make it tomorrow.'

'David, you can't let us down like this! Everything's arranged.'

'I'm sorry, but I've made my own arrangements. Give my best to Father. Cheerio.

'Well, what did you think of that?' he enquired of Kitty, holding her up in front of his face. He was almost shaking with triumph at having carried out something about which other people would not have thought twice. It had been easier than he had imagined.

Kitty's eyes opened wide then closed sleepily as if she was saying she could not understand what all the fuss was about. She was adept at giving humans the cold shoulder.

David lowered her to the floor and set about getting his own supper. He had, during his years alone, become a more than adequate cook.

He usually ate in his small study, seated at the round table by the window which had a view over some playing-fields at the back of the flats. Between the branches of trees which were now misted with pale buds, he watched some boys kicking a football, people walking dogs and couples, hand in hand. As he chewed his food methodically he tried to pinpoint what had caused his unprecedented behaviour. It led him back to John and Giles. Were their lives fulfilling? Did they, too, live under the same cloud? None of them had children – were they as frightened of commitment as he was? Yes, he decided, it was seeing them both which had make him take stock of his own life.

He sat for some time then wandered through to the lounge to see if there was anything worth watching on television. There wasn't, but he switched it on anyway. There was an American film in progress, two blonde females were discussing something trivial. What he viewed as their false charms held no attraction for David. He supposed John's wife would have looked similar. He had become lazy. There were one or two women he was attracted to and with whom he occasionally enacted mental erotic scenes, but he lacked the impetus to ask them out.

He was not sexually inexperienced; the year he spent trekking across India with a group of people his own age had seen to that. There had been a lot of what he thought of as bed-hopping, and he had complied because it was

157

expected of him. He realised how much of his life had been spent doing things for that reason.

'No more. I, David Charles Shawcross, am going to make some changes.' He addressed the two blondes on the screen who were now wearing bikinis. 'It's time I was my own man.' And although he wasn't entirely sure what he meant by that, he felt a lot happier when he went to bed that night.

Giles paced the ground floor of the Georgian house he and Ingrid had purchased just after their marriage. It was situated in what the estate agent's blurb had described as 'a quiet, leafy area'. The house was indeed Georgian, the genuine article, but the street was no longer quiet. Since the wider road which ran parallel had been fitted with humps to slow down the traffic because the residents had complained it was treated like a racing circuit, the inevitable had followed. Vehicles detoured down Giles's street where there were no such impediments and caused the window panes to rattle with monotonous regularity. And as for leafy, yes, once it had been until someone from the Council, in their wisdom, had decided to have the trees pollarded. He had grown used to these minor nuisances and did not know why, that evening, they made him feel so irritable, unless it was because Laura had seemed less welcoming than usual. She had made it clear she was anxious for him to leave and did not seem to take his concern about David seriously.

The Sarah Milton case was, presumably, still open. Paranoia had not set in to such an extent that Giles believed a young journalist called Kathryn Brooks could get to the bottom of it, but Laura had acted like a complete idiot turning up at that hotel.

Giles stood, his hands in his pockets, and surveyed the untidy garden at the back of the house. The sun was beginning to sink and long shadows fell across the grass which needed cutting. The house and garden were large but Ingrid entertained a lot and insisted their guests stayed overnight. He wished she was here now, if only to relieve the hollowness which seemed to exist in her absence. She was an enigma; organised and professional in her work yet totally chaotic at home. Each room bore evidence of her many and varied hobbies. There was a sewing machine on a felt mat on the dining-room table, and papers and manuals scattered around the computer in her study. In the little room which had once been a sort of reception area in the days of carriages and calling cards, there was an old chest and the bits and pieces she required for the process of learning the art of stencilling. Things were a little tidier at the moment because Ingrid had made a token gesture by piling books and utensils into heaps before she went away. Oddly, Giles missed the disorder.

He poured a glass of wine and sat on the love-seat by the window allowing his thoughts to go where they would. The low purr of the telephone interrupted his reverie. When he heard Ingrid's voice he felt guilty, then angry at his guilt, because he had been thinking of Laura instead of his wife whom, minutes earlier, he had admitted to missing.

'You are back, Giles,' Ingrid said.

'Obviously so.' He had not meant to take his anger out on her.

'Are you not well?'

'Why do you ask?'

'Ah, darling, you have very much the English way of answering a question with one of your own.'

'What is it you want, Ingrid? I'm shattered, and I've got one hell of a headache.'

'I'm sorry.' He heard the faint laughter in her voice as she added, 'Did you have one of your – how do you say it – liquid lunches?'

'Don't be so bloody patronising.'

There was a gentle click as Ingrid disconnected the line, which annoyed him further. Had the situation been reversed, he'd have slammed down the receiver. Ingrid refused him the satisfaction of witnessing her anger. 'Oh, shit. She's so bloody reasonable,' he said and drained the glass of wine. He had no sooner refilled it when the telephone rang again. He took a deep breath, ready to apologise because all sorts of thoughts had crossed his mind. Supposing something happened to Ingrid and their last words

159

had been that conversation. He would never be able to live with himself.

'Hello?' His voice was calm.

'Hi, it's John. I got your message.'

'What message? Oh, of course. Thanks for ringing. It's nothing important, at least I don't think it is.' He wanted to keep it brief in case Ingrid was trying to get through. 'David came to see me. It was completely out of the blue, we don't keep in touch. I merely wanted to warn you that he was acting very oddly and couldn't leave the subject of Oxford alone.'

'Oh? What was he saying?' John sounded as composed as ever and he wasn't slurring his words. At seven-thirty on a Saturday night it was difficult to gauge how much he might have had to drink. Background noises suggested he was calling from a pub.

'General talk. About the group and what had become of us. God, I don't know, it's difficult to put a finger on. Then he upped and left without finishing his drink. He was laughing maniacally. It wouldn't surprise me if he was close to the edge.'

'It's not worth worrying about. As long as we stick to our original story, nothing can happen to us. After all this time we're in the clear.'

'Well, we'll leave it at that then, shall we? Thanks for getting back to me.' Giles replaced the receiver, sorry now that he had bothered. John had always been so unflappable.

Ingrid was attending an end-of-seminar dinner and must have rung just before it was due to take place. Giles had no idea how long it would go on, but did not want to go to bed until he had made things right with her. To fill in the hours until he could reasonably expect to find her at her hotel he ploughed through an uninspiring manuscript. It had the makings of a decent novel but would require a lot of work. With a pencil he began making notes in the margins.

It was twenty to one before the hotel receptionist was able to put him through to Ingrid. She had forgotten the incident, she told him, and would be home around lunch-time on Sunday.

Giles was able to sleep with an easier conscience. Easier, but it would never be completely clear.

Chapter 8

For several seconds Kathryn was disorientated. Light was falling across the bed from a different angle and the only sound was birdsong. Then she awoke fully and recalled the events of the previous day. She hoped that the degree of intimacy which had developed so quickly between herself and Harriet Milton would not be regretted and cause awkwardness this morning. She had never confided so freely in another woman and guessed that the same was true of Harriet. A catharsis, perhaps, for them both. She had drunk more than she was used to, but a dry mouth was the only residual effect.

The room was pretty and might have been designed with Sarah in mind, but the crispness of the sheets on the bed and their clean cotton smell showed that no one had slept between them before. The ceiling was vaulted, the exposed beams attractive against the plain white walls. The curtains and duvet cover had a tiny pink flower design but there were no pictures or photographs.

Faint noises filtered up from the kitchen which was beneath her room. It was only ten past seven, but no doubt her hostess had been up and tending to her two horses, on which she gave riding lessons to local children. Kathryn supposed they came from the surrounding farms, but would need to be driven here because she could not remember having passed a house for several miles before she reached Harriet's address.

Making use of the en suite bathroom, which was thoughtfully supplied with toiletries, she showered and washed her hair, towelling it dry because she did not want to bother Harriet for a hairdryer. Having combed it, she tucked it firmly behind her ears and hoped it would not become too fly-away when it dried.

Dressed and ready to go downstairs, she hesitated. Harriet had been a little drunk the night before and might regret having said so much. Perhaps it would be best not to mention their talk. Kathryn herself had gone so far as to disclose her quest for Megan Morris – the reason for her being there at all.

Quite late they had eaten an omelette and salad, perfectly produced by Harriet, whose efforts to please confirmed Kathryn's suspicion that she was desperately lonely. Then, just as they were going to bed, Harriet said there was something she wanted Kathryn to see. Several minutes later, she returned and handed her a shoulder bag. 'This was Sarah's. They found it with the body.'

Taking it in her hands made Kathryn shudder. The dull green leather had not suffered badly from years of exposure, but she suspected the darker green stains might be blood. The gesture seemed macabre – and she could not understand why Harriet had thought she might want to see it.

In the light of day she realised that she had been responsible for bringing Sarah back to life for a few hours, and that the handbag was Harriet's tangible proof that her daughter had existed. Kathryn felt that Harriet was the sort of woman with whom she could become friends, but so much familiarity so quickly might have precluded that possibility.

She stripped the bed then went downstairs, her mouth watering as she smelled grilling bacon.

'Did you sleep well?' Harriet, in the same trousers but a different top, turned to greet her.

'Yes, very. It's such a comfortable bed.'

'It's the wooden base, you can't beat them.' Harriet did not seem in the least embarrassed about anything she might have said. 'Can you eat a bacon sandwich? I didn't think you'd want more eggs.'

'Whatever you're having.'

'Good. Help yourself to coffee. It's over there.' She nodded towards the filter machine. The jug was already half-empty. 'If you need the telephone you're welcome to use it.'

'No, it's all right.' The same offer had been forthcoming the previous night. She did not want to dial her number and hear her own voice on the recorded message, nor did she want to leave a message for Alex only to discover he had not been home to hear it for himself. 'I put the sheets and your nightie in the laundry basket.'

'Thank you. Here you are.' She handed Kathryn a plate and they sat in the kitchen and ate, almost in silence, as if everything there was to be said had already been said.

'I really ought to go now. Thank you, Harriet, for everything.'

'It was my pleasure. I'd like to think you'll keep in touch, Kathryn, even if it's just to let me know what you come up with. Will you do that?'

'Yes, I promise.'

'And any time you're in this area, give me a ring.'

Harriet waved to her from the gate and Kathryn tooted just before she was lost to sight. Whatever happened she would let Harriet know; she had lived through too many years of not knowing.

Remembering the route without difficulty she was soon on the main road. This time she drove faster, without the accompaniment of the radio. She needed to be at home, to put things in perspective.

The brightness of the morning had been deceptive. Already clouds were banking up on either side, and by the time she reached Burnham it was overcast and muggy. There was a Sunday morning somnambulance, broken only by shouts from the nearby tennis courts. Wearily she climbed the single flight of stairs to the flat and put her key in the lock. She had tried not to notice that there was no sign of Alex's car.

'Oh dear God!' The keys dropped to the floor as Alex bounded from the lounge, terrifying her. She steadied herself against the wall, her knees weak.

'Are you all right?' He was gripping her painfully by her upper arms, his face deathly pale.

164

'Yes.' Kathryn's face was equally white with shock. 'Yes, of course I am.'

He released her and they stood mutely staring at each other, neither of them sure what to say. Alex shook his head and ran a hand through his hair. He looked as if he had not slept although he had showered. Kathryn caught the faint tang of his aftershave and the fresh scent of the shirt she had so recently ironed. 'I've made some coffee.'

Kathryn followed him to the kitchen. His hold-all, she noticed, was on the hall floor. The meaning of that was something to consider later. She sat at the kitchen table, steadier now, but wishing she had had some time to collect her thoughts before encountering Alex. He poured her coffee just as she liked it, with one sweetener and a dash of milk. When he took the chair opposite she could not bring herself to look at him.

Alex studied his hands which were clasped in front of him on the table. 'I don't expect you to give me an answer, Kath – God knows, I don't deserve one – but first I want you to know that I've been at the boat-yard – nowhere else, I swear it. I've had a long time in which to think, and I couldn't not come back. I can't tell you how worried I was getting back here and finding you gone. I nearly called the police in case you'd had an accident. I rang Helena, and your mother . . .'

Alex had indeed been worried. 'What did you say to them?'

It seemed irrelevant compared to everything else that was happening, but Kathryn needed to focus on one thing at a time.

'I told them the truth – that we'd had an argument and I didn't know where you were. Helena gave me a measure of her own brand of common sense and said you'd probably gone off somewhere to think. Your mother said that you were always stubborn and that I wasn't to worry; you would do your own thing whatever I thought.'

Kathryn wasn't sure whether to feel flattered or hurt. It hadn't occurred to anyone except Alex that she might be in trouble or need help, but it was reassuring to know

165

that they thought her able to take care of herself. Still . . . stubborn? Was that true?

'Kath, where were you?'

Harriet Milton had taught her something. There was no hesitation, no urge to keep him guessing to punish him for his own absences. 'I went to Gloucestershire, to see a lady called Harriet Milton. I was enjoying her company and we drank too much wine so I had to stay the night. I didn't telephone because I didn't think you'd be here. It's that simple.'

It hadn't been so hard to let him know how she really felt . . . but Alex seemed unable to take it in. His face registered complete incomprehension. She had forgotten that he knew nothing of this latest development. Then she recalled why seeing him had come as such a shock. 'Where's your car?' she asked.

'At the boat-yard. I walked back.' It was several miles but Alex had done this before, striding out to get rid of pent-up energy. 'Tell me, have I killed what we had? Can you ever forgive me?'

Kathryn studied the pattern on her mug as if it had been painted by a master. Bold tulips, depicted by heavy brush-strokes, stood out from the fine white porcelain. The sense of relief was enormous. Alex wanted her; she had simply not allowed herself to believe it lately. And she must be very careful; whatever she said now she had to stand by – there must be no more recriminations later, no bringing up the past at a future date. She was strong enough to stick to it; it was a case of whether she wanted to. Alex loved her. It showed clearly in his face as he waited for her answer.

'Yes, but . . .'

'But what?'

She shook her head and her hair settled round her face, hiding the redness which had come into it. It was no good if she added provisos, no point in adding 'as long as it never happens again'. If she agreed, it was a chance she had to take – just as Alex had to take it with her. She only looked up when Alex reached across the table and squeezed her hand. Instinctively he did the right thing by saying nothing; he could see she needed a minute or two to accept what

166

she had finally done. 'Thank you,' he said, and got up to pour more coffee.

Neither of them felt like eating lunch so they decided not to bother but to go out somewhere in the evening. As the clouds darkened and rain began to fall and the afternoon drew to a close they talked, still in the kitchen, still sitting without touching but both of them knowing they should have done it weeks before.

When they were on their third cup of coffee Kathryn went to the fridge for another carton of milk and saw the food she had prepared yesterday but which seemed like a week ago. It would have to be thrown out, but that could wait.

'Thanks.' Alex took his mug from her hand. 'Do you want to tell me about yesterday?'

Unsure of how much he already knew, Kathryn pieced the story together. Alex listened attentively, genuinely interested. He made no disparaging comments – his way, he realised, of trying to regain her attention. Kathryn's mother was right; she was always going to do things her way and he had better learn to accept it. 'But what can you do about it?' he asked when she finally finished.

'Find the others, the rest of the group.'

'Sounds like the basis of a novel,' Alex concluded, carefully watching Kathryn's face. He was aware of her ambitions in that direction but her expression was a mask. 'Are you going to change?'

Kathryn said she was. She had the same dress on that she had worn for her visit to Harriet.

They went for a Chinese meal but found they couldn't eat it all, and when they got home they fell into bed exhausted from the emotional turmoil and both slept immediately. When Kathryn woke, Alex's arm was flung heavily over her.

The week passed in a pleasant blur. Things were going well at home and Dave was less irritating than usual. They were experiencing a heatwave just like the start of the previous May, and were making the most of it as June was often wet. The office doors and windows remained open all day to attract any draught, and each lunchtime Kathryn sat outside; consequently her limbs and face were beginning to tan. Last year's summer clothes were loose and she planned a shopping trip to Reading. Although she had received a salary increase, Alex had promised to finance it.

She had just finished a human-interest story and started on her column and, to add to her optimism, the octogenarian poet had written her a charming letter saying he was thrilled with what she had written about him. Keith, the other ever-present thorn in her side, had actually gone so far as to compliment her when she wore a low-cut dress into work. She suspected it was not so much the brief glimpse of cleavage but the lack of anxiety in her face and because she had regained her ability to laugh easily.

Her preoccupation with Megan Morris's identity was no longer a driving force but she was still determined to get to the bottom of it. It was simply a question of getting her priorities right. One midweek afternoon she sat at her desk chewing the end of a biro, a habit which ensured Keith kept his hands off the ones which were in a pot beside her. She was up to date and could have gone home, but spent a few minutes thinking of the discrepancies in what Harriet and Michael Jarvis had told her. They had both remembered the same names so she gathered that they were the dominant figures. David, whoever he was, seemed to have left little impression on either of them, but whereas Harriet had described her daughter in what seemed to be an honest way, Michael had referred to Sarah as 'that little tart'.

'Keith?' He was seated at his own desk, his back to the window, his fair hair gleaming in the sun.

'I'm busy.'

'You're not, you're eating a roll.' He was always eating.

'What is it?' He strolled languidly across the new carpet tiles and stood at her desk, cramming in the last mouthful, having assumed Kathryn wanted him to read something.

'Nothing personal here, but when you're out with the boys, what words do you use to refer to females?'

Keith chewed stolidly, his cheeks expanding alternately as he studied Kathryn shrewdly. Having sucked the last of the doughy bread and tuna from his teeth he wiped his mouth on the back of his hand, straightened his wide, flowered tie and sniffed. 'Why?' he asked.

'Just curious.'

'Do you really expect me to believe that? You just want an answer that'll allow you to berate me with that feminist crap of yours.'

'No. I really do need to know.' She kept her voice steady; they were adept at winding each other up.

Keith's expression was sceptical. 'Oh yeah? What do you expect me to say? "Girls, crumpet, skirt" – you know, that sort of thing, I suppose. I've never really thought about it.' He offered one or two more suggestions and although they were not exactly complimentary he did not come up with the one she was waiting for. 'Satisfied?'

'How about "tart"?'

'God, you never give up, do you?' He waited, but realising Kathryn really did expect an answer, thought before he spoke. 'No. "Tart, slag", words like that – well, you only apply them if the cap really fits, if you get my drift. I'm not as bad as you seem to think, you know.'

'Thanks, Keith.'

'That's it? No bollocking?'

'Nope. That's it. You've been a great help actually.' Kathryn tossed back her hair and gave him the benefit of her dimpled smile.

Shaking his head in disbelief, Keith returned to his desk and began demolishing a second roll as he watched her from the corner of his eye, but she did not notice.

Michael Jarvis hadn't been with his mates when he called Sarah Milton a tart, Kathryn thought. He had used the word in front of her, another female, as if he had meant it. In which case . . . In which case she thought she might as well complete her column, then she could take the afternoon off tomorrow and to go Reading.

That evening Alex said that he had heard from Colin and suggested that, if she was willing, they could meet him and Viv in London on Saturday. 'I said I'd have to check with you first.' Colin and Viv had been neighbours, living in one of the flats for a while, but had moved back to

London to be nearer their work. 'I thought we could meet them for a lunchtime drink then do something by ourselves in the afternoon; a gallery or the cinema or the theatre if you like. The weather's supposed to be breaking up but if it's still hot, we can think of something else.'

It was something to look forward to. Like Kathryn's other friends, Viv had been neglected recently and she was good fun. She was a florist and, in partnership with another girl, ran a business which provided anything from table decorations to Christmas arrangements, to bedecking churches for weddings or whole houses for weekend parties. It was an exclusive set-up, run from premises which did not constitute a shop, and there were many well-known names on the client list which meant Viv, when in the mood, was a wonderful source of wicked gossip.

Kathryn had written and telephoned Megan Morris's publishers asking for an explanation as to why the meeting had been set up then cancelled without warning. She hadn't received a reply nor would the woman who answered the telephone put her through to Miss Morris's editor. She could not even elicit his name although she had made it quite clear on the envelope to whom she was writing. That side of things was a dead end. She would concentrate on finding Sarah's friends. It wasn't the story she was after, but something told her she must continue.

Alex rang Colin to confirm the arrangement. Trafalgar Square being easily accessible to both parties, they agreed to meet at twelve in the Sherlock Holmes, a pub they all knew and was within walking distance.

'Say I'm not in.' Giles almost dropped the receiver as he replaced it. Visions of media attention flashed through his mind. They were safe. Surely they were safe! John Atherton might be able to cope with it, but Giles Harris had no illusions about himself.

Temporarily he need not worry. His secretary Lisa would politely lie for him and use one of a store of excuses for his being unable to take the calls, but there was nothing to stop Kathryn Brooks waiting outside the office for him. That young lady was tenacious. Not one of her calls had been returned and he had torn up her letter, but none of this had deterred her.

'Why, oh why, oh why?' he muttered, gazing down on the street below as if the answer were to be found in the paving stones or the striped awnings opposite. If Laura had not been so foolhardy in the first place none of this subterfuge would have been necessary.

Giles moved slowly back to his desk and pushed the morning's correspondence to one side. Eventually his panic subsided and he was able to think rationally. How readily he had jumped to the wrong conclusions. All the girl had discovered was that he was Megan Morris's publisher and that fact was not difficult to glean – She only had to look on the book jackets to find *that* out. And if it had taken her this long to discover his name, then she was nowhere near as bright as Laura claimed. Tension eased from his neck and shoulders. This was all to do with Megan Morris, not Oxford in the 1970s, and he was used to fielding enquiries from all sorts of directions. He almost laughed aloud. The girl was no supersleuth. Even the parochial David Shawcross had tracked him down without difficulty.

Giles buzzed his secretary on the intercom. 'Did Ms Brooks leave a message?'

'It's Mrs Brooks. No, but she left a number and asked if you would call her back.'

'Thank you. Is there any chance of a cup of tea?' Lisa said there was. His tone was placatory after their previous abrupt exchange.

When the bone-china cup and saucer was placed on his blotter Giles looked at the memo slip on which the number was written. So it was Mrs Brooks, eh? He would ring her back and put an end to it, the sooner the better.

Kathryn answered on the third ring. It was her direct line. Her voice was low-pitched and well-modulated, and rather soothing. Highly dangerous – he knew that technique himself. And she sounded younger than he had expected.

'Thank you for getting back to me so quickly.' She responded as if she was in no doubt that he would return her call, but Giles could not know how her hand shook as she reached for a pen.

'You're the journalist at the *Thames Valley Echo* whom Miss Morris agreed to see, if I recall correctly. I must say I was absolutely astounded when she instructed me to make the arrangement, as I knew she had no intention of keeping the appointment. Miss Morris is virtually a recluse but I have never known her to be deliberately rude before. Please accept my apologies on her behalf. I do hope it didn't inconvenience you too much. I'm afraid if it's my client you wish to enquire about, I shall have to insult you with that well-known cliché that I have nothing to say.'

'It isn't.'

Giles felt the sweat break out along the length of his spine. *It isn't.* It was said with such confidence, such finality that he felt dizzy. He listened without comment to what she had to say, but when she asked if it was possible to come and see him, his hesitation was minimal. It would be far wiser to find out what, if anything, she knew, rather than leave it to chance. He had time to come up with something plausible which would prevent her digging further. 'I expect an evening would suit you best?'

'Or late afternoon.' Kathryn would make it, whatever time he suggested. She had had the weekend to prepare herself for this conversation, although she hadn't been sure it would take place, and had timed it so that Giles Harris would have just arrived at his office and be off his guard. She was expecting his final question.

'Why me?' he asked.

Her laugh was soft and reassuring. 'Oh well, once I realised I wasn't going to get anywhere in finding out who Miss Morris was I thought, why not do an article on her publisher instead? You are, in a different way, equally important.' He did not fall for the flattery. 'As many before me must have done, I made enquiries at Oxford University and drew another blank.' She refrained from mentioning that these enquiries concerned Jenny Branagh: she would leave that bombshell for their meeting. 'But once I realised you were also educated there, it gave me the idea.'

Giles hung up. He did not believe a single word he had heard. His hands were shaking as he poured neat vodka over ice from the supply kept in the refrigerated cocktail cabinet normally only produced for the benefit of visitors. He would not usually dream of drinking so early.

He took a sip and felt the shock of the coldness. The sweat had soaked into his shirt and the air conditioning chilled him.

If Kathryn Brooks had not known until very recently that he was Megan Morris's editor, then how the hell did she know he had been at Oxford?

'He's agreed to see me.'

Alex frowned. Giles Harris had money and power and contacts and was not, he told Kathryn quite bluntly, a man to be fucked with. He wanted to know when and where the meeting was to take place, and only when he saw Kathryn's amused smile did he realise that he probably sounded like a Victorian husband. He was simply concerned for her safety. If Sarah Milton's killer had not been found, it might be that her friends had secrets they would not wish to be made public.

Kathryn continued writing a shopping list. Nothing was going to stop her now. Alex could rant and rave if he chose, but she was going to interview Giles Harris. 'Why do you want to know?'

'Because I might have to send in the troops.'

'You can't seriously believe a man in his position is going to do me in in his office, no matter what he may have done in the past! He's going to fob me off, that's what's going to happen. Nothing more.'

But Alex saw that the possibility had crossed Kathryn's mind. 'No matter what he may have done in the past', she had said.

'And don't forget,' she went on, 'the police eliminated them all. Twice.'

'So be it.' Alex raised his hands in a gesture of defeat.

'All right, if it makes you any happier, I'm seeing him in his office at four o'clock on Wednesday. He said he can spare me an hour, and there'll be other people around. Perhaps you'd prefer me to carry a gun?'

'Honestly, Kathryn!' But she was grinning and he couldn't help but laugh himself.

Kathryn was making little headway with her list. Instead of concentrating on items which needed replacing, she kept thinking about Giles Harris. It was thanks to Viv that she had had no difficulty in tracing him.

She had reached the stage where she was beginning to believe it was best to give up altogether on Megan Morris and therefore knowing the name of her editor was irrelevant. Then, over drinks, Viv had unknowingly dropped her bombshell. They had been discussing the theatre and films they had seen when the conversation changed to books. Kathryn said she had enjoyed the latest Megan Morris.

'Me, too,' Viv agreed. 'And Colin did too. That woman's certainly got something. She gets so much into her characters' minds you feel they're people you actually know. We did the flowers for the last launch. She wasn't there, of course, but the publishers still put on a bit of a splash. I would too if I had an author like that – she must be raking it in for them. Still, good luck to them. Giles deserves it, he's a bit of a sweetie.'

'Giles?' Kathryn gripped her glass tightly. It wasn't that common a name.

Viv looked puzzled. 'Yes – Giles Harris. Don't say you've never —'

'Viv, do you know what you've just said?'

'Steady, girl, or you'll have us thrown out of here.' Alex grabbed her drink before she sent it flying over the table. Kathryn had almost left her seat. All three looked at her as if she was crazy. Then Alex remembered the name.

'I think the heat's got to you. You only have to read the papers to know who he is. Oh, you don't bother with the financial pages, do you?' Viv couldn't see why Kathryn was so excited, but then Alex deftly changed the subject.

Later, when the four had parted company, he and Kathryn strolled around as they decided what to do with the rest of the day. 'It isn't because he's Megan Morris's publisher, is it? It's because he was one of the Oxford crowd.'

Kathryn nodded. Giles Harris fitted into both parts of her investigation, and that, without doubt, was more than a coincidence. And now she was going to meet him, but not for another two days. It was difficult to think of anything else.

Giles was also finding it hard to think about anything other than the coming Wednesday. Because he wanted the meeting over and done with, time seemed to stand still. He wished he had been able to arrange it earlier but there were other meetings to attend.

Ingrid had returned, as promised, late on Sunday morning, not at all put out by his rudeness. They had spent a pleasant afternoon together, Giles totally unaware of what was in store. He had excused his outburst by telling Ingrid that he was worried about Megan Morris, and although Ingrid had only a vague idea who she was, she understood how important her work was to Giles.

On Monday evening they had gone out to dinner at an exclusive restaurant where Giles was always able to command a table even when it was busy. He had not been able to bear the thought of staying in. Fortunately, most of Tuesday was taken up with editorial meetings and another long drawn-out discussion over finances where each editor put forward their reasons why their own particular writers merited publishing priority and higher advances.

Finally all Giles had to endure was lunch on Wednesday with an elderly spinster who travelled down from the Lake District once a year specifically for the occasion. She didn't want her face to be forgotten, she said. Giles's amazement did not lessen each time he saw her. Impossible to believe that the frail, grey-haired creature who wore the same baggy suit on every visit churned out such graphically violent fiction in inner-city settings. Either she had a vivid imagination or she had not, as he was led to believe, spent her life amongst the sheep and daffodils of Wordsworth's countryside.

Writers like her were his bread and butter and warranted his time and attention. If the tweed suit ponged of dog and there was lipstick on her top teeth he did not allow her to see that it was affecting his appetite.

She was by no means a teetotaller. She drank a dry sherry before the meal, wine to accompany it and two brandies after it. Giles suspected he was not going to be free of her easily, but he was determined not to mention his four o'clock appointment unless it became absolutely necessary. He did not want to offend her.

Finally, at three o'clock they shook hands and she went back to wherever she was staying for the night.

As Giles returned to the office, the rain which had been forecast for the weekend finally began to fall, if a little late. The soft drizzle clung to his jacket and settled like tiny beads on his thick white hair. He dodged under the awnings, beneath which people were still eating although some were already moving inside, and made it back to the office before he was soaked.

There was less than an hour to go. Giles unwrapped the latest offering from the doggy author and placed it on his desk. Useless to start reading it – he knew he wouldn't be able to take in a single word. Although his publishing company employed readers, especially for established writers, Giles still preferred to take responsibility for what he called his 'own stable'. It was also a task he enjoyed.

'Mrs Brooks is here,' Lisa finally announced through the intercom.

'Would you show her in, please.' It was Giles's usual practice to go down and greet his visitors himself but, illogically, after all the waiting, he found himself needing those few extra seconds to compose himself. And it would also emphasise to Mrs Brooks that she was on *his* territory.

The door opened and he caught a fleeting glimpse of Lisa's face before she closed it again, leaving him alone with Kathryn Brooks. Giles rose from his seat and walked around to the front of his desk. She was not at all what he had been expecting. For a start she was dripping wet, having walked from the tube station. Naturally there would not have been a free taxi the minute it started raining. Her dark hair was plastered to her head and her dress clung to her in a way which made him avert his eyes because he liked what he saw. This chit of a girl could not be a hard-bitten professional. She did not even have the sense to carry an umbrella.

He fixed a genial smile on his face. 'How do you do, Mrs

176

Brooks.' The hand he extended remained steady but it had taken an effort.

'Hello. Thank you for seeing me.'

'My pleasure. Please sit down.' He indicated the chair beside her.

Kathryn eyed it dubiously. The seat had a fabric cover and she did not envy the person who used it after her. There was no option other than to dampen it, for she could not conduct the interview on her feet.

'I'm sure you'd like some tea or coffee?'

'Coffee, please.'

Giles buzzed Lisa then instigated small-talk about her journey and the weather until Lisa brought in a tray containing a large pot of coffee. Giles poured two cups and told Kathryn to help herself to hot milk and sugar. 'Now, I believe you wanted to talk to me about my student days?' His manner was as bland as the warm milk in the jug.

'Yes. Perhaps if I could start with some general questions. For instance, did you enjoy your days at Oxford?'

'Very much. They say that your schooldays are the best, but I disagree.' He took a sip of his coffee which almost scalded his mouth. He must be prepared for anything this girl might throw at him. 'Where did you go, by the way?'

'Reading.' Kathryn smiled and left it at that. It was not her history she had come to discuss. Several more carefully innocuous questions followed and she observed Giles gradually become less guarded.

'Yes, indeed. I've always been in publishing. I can't imagine doing anything else. I started elsewhere, as most of us do, but after four or five years I realised the company was ripe for a takeover or amalgamation and I moved on before I was put in a position where the choice might no longer be mine. I was subsequently proved right and glad I made the move.' His smile was self-deprecating. 'I don't expect they're too happy about it, knowing who my famous client is.' Giles had decided to broach the subject himself. Far better to distract Kathryn Brooks with Megan Morris than discuss his university days. Besides, it was still possible that that was the real reason for her visit. He wondered if he might have panicked, if the girl knew nothing at all and had merely read some press release.

'How did you acquire her?' Kathryn was leaning forward to drop a sweetener into her second cup of coffee. Her hair swung forward and she missed Giles's wry smile. Her dress was already beginning to dry out but she hardly noticed. She was here, with Giles Harris! As he was answering her preliminary questions, which were of no interest to her, she had had a chance to take in her surroundings. The office was comfortable, not unlike someone's sitting room, an impression created by the Wilton carpet and a settee against the wall covered in a matching pale green fabric. The desk was curved, with ornate legs, and the hard-backed chairs had upholstered seats. Only the piles of folders which seemed to be stored on the floor and the window-sill showed that any work was done here. She had imagined something far more functional with the latest technological gadgetry. However, it obviously worked well.

So, Giles was thinking as he waited for her to look up, I was right. It *is* Megan Morris she's after, not me at all. 'One of those chances of a lifetime,' he answered smoothly. 'Pure luck. An unsolicited manuscript landed on my desk, probably because I was the new boy at the time, and, for want of something better to read over the weekend, I took it home with me. It could have sat on a shelf for ever, or been sent back unread. Miss Morris didn't have an agent, you see, nor does she now, by the way. Anyway, I couldn't put it down, I knew almost from page one that I was on to a winner.' He raised his hands, palms uppermost, as if to say: *Why me? Why should I have been picked?* 'It certainly hasn't done my career any harm.'

'No, I don't imagine it has. What happened after that?' Kathryn decided not to change tack for the moment; she might even learn something. She studied him as he composed his face into a thoughtful frown and thought what a good actor he was. They were, she realised, metaphorically circling each other like two animals, whilst sniffing the air for danger as they sized each other up. Despite the untruths she was sure she was about to hear, she quite liked him. There was an innate gentleness about him which he was

178

unable to conceal and he had presence, which she always admired in a person.

'In what way?'

'You wanted to publish the novel, but how did you go about it, if no one could know who the author really was? You must have had to meet her?'

'I see what you mean. But, no, not necessarily. We make a point of personally getting to know all our authors, but it isn't strictly essential. Everything can be done through the post or by fax, and usually it's through an agent. In this case I wrote to Miss Morris by way of the Post Office box number she had given in her letter. I offered her an advance which she accepted, and the usual contract, naturally. I thought the book was brilliant but we couldn't risk going over the top with one novel. Now and then we've been proved wrong – not often, thank goodness.'

'I accept all that, but what about payment? Cheques have to be made out and there's the tax and VAT people.'

Giles held up a finger. 'I'm sorry, Mrs Brooks, I'm not at liberty to divulge that sort of information.'

'No. I realise that.' But for one moment she thought he might have been going to do so.

'Suffice it to say that Miss Morris trusts me to deal with her affairs in a suitable manner.'

'And you've never met her?'

Giles pursed his lips and shook his head. Kathryn chewed the end of her pen. That was, she thought, one lie he did not like telling. 'Have no fears, young lady, my client's identity is quite safe.' He smiled to soften the sternness of his words. 'I believe there's more coffee in the pot if you'd like some. And your clothes are almost dry, I see. I do apologise, I should've offered you a towel.'

There was no more to be said on the topic of Megan Morris but Kathryn was beginning to wonder if Giles Harris was writing the novels himself. It would explain a lot of things. He had been at Oxford, knew the publishing world and its requirements inside out, and it was surely possible that he could arrange to have the cheques made out to his own name. Many authors also held down full-time jobs. 'You are a very successful man,' she began again. 'How do you think you would have fared without a degree from Oxford?'

'Are you asking if I think one mention of those hallowed portals is enough to open doors?' His eyebrows were raised in amusement. 'If so, the answer is yes. Or shall I say it was in my day. However, your hypothetical question is impossible to answer. Perhaps I would still have ended up in publishing, as I already knew people in it.'

'From Oxford?'

'Ah, clever Mrs Brooks. Point taken.' But if he had not been to Oxford, he admitted silently, he would not have met Laura and her first manuscript could have landed on anybody's desk.

'What about your contemporaries?' Kathryn probed. 'If what you say is true, they must be equally successful.'

Giles shrugged in what he hoped was a nonchalant manner. 'I can't help you there, I'm afraid. Lost touch with them all long ago.' He had relaxed now. Either Kathryn Brooks was still fishing because she had been stood up at that hotel, or she really was going to write an article on Megan Morris's editor. Her next question made his mouth go dry and his heart beat faster.

'Really? But I thought you were all so close, the six of you.'

His self-control was amazing but Giles's hands, clasped loosely on the blotter in front of him, tightened. The knuckles were white and his startlingly blue eyes narrowed fractionally.

'Many friendships formed at university stand the test of time; unfortunately and, rather sadly, I was too busy getting ahead in my career to have much time for socialising, other than with clients and people in the same line. For all I know, the rest of my friends from those days are in and out of each other's houses every five minutes. It's a shame, but that's the way life is.'

'Yes.' Kathryn glanced down at her lap, timing her pause for most effect. 'And I expect you wanted to forget them. I think I might, if one of my closest friends had been murdered.'

Giles stared at her, unable to speak, almost unable to

catch his breath. Laura *must* have spoken to her, there was no other way she could know! But to ask would be to reveal that he kept in touch with Laura, and it would also endanger her anonymity. With fear knotting his stomach muscles, Giles heard her list the four names apart from his own. 'And Jenny Branagh,' she added, 'although she wasn't at Oxford with you all. Was it usual for the students to mix with the locals? I always got the impression that Oxford was very much split into Town and Gown.'

'No. *Un*usual, I'd say.' His voice was a croak. He cleared his throat. 'We got to know Jenny because we used the café where she worked. She was a very bright girl, great fun, but had missed her opportunities somewhere along the line.'

'Yes, I spoke to her headmistress. I also spoke to her boyfriend of the time, Michael Jarvis. He's very bitter, even now. He blames you all for taking Jenny away from him.'

'Jarvis?' And Jenny's headmistress. Christ, she has been busy, he thought. This wide-eyed girl with the lovely smile had been leading him by the nose. He wondered what she didn't know. Giles swallowed hard and waited for the worst.

'Mrs Milton, Sarah's mother, isn't going to rest until she finds whoever killed her daughter. Now, for the sake of what I'm trying to do, can you tell me what it was like for you at the time? Did it, for example, affect your studies?'

There was nothing for it but to comply. He answered her questions as best he could without giving anything away. Naturally there were things he wasn't sure about, and never would be, but he would not break his word. He gave Kathryn Brooks the same story he had given the police.

After she had gone, her perfume lingered. Giles suspected he would always smell it in his office. Her visit had lasted only an hour and a quarter, yet it had seemed an eternity.

Suddenly Giles knew what he had to do. He grabbed his raincoat and flew down the stairs and out of the building. It had to be done for his own sake, for all their sakes, and most especially for Laura's.

The blood was pounding in his ears as he was filled with rage. *Michael Jarvis.* The name went round and around in his brain. He had forgotten all about him, but the moment

Kathryn mentioned him he pictured the youth quite clearly. Tall and thin, his face pinched and mean-looking. They had laughed at him with his local accent and his lack of education, but not in front of him, that would not have been wise and, initially, not in front of Jenny either. Michael used to pick her up from the café, his expression suggesting that he'd like to punch her new friends.

Giles was out of breath when he entered the tube station. Having lived in London for so long he knew which route she would be taking if she was going back to Paddington. Relief surged through him as he saw Kathryn's vaguely bedraggled figure on the platform. The indicator board overhead showed two minutes to the next train. Giles edged along, keeping to the back, near the wall where he was sheltered by the waiting crowds. There was a click. He looked up. One minute to go. Positioned immediately behind her he held his breath. He had killed once, he could do it again. The commuter crowds were still surging onto the platform. One quick push, no one would notice, then they need fear no more.

He heard the whistle of the line and felt the rush of wind before the lights of the tube train rounded the bend. Exhaling deeply he slowly raised his hand.

'Danny, don't! I'm so sorry.' A woman clutching the reins of a three-year-old dragged the child backwards. It had stepped on Kathryn's foot.

The screech of brakes on metal and the hiss of the train doors opening drowned out Giles's smothered cry. Three seconds, that's all it had taken for the woman and child to come between Kathryn and the rail. Sweat poured down his back and from his armpits as he gasped for air. He felt as if he was suffocating. Loosening his tie he turned and walked, unseen by Kathryn, back towards the stairs.

It was cool above ground and his skin felt chilled. White-faced, he made his way back to the office not knowing if he would have carried out his plan. That the thought had been there was enough.

Chapter 9

'You're absolutely certain, Laura?'

'Giles, how many times do I have to repeat myself? We talked about her work – a few short sentences, nothing more. Be realistic! You can't believe I suddenly got it into my head to confide everything?'

Laura trailed the long lead of the telephone behind her in order to reach her cigarettes and lighter which were on the table by the window. How close Giles was, in a way, for how tempted she had been lately to do just that, confide in someone. What he had told her had shaken her, but what he had said to Kathryn Brooks disturbed her even further. She sank into an armchair, the telephone in her lap.

'Michael Jarvis ... I'd forgotten all about him,' she said slowly. 'Still, it doesn't matter, he doesn't know anything.'

'That's not the point. How has she got so far without any help? And what worries me more is you.'

'Me?'

'Think about it – there's nothing to stop her making the connection.'

'True enough, but even if she does, she won't know which one of our group is Megan Morris. It's bound to have crossed her mind that it might be a male. And, don't forget, you're the only one who knows my address.'

'That may be so but you *did* turn up that day and you gave the name of Jenny Branagh. She isn't going to stop looking now.'

Laura did not know what to think. Half of her desired everything to be out in the open, the other half told her to run and hide with Marcia. She was suddenly aware of the break in conversation. There was obviously more to come.

'I told her where she could find John.'

'You did *what*?' And Giles had had the nerve to suggest that *she* had been indiscreet!

'He's always enjoyed being the one in charge – let him sort this lot out.'

After she had hung up, Laura chewed a nail. Something was troubling Giles. He had sounded very strange – quite out of breath, in fact. She was worried herself. Too much was going on that she didn't understand. Why should Giles want to drag John into this? 'Oh God,' she muttered, 'I can cope with Giles, but not the rest of them.'

Giles would protect her, but for how long? She felt as if a noose were slowly being tightened around her neck. Something had to be done, and soon. Perhaps it was best left to John. He was always believable, more so when he was lying, and he would charm the pants off Kathryn Brooks – quite literally, if given half a chance.

Filled with tension, Laura waited for the rain to stop. Then she changed into old clothes, went out into the garden and tugged out groundsel and thistles from between the plants. The damp soil yielded the weeds easily and gave off the smell of wet vegetation. Gradually she began to relax.

Only when it was too dark to see did she put her tools away and go inside. Her hands were encrusted with earth and she had broken a nail, but the physical exertion which made her muscles ache had also soothed her. After a hot bath she wrapped herself and her wet hair in towels and poured a gin and tonic then rang Marcia to bring her up to date. Marcia would point out any pitfalls and would certainly reassure her. If she didn't, it would still do Laura good to hear her loving voice.

She had to wait ages for her call to be answered but knew it was unlikely that her mother was out. She never felt the need to hurry. If she was busy, or absorbed in something, whoever was ringing had to be patient. If they hung up it was too bad, she knew they would try again if it was important. Marcia answered on the thirteenth ring. Laura hoped it wasn't a bad omen.

Her glass chinked against the ashtray as she set it down. Her hands were still far from steady.

'I was in the kitchen, cooking for the freezer,' Marcia said. 'Just stews and some curry. Beef's very cheap at the moment so I'm taking advantage of it. How's the novel going?'

'It's fine, I know *where* it's going now. How are you?'

'The same as ever.' Marcia was puzzled. She sensed this was more than a social call and it was unlike Laura not to get straight to the point. 'All right, out with it, my girl, tell me what's troubling you.'

Laura did so and Marcia listened, knowing she must hide her own anxiety. 'You have to stop being constantly afraid, darling. It's all in the past. The police cleared all of you at the time. Yes, I know you lied about what happened that night but you must see that it's over. This girl isn't going to come up with anything the police don't already know. Oh Laura, I can't bear the thought of your being miserable.'

'I'm sorry. I didn't mean to inflict it all on you.' She knew Marcia felt her pain as strongly as if it were her own. She should not have rung.

'It's probably best you got it off your chest. Now look, I was thinking of making a trip to London in the near future. There's a series of concerts I wouldn't mind going to and I'm a little stuck for culture out here. The radio's not quite the same thing. I can do some shopping at the same time. My summer visitors will start arriving soon and I won't get the chance then. How about if I stayed with you? I can go up by train and perhaps, if you're free, you could come with me. We could do all sorts of exciting things. Do you know, I've never had tea at the Ritz? It's about time I remedied that.'

Despite everything, Laura smiled. Dear Marcia. She had probably had no intention of going to London but her enthusiasm was infectious and Laura agreed, knowing it was her mother's way of trying to cheer her up.

'I haven't got the *Times* handy at the moment, but I'll look up the concert dates and let you know. I'll book the tickets on my credit card. You will come, won't you?'

Laura said she would.

* * *

Having made the first step towards mental independence David was uncertain how to progress. There was little he could do about the business; it more or less took care of itself and he didn't want to change things. It was the same with the flat; its vague shabbiness was comforting and he had no desire to move. It was really a matter of changing his life so that it included people other than his customers and family. Apart from books, he realised how little interest he had in hobbies and he had never been much of a sportsman since Oxford. He did not feel the desire to travel so a holiday seemed pointless. David grimaced. He really had become incredibly boring.

As he lay in bed the depressing thought struck him that if he were to die that night, he would have left no mark whatsoever on the world, but as he drifted off to sleep he supposed in a way he had. There were few people who had been involved in a murder and who had sworn to carry a secret to the grave.

He knew that everyone dreamed but not all dreams were remembered. Some of David's were, but he was never troubled by nightmares. The next step came to him as he slept and in the morning he knew what he was going to do.

Alex was pleased that Kathryn had not only agreed to his accompanying her to Cardiff, but seemed eager that he should do so. They would make a weekend of it. From the boat-yard he made a reservation at the Marriott, which was fairly central, and asked for some champagne to be placed in their room, ready for their arrival around six on Friday night. They were both getting away early.

Kathryn had been surprised that John Atherton had assented so readily to a meeting with her, and she was taken aback by his unruffled attitude. She had telephoned Cardiff University first but John was in a lecture. On the off-chance that his number was listed, she tried Directory Enquiries and was provided with a number which she hoped was his. Impatient to make contact, she had caught him at home in the evening but did not know that when she finally got through he was half-drunk and had completely forgotten the conversation by the following day. All he had to let him know it had ever taken place was a barely legible scrawl on the notepad by the phone.

Kathryn assumed that Giles, having admitted he knew where John was even if he denied communicating with him, would make an exception and warn him in advance. It didn't matter; whatever John Atherton told her it would come from a different viewpoint.

Her file was filling out with notes now but she left it in the drawer at home and concentrated on work and Alex. She had finally come to understand that he, too, needed time to recover. Now he was almost the Alex with whom she had fallen in love; gentle and thoughtful and able to make her laugh.

The weekend chores were to be given a miss but it no longer mattered. Alex had finally persuaded her that it was ridiculous to spend precious time cleaning when they could easily afford to pay someone else to come in and do it. Without meaning to, he had brought to her notice the fact that she was guilty of not always listening to what he said or, more precisely, not taking it in. From somewhere she had received the impression that he didn't want a stranger in the flat when they were not there themselves. It seemed likely that she had simply been projecting her own thoughts. Once she was used to the idea she began to look forward to it.

On the Wednesday evening they drove up to Burnham Beeches and strolled through the trees, last autumn's leaves slippery beneath their feet. Autumn, or late summer, was the best time to come when the colours were almost unreal, but they had got out of the habit of walking and it was pleasant to be with Alex, side by side, holding hands as they used to.

'Had enough?'

Kathryn nodded. Alex leaned down and kissed her and she knew that the worst was over as she experienced the tingle that had been missing for some time. 'In that case, you can buy your old man a drink.'

She smiled and they made their way back to the car. In the pub they had chosen because it was old and low-beamed and without juke-box or fruit machines, Kathryn was aware of a pair of females seated on bar stools. One was toying suggestively with the stem of her glass as she blatantly stared at Alex. It had always been the same; women were attracted to him. She silently thanked him for his display of indifference. Kathryn did not know that the reverse was also true, that Alex saw the admiring looks she received and ignored in her turn. He had never been able to define what it was about her that drew the attention. She was attractive, but so were many women; it was more than that – an air she had about her. She came across as confident but sexy, yet there was something incongruous about her femininity contrasted with a certain expression in her eyes which suggested she was quite capable of landing a left hook if the occasion arose.

Because they had the car they did not stay long. It had been a good evening and Alex could have bitten his tongue when, in bed, he reached for Kathryn and, feeling her hipbones beneath the thin nightdress said, 'Don't lose any more weight, I like a bit of meat on my women.' Once, it would have meant nothing and she would have laughed. The plural noun would not have mattered. Since that time there had been Rebecca. And Rebecca was thin.

Kathryn tensed then let out her breath. She said nothing but Alex thought it would not be wise to make love to her that night.

Giles had no intention of warning John – an omission he acknowledged was partly due to malice. John had made so little of walking back into his and David's life, had seemed so uncaring about the past and completely unconcerned when it came to danger. He was also pretty certain that the warning would not have been forthcoming had the roles been reversed. He had passed the buck and that was enough.

After a week, when he had heard nothing, he began to think that Kathryn Brooks had changed her mind about talking to John, but logic told him he was wrong. He had assessed her shrewdly; she was not a quitter.

Meanwhile he had to ring Laura to confirm their monthly lunch appointment. He would not presume to take her for granted even though he was in possession of her latest royalty statements. She surprised him by cancelling. 'Oh, they can wait. I'm sorry it's such short notice, but Marcia's staying with me at the moment.' Giles, unaware that Laura's mother knew as much, and more, than he did, understood.

'And the manuscript?'

'You'll be pleased to hear it's almost ready. Just a few bits to tidy up.'

'That's great news. I'll ring you next week.' He did not mention Kathryn Brooks or John Atherton and tried to forget them himself. He had the distraction of an annual awards dinner at which he was expected to make a speech. Public speaking was a chore he dreaded and it took him hours until he was satisfied with his notes; he always worried he would leave out the name of someone he was specifically meant to thank or congratulate. Thank goodness for Ingrid, who went through them for him and who, for once, was accompanying him to the dinner. Knowing she was there would help.

John Atherton scowled at the piece of paper upon which was written *Kathryn Brooks, Saturday 11.30 a.m. Forte Post House*. He had been looking at it on and off for the past two days. It was another silent admonishment of his drinking habits. Then he grinned. He would turn up; it couldn't be all bad if whoever wanted to see him was female.

The Dean and his wife and one or two other influential people from the university were coming for dinner. The house was immaculate and Sheila, who had thoughtfully brought more flowers from her greenhouse, was still in the kitchen preparing things. He had stopped suggesting menus once he learned that she instinctively knew what constituted an excellent meal and what was appropriate for the occasion. It turned out she had worked for university staff before and it amused him to discover that she held strong views on what she called the class system. She considered herself to be working class, as was her husband, to whom she served plain Welsh food, along with pie and chips and sausage and mash. For the Dean or other dignitaries she would provide delicacies and rich sauces, but she wouldn't dream of going to so much trouble if John was having students in. 'Just give them a drinks party with some crisps and cheese,' she told him. 'That's all they want anyway.' If it was to be a sit-down do she'd knock up some spaghetti bolognaise or chili. John had never met anyone who equated another person's position in society with what they ate.

'Everything all right, Sheila?'

'Yes – as long as you keep out of my way. Here now, don't get started on that too soon.'

John laughed and poured himself a drink. Sheila was the one person who seemed oblivious to his charm and scolded him as if he were a child. 'I don't suppose I can tempt you?' He raised the bottle in her direction.

'It's a bit early for me, Mr Atherton,' she replied pointedly.

He took his drink through to the lounge and sat enjoying its high-ceilinged elegance. The newspaper was neatly folded on the table but he ignored it. Instead he took the sheet of notepaper from his pocket. *Kathry Brooks*. The name meant nothing. As hard as he tried he could not recall a student of that name, not even in the distant past.

Lectures were in full swing and he was pleased he had avoided the temptation of little Tina Parry, especially as her frequent smiles were no longer directed at him but at an emaciated third-year student with a pony-tail. John's status had reverted to that of her tutor and nothing more.

The coming appointment intrigued rather than perturbed him and he wondered why he had chosen an hotel instead of a pub. Perhaps he hadn't; maybe the unknown Kathryn Brooks had nominated the venue. And why a Saturday and not an evening? It suggested she might not be local.

When the time came John showered and shaved and cooked himself a proper breakfast, washing up afterwards because Sheila would not be in again until Monday. These things took time and he realised he was ensuring that he would not arrive too early and have a head start with the drinks.

He was still ten minutes early and there were only two other customers, a couple, seated in the corner. It occurred to him that he would have no way of knowing who she was, assuming she intended showing up.

At exactly eleven-thirty Kathryn walked into the bar and focused on the tall man leaning against the counter. It had to be John Atherton, although he had said he would wear a dark green shirt. He was handsome in a lived-in sort of way and his thick hair curled over his collar in a manner similar to Alex's. When he smiled she felt a warm sensation inside.

'Miss Brooks?'

'Mrs. But I prefer Kathryn.'

'Ah, Mrs. What a shame.' They shook hands solemnly. 'What would you like to drink?'

'Just a half of lager and lime, please, Mr Atherton.'

'Oh, please, call me John.'

'I hope I haven't spoiled your weekend plans.' She felt foolishly tonguetied and vaguely uncomfortable in his presence and began to understand how it was that he was the dominant one of the group. Without doing or saying anything he exuded confidence and power.

'Far from it. I did not expect to be having a drink with a beautiful woman.' Far from it indeed, he thought. This girl was worth the effort. Her looks were natural and she did not need much make-up; the pale blue and white dress she wore was simple and suited her. On her feet were white espadrilles. He guessed her looks and her outward gentleness hid great strength; it showed in her eyes. For some reason he thought he would like to pour all his troubles into her pretty ear before removing her clothes and taking her to bed. She surprised him by offering to pay for the drinks, and as she bent to unfasten her shoulder-bag, he touched her hand to stop her. 'I'll do it.' He could smell her skin and peach shampoo and had a strong desire to kiss the nape of her neck where her hair had fallen forward. This girl left Tina Parry standing. 'Shall we sit down?' It might be safer; he could put some distance between them.

Once seated John took a packet of cigarettes from his shirt pocket and offered one to Kathryn. She shook her head.

191

'I was surprised you agreed to see me,' she said as he lit up. 'Especially as I explained what it was about.'

John smiled enigmatically and wondered what the hell she was talking about.

'Can I just verify one or two things first?'

'Fire away.' He leaned back against the seat and folded his arms, a wreath of smoke trailing from his right hand. His features, he hoped, were arranged in an intelligent and knowledgeable manner. He had no idea what he was in for.

'Out of the six of you, I've only spoken to Giles. Sarah, of course, is dead, but I did see her mother, and I had a brief conversation with Michael Jarvis. I have to admit, I haven't yet been able to locate David or Laura.' Kathryn was not going to let him know that she might have met Jenny Branagh.

You bastard, you sodding bastard, John thought, managing neither to move nor alter his half-smiling expression. Giles could have had the decency to let him know. But had he been sober when he received the telephone call, there would have been no need of that. Amazing that none of this had registered.

Kathryn continued along the lines of tracing the careers of a group of fellow students. 'Giles has clearly done very well for himself. How would you say you've fared?'

This was easier terrain if all she wanted was a potted history. John unfolded his arms and took a sip of his beer. Fully aware of Kathryn's pen hovering over her notepad he refrained from swallowing too much at once. He needed to stay completely sober. She had already written something but as it was in shorthand it made no sense to him. 'It's hard to say. Professionally I suppose I'm a success, but it depends what you mean. I doubt if financially I come up to Giles's standards although, before you start feeling sorry for me, I have more than enough to live on.'

Kathryn wasn't sure whether the remark was cynical or sarcastic. 'And personally?'

'I shall leave it to you to work that one out. My parents seem to have forgotten my existence, my wife has divorced me and my old friends did not exactly welcome me back with open arms. Doesn't that tell you something?'

The grin on his face told her it might well be true but he didn't give a damn. Kathryn tapped her teeth with the pen. 'My old friends,' he had said. An interesting comment if he meant his old Oxford friends. 'Lots of people get divorced, and maybe the others were not really friends to start with.'

It was either an astute comment or Giles had said something along those lines. It had taken John several years to discover that what they had, what had held the group together, was something other than friendship.

'Do you enjoy what you do?'

He was taken aback with the sudden change of direction. 'Enjoy? I'm not sure that I think about it in those terms. The students can be frustrating and, occasionally, exhausting, but there are rewards. There's a lot of satisfaction in imparting knowledge and making people use it to think for themselves – satisfaction, too, when predicted results are achieved or someone does exceptionally well. Yes, I do enjoy it.'

'And the future?'

'I never plan the future, Kathryn, it's a pointless exercise. For the moment I'm happy where I am. This is thirsty work – may I get you another?'

Kathryn had hardly touched her drink. She took a few sips and nodded. This interview might take some time because John was displaying a willingness to talk which had been lacking in Giles. She smothered the thought that she was also enjoying his company.

'How long were you married?' she asked when he returned with the drinks.

'Eight years. We parted by mutual consent. It was not in the least traumatic and there are no added complications because we didn't have any children and my wife is in the States. Believe it or not, we write to each other occasionally.'

Kathryn asked what his wife was doing overseas and John described the course of his career. 'When we realised the marriage was never going to work there were only a few months left on my contract. I knew I was ready to come home and, had we stayed together, Angela would not have been happy over here. She was very much a family girl.'

'So having got settled you decided to go and see Giles?' Kathryn hoped she was right. John seemed quite relaxed.

He had one ankle resting on the other outstretched leg, and a hand behind his neck, his elbow resting on the back of the banquette. It seemed such a natural pose that she wondered if this was how he sat in tutorials.

'Yes. And David. Neither of them has changed much except to become slightly exaggerated versions of their younger selves. I wonder what they thought about me?' He raised an eyebrow quizzically but Kathryn did not respond.

'What's David doing now?'

John explained. 'Typical Shawcross,' he concluded. 'Never had any sense of adventure.'

She had the name at last. 'Tell me about Sarah. What was she like?'

'I thought you said you were writing something about how we've fared since our university days? Sarah's dead, there's no mileage to be had there. Ah, unless – let me guess – you haven't got it into that pretty little head of yours that you can solve the mystery, have you? Perhaps you even think we killed her.'

Kathryn was stunned. She had not expected this openness or an unsolicited admission that such a thing was possible. 'No, it's not that.' And then, for no reason she could think of she added, 'What I started out doing was trying to find out who Megan Morris really is.'

John's laughter filled the room and caused heads to turn. He uncrossed his legs and sat forward, leaning on the table. 'Then you've had a wasted journey, my lovely Kate. I know nothing about the woman. I did, however, try to worm it out of Giles but there was nothing doing. You have had a journey, I take it. Where did you say you were from?'

'I didn't. Burnham. Between Maidenhead and Slough.'

' "Come friendly bombs and fall on Slough; it isn't fit for humans now".'

'John Betjeman.'

'Indeed.' But unlike his Oxford days there was no answering quotation. Nevertheless, he would very much like to play the game with Kathryn Brooks. There were many other things he'd like to do with her as well, and the day was still young.

Kathryn mistook his tone. She thought he was being

patronising. 'There can't be many people who don't know that.'

'You'd be surprised.' John lit a cigarette. 'Look, it's Giles you need to talk to, not me. But as you've already seen him, you know you won't get anywhere. Can I ask you something? What are you really up to? Megan Morris's identity has been a closely guarded secret ever since she started writing – what – ten years ago? You're not stupid, and neither am I, so why not tell me what's really behind all this.'

Inexplicably Kathryn found herself telling him about the woman in the Thames Riviera who called herself Jenny Branagh, and her visit to Oxford which had culminated in speaking to Harriet Milton.

John whistled. 'No wonder you want to question us all! By going about it in a circuitous route you've come to the conclusion that one of us might be Megan Morris. It's not beyond the bounds of possibility. However, it isn't me, I can assure you.'

Kathryn thought it was unlikely if he had been out of the country for ten years. She paused. 'Will you tell me what really happened when Sarah disappeared?'

'Will you let me buy you lunch?'

'Yes.' She wasn't sure if this was a condition or a method of changing the subject. Either way it would be entertaining.

As soon as Marcia arrived Laura began to feel better. She was so practical, so down to earth that her own probably irrational fears disappeared.

Helping her to unpack caused some amusement. The suitcase contained what Marcia called her 'London clothes' and although there was no sign of the famous cardigan or the baggy cords she favoured, they were terribly out of date. It wouldn't have surprised Laura if she'd brought a hat with a long feather in it.

'We were lucky, there weren't all that many tickets left for the first concert. The seats aren't great, but it doesn't matter, it's not like the theatre. The only thing that counts is whether you can hear the music.' Marcia hung a heavy tweed skirt on a hanger.

'I'm looking forward to it. And I expect you're looking forward to a drink.'

'Love one.' Marcia thought it was more likely that Laura needed one. Her face showed signs of strain and she looked older, although she was still beautiful. It was an objective observation; she would never have fooled herself into believing her daughter was beautiful if she was unattractive.

'Are you hungry yet?' Laura asked when Marcia appeared downstairs.

'I had a sandwich on the train. Don't fuss, Laura, I'll eat whenever you usually do.' Marcia sat in one of the deep settees, thinking again how much her daughter liked to surround herself with tasteful elegance. 'The garden looks nice, almost countrified.'

Laura smiled. 'I know, and I cut the grass especially for you. It's the one chore I always leave until last.'

'Laura, now we've covered the social chit chat, please tell me why you're so unhappy. It isn't like you.'

Laura followed the direction of her mother's gaze. 'Do you want to sit outside?'

'Yes, why not? I think it's warm enough.' Marcia gathered together her handbag, glass and an ashtray and they stepped over the narrow ledge at the foot of the window, out onto the paving stones. Over the years moss had accumulated between the cracks. Laura left it there, she thought it looked more natural.

They sat at the wrought-iron table but it was not hot enough to warrant getting the striped umbrella from the shed. A light wind lifted Laura's hair and, lit from behind, it danced around her shoulders like fire. 'This girl,' she began, 'this Kathryn Brooks, she worries me.'

Marcia listened without interruption until she had finished. 'Why did you never tell me about that first novel?' Her voice was pained. She thought they had shared every secret.

'I thought you'd be ashamed.'

'Ashamed?' Marcia sat upright in astonishment. 'You could never do anything to make me ashamed, you should know that.' But she understood. Laura was straightforward and basically honest. The slightest misdemeanour filled her with guilt, but from what she had said there was nothing to feel guilty about. 'Is there anything else?'

'No. That's it. There really isn't anything you don't know now.'

'Then it's time you stopped blaming yourself for everything. If anyone should suffer it's John and, I hate to say it because she's dead, but Sarah was greatly to blame. You have to forget it, darling.' She laid a hand on Laura's which was cold and decided this was not the time to tell her about her forthcoming appointment with a specialist. In a few days, maybe, when they had had some fun.

Laura brushed back her hair. It was a tired gesture which caused Marcia to think that the basic problem was that her daughter worked too hard. She had spent a few days with her at Easter, but otherwise she never took a break. It couldn't be easy, turning out one bestseller after another. She would suggest a proper holiday, a fortnight somewhere by the sea or a cruise. It wasn't as if she couldn't afford it. For now she needed to talk. 'Shall we be devils and have another drink?'

Laura smiled. Dear Marcia, she had a knack of making the most innocent thing seem like vaguely wicked fun.

When they had had their second drink Laura said it was time to go in and eat.

John drained his glass without difficulty. Kathryn was unable to do so. The lager was too gassy. 'Leave it,' John told her. 'It doesn't matter.'

He was already at the doors so she had no option but to follow him. Outside she blinked in the sunlight. Cardiff Castle was almost opposite where they stood and Arms Park was to their right. Without hesitation John began to stride down Westgate Street and Kathryn was glad she wasn't wearing heels or she could not have kept up with him. 'Do you mind what you eat?' he enquired over his shoulder as they made their way between crowds of shoppers into a narrow, pedestrianised street.

'No.'

He held her arm as they crossed St Mary Street and she

197

felt the heat of his fingers on her bare flesh and was glad he could not read her mind.

He had not waited for the lights but steered her to the centre of the road and pushed her forward when they had to sprint the last two yards. He seemed to have no sense of danger.

'Here, I thought this would make a pleasant change. It's basic but good.'

The restaurant was Portuguese with the uninspiring name of Porto's. Inside, all was dark wood and floorboards but the atmosphere was completely Continental, and most of the smartly dressed waiters were foreign although Kathryn could not have guessed at their nationality. It was busy but there were spare tables. John asked if there was one available upstairs. They were shown to one near the window and handed menus and a wine list. 'A litre of the house red, I think,' John said without bothering to open it. 'Suit you?'

As Kathryn assumed he was paying she said it would and it seemed more appropriate in a place such as this.

'We'll have it straight away, please. Now, you may, of course, eat whatever you want but I suggest you try the kebabs.' He smiled but did not enlighten her further. Kathryn agreed; she did not want anything too heavy because she would be eating again later with Alex. She hadn't said when she would be back, only that she would wait in their hotel room once the interview was over. Alex had told her she was not to hurry. They had travelled all that way for the purpose, there was no point in rushing things. He would find himself a cricket match to watch or look around the castle.

The waiter returned with the wine and they placed their orders. John raised his glass. 'Here's to your project, whatever it might be. May I ask what you're finding so amusing?'

'Actually I was just calculating how much alcohol I've consumed since I began what you term as my project.'

'Surely Giles didn't wine and dine you? I imagined he'd have seen you in his office.'

'Not Giles. Harriet Milton.' Had the past affected them so much that they needed to drink, Kathryn wondered.

'Well, that lady may well have need to drown 'em. Now,

Kathryn Brooks, you were asking me about Sarah. I take it you didn't believe what Giles told you.' He lit a cigarette and decided nothing but the truth would suit his dining companion. She would probably spot a lie but he could be economical with the truth. 'It started as a game,' he began.

Kathryn leaned forward, her elbows on the table, her hands under her chin. She knew with certainty that she was about to hear something important.

'People make new friends at university. They're away from home, perhaps for the first time, and anxious about all sorts of things, but at least they soon learn that they're all in it together. These friendships are very important – even, I suppose, character-forming, but what we had was far more than that. You have to understand that, Kathryn, if you're to make any sense of things.' She nodded but did not speak for fear of distracting him. 'There were five of us initially, then we got to know Jenny from the café and she just fitted in. She and Sarah were close, they could've been sisters. I'm not really sure how it happened, but it did. We used to meet . . . oh hell, it all sounds so juvenile now. We found a place, you see, in some woods where we were foolish enough to believe no one else ever went. Later we learned that other groups of students used it too, and it was the first place the police searched. Anyway, we used to take booze there, and sometimes food and then Jenny introduced us to drugs. Not hard drugs, although in the end I think she did take them. We used to play games, games of mental skill. One was to employ quotations; we used to look them up furiously, probably to the detriment of our studies, but no one wanted to be outdone. It was an ongoing thing. You had to have a quote for every occasion, and preferably be able to find another one along the same lines or to contradict it. Jenny was no good at it at all; she'd failed most of her exams and dropped out of school. It was sad – she was intelligent enough to have done well and she certainly kept up with us on the other games. You might think I'm digressing but you need to know the whole background. You see, Sarah's death – it started with a game . . .'

With the timing of an actor the waiter appeared at that moment with their meals. John watched Kathryn's face and

199

was not disappointed when her eyes widened in surprise and her lips twitched with a smile. On the table were bowls of salad and a huge portion of chips, but the second waiter bore meat-laden skewers all of three feet in length which he hung from hooks suspended from the ceiling over the table. She had not noticed them before and now realised that all the tables had them. He reached up and squeezed something over the top which ran down the length of the skewers over the pieces of lamb. 'I shall never eat all that.'

'Rather unusual, though, isn't it?'

They put some of the food on their plates and ate a few mouthfuls.

'You were saying that Sarah's murder began as a game?' Kathryn hoped John Atherton was not playing a game of his own just then.

'Yes. I always considered it as healthy competition – you get used to that if you've been to public school. I wasn't very happy there,' he told her, apropos of nothing. 'Sarah took things far more seriously than the rest of us; she always had to succeed, to try to be the best. I don't know if she was insecure, you don't think of things like that when you're young, but she seemed terrified of failure.'

So far what he had said fitted in with Mrs Milton's assessment of her daughter. What followed did not.

'It was always Sarah who wanted to take things too far. She went about things the wrong way, somehow. Her fears were misplaced – for instance, when there was real danger she didn't turn a hair. I think she was a compulsive liar, too. She used to go on and on about her parents, how awful they were to her et cetera, but it didn't ring true. I always thought it was just her way of gaining attention. Or sympathy. The final game, the one that led to her death, was her idea.' John paused to lever some more meat from the skewer. Kathryn ate a bit more but she no longer felt hungry.

'She came up with this idea that we all had to present a way in which we could disappear without trace – you know, like Lord Lucan – except you had to be alive and living a normal existence but under another name. It was quite fascinating trying to work it out. It does happen, but usually to people whom no one cares about and therefore they aren't looked for and tracked down. Everything I came up with was flawed. I went through the usual things, like the John Stonehouse case – remember that? He was duly found though, in Australia, wasn't it?'

Kathryn nodded and saw that he was already refilling his empty glass. He topped hers up without asking if she wanted more. 'So what happened?'

'Sarah confided in me. She—'

'But what was the point of that?' Kathryn interrupted. 'Surely you had to surprise each other. And how did she know you wouldn't steal her idea?'

'My dear Kathryn, public-school boys at Oxford would not *dream* of doing such a dishonourable thing.' His smile was mocking. 'Later, of course, when they go into business, it's a different matter.' He raked his hands through his hair then sat back and belched quietly, without embarrassment or apology. 'In those days we were full of shit. We had grand ideas about principles and integrity and honesty and changing the world. Oh, the things we railed against – life's injustices, the poor – ironic that, when we were all loaded. Had we been asked to share our wealth around and live on a meagre grant I expect it would've been a different story. But, no, Kathryn, I wouldn't have stolen her idea. She told me because . . . well, because she happened to be in my bed at the time and was probably deeply satisfied and filled with gratitude.'

Kathryn laughed even though she wasn't completely sure that he was joking. Despite the egotistical comment she liked him and suspected he was not afraid to relate anecdotes against himself.

'She'd been after my body for a while. She made it pretty obvious and I was incredibly vain. It was unkind of me because I was seeing Laura at the time. I hoped Sarah had the sense to keep her mouth shut, and suspected that she only did it to have one up on Laura. Anyway, if she ever said anything, there were no repercussions.'

John had managed to finish his meal and to eat half of the chips. Kathryn had not touched them but picked at the salad and got through half of the meat. It was far too much. She laid her knife and fork together on the plate.

'So what was her plan?'

'It was a little impractical but it had its good points. She had planned her own murder.'

'*What?*'

'I thought that might shock you. However, it wasn't to actually be her own murder – only to seem that way. And, as I said, it was only a game. That's why I didn't panic that night. I honestly didn't think anything was wrong other than that she had, in her interminable way, gone too far and tried to frighten us by acting it out. I really did believe she intended to disappear, but only for a day or two then come back, laughing at us for our gullibility.'

Kathryn waited for John to light a cigarette. He then explained that they had all gone out to the woods. They had drunk more than usual and whatever Jenny had provided them with seemed to have an extra kick. They paid her for whatever they smoked and John said he suspected she made a tidy profit. 'None of us could remember later what had really happened – other than that very late on, Sarah stood up. She was covered in blood and there was a knife on the ground. Jenny screamed but it wasn't until Sarah fell down that the rest of us noticed anything was amiss. We were in that bad a state.

'I cursed her solidly and went over to her. God, you won't believe this, no one would believe it, that's why I made them all keep quiet. You see, when I bent over her I was sure that she winked at me. I was furious, it was a stupid trick to play! David was out of his head, Jenny was hysterical and Laura was crying. Giles seemed in a state of shock but his main concern seemed to be comforting Laura. I blame myself.' He paused at that point and gave a long, regretful sigh. 'Things could have been so different. I decided to punish her, God forgive me – to leave her there and take everyone else back. I did so, and calmed them all down by explaining what she was up to. I'd dropped Jenny off where she was staying; she was fine by then, then I went back to collect Sarah. I thought she'd have had a bit of a shock herself, being left in the woods alone.' He stopped and tapped the end of his cigarette, watching the ash fall off.

'And?'

'She wasn't there.' John was staring blankly as the dark woods arose to confront him once more. 'I looked around, called her name – I suppose I was there the best part of an hour. Finally I realised that the little bitch really meant to go ahead with her plan. No, not the real plan, but to act it out.' John signalled for the waiter. Kathryn was disappointed. She assumed he was going to ask for the bill. They would leave and she would learn no more. However, the wine bottle was empty. He ordered another.

'No, please. I've had enough,' she told him.

'You may have, my lovely – I haven't. One more glass won't hurt you.'

She thought that perhaps this was the first time he had discussed what had happened for many years. In his position, she, too, might feel the need of some bolstering.

'The next day we all went straight down to the café as soon as it was open. Jenny was there, looking none the worse for wear. I don't know how she did it. In the broad light of day, so to speak, things didn't seem as bad, but then I suppose they never do. The café was quiet which meant Jenny could sit with us for a while. Sober, we were able to discuss it rationally. Knowing Sarah as we did, we thought we'd let her get on with it. She'd missed lectures before, no one would be any the wiser. But she never came back.

'After a week I knew something had gone dreadfully wrong. Her parents had been on to her college and people began asking us questions. We stuck to the same story – that we'd last seen her some time earlier in the evening that she disappeared – except only we knew it was that evening. We had to keep as near the truth as possible in case anyone had seen us together. And that, Kathryn, is the whole story. Make of it what you will. If you go to the police, none of us will say anything other than what we told them at the time. But, more importantly, I know *I* didn't kill her. God, I've thought and thought about it and I'm certain she was still alive when we left her, and if you'd seen the state of the rest of them you would know by their reactions that they were as stunned as I was.'

'Do you remember what her original plan was – I mean, the game?'

'More or less. She said if she faked her own murder then killed someone of the same age, someone who would not be missed, and hid the body where it would not be found for years, she would take over that person's identity. Oh, the details escape me now, but everything she said was plausible. The main part was in convincing someone they had killed her and then making sure only a skeleton was ever recovered.'

'Only a skeleton was recovered... Do you think she actually succeeded? I mean, that she really went ahead with the game after all?'

'I don't know. I honestly don't know. The police seemed satisfied that the corpse was Sarah.'

'How cruel if she did succeed.' Kathryn shuddered. 'How awful for her parents. They split up over it.'

'And how awful for the victim. What a lonely person *she* must have been not to be missed by anyone. And what an awful reason to die – for someone else's vanity.'

'What I don't understand is why, if she had so much going for her, Sarah would choose to take on the identity of a girl who had so little going for her. And why give up the chance of a degree?'

John shrugged. 'I doubt if we'll ever know.'

'Wait a minute... The report I found in the paper said her body had been found in the woods. How come, if the police searched them almost immediately?'

'Perhaps they were not as thorough as they might have been. Perhaps she was nowhere near where we left her. That's what makes me wonder if she did go ahead with it; disappear that night and kill someone, hiding the body later, after the police had searched. She was very fit, and she had her own car.'

Kathryn felt a sense of unreality, as if none of this could be happening to her. It was possible, though, that John was making the whole thing up.

'There was something else,' he said quietly.

'Oh?'

'Sarah told me she was pregnant – that the child might be mine.'

'Might be?'

'I suspect there were several candidates.'

'She was pregnant, the police confirmed it.'

John saw that she had not wasted much time. 'The girl they *found* was pregnant,' he corrected her. 'What if it wasn't Sarah? What if she had told me that because she had already picked her victim?'

'No one could be that callous.'

'You didn't know Sarah. But don't you see, if it was her, it gave me more of a motive than anyone. No bright student with a brilliant career ahead of him wants to be saddled with a wife or having to pay maintenance for the next sixteen or so years. It was another reason for keeping quiet; I didn't want to face all the questioning. I know there's such a thing as abortion, but the subject didn't come up. I didn't do it, Kathryn, I swear I didn't.'

She ignored his denial because she needed time to think things over. His presence was too strong to judge what he was saying rationally. 'Why did it take so long to find her?'

'Oh, that's simple. The woods are dense in parts and there were no houses in the vicinity but eventually the inevitable happened – some of the surrounding land was developed. Kids started going in there and people walking their dogs. It was a dog owner who found her – or rather the dog did. She'd been buried in a ditch. It was completely overgrown by that time. If the dog hadn't gone rummaging, she might still be there.'

Kathryn picked up her drink and took a small sip. It all fitted except for one thing. How was John in possession of these facts when he had been in the States at the time? 'Why have you told me all this?' she asked him. 'How do you know I won't go to the police and drag the whole thing up once more? You'd be questioned again.'

He smiled. 'True, if they believed what you told them. And anyway, "He's half absolv'd who has confess'd". Matthew Prior.'

Kathryn refused to be drawn into his games. 'I think they

would take notice. One of the officers originally on the case still has a thing about it. He—'

'But you won't, will you?'

Nothing seemed to daunt him. He sat grinning at her, as relaxed as when she had first set eyes on him. He was right, of course. If only for the time being. Kathryn was not going to make any decision until she had spoken to them all. She averted her eyes from his mocking perusal of her.

John asked for the bill and as he signed the credit-card slip, asked if she would like to join him for a drink in his local.

'Thank you, but no. I'm meeting my husband.'

'So Mr Brooks is here too.'

'Yes. The meal was lovely, thank you, but I really must go now.' She was very glad Alex was with her; the temptation to spend a few more hours with John would have been hard to resist.

'Yes, I suppose you must. Sadly, I understand. You'll be seeing David, I take it, in which case, to save you the trouble of finding him I'll give you his address.' He wrote the name of the shop and the street on one of the paper serviettes. 'You know, either it is or it isn't Sarah who is dead, but *someone* killed that girl. It's the same crime, whichever way you look at it. I just pray it wasn't one of us.'

Once more in the brightness of the streets John took her hand and held it for several seconds. 'I enjoyed meeting you, Kathryn Brooks. I hope your life is a happy one.'

Before she could answer he was striding down the street, his hands in his pockets and she had no idea what to make of the interview.

Chapter 10

Kathryn strolled back to the hotel having got her bearings the previous evening when she and Alex had wandered around whilst they decided where to eat. Neither of them was fond of hotel restaurants. She smiled to herself at the idea of going back to Porto's that night and being served by the same waiter. Alex would enjoy it, he was a great meat-eater.

At Reception she asked for the key card and went up in the lift. She shook her head. It was the same in every hotel in which they stayed – the chambermaids persisted in closing the windows. She opened theirs as far as it would go and sat on the bed. If Alex had found a cricket match he might want to stay until the end.

Feeling the effects of the wine because she was not used to lunchtime drinking, Kathryn thought a shower might be advisable. Stepping out of her clothes she set the dial on a low number and let the tepid water stream over her, closing her eyes as she shampooed her hair. She did not hear Alex come in and jumped when he spoke to her. He was leaning against the side of the door, eyeing her appreciatively. 'Mind if I join you?'

He unbuckled his belt and took off his jeans, leaving them on the floor, then removed the rest of his clothes.

'I'm glad you're here,' she whispered as he stood under the shower beside her. He kissed her, water running down their faces and into their mouths. Loving Alex, Kathryn had still been attracted to John Atherton – more than attracted. If Alex had shut her out for months on end there was the strong possibility that she wouldn't have refused John's offer of another drink and whatever it might have led to.

Later, wrapped in the hotel's enormous white towels, they lay on the bed and watched the Channel 4 news summary. Alex's hair, untamed even though it was wet, left damp patches on the pillowcase. 'What was he like?' He did not take his eyes from the screen.

Kathryn wondered if she detected a hint of jealousy. She had told him John had bought her lunch. 'Intelligent, witty, charismatic and good-looking, in a raddled sort of way.'

'Hum. Just like me then.'

'Honestly.' She thumped him on the chest with her pillow.

'Come on, we'd better get dressed if you require feeding again.'

Kathryn put on one of the dresses she had hung neatly in the wardrobe. It was sleeveless, with a boat-neck and fitted bodice; the skirt flared out from the hips and ended at knee level. Against her faint tan and the darkness of her hair and eyes, the canary yellow was perfect.

'You look lovely,' Alex told her a little sadly, knowing what he had almost lost. 'Here, I think these will go with it.' He handed her a small paper bag decorated with flowers. Inside was a string of amber beads which changed colour with the light.

'Thank you.' Kathryn put them on, tears pricking at his thoughtfulness. She was not completely over Rebecca and there were times when she did not know whether she was nearer to laughing or crying. They were both, she realised, still a little unstable emotionally.

In the street he took her hand and squeezed it but did not relinquish it as they walked towards the city centre.

That night a dream woke her. She was sweating, it had seemed so real. Six faceless people were chasing her, coming at her from different directions. She had hidden in an alley, her heart racing. But she was confused because in *her* hand was a gun and her pursuers were unarmed.

Quietly getting out of bed to splash her face with cold water in the bathroom, she realised the significance of the dream. Alex was right, she may well have placed herself in danger by getting too close to the past, but the reverse was also true. John Atherton had given her the ammunition and Kathryn, metaphorically, was holding a gun to their heads. Scared she might be, but she would not lower the barrel until she found out exactly what had happened all those years ago.

David had begun what he jokingly called his 'rehabilitation programme'. From now on he would have a drink once a week in the pub around the corner from his flat. That way he would probably meet some of his neighbours and eventually become known as a local. Initially he was greeted with a nod and found himself inordinately pleased when, one weekday evening, the landlord picked up a glass and drew a pint of the bitter he drank without waiting to be asked. One by one the other regulars began to greet him and finally engaged him in conversation. None of it was as arduous as he had imagined.

Having discussed the latest cricket results with a man he now knew as Richard, David went home to feed both Kitty and himself. Kitty performed her usual slalom between his legs as soon as he opened the door. The light on the answering machine glowed red in the dusk but the green light which flashed when there were any messages was still. It was a sad reflection that he received so few personal calls. Even his mother had not contacted him since his refusal to go down for the weekend. But he was optimistic because he knew he had already made progress. It was a gratifying feeling to be part of the crowd in the Montgomery Arms, and it was so different from his acceptance into the Oxford crowd. In the pub he felt he had been received because he was one of them, a local, an ordinary man who liked a beer after work. At Oxford it had more to do with elitism. He was sure John knew about the brilliant results he, David, had achieved at school and the predictions for his future – and that was why he had been included.

He put the other half of the casserole he had made the previous night in the oven and opened the evening paper, wondering whether he would receive any response to his advertisement. After he had eaten he checked over a first edition he had ordered on behalf of Mrs Bradden, one of his most profitable customers and, satisfied it would meet her requirements, went to bed.

Mrs Bradden did not arrive at the shop until after five the next day, and he wondered whether she had changed her mind. He was in the process of pointing out the book's merits when the telephone rang. David swore silently. Mrs Bradden might be a good client but she was pernickety and demanding, and they usually had to go through the pretence of his persuading her to buy something which he knew she was desperate to acquire. This was one transaction he did not want to mess up. 'Excuse me for just one minute,' he said with his most winning smile.

He pushed his glasses up his nose and picked up the receiver. 'Yes. Yes. Really? Uh, that'll be fine. Goodbye.' David scribbled on a piece of paper and hung up. The call was baffling but he would think about it later. Mrs Bradden was fidgeting and glancing pointedly at her watch.

'I'm so sorry. Now, what do you think? You have to agree it's in excellent condition considering the age of the volume.' She warranted his best sales pitch. The book was in good, rather than excellent condition, but it no longer mattered. Mrs Bradden was unclasping her ostentatious leather bag and searching for her chequebook. The cheque safely in the till, David parcelled the book up with care and handed it to her once he had escorted her to the door. Two students were still browsing through the second-hand Penguin classics so he made no rush to close the shop. They might not buy anything today, but they were possible future clients.

The following morning he received two answers to his advertisement and made arrangements for interviews the following week. Meanwhile there was Friday to think about.

Saturday morning would have been more convenient for Kathryn as Alex had to be at the boat-yard but she understood that it would be one of David Shawcross's busiest times. She had spent the whole day in the office, including her lunch-hour because Dave was away and she was covering his work along with Keith. She had also wanted to go over all that John Atherton had told her, to have it absolutely clear in her mind before she confronted David. They had agreed to meet at six-thirty in the Regent Palace although he had sounded abstracted at the time. She hoped he would not forget but did not want to make a nuisance of herself by telephoning again.

Kathryn had decided to take the car home then catch a train from Burnham. There was no point in driving up the M4 in rush-hour traffic and then having nowhere to park when she arrived.

She said goodnight to Keith, picked up her bag and her jacket and skipped down the stairs. The air was cooler than it had been the previous few days and she shivered. Crossing the car park, she had a sudden feeling that she was being watched. She looked up to the window of the office she shared but no one was staring out. Goose-flesh stood up on her arms and she knew it was not solely to do with the weather. Hurrying towards the car she got in and, feeling rather foolish, depressed the button that locked all four doors.

Leaving the car outside the flats she walked to the station, having already checked the train times. There were several people on the platform, but had she been followed there was no way in which they could have got there before her or known her destination. She stood close to two middle-aged females although she no longer felt in any danger.

By the time she reached Paddington and was fighting her way to the tube station with the other commuters she had forgotten all about the strange feeling.

Piccadilly Circus was as crowded as ever. Tourists milled around and blocked the pavements as they studied street maps, and others, in a hurry to get home, pushed past rudely. Having stepped into the daylight after the tenebrous netherworld of the Underground, Kathryn was temporarily disorientated and realised she had taken the wrong exit. She knew from experience that standing in the middle of the pavement at that time of the evening was not a good idea. The traffic was at a standstill so she crossed the road between two taxis. As much as John Atherton's admission had surprised her, she had not allowed it to interfere with work and had so far only given Alex the bare bones of the story.

211

In the foyer of the Regent Palace Hotel was a man who could be no other than David Shawcross, but she did not know why she was so certain. Perhaps the way in which both Harriet Milton and Michael Jarvis had written him off had something to do with it. Amongst the smartly dressed businessmen and women and the guests he stood out considerably. He was studying souvenirs in a glass-fronted case, his back to the entrance, but she could see his reflection. She approached slowly, giving herself time to take in the sloping shoulders which did not quite fill his jacket, the thinning hair which needed cutting and the wistful expression on his face.

'David Shawcross?'

He turned and frowned and adjusted his glasses, then offered his hand. His skin was sallow but his eyes looked healthy enough.

'Mrs Brooks. I thought it was you.'

His palm was damp and Kathryn resisted the temptation to wipe her hand down the side of her skirt. 'Did you?'

He nodded towards the showcase. 'I saw you come in.'

She smiled. So they had been assessing each other.

'We can't very well talk here. Would you like a drink, or coffee? We can get either.'

'I think I'd prefer a drink. It's Friday night, after all.'

'Yes.' The faint humour was lost on him. He led the way into the bar with a frown on his face. David ordered dry white wine for Kathryn and a bottle of light ale for himself which he carried to a table away from the bar where conversation could be conducted in relative privacy.

'I hope you didn't think me abrupt on the telephone. I was in the middle of dealing with one of my best customers. You said you wanted to ask me some questions about my career. Does your paper cover rare books?'

'No.' Kathryn paused. Like John, David seemed not to have understood the contents of their brief telephone conversation. 'It's more to do with how your life has been affected by your Oxford days – more of a personal thing really.'

'I don't understand.' Apart from his trip to India and a

broken engagement David believed he had led a dull life. Unless she was referring to Sarah's murder ...

David Shawcross struck Kathryn as a man consumed with insecurities and anxiety. He was so very different from Giles and John. His body language confirmed his tension; he seemed unable to get comfortable in his seat and he worried away at the skin around his nails.

'I'm interested in a group of people with whom you were at university,' she explained. 'I've already spoken to John Atherton and Giles Harris.' She had plunged straight in and noticed how his skin had paled to an ashen grey. She decided a gentler approach would be more appropriate and told him how she had been trying to discover the true identity of whoever wrote the Megan Morris novels. Talking about books might help put him at ease.

'My business mainly concerns rare and ancient books, Mrs Brooks,' he said finally. 'I have read Miss Morris and greatly admire her work, but I don't stock bestsellers, and if you've come to me because you thought I could help you then I'm sorry, because I can't.' This time he pushed his glasses into position firmly, having surprised himself by his bluntness and his refusal to fear this young journalist.

'Yes, I understand that. But there's more. Both Mr Atherton and Mr Harris have given me their version of what happened on the night that Sarah Milton disappeared. Would you be prepared to give me yours?'

David swallowed noisily. So this was it. Just as soon as he'd decided to wipe out the past and get on with his life, someone came along to resurrect it. He fought down the urge to simply get up and walk out. What puzzled him was why someone from a local newspaper had any interest in Sarah's murder when the nationals had forgotten it years ago.

'I know about the game,' Kathryn prompted quickly.

'Then you probably know as much as I do.'

Kathryn thought he was lying – that David Shawcross, of all of them, knew the most. Perhaps they had all been in it together. What better reason for them continuing to back each other up by sticking to the same story? Acting under the influence of drink and whatever else they had been on, perhaps John wasn't far wrong when he said the game had got out of control. Five of them would have had no difficulty in removing a body and hiding it until any likely search was over. Yet assessing the man opposite her, Kathryn found it hard to imagine that he would have been able to live with the guilt. 'Please, Mr Shawcross, this is very important to me. Isn't there anything you can remember about that night?'

'No. Only seeing her with blood on her dress. Mrs Brooks, I'm sorry, but I really don't wish to discuss this subject further.' David saw he might have fallen into a trap. Kathryn Brooks needn't have known anything about that part; she had only mentioned the game. Then she asked about the knife and he felt safer. John would have told her; John would have given her some story which exonerated them all. 'We didn't know how it got there. None of us had brought it with us. It was never found afterwards, you know.'

Kathryn didn't know. It was one more piece of information to add to her file.

'I'm prepared to buy you one more drink, Mrs Brooks, then I really must go. I hope you didn't come to London specifically to see me, because there is nothing more I can add.' He stood and took their empty glasses up to the bar.

Kathryn knew it was useless to persist. If David Shawcross was not prepared to go as far as first-name terms, he was certainly not going to tell her anything more about that fateful night. She would have the second drink. There was no rush; Alex was not expecting her back until late.

Only when she was on the train going home did Kathryn realise how accurate her assumption must be. If Megan Morris was adamant that she did not wish her identity to be known, she would only entrust her manuscript to someone she knew could keep a secret – someone, for example, who had already proved they were able to do so ... Surely this meant that whoever Megan Morris was, she too had been there the night that Sarah disappeared. Could that someone, so filled with restlessness and tension, be David Shawcross?

Kathryn's last question had been to ask if he had any idea where Laura Tennyson was living. At this he looked genuinely surprised. 'As far as I know, she left London years ago,' he told her. And Kathryn believed him, for the simple reason that he had admitted that at one time he had known where she was.

David watched her leave, relieved that the ordeal was over and that he had managed not to say anything she might misconstrue. He had never met a woman like her before and he doubted that she would be satisfied until she got to the bottom of things. But what then?

He shook his head. She was a reporter, not a police-woman, and the police had not been very successful all those years ago. Still, it bothered him. He had been right; he knew that once John was on the scene, things would start to happen. The question was, what could he do about it? Kill her? He smiled to himself. Why not?

Remaining in his seat he realised that prison held no real fears for him. He was sure it would be worse than he imagined it to be, but it did not terrify him the way it once had. And there would be books; there always was a library. It was a tempting thought, if only to hit back at his parents. His mother would never live it down!

He knew he must think things through seriously, that danger lay ahead, but he partly blamed himself. He should never have agreed to meet John, and he should have refused Kathryn Brooks an interview. Suddenly he had a desire to be safely at home with Kitty.

His block of flats was built of red brick and back in the 1920s and 1930s had housed married couples or single people who could afford a live-in servant and probably other daily help. David liked to think that he was carrying on the tradition, although not in quite the same style. He had purchased the flat outright, at a time when they were difficult to sell because they were unsuitable for families, there being no lift or garden, and all the rooms above ground level had long windows which opened inwards with only a low iron railing to prevent the occupants from toppling to the pavement. None of them had central heating and his had been badly in need of decoration – work which he had carried out before he moved in. It had not been touched since.

215

David stopped on his way home to buy six tins of cat food from a mini-market, not caring that he was paying extra for the privilege of shopping after eight o'clock in the centre of London. To erase the encounter with Mrs Brooks he calculated the difference between what he had paid and what he usually paid. It didn't matter, he could afford it and Kitty was worth every penny. He had nothing else to spend his money on.

In retrospect, David saw that he could have been more generous with Nicola. He felt ashamed. They had continued to live like students, buying alternate rounds and sharing the cost of meals even though he was earning more than her at the time. In his favour he had little experience of women and Nicola had never complained. His presents, he realised now, had always been practical rather than luxuries. Would she have stayed if he had showered her with perfume and jewellery or items from the Ann Summers shop he passed every evening on his way home? He frequently saw men enter it and wondered how they had the nerve. Of course, he knew his relationship with Nicola had become habit and that neither of them had progressed as far as suggesting a date for the wedding, presumably because they both realised they had not really wanted marriage. If he did find someone else he would treat her very differently.

Although these thoughts were uppermost he was still thinking about Kathryn and what could be done about her. Was John in league with her? Was that his reason for coming to London, to prepare them for another of his games? If so, then David acknowledged that he was ready to join in.

Focusing only on the music, letting it flood her mind until there was no room for Kathryn Brooks or her own *alter ego*, Megan Morris, Laura began to enjoy the concert. Now and then she glanced at Marcia who, quite rightly, had said that it did not matter where they were seated as long as they could hear. Her eyes were closed and she might have been sleeping except she sensed Laura's eyes upon her and turned her head and smiled.

Laura experienced a tender sadness. In the dimmed lights of the auditorium she noticed the relaxed muscles of

Marcia's face. They gave an indication of how she would look as an old woman. Laura, approaching her fortieth birthday, did not consider sixty-one to be old.

They did not delay after the concert but made their way to the tube station, Laura hurrying to keep up with her mother's brisk walk. There was a train leaving almost immediately which they caught with seconds to spare. At Maidenhead station Laura suggested a taxi; there was a whole rank of them queued up.

'Good gracious, it's a twenty-minute walk at most, girl. It'll do us good. We've been sitting all evening.'

There was a dampness in the air and veils of mist swirled under the streetlights. The moon, which was almost full, was obscured by cloud cover but it wasn't cold.

They waited at the pedestrian crossing where the lights had never been synchronised with the ones which controlled the traffic. Marcia, who was always hungry, heard her stomach growl as a mixture of Indian food and kebabs assailed her nostrils, but there was a cold supper waiting which Laura had prepared earlier.

The porch-light was on and the one in the hall which was set on a timer. Neither woman worried about the lateness of the hour. Marcia needed little sleep and Laura could work the hours that suited her. Apart from which, Marcia had insisted she take the week as a holiday. It was doing her good.

Similar in so many ways, they felt no need to discuss the concert. They both preferred to simply listen to and absorb the music and remember its effect without need of criticism or a dissection of individual players' performances.

'Do you need the fire on?'

'No, darling, I'm quite warm enough. I'll get the tray, shall I?'

'Thank you. I take it you'd prefer whisky to coffee?'

'Indeed I would.' Marcia placed the tray on a small table between them and helped herself to ham and pickles before spreading butter on the baguette she had halved. Her appetite always astonished Laura until she thought about how far she walked.

Marcia was thoughtful as she ate. She sometimes forgot

217

that Laura had not always been a writer; it was only ten or eleven years since she had had her first novel published. She could not recall her ever having expressed a wish to be an author, but maybe it was something she had felt shy about. Brief flirtations in the business world had not suited her but Marcia had had to let her find out for herself; however she had quite enjoyed her stint in publishing – a job, Marcia suspected, that Giles had had a hand in procuring. Maybe Laura's divorce had been the catalyst, because it was a little after it that her first book had appeared on the shelves and was receiving critical acclaim. She was so proud of her.

'Tell me.' Marcia licked some pickle from her thumb. 'What got you started?'

Laura stared at her blankly.

'What you were telling me the other day – about the manuscript. How on earth did you know you could do it?'

'I didn't. It was a chance I had to take.'

'In more ways than one, Laura. Still, it paid off.'

Laura put down her plate, her food hardly touched. 'I'll be back in a minute. Help yourself to some more.'

It had not been one of Peggy's days but the attic stairs were folded into the ceiling. Laura pulled them down with the hook which she must remember to put in the shed in the morning. There were no blinds or curtains and she caught a glimpse of her reflection in the blank panes of glass. 'I look like any other woman,' she said, too modest to realise she was far more attractive than most. 'Whoever would believe it?' Then, 'Oh, for Christ's sake, woman!' She picked up the completed draft of her manuscript and carried it downstairs.

'Would you read this for me?' She placed the pages next to Marcia on the settee.

Her mother frowned. 'Are you sure?'

'Yes. I want your opinion, and I need to know what you think of the ending.'

Marcia picked up the manuscript, surprised at its heaviness and felt unusually sad. She very much wanted to read it because she wasn't certain that she would still be around when the book was finally published. She did not look up;

she did not want Laura to see the pain in her eyes – not physical pain, for that was to come – but the pain of being faced with the loss of her daughter. Had Laura guessed? Never before had she been allowed to read anything until it was in print. No. When she did look up, Laura was smiling. 'I'd love to, my darling. Nothing could give me greater pleasure at the moment.' And she meant it, although it was the nearest she came to telling Laura that she had cancer.

They cleared up and stacked the dishwasher then Marcia went up to bed. She was, she said, going to start reading it immediately.

Laura remained in the kitchen for five minutes, wiping surfaces and putting coffee in the machine ready for the morning before going through to the lounge and pouring another small drink. She sat for half an hour not knowing what was wrong, not understanding why she was filled with a dread that had nothing to do with Kathryn Brooks or Sarah Milton.

It was two-thirty before her eyelids began to feel heavy and she took herself upstairs. She listened outside Marcia's door but there was only silence and no light showed beneath it.

In her own room she took off her shoes and had a quick wash and cleaned her teeth in the adjoining bathroom where, thanks to Peggy's efforts, the white tiled walls and chrome accessories gleamed harshly under the lights.

Laura undressed and got into bed between the white cotton sheets she had always used. The floor was thickly carpeted in a shade of fawn which matched the curtains and lampshades. The paintwork was white but there was no suggestion of drabness because the bed was covered with a hand-made patchwork quilt which Marcia had taken eighteen months to complete before presenting it to Laura.

On the walls were several small oils. They had not been chosen because they matched the decor or had any great value, but because Laura liked them. They depicted women from various ages throughout history, including one which was fairly modern, and they all had one thing in common: their faces expressed serenity and hidden strength. In a way, they all reminded her of Marcia.

Dreading another bad night, Laura switched off the bedside lamp and was surprised, when she opened her eyes, to see her mother, fully dressed, standing by the bed with a cup of tea in her hand. 'It's after nine, madam,' she said with mock severity but was pleased to see that Laura looked rested.

Marcia drew the curtains and the room was filled with light. The sun was already high in the sky and reflections from the river rippled across the ceiling. All the uncertainty of the previous night had disappeared.

'Look, I'm having a drink with Anna after work. Shall we make do with a takeaway?'

Alex, his jacket hooked over his shoulder, was just on his way to work. 'Yes, or I could meet you somewhere?'

'No, I don't intend being too late and I could do with an hour or so in the flat. I don't seem to have seen much of it lately.'

'Whatever you say, beautiful.' He kissed the top of her head and went out, swinging his car keys.

Kathryn was about to fill the washing-up bowl then realised there was no need. Mrs Jackson felt insulted if there wasn't enough to do. It was still terribly formal. She insisted upon calling her 'Mrs Brooks' and Kathryn thought she felt happier with some distance between herself and her employers. She had two and had been recommended by the other one, a lady who lived further up the road and with whom Kathryn chatted if they met in the street.

She arrived at the office early, checked her column which she had completed the following day, and when she was satisfied that there were no mistakes or grammatical errors, she left telling Keith she would be back after lunch.

The early morning mist which had lain low over the fields had burned off, but there were still drops of moisture which flashed like diamonds on the grass in the meadows she passed on her way to Cookham. She was going to interview a woman who had recently returned to the village of her birth after many years in an African settlement where she had worked as a doctor. Derek, one of the paper's photographers, had arrived ahead of her and was just leaving. He had, he said, got several good poses of Mary Patterson

220

seated at the table holding a framed photograph of the hospital where she had worked.

Kathryn waved as he got into his car. In itself Mary Patterson's story was interesting, but she had also survived a serious tropical disease for which she was treated in her own hospital, and an attempt on her life by some renegade natives. Kathryn had timed the interview to last approximately an hour.

Mary Patterson was charming and modest and seemed to find it odd that anyone would be interested in her story. 'Hundreds of people do the same thing, and some in far worse conditions than I was fortunate enough to experience.' She produced some photographs of the bungalow-style buildings of the hospital, some with beds on the verandahs. Others were of staff on her team or the smiling black faces of patients she had treated. 'We could only push the beds out in the cooler season,' she explained. 'Now, I'm sure I've been rambling too long. Please don't let me detain you.'

The interview had given Kathryn a fascinating insight into the woman's character as well as some good copy. Mary Patterson had worn well, or perhaps her looks were a result of living a good life and putting others first. Her skin was flawless and hardly touched by the harsh African sun. Her almost-white hair was cropped short but thick and healthy-looking. She said she was going to grow it a little longer now.

Kathryn had suggested she wrote about her experiences. 'It would make a terrific autobiography,' she said.

'No. All I want to do now is rest and to appreciate my own country for the time I have left. But, my God, I'm going to miss Africa.' She brushed away a tear.

Kathryn put her notepad aside and glanced at her watch. 'I don't have to be back in the office until two. I can give you a lift, if you like?' Mary Patterson had said there were things she wanted to do in Maidenhead. She hadn't got around to buying a second-hand car yet, but there was an hourly train service.

'How very kind. Thank you.' She reached beneath her chair and picked up a raffia handbag. 'All right, dear, I'm ready if you are.'

Kathryn smiled at the simplicity of her preparations but Mary was used to an uncomplicated, albeit hard-working, life.

The sun was directly overhead and glinted off the bonnet of the car as Kathryn eased her way through the congestion of Cookham High Street. Vehicles lined one side of the road where parking was permitted but others were left randomly on the double lines. A brewery lorry, delivering to one of the pubs, added to the confusion and it was some time before traffic in the opposite direction gave way to allow her through. At the junction of the Bourne End road she had a further wait until it was safe to pull out. It was somewhere to be avoided in the height of summer. Customers from the pubs would overflow onto the pavements, and the grass in front of the Crown would be heaving with bodies in various states of undress.

Mary Patterson did not speak as Kathryn negotiated the tricky right turn. Further along the road cows had strayed into the swampy fields and stood hoof-deep in water, flicking their tails and gazing mournfully at the passing cars. Only when a motorbike roared dangerously past did they panic and lumber further away from the fence.

'I'm finding it difficult to adjust to the smallness of everything,' her passenger commented. 'And to so many people and so many shops. But more than anything it's the colours. Everything seems so fresh and light compared with what I was used to.'

Kathryn was only half-listening. She had already guessed that Miss Patterson would have a lot to come to terms with. They were alongside the river, heading towards Maidenhead Bridge when a car coming from the opposite direction indicated left and slowed. The only reason that Kathryn noticed this was because there *was* no immediate side turning. Veering slightly and causing Miss Patterson to give her a quick sideways look, Kathryn took a deep breath and concentrated on her driving. There were two women in the car which had turned into one of the houses. She had recognised one of them.

Had Dr Patterson not lived in Cookham itself, but further up in Cookham Rise or Cookham Dean, Kathryn would have taken a different route into Maidenhead, via the wider Switchback Road. 'Pardon?'

'Are you all right, dear? I said you can drop me anywhere you like.'

'You mentioned you wanted the Town Hall – well, I've just remembered I have to go to the library. I can take you all the way.' As she turned into St Ives Road, a car pulled out from one of the restricted parking places. Fate was on her side. She reversed neatly into it and said goodbye to Mary Patterson, who thanked her and hurried across the road to attend to her business.

The library was built of red brick and beneath the modern roof were exposed metal tubes like scaffolding which gave it an unfinished appearance. Kathryn wasn't sure whether they were supposed to be decorative or an essential part of the construction. In the coolness of the interior she hurried towards where she knew she would find the Register of Electors. This time she had the name of the road but not the number. It would take only minutes to run down the list to see if there really was a Jenny Branagh.

She could hardly bear to open the booklet. The woman, whoever she was, might have been giving her passenger a lift home or they could have been visiting someone. Yet she had taken the awkward turn with the ease of long practice, swinging the car out to the necessary angle. Her hands were damp and she felt her heart hammering with excitement. She ran her finger down the list. 'Oh, Jesus!' She was unable to prevent the exclamation and ignored the disdainful glance of a woman seated nearby. She stared at the name, afraid that she had misread it or that it would disappear off the page. There it was in black and white. Not Jennifer Branagh but *Laura Tennyson*.

She was shaking so much that when she pulled out in her car, she slipped the clutch. The last thing she felt like doing was returning to the office but there were deadlines to meet. It was a sparse week for news, so the Patterson story would probably be required.

Lunch forgotten, Kathryn survived the afternoon on black coffee and adrenalin. The day finally came to an end.

223

She slung her bag over her shoulder then stood beside her desk, her head in her hand. 'Damn.'

Keith, in typical pose, was leaning, buttocks against his desk, his legs stretched out in front of him for everyone to trip over. 'You have a problem?'

'Mind your own business,' Kathryn told him. She had just remembered she was meeting Anna. All she wanted to do was to go home and plan her next move. Twice, recently, she had let her friend down at the last moment and she did not intend doing so again. But there was so much to think about; David Shawcross and now this. Oh well, it would have to keep.

The two women hadn't seen each other for a while so there was a lot of news to catch up on. Kathryn mentioned her trip to Witney but said nothing about Megan Morris or the Oxford students. She did not dare. If she started on that she would bore Anna to death. Knowing they would be having a few drinks she had left the car at the office and intended to get a taxi home. She was relieved when Anna said she couldn't stay long. Kathryn telephoned her order through to the Indian restaurant from the pub. She knew Alex's preferences, although he wasn't fussy. Then she ordered a taxi to take her there to collect it and then to continue to Burnham. She promised Anna she wouldn't leave it so long next time.

Alex had the radio on but did not seem to be listening as he was studying some designs which he had laid out on the floor. 'Enjoy yourself?' He raised an eyebrow. 'I think you did.' She was aglow and he thought she might not be entirely sober. 'You'd better let me see to that.' He took the brown paper carrier out to the kitchen. There was an ominous yellow stain on the side but the smell of chicken dansak was mouthwatering.

Later, in bed, Kathryn's hand moved slowly across Alex's chest, massaging the firm flesh. The hair beneath her fingers was strong and wiry. She slid her hand lower, caressing his thighs until he pulled her to him. It was only the second time she had initiated sex since Rebecca and she suddenly thought it was as well that Alex did not connect the two occasions. The first time was in Cardiff, when she had learned about the game and the people involved, and today she had found Laura Tennyson.

John was seriously considering remedying his drinking habits although he refused to accept he had a problem. He rationalised his delay in making a start by telling himself he was always sober on university premises and it was not affecting his work. Both observations were true. He also considered he must have the constitution of an ox because, outwardly, his health did not seem to be affected either. Deep down he knew the main reason for his procrastination was because he enjoyed it. There was nothing like the buzz which came after a day's work when he sank the first couple of drinks, then the pleasant, relaxed state when his mind felt sharper than ever after five or six. He tried to leave it there but was mostly unsuccessful. At least he was guaranteed a good night's sleep.

Intellectually he recognised his weakness but could not envisage a life in which alcohol was absent; a life of work and meals and the television or a book and the occasional trip to the theatre. And if he stopped drinking, he might find himself left with the real John Atherton. 'Come on – admit it,' he told his foam-covered face as he gingerly shaved, the morning after a particularly heavy session. 'Anyone who had to live with me would be driven to drink.'

To distract himself he thought about the smooth roundness of Kathryn Brooks's limbs as he strolled through the sunlit city streets to his first lecture. There was no sign of over-indulgence there, not with her bright eyes and that gleaming hair, and none of the tell-tale red veins which heightened his own complexion. He was in possession of her business card which she had handed him after he had paid the bill but, tempting as it was to ring her, he knew there was little chance of a tumble with her.

He had no regrets about confiding in her because there was nothing her paper would dare print without the headache of possible litigation, and he had known from the start that she would not go to the police. Whatever she was after, she wanted to find it alone. She was, he thought, a kindred spirit. Shame there was a Mr Brooks.

It was possible that she might even let the matter drop. David would say little, if anything, and it might be that she really meant it when she said that she merely wanted to find Megan Morris. That was a non-starter, of course; there was no way Giles would allow *that* to happen.

For once he was early and found he had half an hour until his students would begin to arrive. As a sop to his conscience, John bought himself a proper breakfast and ate it all. He did not intend letting Giles know that Kathryn had been to see him, nor would he inform David. They could, he thought, stew.

Later, his thoughts still on Kathryn, he picked up a woman in the second bar he went into. She was good fun. They shared a few drinks and she told him she was thirty-five and divorced. In the murky light of the pub she was not bad-looking. He took her home to bed.

There were no formalities. Before she had time to admire the spacious hallway, he took her by the hand and led her up the ornate staircase where mutual need or alcoholic disinhibition took over. With the curtains still open they coupled like animals in the jaundiced glow of the streetlights.

In the morning John surveyed the sleeping head on the pillow beside him. Daylight and sobriety suggested that the woman had under-estimated her age by about ten years. He made them both coffee but avoided conversation and the question of them meeting again, then he ordered her a taxi and gave her the fare, which she did not refuse.

She left without once meeting his eyes, leaving John aware that she had no desire to see him again either, and that she could probably not even recall her fleeting partner's name.

Alex had taken a rare couple of days off to escort some clients to Lords. It was an outing he organised every year. Kathryn did not expect him home until late on either night and he would have eaten. There would have been lunch and tea, and when the light faded and play was stopped for the day, they retired to a restaurant where Alex had booked a table. A mini-bus was arranged to take them and to bring them home.

The flat was stuffy when she got in from work, and a bluebottle buzzed against a pane of glass. She let it out then opened the other windows. It was too soon to eat; she always needed an hour or so to unwind first. 'White wine do you think, handsome?' She patted the tuatara. It had become a symbol of luck.

She sipped a glass of chilled Australian white as she prepared a salad. Feeling lazy she had bought a piece of cooked chicken to go with it. Mrs Jackson had made such a difference to her life. It was bliss to come home to a spotless flat and to find the ironing done.

Leaving the salad on the kitchen table she took her drink through to the lounge and opened the file. Details were building up. She read through everything again. David had been right – the knife had never been found.

Her dilemma now was how to approach Laura Tennyson. Having met her once she would know that Kathryn had gone out of her way to find her, but the element of surprise might be best. There was a shirt Alex wanted changing because it was a half-size too small. She would offer to do it on Saturday morning and call at the house in Ray Mead Road at the same time.

Marcia was back in Shropshire and telephoned to say she had arrived safely. She felt cowardly for not having confided in Laura, but the more worry she could protect her from, the better. She would have to know at some point, but later, when she became obviously ill.

After a week Laura had become used to having her mother around the house, and was at a loss for the following twenty-four hours, but it was time to get back to work and she was looking forward to it. The break had done her good. Revitalised, she decided to spend the day reading the finished manuscript and correcting any errors. Marcia had told her it was the best yet, and Laura knew she would not dish out empty compliments.

Carrying a mug of coffee she was halfway up the stairs to the first floor when the door-knocker rapped sharply. She jumped. The postman had already been but she was expecting some unusual plants she had ordered from a magazine. If it was them it would give her something to do tomorrow afternoon. She did not write on Sundays.

She turned around, trying not to spill the coffee, and opened the door. 'Oh my God!' As her hand shook the coffee did spill, splashing over the rim of the mug onto her jeans and the hall floor.

The two women stared at one another speechlessly. Kathryn saw that Laura was shaking, but not as much as she was herself. Of all the unacceptable excuses Kathryn could come up with, she had whittled it down to one. The paper was running a series about riverside homes, but it was not her feature and the ones they were using were further along the river where the rich and famous lived. They had gardens with landing-stages and diversified between the sumptuous and the tasteless. Seeing Laura's expression she knew it was too feeble an excuse for appearing on her doorstep; it would not be believed.

She took a deep breath but it was Laura who broke the silence. 'I think you'd better come in, Mrs Brooks.'

Kathryn followed her out to the kitchen. The whole of their flat, she thought, would almost fit into it. It was a lovely house. She sat down without waiting to be asked because her legs felt as if they might give way. It was too much to hope that she had finally stumbled on one of the best-kept secrets, and all the way over she had convinced herself that Laura Tennyson would not be at home.

Laura was pouring coffee. Kathryn noticed that her hostess was as elegant as her surroundings. She may have been wearing jeans but they fitted perfectly and were flattering, and the short-sleeved top was pure silk. Today her hair was tied back in a scarf which matched the shirt.

A mug of coffee was placed in front of Kathryn and, silently, milk and sugar were put within reach. 'How did you find me?' Laura asked in a quiet voice, thinking how stupid she had been to have turned up that day. How idiotic to think that, having once shown her face they would not, at some point, run into one another again.

As if to prove her right, Kathryn said, 'You might not believe me, but it was pure chance. I saw you pulling into your drive. I . . .' The words trailed off. How did you find me? Laura had asked. Was that an admission that she was Megan Morris? Before she was thrown out, Kathryn had to make sure. As with John, she felt drawn towards Laura in a way she could not define. She sensed her strengths but also a degree of unhappiness. Kathryn hesitated. The wedding ring was still in place. Had she made a dreadful mistake, or had Laura retained her maiden name after marriage? 'Miss Tennyson, are you Megan Morris?'

'Kathryn – may I call you Kathryn?' The full-lipped mouth was smiling and there was a light in her eyes which had not been there seconds ago. 'Before you ask me all the many things you obviously want to know, I must tell you something. Megan Morris is dead. She died in 1985.'

Kathryn felt her jaw drop. It was impossible yet it answered so many questions. Miss Morris had written a number of books which had not been published until after her death, but as a selling point Giles Harris had made a mystery of her identity. The royalties presumably went to her family who were happy enough to go along with the myth. In which case, how many more novels were there and what would happen when the source ran out? 1985. That was the same year Sarah Milton's body was found. But Sarah could not have been the author; she had already been dead for six years and her life had been too short to complete so many books. Unless, of course, it wasn't Sarah they found . . . It was so confusing. She shook her head.

'Yes, I thought that would surprise you.'

'Miss Tennyson, would you be prepared to tell me what you know about Megan Morris?'

Laura lit a cigarette and got up to take a deep crystal ashtray from the work surface behind her. 'I think you'd better call me Laura. And yes, I also think I might as well because I'm sure you'll find out for yourself and I would prefer you heard the true version.'

Kathryn's notebook remained in her bag. She knew there was no chance of her forgetting a single word Laura Tennyson said.

By the time she left, the coffee pot was empty, the ashtray was full and Alex's shirt had been completely forgotten.

Chapter 11

In London and the Home Counties, the temperature
increased with each passing day. Already the grass was
yellowing in suburban gardens and there was talk of a hose-
pipe ban. The metal of cars glinted cruelly and blindingly
and heat rose from the pavements in waves.

London was unbearable. The noise and the heat frayed
tempers, but worse was the dirt and the smells. The slightest
draught disturbed the dry grit which lay in the streets. It
stuck to perspiring skin and was blown into unsuspecting
eyes by the rush of air from passing traffic. At the end of
each day David needed to shower and change his clothes
again. Diesel fumes, plus the stench of fried food and stale
drains seemed to cling to him and seep into his skin. To
open the door of his flat was a welcome relief. It was shaded
by other buildings which made it dingy in winter, but the
coolness was bliss at this time of year.

He had bought a fan for the shop but it only seemed to
circulate the dusty stale air. He had a sudden, unusual desire
to get away from it all, to go to the Highlands or somewhere
where there was only open countryside and cool streams.

He had interviewed two females that day. His advertisement had stated that no experience was necessary and no
knowledge of the book trade required, which he considered
to be fair because he was not offering an enormous salary
and the job had no prospects.

The first applicant was a middle-aged woman in a sensible
grey skirt and a white blouse who did not seem to be
affected by the heat. She wore her glasses on a chain around

her neck and they rested on her ample bosom. All these things reminded David of his mother so he gently turned her down, kindly adding that he was certain she could do much better for herself than work in his shop.

The second candidate was young, no more than twenty, and her name was Polly. She was a confident girl and studied him knowingly from slightly smudged charcoal-ringed eyes. Her pink lips glistened and her bouncy yellowish hair was hoisted on the top of her head in a towelling band. David took her on. He doubted if she would stay long but she seemed bright enough to be able to chat to customers.

In the morning David left the flat early. It meant he would not be too hot by the time he reached the shop and he wanted to make sure he had enough tea and milk for both of them.

Polly turned up in jeans. It was not a good start. David adjusted his glasses prior to telling her he did not think her attire suitable but Polly forestalled him. 'I wouldn't normally,' she said, catching the direction of his glance, 'but I didn't want to wear a skirt until I've cleaned the place up a bit. There's dust everywhere.' She ran a finger along the ledge of a shelf to prove her point.

David was taken aback. She must have been assessing the shop and himself yesterday without his noticing. He wasn't sure he was comfortable with the way she eyed him from beneath her mascara-ed lashes. One thing was certain, she wasn't going to be allowed to touch the expensive stock or interfere with his cataloguing system! He started by showing her where the tea things and the toilet were, saying he hoped she didn't mind that they had to share it. 'I've got two brothers,' was her only comment.

When she had volunteered to make the tea he explained how the till worked and left her to look around and familiarise herself with the books. He checked the necessary documentation she had brought with her and it all seemed in order.

'Why do you need an assistant?' she asked, perched on the side of his desk.

'I thought I might go out sometimes. It gets a bit much, being in here all day long.'

This explanation seemed to satisfy her although David had no idea where he might take himself.

Two weeks passed and Polly settled in. She showed no signs of dissatisfaction and he became used to her presence and her ceaseless chattering. By then he trusted her enough to leave her for an hour.

'I sold two books,' she told him excitedly when he returned from a pointless stroll along the Embankment. 'Look!' Proudly she showed him the note she had made of their titles for the sake of re-ordering and he was amazed to see that she had spelled Solzhenitsyn correctly, although she had probably had the sense to copy it from the cover of the book. Her handwriting was large and childlike.

'Well done.'

Beaming, she went off to make some tea by way of celebration.

David had come to the conclusion that he did not know how to use his spare time, but Polly had become part of the furniture and he would miss her if she was no longer there. He supposed he must be benefiting from the walks he felt obliged to take to explain her presence, and his skin was no longer sallow thanks to the fresh air.

One baking afternoon when London seemed to be taking a siesta, he returned to the shop to find Polly balanced on the mobile steps. He caught his breath when he saw the piles of books on the floor.

'Don't.' Polly held up an admonishing hand as he bent down. 'Don't touch them. And don't worry. They're all in the order I took them down. If you want, you can pass them up to me. Those on the right first.' She draped a duster over her shoulder and methodically replaced the stock.

Later, as he turned the sign on the door to Closed and watched Polly as she bounced down the road, he decided she was good for him. Her tales of her numerous friends and family members fascinated him and he began to feel he really was part of the human race.

Polly possessed South London vowels and a part-share of a flat in the Elephant and Castle but, he was sure, no boyfriend or surely she would have mentioned him. David was not remotely interested in her sexually himself but he was curious why such a lively, pretty girl was on her own.

Despite his misgivings the shop was now considerably cleaner because Polly did not hold any grandiose ideas as far as her job description went. 'Yes, I love it,' she had said, sounding surprised when he asked her if she liked the work. This had followed an occasion when he was in the back room attending to some paperwork and had overheard an almost verbatim reproduction of his own sales pitch.

He called in to what he now thought of as his local before going home. Polly's wholesome presence had managed to eradicate any lingering worries he had suffered concerning John and Giles and Kathryn Brooks.

The weekend seemed never-ending. It was too hot to work in the garden on Sunday and Laura was too restless to write. It was imperative that she spoke to Giles, but he and Ingrid were away. She tried his home number until 10.45 p.m. then gave up. Neither of them would thank her for being disturbed any later, especially if they had had a long journey.

At nine o'clock on Monday Laura rang the office, only to be told that Giles was not expected in until ten. Having been unable to eat the previous day she felt nauseous and dizzy as the minutes ticked by. Finally, at ten past ten, she got through.

'Laura! Is something the matter?' Her telephone calls to the office were rare even though she had his private number.

'Can you come down here?' Her voice was hardly louder than a whisper.

'Yes, of course. Are you ill?'

'No. But it's urgent.'

'When were you thinking of?'

'Now.'

Giles was startled by the vehemence expressed in the one word. 'Can't it wait? I've got a meeting to attend.'

'No, it can't – not for long anyway. Kathryn Brooks came to see me.'

Laura could picture his face as he took in this news. 'All

right,' he said. 'I'll cancel the meeting and get away as soon as I can.'

Once more Laura prepared herself to wait. Having calculated the shortest possible time it would take him to get here, she knew she had to be active or go mad. At seven-thirty she had rung Peggy and asked if she could come in on Tuesday instead – to which she had agreed. Peggy would be astonished to discover that Laura had done the ironing, but she found it soothing, leaving her mind free to think whilst her hands were occupied.

'Thank goodness you're here,' were her words of greeting. 'Come in.' Laura shut the door quickly behind him and Giles stepped into the coolness of the hall and followed her into the lounge. She immediately poured a drink for each of them and handed one to Giles. 'Don't look at me like that. Take it, you're going to need it.' She lit a cigarette and offered the packet, forgetting in her anxiety that Giles had given up some years ago. 'Before you say anything I want you to know that I now realise you were right, that I should *not* have gone to the Thames Riviera that day. However, the damage is done. Kathryn found me again quite by chance, but I want you to hear what she told me before you make any judgments.'

For almost half an hour Giles listened, taking an occasional sip of his drink. Kathryn Brooks had achieved her aim even if she had gone about it in a peculiar manner. She, too, then, had her suspicions that the dead girl might not be Sarah. If she could prove it, they would all be off the hook. Laura was right, it was probably best not to try to stop the girl now.

'She also knows that we were once married.' Laura waited. 'Aren't you going to say anything?'

'Such as what? It seems that between the pair of you you've done enough talking.'

'It isn't all down to me, Giles. You sent her to Cardiff after John.'

'So what happens now?'

'What do you mean?'

'As far as publicity goes. Mrs Brooks is certainly going

to make a name for herself. She'll certainly get some offers from the nationals now.'

'She promised she would keep my identity a secret.'

'Oh, come off it, Laura – you're not *that* naive!'

'She means it. She has her reasons.' But Laura refused to say what they were. 'In return, I promised her that when this is all over, she will be the one to be credited with the story.'

'So, in one meeting the pair of you are bosom buddies.'

Laura smiled. She had known it would be impossible to convince Giles that it was better this way, that in the end they would all be free. 'Another drink?'

'No, I can't. I drove down.'

Giles looked as though he needed one. He was badly shaken. 'I'm going to. There's more, you see, Giles.'

He groaned and rubbed a hand wearily across his eyes before holding out his glass. 'I'll have to leave the car here, then. Oh, what does it matter? Everyone's going to know who you are soon.'

Laura ignored the comment and sat down opposite him. 'I want to tell you how I started writing, and how the pseudonym came about.' She leaned against the padded back of the chair and crossed her legs. It was a time of confessions; she might as well get it over with in one sitting. 'There's something that only I know. Just after Sarah's body was found, someone came to see me. We were divorced by that time and you'd moved out of our London flat. There was no reason to change the telephone number; it was still listed under Harris and that's how she found me. Or, rather, how she thought she'd found *you*. You were beginning to make a name for yourself at that point and this girl wanted a favour – one, she said, that would guarantee her silence. She told me her name was Megan Morris.'

'*What?*'

Laura nodded. 'I didn't recognise her at first as Jenny Branagh. She was such a mess and she'd aged considerably. Her arms were like matchsticks and she'd cut her hair very short and dyed it brown. I'll explain about her change of name later, Giles. It was you she wanted to speak to, and she wouldn't believe you no longer lived there. I wasn't going to give her your new address or the address of your firm although, looking back, she could have gone through any one of the writers' reference books and found you because you were Editorial Manager at the time and your name would have been listed. Anyway, she said that she was flat broke but that she had written a novel which she wanted you to publish. She handed me what, I suppose, was the prototype for *Remembrance*.'

'My God!' Giles was on his feet. 'Are you telling me you haven't written any of the novels yourself? That they are by some other woman – *Jenny Branagh*?'

'No, of course not.'

Giles sank back into his chair, shaking his head in bewilderment. No, it couldn't have been anyone else. Obviously Laura had written them: her style was unmistakeable.

'I read the manuscript,' she went on. 'It was abysmal but there was a germ of an idea there. I did it to protect you, Giles – you have to believe that. Or perhaps it was for *all* our sakes, really. I rewrote it completely then handed it to you.'

'I still don't understand.'

'It wasn't even plagiarism – it had to be totally reworked. You see, if you didn't publish it she threatened to go to the police and you might have been ruined. If you gave in to her and published it as it was, or with only minor changes, you'd have been a laughing stock. She also told me that Sarah wasn't killed that night but, if necessary, she could provide the police with a story which would prove we were all guilty.'

'And you've known this for eleven years. Why, oh why, didn't you tell me before?'

'At the time I fooled myself into believing that if I managed to get the book published that would be the end of it. It didn't occur to me that blackmailers, once started, are not inclined to stop. Conversely, the worst that can happen is that they'll carry out their threat, and there's nothing to stop them doing so anyway once they've received their payment or whatever. Well, I'd explained she couldn't expect a result overnight, that these things took time, and I convinced her that three to four months was the average

236

time for anything to start happening. I promised I would put her case to you, saying that I was sure you would comply and that I'd let her know how things were to be arranged.'

'You told Kathryn Brooks all this?'

Laura avoided Giles's eye but he did not miss the faint flush rising in her cheeks. 'Yes, but I embellished things a little.'

'Okay. So you say you've written all these books . . . how come she isn't on our backs any more? God, you don't pay her, do you?'

'No. You see, Giles, in the end there was never any need.'

'Are you sure you know what you're doing?'

'I'm positive.' Kathryn was pushing the food around on her plate. Her appetite had almost disappeared. The constant fear with which she was living was draining her. She shook constantly and sleep only came with difficulty. But four other people had lived that way for seventeen years and they had survived. She had to know and she had to find out alone. Alex was right, her mission was becoming an obsession. At times the danger did not seem to matter; it was only when she was at home, when she should have been relaxing that she realised the risks she was taking.

She had found Brian Morris, the husband of Megan, and had taken a day off in order to see him. A day in London in the soaring temperatures was not something she was looking forward to, but she had come so far now that she could not let it go.

Alex had great admiration for what she had already achieved, but he thought it was making her ill. He also knew it might lead to a job on one of the nationals. Five long days had passed since Laura's confession and he would be glad when tomorrow was over. Kathryn seemed to have lost more weight and there was a strange brightness in her eyes as if she was burning inside. Her intensity frightened him. He did not know what was driving her, but then she had not told him everything.

Kathryn seemed not to register his kiss as he left for work the next day. 'Take care,' was all he said. She nodded, but didn't speak.

Once Alex had gone Kathryn made more coffee. It was too early to leave so she got out the folder and read through the notes she had made after she had spoken to Laura. Laura, too, was of the opinion that Sarah Milton might still be alive and that it was not beyond the bounds of possibility that the girl who had turned up at her London flat that day with her tatty manuscript might not have been Jenny, but Sarah herself. People's looks can change over a period of years – especially women's . . . and if Sarah had continued taking drugs her appearance may have altered drastically.

Personally, Kathryn doubted that the mysterious caller was Sarah. Whatever may have become of the girl, however desperate she was, Sarah had been well-educated, had gained a place at Oxford. She would therefore surely have been able to produce something better than Laura had described. Being an Oxford undergraduate did not necessarily give someone the ability to write a novel but Laura had said that there were basic grammatical and spelling errors in the typescript.

Whether it had been Jennifer Branagh or Sarah Milton who had turned up on Giles's former doorstep no longer mattered. Whoever it was, was dead. The rewritten novel had been a success and Laura had decided to stick with the name Megan Morris. Kathryn had finally come to understand the constant fear under which Laura lived. If Sarah *was* still alive she would recognise Laura's name and more problems might ensue. Yet Kathryn felt something was still wrong. If, as John had suggested, Sarah *had* carried out her plan to 'murder' herself, she could not afford to risk turning up because then the tables would be turned. The rest of the group would be in a position to denounce her and to prove their own innocence.

Laura had been open and honest, and seemed relieved to be able to confide in someone, yet she was holding something back – something very important which prevented her from confiding in Kathryn completely. Why else was she still so afraid?

Laura had apparently gone through and revised the manuscript in record time. She told Kathryn she was amazed at her ability to write because it wasn't something she had ever thought of doing. And then, after Giles had accepted *Remembrance*, astonished and delighted by his ex-wife's sheer talent, Laura tried to contact Megan Morris to tell her of this and to get the contract signed.

'At the time I intended telling Giles – then, after I learned she was dead, I simply carried on and wrote the sequel.' Laura had explained that the girl had rung once or twice to enquire what progress was being made and that they had arranged a date to meet. 'I was to go to her flat. When I got there, there was no answer. I was so worried, almost frantic, because I didn't know what the hell was going on. I kept knocking and finally a man living in the room next door came out and told me I was wasting my time, that she had died a fortnight previously. It was a drugs overdose – accidental, I imagine, if she'd gone to so much trouble with the book. Heroin. I didn't believe him; it seemed impossible that it had happened at that time. It sounds so callous, but I wasn't sorry. It meant we were all off the hook again. This man, he could see I didn't believe him. He told me to wait and he went back into his room and finally came out with a copy of the local free paper. There was just a small piece saying she'd been found dead by her ex-husband, Brian Morris. He lived nearby, apparently, and used to go and see her now and then.'

Laura then produced an old photograph from their Oxford days. Sarah Milton and Jennifer Branagh both had long fair hair and were not dissimilar to look at. Was it possible that Laura really didn't know which of them was claiming to be Megan Morris?

If Sarah had succeeded in her plan – if she *had* killed a young pregnant Megan and taken on her identity only to die a heroin addict – it could be argued that justice had been done. Would talking to Brian Morris prove anything, or simply cause him pain? He had agreed readily enough to see her.

At the back of her mind Kathryn kept thinking about Harriet Milton. It was a moral dilemma trying to decide – if Megan Morris *was* Sarah – whether or not to tell her herself, or whether to leave it to Inspector Forbes. She would, of course, have to inform him of the latest developments.

How ironic that Megan Morris should die shortly after the body in the woods had been discovered!

Wearing a loose cotton dress and flat shoes, Kathryn thought she might survive the heat of the city. She pinned her hair into a French pleat so her neck would be cool and set off for the station to catch a Paddington train. Once seated she checked the tube map in the back of her diary and saw that she needed to catch the Circle Line to Liverpool Street then the Central Line to Bethnal Green. It was not an area with which she was familiar, but Brian Morris had given her directions.

He had been relatively easy to track down. Laura had said that at the time of Megan's death he had been living quite close. Kathryn had used the London telephone directories in the office and, with the aid of an A-Z had rung anyone with the name of Morris in the vicinity. It was his mother with whom she first made contact, and she said she would give him the message and get him to call Kathryn back. It was two days before the call was returned and although he had sounded puzzled, Brian said he was willing to talk to her.

Kathryn felt dirty before she had completed half of the journey. Gusts of warm air rushed through the Underground tunnels and the trains were busy. Alighting at last she stepped into the airless streets.

Having learned of the squalid conditions in which Megan had been living, she was unprepared for the modern semi-detached residence where her ex-husband lived. She was more surprised when a man in a lightweight charcoal and white striped suit opened the door. His hair was sandy-coloured and very fine, and he smelled coolly of citrus aftershave. 'Mrs Brooks? Please come in.' Another surprise; there was no trace of the metropolis in his accent.

The house was clean but lived in. There were books and magazines and a child's colouring book and crayons on a chair.

'Would you like something to drink? Coffee, or something cold?'

'Coffee's fine, thank you.'

'Have a seat, I shan't be a moment.'

Kathryn did so, needing those few minutes to adjust to her surroundings. It was a lot to absorb. She was sitting in Brian Morris's house, the man who had known and married one of the Oxford group, either Sarah or Jenny, but how much did he know about his ex-wife's background? He was so different from how she had imagined him. She had automatically pictured him as someone like Megan, who used drugs or scraped along on a pittance. Brian Morris was obviously not affluent, but he certainly had enough to live on.

On a table against the wall were two framed photographs. One showed two small smiling boys, the other the same children several years older and in school uniform. Kathryn stood up to look more closely.

'Great, aren't they?' Brian had two mugs in one hand, in the other were a couple of coasters. It was unusual to find a man so thoughtful of the polished wood surfaces. 'They're not mine, they're Jilly's. We got together about seven years ago.' Kathryn had been wondering if they were Megan's children and how sad it would have been for them if they were. She had no way of knowing when the pictures had been taken. 'I hope you didn't mind me asking you to the house. I mean, I'm a stranger and, well . . .' He shrugged, not liking to say what was in his mind. When Kathryn smiled reassuringly, he went on: 'My office isn't really suitable, it's open-plan and everyone's on top of one another. I'm in insurance and I'm out and about a lot so this wasn't difficult to arrange. Anyway, about this article . . . can you tell me more about it?'

'There's no guarantee it'll be printed and this is just groundwork. What I'm looking at is a general view of how drugs affect the friends and families of those who use them.'

'So I gathered, and I'm really pleased I might be able to help. I was lucky, I was never tempted myself, but if you could've seen what it did to Megan . . . And now there are the boys to think of. They'll be teenagers soon and it's such a vulnerable time for them. I would do anything to prevent another pointless death.'

241

Kathryn got out her pad and pen. She needed to appear professional and she did not want him to suspect she was after anything other than what she had told him. 'Were you aware that your wife was a user?'

'No, not for some time. You see, Megan was a creature of moods, it was part of her fascination. When she was happy she made everyone around her feel the same. Unfortunately the reverse was also true. I couldn't believe it when she fell for me. I know my limitations, I'm solid and hardworking but I don't think anyone would describe me as exciting. Megan provided the excitement in my life. She was funny and attractive and I was hooked from the moment I saw her.'

Kathryn was watching his face closely. She felt that his self-assessment was honest and accurate and that he still felt his loss. 'What happened?'

'I'm not really sure. As soon as we were married things started to go wrong. She began to criticise everything I did and complained we didn't have enough money. She also said the people we mixed with were boring. Later, when I realised the types *she* was mixing with, I couldn't believe it. She'd been leading a sort of double life – I think she got her kicks that way. She said she was leaving and nothing I could say would persuade her to stay. Finally I saw that she would not be happy until I gave her a divorce. Then the opposite seemed to happen; she went downhill rapidly.'

John Atherton had said that Sarah was wild, yet the same could be said of Jenny Branagh. They had more in common than Kathryn had realised. 'But you stayed in touch with Megan?'

'Yes. I still wanted to protect her – from herself more than anything. I tried reason and threatening her with the police. I offered to pay for medical help. Nothing worked. Do you think I should've gone to the police?' He paused, distressed, then collected himself. 'No, I had no business asking you that. Sorry. I just hope you're never in the same position.'

Kathryn smiled weakly. She *was* in exactly that position. She now knew most of the events of that summer night; the group had lied about them to the police, but if they were not guilty, did it matter now? And what about Harriet Milton, having it all dragged up again only to experience more disappointment? There was a lot to be said for letting sleeping dogs lie ... but the final decision could be made later. 'At least you did try to help her,' she said gently. 'Some men would have simply washed their hands of her.'

'I suppose so. When she first told me, I insisted she stay with me until she'd got alternative accommodation. We found her a flat but she stopped paying the rent and got thrown out, although she was working at the time and could afford it. From there she went to a bed-sit and it took me a fortnight to find her. Give her her due, she didn't try to rip me off or force me to sell the house, but I foolishly gave her a lump sum. I now know where it went, of course. And I let her keep her car, which I continued to pay for. She rarely used it though, and it rusted away.'

Kathryn thought it possible that Megan had run through the money quickly because she might have been in debt to people who were not prepared to wait for payment. Then the implication of what Brian Morris had said sank in. 'The house? You mean she lived here?'

'Yes. I was already in the process of buying it when we met. She seemed happy enough at first.'

If his wife had been Sarah it was the closest Kathryn had been to her because she had never lived in the Miltons' place in Gloucestershire.

'Anyway, not long after she left, a kind friend told me he'd seen her out with someone else – a man with money to burn, by all accounts. It didn't last and when he dropped Megan she was livid. Knowing what she was spending it on I stopped helping her out with cash but I used to take food around – tinned stuff that she might be bothered to heat up.' He paused. He was sitting on the edge of his chair, his hands clasped between his knees and Kathryn guessed he had not stopped loving his wife despite the way she had treated him. Other people, she realised, put up with a lot more than she had had to endure from Alex and, to be fair to him, his behaviour had some slight justification. Even now he was not complaining; he knew that her mission, as he called it, had to be completed.

'She got quite violent at times, screaming and hitting me when I wouldn't give her cash. You see, for a while I harboured hopes that if I held out, she'd come home again. She could be really hurtful; she said if I loved her I'd give her money. Things got worse and there came a time when I realised that if I wasn't careful I would sink with her. My work was affected and I couldn't sleep. I decided I would see her once a fortnight to check she was all right; other than that she had to get on with it. But there are still times when I think I could have done more.'

'I doubt it, not from what you've told me – not without damaging yourself as well.'

'It's kind of you to say so, Kathryn. I cried bitterly when she died but it was a relief, too. She was finally out of danger. Silly, isn't it, to carry on loving someone when they despise everything about you? But if you print any of this, warn people to look for the signs before it's too late. I know everyone's supposed to be aware of the problem these days, but it doesn't prevent it from happening.' He stopped talking, aware of things he had not said. 'Please don't think I don't love Jilly and the boys. I do, probably more than I loved Megan. Jilly knows about her. Anyway, before you go I'll show you a photograph.'

Yes, Kathryn thought, Brian Morris would have told his new wife everything. He was not the sort of man to go into anything without being completely honest.

'That's Megan.' He held out a snapshot. Kathryn studied the slender figure in a bridal gown. Her short brown hair was cut in points around her face. She looked nothing like the Jenny or Sarah in Laura's picture, and that was before the effects of the heroin had taken over. Laura's story suddenly seemed more plausible.

'Do you have a picture I could borrow?'

'You can take this one. I've got plenty more.'

Kathryn did not miss his anxious glance at the clock. She had taken up a lot of his time but needed to know one or two more things.

They had met, he said, at a dinner and dance. Megan had come with someone else but it was obvious there was no sort of relationship between them. 'She once told me she'd

244

come to London to be a model, but I think that was wishful thinking. As to her background, there's not much I can tell you. As you say, it could be important if it made her the way she was. All I know is that she'd lost touch with her family and refused to discuss them, except she once told me she'd lived in Oxford. Her funeral was the saddest affair I've ever witnessed. There was just me and two people from the place where she was living. I couldn't contact her parents and from what she told me I doubt if they'd have turned up. Kathryn, I'm so sorry, but I really do have to go now.'

'Of course. I'm sorry if I've made you late.'

'Can I give you a lift to the Underground? It's all right, it's on my way.'

It was a short journey and Brian's car was comfortable and air-conditioned. 'What kind of car did Megan have?' The question was irrelevant, merely an introduction to another one. Kathryn had been thinking about it since her meeting with John Atherton and she was beginning to see how a change of identity was not that difficult to accomplish.

'Only a runabout, a second-hand Fiat. She used to love it – she passed her Test in it.'

She passed her Test in it. What did that mean? Sarah Milton had taken a test when she was seventeen but a driver's licence was another document to prove one's identity. They chatted about the weather then Brian double-parked briefly to allow her to get out of the car, and then he was gone and Kathryn was still none the wiser.

On the homeward journey she tried to view the problem from both sides. She started with a supposition. According to Laura, Sarah had disappeared in 1978, reappearing in London under the name of Megan Davies. Within a short time she had met and married Brian Morris, using him as a stepping stone to further her new identity by way of a marriage licence. Next she applied for a provisional driving licence under her new name. She had re-sat the Test, maybe without even taking lessons. It fitted, but the question was still *why should someone like Sarah want to do such a thing?*

Let's say it isn't Sarah but Jenny, she thought. What reason would *she* have had to change her identity? 'I see.' She had spoken aloud. Kathryn hid a smile as the man next

245

to her buried his head in his newspaper, believing he had drawn the short straw and got the seat next to a nutter. There was a more plausible explanation. Supposing Jenny had killed Sarah? She could not have taken her place as a student but she might have had other plans which had backfired . . .

Once she started thinking along those lines, the possibilities seemed endless. What if Laura wasn't who she claimed to be, but one of the other girls? Her mind was spinning but Kathryn was still careful. She checked the platform before alighting from the train and walked home quickly although she did not sense she was in any danger.

She was hot and tired and needed to sit somewhere shady and give her brain a rest. The enclosed area of grass at the back of the flat should be safe enough as she could hear the voices of other people sitting there.

Relieved to be home, she hung her bag over the back of a kitchen chair and filled the kettle to make tea. While it boiled she sat in the lounge enjoying the faint breeze coming through the open window. The telephone rang. It was Alex. 'It's me,' he said. 'I thought you were never going to get back. I don't mean to be a nuisance but could you jump in a cab and come over to Slough?' He sounded extremely apologetic.

'Slough?'

'Yes. Wexham Park Hospital actually.'

'Alex!' She felt sick. Had some harm come to him because of what she was doing? If it had she would stop immediately. Nothing, she realised, mattered as much as he did.

'Don't panic, just a few stitches. The stupid thing is I came in the car and the damned thing's stuck in the car park here and I don't think I can manage to drive back.'

'I'll be there as soon as I can.' She hung up and checked that she had enough cash for the fare then stood by the window waiting for the cab to arrive. As she left the flat the glare of the sun caught one of the tuatara's eyes. It seemed to be winking at her.

Chapter 12

The heat lasted another couple of days then came the reprieve. Just as the skies darkened and the first roll of thunder reverberated through the air, Laura rang Kathryn to find out what she had learned from Brian Morris. She was sure that Sarah had had no hand in the original manuscript but desperately wished it to be so because it would put them all in the clear. If Kathryn proved that Megan Morris was Jenny, then they were back where they started. Deep down she knew that the police would not have allowed the name of the dead girl to be published unless they were certain who she was.

'Can you come over?'

'I'm sorry, Laura, I can't. Alex has hurt himself and I've got a couple of other things to see to.' Frustrating as it was, Kathryn knew where her priorities lay. Alex had played it down, just a few stitches, he had said, but the wound was deep and he was in pain. A steel hawser had snapped and wrapped itself around his arm. He was lucky it wasn't broken. The fault lay with a new man they had taken on and who had already been spoken to about his carelessness. He had now been asked to leave.

At first Kathryn was furious that no one had volunteered to drive Alex to the hospital but, to be fair, neither they nor he had realised the extent of his injury. He had swathed his arm in a towel and covered that with a polythene bag, assuring everyone he was all right. The hospital had done their bit then provided him with painkillers. He was advised to remain at home for a week until the sutures were removed by his GP. For the first two days he was grey with pain then, as the wound healed, Kathryn saw the signs of restlessness but refused to let him go into the boat-yard even though he promised to do no more than look over some paperwork. And then Kathryn, having cut Alex's food up into fork-sized pieces, looked at it and felt sick.

'I can't eat anything,' she said faintly, and found herself off work, too, with a dose of whatever bug was doing the rounds.

It only lasted forty-eight hours and just as she was on her feet, Laura telephoned. She wasn't strong enough yet to deal with her, and it was true – she did have other things to follow up. If what she had surmised was correct, then the whole thing would soon be out in the open. And then . . . Kathryn did not complete her thought because it was tempting fate to do so.

Alex had been worried about Kathryn, about her lack of appetite and her weight loss, but he was reassured when he rang the newspaper to say she was ill. 'Oh no, not another one,' Keith groaned. 'There's hardly anyone left here. I hope she's done her column.'

'Sympathetic lot you work with,' Alex told her, smiling, when he had relayed the message that it was on her terminal and ready to be edited.

Although she felt extremely weak Kathryn was glad to be out of bed. Alex's attempts at nursing were well-intentioned but irritating. All she wanted to do was sleep but he kept bringing her fluids or barging in to ask if there was anything she needed.

At last Alex's stitches were removed and he said he was going into work.

It was strange being in the flat alone. Kathryn pulled on jeans and a T-shirt and made the first cup of coffee she had been able to face. The heavy showers which had accompanied the storms had passed over leaving in their wake, not the cleansing freshness she had hoped for, but a grey mugginess and air so still and thick it was almost tangible.

Ahead of her was a whole day to make some sense of 'the Oxford file', as she now called it. She knew the identity of the writer known as Megan Morris, but this did not give her the thrill she had anticipated. Other events had overtaken that part of the chase. She had already planned how she would write the revealing story, and intended to show it to Laura at the appropriate time.

From the file she produced the group photograph Laura had lent her, and the one of the real Megan Morris on her wedding day. As hard as she tried to decide which of the two girls it might be, she could not come to a decision. And then she realised that Mrs Milton must have one of Sarah on her own where the details would be clearer. She picked up the receiver and dialled Harriet's number, glad to have written it down even though, at the time, she hadn't thought she would ever need to use it.

'I'll put one in the post today,' Harriet told her. 'Have you found out anything?'

'I'm not sure. I'll need a couple more weeks but I'll be in touch, I promise.' As Kathryn heard herself use those words she knew that she had committed herself.

The group picture had been taken outside one of the colleges. Sarah and Jenny were both mugging at the camera, Sarah with one hand on her head, the other on her jutting hip and a leer on her face. Jenny was poking her tongue out. They looked happy and now they were both dead. *Or were they?* Giles appeared relaxed. There was a cigarette between his fingers and his eyes were half-closed against the sun. There was no mistaking John, who had altered so little, and Laura must have been distracted by someone passing by because she was facing sideways on, her hand raised in acknowledgement. Only David seemed uncomfortable, his expression relaying a reluctance to be photographed. There were no clues to be found at all. Then she remembered something Laura had said about the manuscript. 'The only part which rang true, as if it might have been written from experience, was a chapter set in a psychiatric hospital.' What did it mean? That whoever had written the novel had first-hand experience? If it was Sarah then it might explain the anomaly of the book if she was being treated with psychiatric drugs. On the other hand, Jenny might have been undergoing treatment for drug abuse, although Brian Morris had said she'd refused treatment. However, there were three years in his wife's life that were unaccounted for.

Kathryn knew what she had to do but guessed she was going to be disappointed. The question was, where to start?

David turned up the collar of his summer jacket but it offered no protection from the deluge. Litter was swept along the gutters and water gurgled down the drains. The smell of wet, hot tarmac was in the air. He sheltered along with several other people in a shop doorway, but drips from a leaking gutter pattered onto his head.

It was Polly's birthday next week and she had asked him to join her and her friends for a drink. Imagining the invitation to have been made out of politeness, he declined but was pleased and flattered when she insisted that she wanted to introduce him to her mother and sister. He was going to buy her a present, something frivolous, something she would enjoy.

Abandoning the hope of sheltering properly he continued on his way home trying to decide what might appeal to Polly. He fed Kitty and suddenly realised that Polly favoured large, ostentatious earrings which swung wildly whenever she turned her head. Mostly she wore her hair held up in a high pony-tail which showed her neat earlobes and graceful neck to advantage. There was a jeweller's in the street which ran parallel to the shop. In the morning he would go and choose something.

The card he bought was unimaginative; there were flowers on the front and *Happy Birthday* printed inside but the humorous cards were too suggestive or too personal and the verses in others were sentimental or mawkish. The present was a different matter. On a tray were a pair of earrings that might have been made for Polly. They were for pierced ears, and from each circle of marcasite hung three glittering strands of gold. David said he would take them and produced a credit card, guiltily recalling his gifts to Nicola. It also reminded him that his mother's birthday was in a few weeks' time, but her tastes were more conventional. He asked for the earrings to be gift-wrapped.

Feeling reckless he stopped at a sandwich bar and purchased two large, filled rolls. Polly would be surprised because she made her own lunch arrangements, although he had no idea what they were unless she had bought something new to wear during that period. On those occasions she would pull the article eagerly from the bag and drape it against herself for his approval. He was gradually becoming used to her spontaneity and her readiness to share her pleasure.

Polly's eyes widened in surprise when he handed her the paper bag but he did not know whether it was because it was the first time he had paid for her lunch, or because he told her he would love to have a birthday drink with her.

On the appointed day he waited until mid-morning when Polly had made them both coffee, then he handed her the card and present. With typical impetuosity, she ripped open the envelope containing the card and squealed with delight when she lifted the lid of the velvet-lined box. 'I'm going to try them on,' she said, going out to the back where there was a mirror. David reddened when she kissed him on the cheek and said they were wonderful and that she was going to keep them on.

He felt a little self-conscious as he walked with her to meet the rest of the birthday celebrants. Polly was half his age and he thought people might assume he was taking out his secretary although, in the rush-hour, no one took any notice of them. The pub was a tube ride away and had been chosen because it was near the restaurant where they would later be eating. It was basically furnished but had successfully retained the air of a local which was atypical of many of the West End bars. In one corner sat what looked to be about twenty people but Polly's sister was instantly recognisable.

'This is my boss, David,' Polly announced with a touch of pride. 'And that's my mum, Vicky, and my sister, Pauline.' By the time the introductions were completed David had lost track of who was who, apart from Polly's immediate relatives. Vicky Stevens shook his hand and smiled with such warmth that he knew his presence was welcome. There was no Mr Stevens – he had died some years ago in an accident. At first glance Vicky might have been her daughters' contemporary rather than their mother and she had the same blonde curls.

The noisy circle somehow expanded to allow room for David and Polly to sit down and he found himself next to Vicky as if, by silent consent, it was agreed that the two members of the older generation ought to be together. David had no objections; Vicky Stevens was an attractive woman.

After a couple of rounds of drinks Polly said it was time they were leaving for the restaurant. It gave David a jolt to realise he was sorry that the evening, for him, was over already – then discovered that he was expected to go with them. 'You must,' Polly said earnestly, with one hand on his arm, 'mustn't he, Mum?'

'Of course.' Vicky looked at her daughter, trying not to let her enthusiasm show.

'Please?' Polly added, almost bouncing on the spot.

'All right then. Lead on.'

A table had been booked at a nearby Chinese and, to save confusion and any arguments over the bill, they were all having the set menu. Once more David found himself seated beside Vicky. 'She enjoys working for you and I'm pleased she's settled down at last. It isn't that she's not bright, but unlike Pauline, she's a bit of a butterfly,' she said.

David was flattered but wondered if Polly would remain content. The job had no career potential.

'The girls' birthdays are usually females only affairs,' Vicky informed him when David queried his presence as the only man. 'You're honoured.' He had to look away because her smile was doing strange things to him.

As the night progressed the group became noisier, and high-pitched laughter filled the room. Once the meal was over the bill was divided equally, which was a relief because David feared Vicky or Polly might have intended paying for everyone.

'I'm going to make a move.' Vicky stood up. David immediately did so too and helped her on with her jacket.

'They're off to some club now which, as they say, isn't my scene.'

'I'll walk you to your tube.'

'Thank you.' His courtesy surprised her.

They strolled through the streets which were quieter now as performances at theatres and cinemas were still in progress. Vicky spoke of Polly and Pauline and what she had always hoped for them. She came across as down to earth and realistic about their present and possible future achievements. She was so different from his own mother, who had never taken his personality or his wishes into account.

On the platform he waited until the train pulled in then, quite out of character, said he would see her all the way home. 'Does Polly have a boyfriend?'

'No, not at the moment.' Vicky laughed. 'I think she wears them out. You know what she's like, always on the go. Do you?'

'Me?'

'Have a girlfriend, or a wife?'

David was aware of the heat from her body and her flowery scent. He stared ahead of him and their eyes met where they were reflected in the blackness of the window opposite. 'No,' he said quietly. 'Do you?'

Vicky shook her head. 'Oh, we're here. It was very kind of you. I'm lucky, it's only a two-minute walk to my house from here.'

'It's dark. I'd better see you home.' He felt as if he was watching himself. David Shawcross was not the sort of man to be so forward!

They reached it in four minutes because they had been walking slowly, both wishing to prolong the meeting. Outside the front door Vicky hesitated then said, 'If you're ever over this way, call in for a cup of tea.'

'I wouldn't do that, not without telephoning first.' He was as startled by the invitation as he had been at his own behaviour, and hoped he had sounded neither rude nor gauche but it was hard to decide what she might be suggesting. As her daughter's employer she might have felt obliged to issue the invitation to him. But it was Vicky who sought clarification. 'You don't have my number.'

'I do – as Polly's next-of-kin. But if it's all right to use it . . .?' He let the question hang in the air.

'Yes, I should like that. Goodnight, David.'

Before he could say anything else she had unlocked her front door and disappeared inside. How odd, he kept thinking as he waited for a tube to take him home. Of all the half-hearted plans he had made for meeting new people, it was Polly's mother with whom he had, hopefully, tentatively, made a date. What on earth would his own mother think? It doesn't matter a damn. It isn't, and never will be, any of her business, he thought. Some subconscious process had been at work because by the time he reached home the question was no longer *if* he would telephone Vicky, but *when*.

It was a long time since he had stayed out late. Kitty did not budge from the armchair and stared at him in disdain through the slits of her eyes. David rattled a spoon against the side of her dish but there was still no response. In her own time Kitty strolled out to the kitchen and began to eat, stopping now and then to glance over her shoulder, making clear her indignation at having been left alone for so long. But Kitty was not uppermost in David's mind. He was marvelling at how easy it had been to make conversation with Vicky, and how his crippling shyness had not been in evidence.

He sat upright in his chair as a shudder of fear ran through him. Luck had tapped him on the shoulder tonight, but what if Vicky found out about his Oxford days? She wouldn't want to see him again if she did . . .

All night he was restless as he tried to find a way to remove the possible impediment to his future happiness.

Although it was posted first-class, it was two days before Kathryn received the photograph which Harriet Milton had promised to send. With a thrill of excitement she took it to the kitchen window and compared it with the others in her possession. Here was a happy, smiling Sarah but even so, Kathryn was unable to tell if it might be the same girl as the one in the wedding dress. She tried to imagine Sarah with cropped hair, coloured brown, and about a stone lighter, but it was impossible. But did Laura know? That was the important question, and Laura was holding something back, she somehow sensed it.

Almost recovered, she knew she must return to work the following day. She had wanted to go in sooner, but had been advised to stay at home until she felt one hundred per cent fit because they could not afford any more casualties of the virus. Armed with a mug of strong coffee, Kathryn pulled the file towards her. There were still too many unanswered questions. Why had Laura confided in her? Why had she given her the original manuscript to read? And why had she kept it in the first place? Surely not, as she said as proof that she was not guilty of plagiarism. And Jennifer Branagh – what relevance did she really have? Obviously some, if it was the name Laura had used on their first meeting. And who was Brian Morris's wife? Whichever of the girls had taken the name of Megan Morris, she was beginning to see how easily it could have been achieved. If Sarah was a murderess, she only had to apply for the birth certificate of the dead girl. They were provided without the necessity of proof. Using this, a marriage licence could be obtained *and* a new driving licence. In fact, Kathryn realised, you did not necessarily have to kill anyone. As long as you knew the details of someone's date and place of birth and their father's occupation, you could apply for a birth certificate. Those details would not be hard to acquire even on a first meeting, if you went about it in a conversational way.

Kathryn fetched the telephone directory and looked up the number for Maidenhead Town Hall. She dialled it and asked to be put through to the Registrar. After a brief, but revealing conversation, she said her thank yous and hung up.

'So it's that easy,' she muttered, tapping her teeth with her pen. 'I was right.' To get married, all that was required was a birth certificate. This, you took to the Register Office and there, having booked a date, signed a declaration to the effect that you were who you said you were. If you had not been previously married, no other documentation was needed. The lady to whom she had spoken had told her that it meant you would need to lie, and that, if caught, you could be charged with fraud. But apparently no checking or cross-checking took place. The birth certificate you provided and the declaration you signed were taken at face value. It was even possible that two or more people could use the same birth certificate with which to get married, provided the parties in question did not choose the same venue. The hows were becoming obvious; it was the whys which remained enigmatic.

Using the last of her time at home, Kathryn rang her GP with whom she was on friendly terms although she hardly ever required his services, and he said if she called into the surgery when he had finished for the day he would see what he could do.

For the remaining couple of hours Kathryn read, although she wasn't fully concentrating because at the back of her mind she knew she ought to contact Laura but did not yet feel ready to do so. She still had to return the manuscript, too, but another day or so would not matter.

The dull sky had lifted and sunlight filled the lounge as she turned the pages of her library book. Surfaces gleamed as everything had been thoroughly polished the previous day. Even the tuatara seemed to have acquired a sheen. She would get used to it but Kathryn still enjoyed the freedom of not having to bother with housework.

At the end of afternoon surgery she sat in the waiting room under the suspicious eye of the receptionist, one of the breed who believed doctors were to be protected from troublesome things such as patients. Finally John Beard came from the nether regions of the building and smiled broadly. He had not forgotten he had said he would see her.

'A strange request, Kathryn, but this may be of help. It's not the latest edition, but things don't change that rapidly.' Over the telephone he had already confirmed that the treatment described in one chapter of the manuscript Laura had been handed all those years ago, was that prescribed for drug abuse during that period, and would not have been suitable for any of the actual psychiatric illnesses. Sarah might have undergone such treatment and so might Jenny,

256

somewhere between leaving Oxford and meeting Brian Morris. 'You needn't go through it now,' he added. 'You can take it home with you as long as you bring it back.'

Kathryn took what looked like a catalogue, thanked him and promised she would return it the following day.

At home once more she made a note of all the psychiatric hospitals which also had a drugs unit and places where they specialised in the treatment of drug abuse. She only listed those that would serve the Bethnal Green or Oxford areas because she had to hope that was where Sarah or Jenny had been admitted. Her only fear was that the information had been gleaned from someone else and that she would be wasting her time but, like Laura, she felt it was the only part of Megan Morris's book which rang true and which, surely, had been written from personal experience.

For almost an hour she worked out her approach. Information regarding patients or ex-patients was confidential and she was not sure which name she should be enquiring about.

The first five calls to hospitals in the Oxford area were abortive. The sixth was not. Having gone through the rigmarole of who she was and why she required the information, Kathryn was asked to wait. She had kept to the theme of following up friends and families of known addicts, and claimed that she had permission from the late Megan Morris's husband to speak to the doctor who had treated her, if she had been treated in those missing years. She would, she said, provide proof of her identity and a letter written by Brian Morris (whom she had had the foresight to prime and who had agreed willingly to write such a letter). She was finally put through to Medical Records.

The woman who took the call was surprisingly helpful but said she was not in a position to give any details regarding patients past or present. However, she said she would contact the man who had been the consultant psychiatrist during the relevant period and ask him to ring her if he felt it was appropriate. Kathryn had not expected such cooperation and was duly grateful, but she still did not know if Megan Morris had actually been a patient there. All she

257

could do was to wait and hope that the man was not too busy to get in touch with her.

Despite Alex's gentle early morning love-making, Kathryn went back to work with a vague sense of unease, as if something momentous was about to happen; but in the chaos of the half-staffed office it was soon dispelled.

Just as she was placing the plastic cover over her computer, a call came through from the main switchboard. 'Mrs Brooks? It's Michael Steiner.' The name meant nothing. 'I believe you wanted to ask me some questions relating to some research you've undertaken.'

Kathryn gasped. She hadn't dreamed the consultant psychiatrist would be prepared to speak to her, let alone get in touch so quickly. 'Yes. Thank you for ringing. It's a chance in a million . . .' She paused, feeling foolish as the probability of him remembering one patient from the distant past was almost laughable. 'I don't suppose you'd remember if you ever treated a girl called Megan Morris. No, sorry – Megan Davies.' She would not have been married at the time.

'No, I'm afraid I don't.' He laughed. 'They say it affects your brain – working in psychiatry, that is. But strangely enough, even though I usually can't remember what I've had for lunch I rarely forget a patient. When would this have been?'

'Around 1980.'

'Megan Davies . . . Just a minute.'

Kathryn stood motionless. Time, too, seemed to stand still. She felt the heat of the sun through the window she had recently closed and heard the engine of a car in the carpark below as it spluttered into life.

'Are you sure you haven't made a mistake? You see, I knew a nurse called Megan Davies. She was on my team around that time. A ward sister, and a very good one too. We were sorry to lose her.'

'Lose her?' Kathryn could hardly get the words out.

'She left when she got married, because of her husband's job, if I recall. We worked together for eight or nine years.'

'Thank you. I must have got it wrong. Someone told me she had been a patient.'

'Perhaps it's a coincidence – it's not that unusual a name. Of course, if we did have a patient of that name, Megan would remember.'

'Do you know where I could find Megan now?'

'Churchill.'

'Pardon?'

'Churchill, that's her married name. I don't know where she lives but she shouldn't be too hard to find. She did what many nurses hope to achieve, she married a doctor. He's a surgeon, he'll be listed if he's still practising.'

Kathryn replaced the receiver and looked at her watch. The library would still be open. Having got so far she had to keep on trying, but it was useless to expect Megan Churchill to have had any connection with the Oxford group.

Halfway to the door, Kathryn saw what she was doing and made time to leave a message for Alex to tell him she would be home later than usual. Then she drove to the library.

That evening, Alex peered over her shoulder with a frown on his face. 'Kathryn?' He had seen who the letter was addressed to, and for a moment his fears about her health returned.

'It's the only way I can get in touch with Megan Churchill – well, the only way I feel is acceptable. No one's going to give her husband's home address. I'll send it to the Royal College of Surgeons and they can forward it.' She had already decided to wait and see if she received a reply before trying other hospitals. Meanwhile she really must get in touch with Laura, and there was her main preoccupation to consider.

Laura tutted with annoyance. It had been hot and sticky in the attic room and she was about to step into the shower at the end of a day's work when the telephone rang. Although the answering machine was on she found it very hard to ignore the seven insistent *brrs* before it clicked into action. It was one area of her life about which she was always optimistic. She always believed she was about to hear good news. For once she was wrong.

259

'Hello, darling.' Laura smiled. It was always a pleasure to speak to Marcia. 'Now I don't want you to worry for one moment, but I thought I ought to let you know I've got to go into hospital for a couple of days.'

'What is it? What's wrong?'

'There, I knew you'd react like that.' She had heard the panic in her daughter's voice and felt so sad. It would have been better to tell her face-to-face. Except her own panic might have been too obvious. 'Just a few tests.'

'I'll come up right away.'

'No, Laura. Stay there, I insist.' Her own voice sounded firm and steady and, with a wry humorous smile she wondered if she ought to have gone on the stage. 'You know what it's like, and I'll only be in two nights at the most.'

'When are you going in?'

'Tomorrow.'

'Tomorrow? Why on earth didn't you tell me before?'

Because, my darling, you'd have come up and asked the doctors all sorts of penetrating questions and I don't want you to know just yet, Marcia thought. 'Because I didn't think it was that important,' she said aloud. 'Anyway, I'll give you a ring tomorrow evening.'

Marcia made small-talk for several minutes then hung up. She hadn't told Laura which hospital, nor had she given her the chance to ask what the tests might be for. 'You're a coward,' she said, but was unaware that Laura had something else to divert her from her worries.

Laura walked slowly to the bathroom, chewing the inside of her lip. Marcia had sounded all right but it was unlike her not to have mentioned it if she had felt unwell or needed to see a doctor. Before the implications could hit her, the telephone rang again. Thinking Marcia had forgotten to tell her something she quickly retraced her steps and answered it.

'I'm sorry I haven't come back to you sooner, but I've got some news. I've also got your manuscript to return.'

Kathryn Brooks and what she was up to had temporarily become of secondary importance, but God knows, Laura needed some distraction. 'You could come over tonight, if you like,' she said abstractedly.

The arrangement suited Kathryn as Alex was taking his bank manager out to discuss further expansion of the boatyard. 'What time?'

'I'm just getting in the shower. Can you give me an hour?'

'Of course.'

Laura was watching from the window and saw Kathryn make the awkward turning into her drive. There was just enough room to park behind her own car which she rarely bothered putting in the garage, an omission she recognised as laziness and one which would not please the insurers if it was ever broken into. She had put a bottle of Chablis in the fridge immediately before her shower and, seeing the expression on Kathryn's face and the jaunty way in which she approached the front door, felt she might need it.

This time Laura was more formal. She showed Kathryn into the lounge where the tall windows were open onto the patio. The sun, still bright, shone through from the front but the garden was now in the shade. 'Do sit down. Would you like some wine? I'm having some myself,' she added.

'Thank you.' There would be no repeat of her experience with Harriet Milton. She would drink no more than two glasses at the most.

Laura returned bearing two misted glasses and a bowl of nuts which she placed on a table between their two armchairs. She sat down and lit a cigarette then crossed her legs and gazed expectantly at her guest.

'Oh, here's the manuscript.'

Laura took it and stuffed it unceremoniously down the side of her seat. 'Thanks.'

'What you said about the bit in the psychiatric hospital – well, you were right. The thing is, Laura, whoever gave you that manuscript *did* have first-hand experience and they were not lying about the name Megan Davies.'

Laura's skin paled beneath her light tan. 'Who was it, Kathryn, Sarah or Jenny?'

Kathryn sipped the wine. It was cold and delicious. 'Megan Davies existed. Still does exist. She was a psychiatric nurse and is now married.'

'Are you telling me that either Sarah or Jenny was a *nurse*? Never in a million years. They were both far too selfish.'

'No. Megan was the nurse but she wasn't killed. She's now happily married and living back in Oxford with her husband and two children.'

'I don't understand.'

'Neither did I at first, but it's far simpler than I realised. I can tell you now that the girl who turned up at your London flat with that manuscript was *definitely* Jenny Branagh. It wasn't Sarah – which means we have to assume that it really was her body they found.'

'Then Jenny killed her. But why take someone else's name? Of course, how stupid of me! Jenny used the game for her own ends, I suppose, then realised how dangerous it would be to call herself Sarah Milton.'

'Do you think so?' Kathryn had her own ideas but she saw that Laura was stunned. 'I traced Megan Churchill, that's her married name, through her husband who's a surgeon. She wrote to me and agreed to see me. She was mystified and said that naturally she'd remember if she'd ever nursed anyone with the same name. I realised then that Jenny, during the course of her treatment would have got to know her well, well enough to be able to use her details to apply for a birth certificate. However, I was wrong on that score too. I really do seem to have gone about this the wrong way around. Anyway, Megan, the real Megan, had never heard of Sarah Milton and only vaguely recalled the story about her disappearance when I spoke of it. She had been living in Oxford at the time but when her body was found had already moved away. She did remember Jennifer Branagh, though, and said she had been a patient at the unit where she worked in Oxford. She couldn't be too specific about the dates but it would have been before 1982 when she left there. Although she was later proved wrong, she thought that Jenny was one of the more successful cases, that she had been weaned off drugs when she left the unit. This would be why her family didn't know where she was and immediately after her release she went to London.'

262

'How does this Megan person know that?'

'She doesn't.'

Laura toyed with the stem of her glass then flicked ash into the ashtray. Kathryn Brooks seemed to be enjoying herself. 'Go on.'

'I wrongly assumed that if Sarah was Brian's wife she had retaken her driving test in order to get a new licence. That wasn't the case. Jenny had never learned to drive until after she was married. You see, it foolishly didn't occur to me when I met Brian to ask what his wife's maiden name had been.' Kathryn put down her own glass and hooked her hair back as her enthusiasm strengthened. 'As Jenny had told you her name was Megan Davies I could hardly ask him if she was really called Milton or Branagh. God, I could've saved hours of time! Anyway, Jenny had formed a close relationship with Megan and, perhaps, as you did with me, chose a name which meant something to her.' Laura turned her head towards the garden to prevent Kathryn seeing her embarrassment. 'I believe that Jenny knew you wouldn't be able to positively identify her. I also believe she did not know, any more than you did, whether Sarah was alive or dead but she did know you were afraid and she played on this. By that time she was pretty desperate.'

'I can see that. I wanted to believe it was Sarah because that would put us all in the clear, but deep down I suppose I knew it couldn't be. Have you spoken to Brian Morris again?'

'Yes. I asked him outright what was written on his marriage certificate. He said his wife was recorded as Megan Branagh, formerly known as Jennifer Branagh. It's perfectly legal. According to him, she did not like her Christian name, and as she had once met someone who was very kind to her, someone called Megan, that's the name she wanted to be known by. Now I think about it, everything else fitted. She hadn't lied to him. She told him she came from Oxford and that she had lost touch with her parents. There was no real mystery, after all.'

'Then Sarah is dead. But who killed her, Kathryn? It's worse now than before. If you believe that it wasn't Jenny, it has to have been one of us.' Laura held her head in her hands. It was too much, this news coming on top of Marcia's.

'We could try to find out.'

'What!' The ejaculation was almost scornful. 'After all this time, and when the police have been unsuccessful?'

'I'd like to ask you a favour. I have, as you know, kept my word regarding your identity.' Kathryn knew she was being unfair, using this as a method of persuasion. 'Would you invite them all here, John, David and Giles?'

'Whatever for?'

'I think it might be a catalyst, your all being together again. You see, someone might remember something or say too much.'

'Christ. You really do think it was one of us.'

'I don't know *what* to think, except that since I started asking questions I've had the feeling I'm being followed, that someone is very much afraid I'm going to find out too much.' She hadn't mentioned this to Alex because she knew he would try to stop her.

'All right, I'll do it. I'll invite them all here but if your fears are justified, I can't guarantee your safety.'

'I understand that.'

'In which case, Kathryn, I think it's time I spoke to Giles and time you published your scoop about my identity.'

'Really?' She couldn't keep the excitement out of her voice.

'Yes. If I'm to invite the others, they'll soon know anyway. John's bound to suspect; he'll realise that Giles and I have never lost contact however much we might try to disguise it. Go on, write your story.'

Kathryn nodded. Even over her own exhilaration she saw how tired and defeated Laura was. Did she know who had killed Sarah? Refusing a second glass of wine, she left. She couldn't wait to tell Alex the news.

It was not a long drive home, no more than a few miles, but as she approached the railway bridge under which only one line of traffic, regulated by four sets of lights, could pass at a time, Laura's words about her safety came back to her. The driver of the car behind put his headlights on full, revved the engine and accelerated and seemed to want

264

to overtake her beneath the bridge. Instinct made Kathryn swerve to the left. She heard the scraping of metal against the bricks of the arch. Sparks flew like miniature stars and as the car impacted against the wall she was flung to the right, hitting her head on the window beside her. For several seconds she was unable to move. Her head was spinning and she couldn't remember what had happened.

The seat belt seemed to be strangling her. It had locked, but the distance between herself and the window had been too little to prevent injury. A man from one of the bungalows along the road had heard the crash and hurried out to help. He called the police and an ambulance, although when the latter arrived Kathryn knew it was not necessary. A queue of cars had formed behind three sets of the lights, and a young policeman was clumsily redirecting the traffic. 'It was an accident,' she kept repeating, hating to be the cause of so much trouble. The driver of the other car had not stopped.

'It was an accident,' she repeated shakily to Alex when she arrived home in a taxi, unharmed apart from some bruising.

Kathryn had told him about what had happened at Laura's and therefore he believed her, putting the accident down to lack of concentration on Kathryn's part. He refrained from pointing out that her obsession was endangering her, aware that she was too shaken up to take a scolding.

Only when she was falling asleep did Kathryn realise it might have been a deliberate attempt on her life.

Laura was awake for most of the night and only fell asleep as dawn cast its light on the Thames.

Immediately she woke, she rang Giles and explained what she intended doing. She was unable to gauge his reaction to the news that she had decided to hold a reunion party, but his astonishment at her revelation that she was ready to let the public know who she was, carried down the line in the form of four-letter expletives.

'I promised the girl.'

'Yes.' Giles had calmed down; he was thoughtful. Laura

would keep her promise. But if they were all together again, they could plan how to deal with it. It would, he thought wryly, be just like the old days.

'This is what we'll do.' Laura began to outline her plan. Giles took down the details. He was filled with a mixture of dread and anticipation. It would make a wonderful piece of publicity, but they could not let Mrs Brooks delve any deeper. However, the reunion would be the time to make decisions.

Kathryn, having recovered from the shock of the accident and in possession of a hired car until her own was repaired, was out interviewing a lady who had built up a catering business from scratch. The food she used to provide for her husband's business associates at dinner parties had proved so successful that she had branched out and gone to other people's houses to do the same. Seven years later she was employing a staff of twelve who worked in pairs. She had recently won a businesswoman's award.

Keith took the call that came through on Kathryn's private line and conscientiously wrote down the message.

'How was it?' he asked when she returned.

Kathryn shrugged. 'So-so.' The woman in question had proved she was enterprising but lacked the personality to make her story interesting. She would have to tart it up herself. But her mind wasn't on the article; she couldn't stop thinking that someone had tried to kill her. 'What's this?' She picked up the note.

'What it looks like – a message.'

Interesting. Giles wanted to speak to her. Shaking slightly, she picked up the telephone and dialled his number. She listened to his proposals but for some reason they did not sound sincere. Then she made a proposal of her own, one which she had already discussed with Laura.

Sitting at her desk with her chin resting on interlaced fingers Kathryn was unaware of Keith's furtive glances. She was thinking that it was all too good to be true, that something was amiss. All of the group knew her now, all of them presumably could drive. Which one of them had tried to put a stop to what she was doing? David was odd, Giles

266

was cunning, Laura might be leading her on . . . and John? Well, she wasn't too sure what went on in *his* mind.

She sighed. She could not tell Alex, not yet, and for the moment her job must come first.

Chapter 13

David waited two days before he telephoned Vicky. His hand hovered over the receiver until he finally steeled himself to dial the number. He had not wanted to conduct the conversation at the shop in Polly's presence so waited until he got home, and only then did it occur to him that Vicky probably went out to work during the day.

'Yes, I'd love to,' she said, when he suggested they spent Sunday afternoon and evening together.

Feeling foolishly smug he grabbed Kitty and regaled her with feeble jokes. The following morning he told Polly of the arrangement. 'I'm taking your mother out at the weekend,' he said without preliminaries and without making eye-contact.

'You're never! That's great. Where're you going?'

'I hadn't really thought about it.' It was true and the idea worried him.

'Take her to the zoo. She's always saying she hasn't been there since we were kids. Go on, she'll love it.'

'Are you sure?'

'Positive. I won't mention it, honest. Mum's the word.' And giggling at what she believed to be her repartee she went off to make coffee.

Vicky was refreshingly different from the females with whom he had come into contact through his parents' circle of friends, and she shared Polly's enthusiasm for life. David watched her delighted face as they strolled through Regent's Park after several hours in the zoo. She was wearing a summer dress which was simple and ladylike, although he guessed she probably did not have more than an adequate income. By the time they were seated in an Italian restaurant he had learned that she worked part-time in a building society but her house had been paid for upon her husband's death.

He saw her home again and kissed her lightly on the cheek. She did not invite him in and he was glad. He needed time to accept what was happening to him. They agreed to meet one night in the week.

It was some time since he had heard from his mother and David had already decided he was not going to make the first move. As if she had read his mind, she rang on the Monday after he had taken Vicky to the zoo and invited him to her birthday dinner the following weekend. Sonia Shawcross's birthday party had become a tradition. The guests wore evening dress and after the meal there was dancing. Because it usually went on into the small hours it was always held on the nearest Saturday, and many of those invited stayed overnight.

'I hadn't forgotten,' David said, 'but I'm not sure if it's convenient.'

'Oh?' Sonia managed to express several nuances in the one word.

'I'm seeing someone actually and I've already arranged to take Victoria out.' He smiled. Two daughters of his parents' friends were called Victoria, but they were nothing like Vicky. His mother was in for a surprise. He knew instinctively that she would want to vet his girlfriend, and said he would like the invitation to be extended to Victoria as well.

Vicky agreed to go but David sensed her nervousness and reassured her that if she was not happy, they would leave immediately. She smiled and said she was being silly. They had gone to see a film, something David rarely did and he was surprised at how much he had enjoyed it. 'Will I see you before Saturday?' he asked, so naturally that he knew she was right for him and that if he never saw her again he would be more hurt and upset than when Nicola jilted him.

'Tomorrow, if you like. Come over for a meal. I can't let you keep paying for everything.'

269

On Saturday evening they met at Victoria Station and caught a fast train to Brighton. Once there they climbed in a taxi and David gave directions to his parents' house.

'My God, is this it?' Vicky whispered as the cab turned into the driveway.

For the first time David saw how the house must appear to someone who had not been born and brought up in it. It was more imposing than impressive. There were tall windows reflecting the sun, and a stone balustrade ran the length of the front, divided by three steps onto the terrace.

The door was opened by a woman in a black and white uniform. Vicky smiled. Her family all had keys to her house and were free to come and go as they pleased. They were shown to their rooms and David said he would knock on Vicky's door in about fifteen minutes. She nodded, puzzled, imagining she would have been introduced to his parents immediately.

David changed into his evening suit and went to collect Vicky. 'You look terrific,' he said. Her black dress plunged daringly at the back but otherwise modestly covered her arms and shoulders. It was the first time he had seen her with her hair loose, and it fell contrastingly over the black velvet. Her only jewellery was a pair of pearl stud earrings and her wedding ring. He took her hand and led her down the staircase. He could feel her trembling.

The folding doors which separated the lounge from the drawing room had been pulled back. The carpet had been rolled up to reveal the parquet floor and there was an abundance of flowers. Behind a trestle table at one end of the room two men were serving drinks. The meal would be served in the library. Vicky looked around and found it hard to believe that David came from such a background. There were already a dozen people present and, observing them, Vicky saw that they were used to this sort of occasion. She hoped she would not let David down.

David guided her across the room, nodding to acquaintances casually. 'Hello, Mother.' He bent to kiss the cheek of a dumpy woman in emerald satin whose heavily framed glasses were strung around her neck. She put them on to inspect David's guest. 'This is Vicky Stevens. Vicky, this is my mother.'

'I'm pleased to meet you, Victoria,' Sonia Shawcross said pointedly.

'How do you do.' Vicky extended her own hand, prepared to give a firm handshake, only to have her fingertips briefly touched by the older woman.

'Ah, here's Cyril.' More introductions were made when David's father joined them.

Cyril Shawcross was more welcoming than his wife had been although he seemed a little preoccupied. Only David knew that was because he did not enjoy large parties and especially dreaded his wife's birthday. 'Enjoy yourselves,' he said. 'If there's anything you want, just ask. I'll leave David to do the honours as far as the rest of them are concerned.' He waved a hand to indicate the other guests. 'Well go on, son, get your young lady a drink.' Mr Shawcross then disappeared to the library where he kept his malt whisky. Not for him the wine and champagne which most people were sipping.

'What can my son be thinking of?' Sonia Shawcross said, loudly enough for David and Vicky to hear as they went over to the makeshift bar.

David felt his face redden but said nothing. He was sorry now he had brought Vicky; it would have been nicer to spend the evening with her alone. She was vulnerable amongst these sort of people, some of whom had money but no manners and one or two, like his mother, who were unbearably arrogant. He bit his tongue. They were in the minority. It was really his mother with whom he was angry.

'Why don't we go and wander around the grounds?' he suggested.

'No, David.' Vicky touched his arm. She knew he was trying to protect her but she refused to be cowed.

Each fortified with a large gin and tonic, they made the rounds of the room and he introduced her to the guests that he liked. Later they sat at the long dining table and made small-talk with their neighbouring diners. The meal seemed interminable but finally it was over and more guests arrived for the dancing.

They stuck it out until 1 a.m. then said their goodnights. David lay fully clothed on his bed and waited until he heard the last stragglers depart or make their way to bed. He had already told Vicky to be ready early in the morning although he gave her no reason. He made his way downstairs.

The hired staff had almost finished clearing up. David poured himself another drink and waited for his parents to come from the front door where they were seeing the last people into taxis. He heard his father's gruff voice and knew that he had gone straight up to bed.

'David! I thought you'd be asleep by now.' Sonia was genuinely surprised to see him.

'I'm not tired. Not physically, that is.' He gulped at his drink. This was going to be harder than he had anticipated. 'I just wanted to tell you that your behaviour did you no credit tonight.'

'What on earth are you talking about?'

'The way you treated Vicky. You've always drummed into me that good manners is a sign of good breeding ... well, your manners were appalling.'

'David, she's hardly suitable!'

'She suits *me*, Mother, and that's the only thing which matters.' His voice was louder than he had intended it to be. 'And you needn't expect us for breakfast or lunch. We're leaving first thing.'

'You can't. You'll leave me two short.'

'Is that all you care about – your damn seating plans?'

'Don't be ridiculous.'

'Under the circumstances it would be more ridiculous to stay. Goodnight, Mother.'

Sonia Shawcross stared at her son as if he was mad as he stomped across the room and shut the door with quiet deliberation.

At the foot of the stairs he took a deep, satisfying breath and knew that another phase of his life was over.

The bar of the Thames Riviera was cool after the blinding heat which had been building up all day. With a touch of irony Kathryn had suggested it to Giles as their meeting place. He wasn't there yet but she was a little early. She perched on one of the high stools which surrounded three sides of the rectangular bar. A wall, lined with shelves containing drinks, provided the fourth side. From where she sat she had a view of both entrances and was immediately reminded of that first meeting with Laura Tennyson.

Before she left the office, Kathryn had telephoned Helena to bring her up to date and to explain what her meeting with Giles was about. She did not mention that Megan Morris was about to reveal herself although she had hinted at it. 'Just watch the main news next Wednesday,' she told her cryptically. Helena had no time to enquire further as she was driving Gerald to the airport and was trying to organise the children first.

Helena had said to give her love to Alex and that she hoped everything was all right. Kathryn did not mention the accident, because she knew Helena would guess intuitively that it had been no such thing. She was a little piqued that her friend had no time to listen, then immediately felt ashamed. She had neglected Helena over the past few weeks, having neither telephoned nor written. And Alex, she thought; she must be very careful there. He was immersed in discussions and plans for expansion but Kathryn had not yet asked him how they were progressing. Tonight she would remedy that.

She composed herself, sitting with a straight back as the minutes ticked away. Was it her potential killer she was about to meet? She couldn't work out if it was safer to leave first when the meeting was over, or to let him go.

Giles arrived ten minutes after the appointed time and blamed the traffic for his tardiness. He ordered a drink and asked Kathryn if she would like another then suggested he buy her dinner.

'Thank you, but no. I'm meeting my husband.' The polite formalities over with, Giles explained what was to happen the following Wednesday night.

'About the other thing – you intend going ahead with it?'

'Definitely,' Kathryn said, meaning it but wondering why he was looking at her in such a strange way.

'I can't talk you out of it?'

273

She shook her head and her hair fell forward, hiding her expression. Was it Giles, then, if he was against it?

'In that case may I ask you a favour? Will you come to me first?'

'Yes, of course. But I can't start until after your reunion, for obvious reasons. Did Laura mention that she wants me to be there?'

'She did.' Giles's smile was urbane.

'Good. Thank you for coming all this way to see me. I have to go now.' As they shook hands she was aware of his scrutiny and the way in which his eyes flickered to the yellowing bruise on the side of her forehead. Had he tried to kill her because he had also killed Sarah? Kathryn could not decide how far a man in his position would go, how many risks he would take to preserve it. Whatever happened she was not going to take any chances. Not with him, not with any of them.

She couldn't help glancing behind her as she left and locked all four car doors the moment she was behind the wheel. The traffic was still heavy; she would have little chance of knowing if she was followed.

It was overbearingly humid and the sky had a peculiar yellow tinge but no rain or storms had been forecast. One day she would have a car in which the air-conditioning worked properly.

Kathryn went over what Giles had said. It was an enlargement on Laura's story. The method of payments to Megan Morris was more simple than she had imagined. 'When we were married, we had a joint account as well as individual ones,' Giles had said. 'I agreed to keep the joint one going until after the divorce was finalised because I had promised to pay in a monthly cheque to enable Laura to cope until our financial affairs were settled. Meanwhile she produced her first novel, under the name of Megan Morris. She signed an agreement which stated that all monies pertaining to her career were to be made over to me. I then paid them into her account under my name. The account still exists. Laura knew I would never let her down or make a withdrawal from that account. There's nothing illegal, you understand. You can use any name you wish as long as it isn't for

274

fraudulent purposes. Our accountant sorted out the Inland Revenue side.' As he spoke, Kathryn watched his expression. It was obvious how much he loved Laura, even now. It was also obvious how useful it had been to Laura to have married Giles. She wondered why the marriage had not lasted.

Rounding a bend and indicating right, Kathryn was aware of headlights close behind her and the flashing signal of the car. She held her breath. When she made a subsequent turn into the road where her flat was situated, the car behind seemed to slow then accelerate before carrying on in the same direction. From the corner, the lights shining from her flat were visible. 'I'm getting paranoid,' she told herself as she ran from the car to the entrance.

Alex looked exhausted. He smiled wanly but did not get up from where he was sprawled on the settee. 'Fancy pouring your old man a drink?'

'Beer?' She was glad of the excuse to go to the kitchen. She didn't want Alex to see that she was frightened.

'God, this weather. I hope it breaks soon.'

'So do I,' she called back. I must ask him, she thought. I mustn't let this business ruin everything again. 'How's the deal going?' she said as she handed him an ice-cold glass.

'It's not.'

'Oh, Alex!'

'I know. One of those things. Having thought it through carefully, I can see the pitfalls. However, I've got other irons in the fire.'

'Such as?'

His grin changed his whole face. He ran a hand through his hair then pulled her to him, kissing her hard on the mouth. He tasted of beer and his lips were cool. 'Not just yet, my little tuatara. I'll discuss it with you in a week or two.'

'Come on, tell me. Please?'

He laughed again. He knew just how much Kathryn hated not knowing things; how much stronger her curiosity was than his. 'Not until after the big revelation.' He wanted her to have her moment, especially as, if she agreed to his proposal, their lives might alter dramatically.

275

Kathryn went to the kitchen to prepare a meal, something light as neither of them was particularly hungry. When they were seated at the table by the open windows in the lounge she realised that there was no longer any tension between them, that somehow or other it had simply evaporated. When she and Alex made love that night, it was for no other reason than they wanted each other.

The debilitating humidity lasted another forty-eight hours then, without warning, came the rain. The plants in Laura's garden were washed clean of dust and the lawn, already parched and yellow, sprouted new tufts of green. Damp smells wafted in through the open windows and Laura changed out of a summer dress into jeans and a blouse when the goose-flesh rose on her arms. *Tonight*, she thought, unable to believe it was really going to happen.

There was a gala dinner and presentation in London, one at which the rich and the famous would be present in order to honour those in the literary world. The guest speaker who would be presenting the main awards was to be Megan Morris – *in person*! This news had created great excitement, and press speculations were once more rife. A reporter on a Berkshire weekly, Kathryn Brooks, had apparently made the discovery single-handed and had, herself, been subjected to interviews.

Kathryn had telephoned Laura that day. 'I'd no idea it would be like this,' she said. 'And Alex keeps teasing me.' Her picture had made the front page of the tabloids. Even Keith had said she would not look out of place on page 3. The gala dinner was that evening, but Kathryn was not attending in her professional capacity.

Laura was finding it impossible to work. She showered and lay on her bed, almost ready, hours before she was due to be picked up. At five-thirty she put on underclothes and made up her face. Every muscle in her body felt knotted.

The curtains fluttered inwards but the coolness was welcome to Laura's hot face. A crack of thunder made her jump and she wondered if the gods were angry with her. Finally deciding she was shaking too much to pin her hair up neatly she left it loose, the sides held back with combs. At six she rang Marcia, who would only say that she was still awaiting the results of her hospital tests.

'Good luck, darling. I'll be watching the news. If you're nervous, drink some of that herb tea I gave you.'

'I wish you were coming with me.'

Marcia chuckled. 'You can't really imagine it's my idea of a night out, can you?'

'No. Not really. But I'll be thinking about you.'

Laura stepped into her dress and stood watching until the chauffeured limousine drew up outside the house. It could not be seen by her neighbours and there were only the ducks on the Thames to witness her departure. With a satin stole around her shoulders she stepped into the back of the car and the driver closed the door.

The tarmac of the road glistened as they headed towards London and she was unaware of the stares of other motorists and their passengers as they progressed up the M4. She had plenty of time to think about the consequences of her actions before they reached their destination.

The chauffeur smoothly negotiated the traffic and pulled up outside the hotel in Park Lane. The press were everywhere, peering into the car before Laura had a chance to get out of it. A carefully fixed smile broke into a genuine one as she saw Giles approach. He took her arm and led her up the steps and into the building. 'Keep smiling,' he whispered. 'The worst is already over.'

A path to their table magically appeared as people stepped backwards in deference or awe. Laura had expected them to surge forwards. Her senses seemed not to be in working order because she recognised no one and could not recall any of the sounds of those first few minutes. Only when she had a drink in her hand did she notice the excited babble of conversation and the colourful dresses of the women. There was one more obstacle before she could try to enjoy the evening.

'This is Ingrid,' Giles announced as he steered her towards a group of people. The sea of faces receded as Laura shook hands with her replacement.

'I did not know that Giles's first wife was so beautiful and so talented,' Ingrid said generously. 'He has kept two secrets from me.' There were no signs that she minded the fact that Giles, unknown to her, had continued seeing Laura.

'Thank you. I'm pleased to meet you at last and at the risk of this sounding like a mutual admiration society, you look stunning.' Ingrid's dress was icy white with silver threads running through it which caught the light. It was held in place by straps no thicker than shoe-laces.

Giles was looking from one woman to the other with a bemused smirk on his face. He had not expected them to react well to one another but they were opposites in almost everything, which might explain why there was no antagonism. He had taken a chance in bringing them together on such a public occasion, but had worked on the principle of there being safety in numbers. He considered himself to be a lucky man; both of his wives were beautiful. Laura's long black dress accentuated her sensuousness and sexuality. Ingrid was as slender, although without the same curves and her hair, cut straight just below her ears, was so pale it was like a child's. The introductions over they sat down and Laura saw Kathryn wave from across the room.

After the meal, at which Laura only picked, she was escorted onto the platform to thunderous applause and made her speech. At the end she said she would not have been there if it wasn't for the persistent efforts of Kathryn Brooks. She presented the awards in the continuous glare of flashbulbs and was vain enough to hope that the journalists used the most flattering photographs.

'You are very brave. I couldn't have done that,' Ingrid said, laying a hand on Laura's when she returned to the table. Laura realised there need be no more secret meetings with Giles, no more aloofness in her relationships in case people came close to the truth, and no more anxiety about being found out. She was free at last. Or almost free. She began to enjoy herself.

By the time she was in bed she was exhausted and reaction had set in. She spoke briefly to Marcia who had seen her on television, then switched off the light.

In the morning she heard the paper drop through the letter-box as she was making coffee. She had the *Telegraph* delivered and had been right not to expect more than a few lines alongside a photograph. Later she would buy the tabloids and see what they had made of it. Sipping coffee and smoking her first cigarette of the day, Laura laughed. There would be little housework done that morning. When Peggy arrived armed with the *Sun*, she would be breathless with excitement, having learned through its pages who her employer really was.

Kathryn watched Laura from across the room. She was radiant and beautiful but she knew that beneath the outer confidence was a layer of raw nerves. Other press people were there. It was not up to Kathryn to gain an interview; she had already played her part and taken the credit for it. She did not stay until the end.

Unobtrusively leaving the banqueting suite, she collected her jacket and went outside. The clear night air was welcome after the stuffiness of the building. She took a couple of deep breaths and began to walk towards her car which was parked at the back of the building. She stopped, suddenly scared. The silence was only broken by moving traffic. Her heart began to beat faster and her breathing was shallow as adrenalin flooded her body. *There was someone there.* She knew without doubt that someone was watching her.

As she began to walk faster she heard the footsteps. Her car keys were in her hand ready to open the door. She started to run. The high heel of her shoe bent beneath her and the ground rose up, in slow motion, as she landed on her knees. Tiny bits of surface stone grazed her legs. She felt nothing. Lurching forward she made the car, fumbling for the lock, trying not to faint. A shadow fell across her as she flung herself inside and slammed the door, pressing the central locking switch as she did so. Her foot slipped off the clutch and she scrunched through the gears as she made it to the exit barrier which rose so slowly before her. A man had grabbed for the door-handle – a tall man in dark clothing with a baseball cap pulled down low on his forehead. She hadn't seen him, not properly, but there was something familiar about him.

Negotiating through the other parked cars she had tried

to catch a glimpse of him in her mirrors but he must have ducked down somewhere.

Seconds, she thought, only seconds away from injury or worse. The thought made her feel sick. She wanted to stop the car, to sit with her head on the steering wheel and weep but she dared not. 'Oh God,' she said as a light changed to red ahead of her. 'What if he's got a car?' There was the motorway to contend with. There would be traffic, there always was on the M4, but not much, not enough to prevent someone running her off the road.

An inner strength Alex had always known Kathryn possessed came to her rescue. It was pointless taking risks, trying to run through red lights or driving too fast – she'd only end up injuring herself or someone else. She drove as carefully as her trembling would allow. The motorway was safer than the A4, she decided. Her car was good enough not to let her down and could probably out-distance a lesser model. At a steady seventy-five she made it to the Slough junction. Nothing turned off after her.

Weak-kneed, she reached the entrance to the flats and leaned against the door once she was inside. The next problem was whether to tell Alex. She had given her word that she wouldn't go to the police, not until after the old crowd had met up again at Laura's place. It was tempting to break it, but then she might never know. Hold on, she told herself, it isn't long now. I won't go anywhere alone. She felt quite sure that whoever was tailing her would not break into the flat. The risk of a neighbour seeing or hearing something, or of Alex being at home, was too great.

Breathing deeply to steady herself she went up the stairs and into the flat. Alex was waiting up for her.

'You okay? You're a bit pale.' He kissed her as she nodded. 'You don't know how proud of you I am. Now, tell me all about it.'

She did so and hoped he would put her confused version down to excitement.

Helena rang early the following morning. 'I got your message,' Kathryn said, 'but it was too late to ring you back.'

'What does Alex make of it all?'

'Oh, he's doing his quietly-proud, I-knew-you-could-do-it bit.'

'Is something wrong?'

'No, why?'

'I don't know. You don't sound your usual self.'

'It's a lot to take in, Helena. Look, can I give you a ring later in the week?'

'Of course you can. Go on or you'll be late for work.'

Kathryn replaced the receiver. There were nine days to go before the reunion. She vowed she would get through them and she would do it alone.

John Atherton rarely watched television and knew nothing about the gala dinner until he saw the paper the day afterwards. His stomach contracted when he caught sight of Laura's smiling face. He studied it for ages, hardly able to believe the story. 'Well, damn me,' he breathed still reading as he walked towards the university, the paper folded in his hand. Seventeen years had passed yet he had recognised Laura instantly. It was typical of Giles that he had kept the secret from him.

John was slightly shocked to learn that Giles had been married to Laura – and that he, John, had not been the only love of her life, after all. All those times he had criticised her essays yet he had not spotted her style when he had finally read a copy of *Homecoming*. Of course, her arguments and organisational skills had been superb, but he had never told her so, preferring the others to believe that no one was better than himself. What a prig I was, he thought.

A student was waiting to speak to him about something. John rolled up the paper and shoved it into his back pocket. 'Lincoln had it right,' he said.

'I'm sorry?' The myopic student was gaping at him through round, steel-rimmed glasses.

'Lincoln. You've heard of him, no doubt? Laura and Giles. They fooled all of the people for a very long time.'

'Er . . .'

John roared with laughter. 'It's all right, I haven't taken

leave of my senses. Here,' he slung the paper down on the table, 'Laura Tennyson. My ex-lover.'

The student blinked. 'Oh. I see.' His expression showed that he clearly did *not* see and thought it might be better to come back at another time.

John had a lecture scheduled for eleven on the merits of various British poets. He hoped at least a couple in attendance would have bothered to have read them. On his way to the hall, Tina Parry hurried past without bothering to acknowledge his existence. She wore a very short skirt over what seemed to be cycling shorts. He would have enjoyed boasting to her about his relationship with Laura although he doubted if she would believe him. And how much more glamorous would he appear to his colleagues if they knew. Except, he thought, it's unlikely they would believe me.

Rereading the article had delayed him slightly, and students were already filling the lecture hall. Some were gossiping; others, unable to accept that university was not an extension of school, had their books open studiously. They were in their second year now and had apparently not learned how to have fun as well as study. There was no time now to ponder over the mystery surrounding Laura and Giles, but it crossed John's mind that Laura's reluctance to subject herself to the public eye might be connected to that summer night, seventeen years ago. *I know*, she had written on that final postcard. But what did she know?

'Are we ready?' John asked, his smile falsely benign as he cast an eye over the disparate assemblage. Experience enabled him to pick out the attentive from those who had called in to catch up on some sleep. One or two appeared languidly bored but they, he knew, were like himself at their age – affecting apathy to disguise their burning ambitions.

A large cloud passed overhead and a sudden breeze funnelled through the building. 'If someone would like to close the door, please? We don't want to freeze our balls off, do we?' After a few titters the lecture began.

When it was over John decided he would try to contact Laura. If she used the name Tennyson she had presumably not remarried and she might, if he was lucky, consider taking up where they had left off.

By the time he had decided that the only way to approach her was through her publishers, he had received a short letter from her inviting him to lunch.

Vicky had told David she could not see him on the Wednesday after the awkward birthday party but immediately reassured him it was nothing to do with his mother. 'My son and his wife are coming down from Leicester and they're taking me out for a meal. What about Thursday?'

He agreed with alacrity, pleased that the suggestion had come from her.

At home that evening he stood in the kitchen listening to the noises filtering up from the streets below him as he gave serious thought to his future. He already knew that without Vicky it would be bleak – and realised that he had never loved Nicola, not in the right way; she had been more of a sister. Now he had sudden urges to splash out on champagne, to give Vicky all the things he guessed she had never had, but she only smiled fondly at him when he made what she considered to be rash decisions.

The rain had stopped but the air was humid. David thought a glass of wine would be preferable to the coffee he had been about to make. He hardly went to the pub around the corner now and had taken to keeping drinks in the flat. Vicky had been inside once or twice and expressed her approval, which surprised him because her own house had been modernised internally and was very tidy.

Taking his drink into the large living area, David tore open the bank statement which had arrived that morning. It was his personal account. Never before had he really thought about money, but he saw that although he did not stint himself he was, in fact, quite rich. There were also several building society accounts. He meticulously checked the items listed against his chequebook and cash withdrawal slips, then filed the statement in his desk. He was restless, unsure what to do with himself and knew it was because he was becoming dependent upon Vicky's company, but he must not fall into the trap of becoming *over*-dependent.

For something to do he switched on the television and picked up Kitty who was reclining on the floor. The newscaster was running through the headlines as a preliminary to reading the news. The words *Megan Morris* made him raise his head and stop stroking Kitty. How strange that the name should have cropped up three times recently! And then, disasters and politics out of the way, he held his breath as the newscaster said, 'The identity of the best-selling novelist, Megan Morris, was revealed this evening at a literary dinner in London. Miss Morris, whose real name is Laura Tennyson, was accompanied by her publisher, Giles Harris.' The words were read over footage of Laura getting out of a limousine and being escorted into a grand hotel on Giles's arm. David thought she was as beautiful as ever. The sequins on her black dress were dazzling. Inside the building the other guests parted like the Red Sea as she was led to the ballroom. The next shot showed her at the end of her speech and she blushed slightly as the applause broke out.

It's finally over, David thought. If Giles and Laura have gone public there can be nothing to fear. He wanted to telephone Vicky to tell her that these were old friends of his from university, but she was out somewhere with her son. He would let her know tomorrow, after he had read the paper, and he would also speak to Giles to find out what had happened to cause this unveiling of such a well-guarded secret.

On his way to work he purchased several newspapers. Laura's face was splashed over the front pages of several of them. He read each article thoroughly then tried to reach Giles but was told he wouldn't be in the office that day.

'Amazing, isn't it?' Polly said, nodding towards the papers spread over the counter when she arrived for work. 'I've read all of her books, she's brilliant. I didn't imagine her to look like that, though. She's lovely.'

'I know. I was at Oxford with her.'

'Never!' Polly's eyes lit up. 'Just wait till I tell my friends.'

David went to serve the first customer of the day leaving Polly to scan the papers, vainly hoping to see a mention of his name. He was amused at the idea of being, in her eyes, famous by proxy.

'What was she like?' Polly asked during a quiet period.

'Intelligent and kind and gentle.'

'Here, I bet you were in love with her.'

'I was a little. But so were many others. Unfortunately, she was in love with someone else.' He paused but was unable to resist a little harmless pride. 'I kissed her once.'

Polly treated him to one of her delighted squeals. 'You didn't!'

'Only on the cheek. It was very chaste.' Polly's face fell. 'I could only worship from afar. She came to me for comfort after she discovered her boyfriend had been unfaithful.' David wasn't sure why it was him she had chosen to confide in when she had always been closer to Giles. Having learned from the papers that Laura and Giles had been married he began to understand. Laura must have known how Giles felt about her, and on learning that things were not working out with John, he might have felt encouraged. In the end Giles had got what he wanted even if it hadn't lasted.

'And they talk about the younger generation,' Polly said. 'I suppose you'd all have been hippies back then.'

Back then? Did he seem that old to her? Then he laughed. 'Me, a hippie?'

Polly's eyes travelled the length of his body. 'No, perhaps not,' she said rather dismissively before unpacking and pricing some new stock.

Giles had decided to hold the press conference at his own home rather than disrupt the office routine. He had already received several calls from his secretary Lisa, saying there had been numerous demands for Laura to attend signing sessions, and Radio Berkshire wanted to interview her. He said it would all have to wait although he rang Laura to warn her what to expect. 'Oh, by the way, Ingrid has suggested you might like to come for dinner one evening.'

Laura sensed by his tone that it was none of his doing, that he felt the idea to be vaguely incestuous. 'But you're not keen?'

'I didn't say that. It's just . . .' but he could not say just what it was. 'However, I must warn you that although Ingrid has many strengths and virtues, I cannot recall more than a handful of culinary successes.'

285

Giles had always enjoyed his food and Laura's cooking in particular. It was difficult to imagine him married to a woman who, apparently, did not know the difference between a potato peeler and a garlic press. 'Tell her I'd love to come,' Laura said firmly.

Giles managed to hang up without making a commitment.

Laura's day had been chaotic since the moment of Peggy's arrival. As she had suspected, little housework got done because Peggy kept staring at her and shaking her head and coming out with phrases such as, 'Well I never!' and, 'Who'd have believed it?' Laura had finally shown her the attic room to put an end to any further speculation.

'I knew it was there, of course, because of the window. But I thought it was a store room or something.' Peggy, clad in her fuchsia nylon overall, had touched the electronic typewriter with awe. 'I don't know how you do it, all those words. It takes me an hour to write a letter.' Peggy was given permission to vacuum the attic room, but Laura made it clear she was not to touch anything else.

Neighbours from both sides had called in, unable to believe what they had either seen or heard, and congratulations were offered. Champagne provided by Pam and Jos was duly opened and drunk. It was early evening before Laura had a chance to sit down and compose a short, identical letter to John and David, inviting them to lunch. She did not tell either of them that the other would be present.

She sealed the envelopes and placed a first-class stamp on each then walked to the nearest post-box. She had been confined to the house all day. Stopping to watch the soothing water of the Thames, she wondered if they would guess there was more to it than she had implied. They would know that Kathryn Brooks had been involved in it all and she had spoken to them both. There was nothing now to do but wait.

Forewarned by Kathryn, Harriet Milton had watched the news. For the first time in many years she cried, properly cried, hot tears flowing down her face. Seeing Laura and Giles had brought it all back. Yet she felt a vestige of hope. If Kathryn had succeeded in tracing Sarah's friends and had achieved what no one else had been able to in ten years, dare she believe she might also succeed in other directions?

One other good thing had come out of it. Jim had read the papers and recognised the names and had telephoned Harriet immediately to see if she was all right. He had offered to come home for the weekend. 'No, Jim,' Harriet had said, 'I'm fine.' She did not want his pity and she had to admit she had grown used to not having him around. Later she would telephone Kathryn.

'How does it feel?' Alex asked, not for the first time.

'I can't explain it. In one way it's great, but it's also frightening.' Far more frightening than she could allow Alex to guess. Each hour seemed to drag. Laura had told her that the four surviving members of the Oxford group would all be present on Saturday. Surely she would learn then which one of them was so terrified of the past that they intended silencing her.

Kathryn had been inundated with calls, from other journalists who wanted her own story, and from newspapers who were interested in employing her. Now her ambitions were about to be gratified she needed time to think. Alex agreed; he said it was best to wait and not rush into a job in a fit of euphoria. But she was feeling far from euphoric. The only thing she could think about was the forthcoming reunion.

'All hell's been let loose,' Giles commented when David got through to him in his office on Friday. 'Ingrid was marvellous. She took the day off work and spent it providing the press with tea and coffee. I take it you'll be at Laura's?'

'I wouldn't miss it for anything. Look, can I buy you a drink this evening?'

'Yes, why not?' Giles was taken aback. There was none of the old hesitancy in David's voice. There had been no repercussions, despite the enormous amount of publicity; the word 'Oxford' hadn't even been mentioned, and there was no reason why the police should make any connection between a best-selling author and a murder which had taken place seventeen years ago. They were safe and Giles was beginning to relax. 'Why don't we make it the American Bar at the Savoy? It's almost on your doorstep,' he added a little unkindly.

Giles arrived before David and was seated at a small round table puffing at a cigar. He stood when he saw David and waved him over, much to the displeasure of the waiter whose job it was to show people to their tables. 'I've ordered champagne,' he said immediately. 'I hope you don't mind. You can have something else if you prefer.'

'No, that's fine. It certainly shook me up, seeing you and Laura on television.'

'I couldn't warn you – it had to be a complete surprise. Laura had promised Kathryn Brooks it would be that way.'

David had wondered about that. He had read about her part in it all but could not see why, if Laura was afraid of the past, she had suddenly come forward. 'Yes, I met Mrs Brooks.'

'You did?' Giles had laid the cigar in the ashtray and was in the process of picking an olive from the tray on the table. 'In that case, she's spoken to us all. I wonder what else that young lady has managed to discover? She'll be there, at this reunion.'

David did not answer because just then a white-jacketed waiter appeared bearing the champagne and went about his business with cork and serviette. 'That's fine, thanks,' Giles said, then began to explain to David how Kathryn had found each of them. 'So you see, we know that Jenny's dead and it looks now as if it *was* Sarah's body that was found in those woods. The only mystery is, who killed her, and why? If what Jenny told Laura is true – and we have to remember she was the sort of girl who might make things up – then she wasn't killed the night we were all there. That, thank God, rules all of us out.'

'I see. So that's what this is about, us all meeting at Laura's. Is it to prove we couldn't have done it?'

Giles shrugged. 'The reverse could also hold true, but I do keep wondering if Sarah could have carried out her plan. Anyway, drink up, old boy, it's all in the past.'

David did so. The 'old boy' no longer sounded offensive;

it was just the way Giles was and he, David, was less sensitive since Vicky had appeared on the scene.

For several minutes they sat in silence and watched the other drinkers in the American Bar. Most were smartly and expensively dressed; couples and businessmen enjoying a pre-dinner drink. A pianist sat at one side of the room playing Gershwin melodies. 'I suppose,' David mused, 'if Sarah *did* kill someone, she must have left her own identification with the body, but I still don't see how the police could be mistaken.'

'A lot of time had elapsed.' Giles re-lit the cigar. He wasn't really enjoying it but was in a celebratory mood. 'There were obviously no scars or marks on the flesh to work from, and,' he paused, 'there were no dental records fom which to work. Whoever killed her, kicked her teeth in afterwards.'

'My God!' David felt faint.

'Precisely. And that's why I'm sure it couldn't have been one of us.'

They were both thinking the same thing. It was David who voiced it. 'But it could have been Sarah.'

'Yes.'

She was the only one who was callous enough to have done such a thing to cover her own tracks.

David changed the subject.

'How did you and Laura come to be married?'

Giles poured some more champagne. 'We'd both come to London to find work. I'd rather liked to have remained in Oxford, but after that night I knew I couldn't. Anyway, we met now and then for drinks and Laura told me she wasn't happy where she was working. I arranged an interview for her and she got the job. It was on her own merits, I didn't pull any strings. Anyway, to cut a long story short, she bought me a meal in return for the favour and things progressed from there. John was no longer on the scene by then and, I have to admit it, I was pleased when I later heard he'd gone to the States. I was a lucky man. Unfortunately it didn't last. Around the time of our divorce, Laura presented me with her manuscript and when it was accepted she moved to Maidenhead to write full-time and reverted to her maiden name. I went along with her about keeping her identity a secret; I didn't want to lose her as an author.'

'Why didn't she simply write under the name of Tennyson?'

'Do you know, she's never told me.' Giles didn't want to go into the details of how the first manuscript came about.

'Will you allow me to repay your hospitality?'

'What?'

'Champagne. Can we manage another bottle?'

'Good God, man, I've never known you push the boat out before. But, yes, you certainly can. Ingrid's latest hobby is bridge and I can think of nothing worse than a houseful of women squabbling over cards.'

'That's rather a sexist comment, Giles.'

'What?' Heads turned as Giles's laugh echoed around the room and for a split second there was a lull in the discreet murmurings of conversation. Only the pianist remained oblivious to the hiatus. 'You're the last person I'd have associated with isms.'

'It's Polly's fault. I have to be careful in her presence. You might say, "An' I learned about women from 'er!" '

'Well, I don't know who this Polly is, but she seems to be doing you some good. You're developing a sense of humour. But look here, I've had two wives and therefore consider myself to be a bit of an expert. "So be warned by my lot (which I think you will not), An' learn about women from me." Kipling certainly knew what he was on about, didn't he? And surely he also said something along the lines of a woman being only a woman, but a good cigar is a smoke?' Giles stared thoughtfully at the glowing tip of his own cigar. 'I'm not so sure he was right there. So, tell me, who is Polly?' Giles listened in amazement as David described the strange creature who had come to work for him and who had brightened up his life. He was even more amazed when he heard about Vicky.

They were halfway down the second bottle of champagne when David felt a foolish grin spreading over his face. He loved talking about Vicky and Giles was laughing at his anecdotes. He had had no idea he could be so entertaining.

* * *

Michael Jarvis had heard nothing further from Kathryn Brooks. He was not particularly intelligent but he was streetwise. He had known at the time that no way was she making a documentary, although she certainly was a reporter; she had left her business card. He felt no qualms about taking the ten pounds from her and would have demanded more if he thought he could have got away with it.

Later he went through it again. Why should someone like her be interested in himself and a group of Oxford students? The more he thought, the more sure he became. He needed to find out exactly what she was up to. He hated her. Not personally – he couldn't give a toss about Kathryn Brooks as a woman one way or the other – but she had brought it all back to him. He had loved Jenny; she had been his world. There wasn't a single day when he didn't regret the past, when he did not remember it, but it was in his own head that he lived it. He did not want anyone else soiling his memories.

The woman had not come back to him, not even with a false excuse, but he could not get her out of his mind. He needed to know what she was up to. He knew he must do something about it.

The day after the gala dinner he read the newspapers. The room span and he wanted to vomit. He had not expected to see Laura's face smiling up at him, mocking him. There was another picture, one of the Brooks woman. She, too, was smiling. Dressed in their expensive clothes, beautiful and rich, they provided a dreadful contrast to the woman Jenny had become. Nothing ever worked out for Michael Jarvis.

The job he had recently obtained as a courier was not going well. Sometimes he took too long over deliveries; sometimes he was late for work. The items he was respons- ible for were either too large to post or were required in a hurry. It was supposed to be a rapid service he was pro- viding. There was a certain amount of freedom in his work which was why he had applied for the job. It was also reasonably well paid. He would miss the money, for he knew that he was in danger of being sacked but it no longer seemed to matter. Since he could never have Jenny, nothing really had ever mattered.

He studied the paper closely, fury mounting inside him, then he screwed it into a ball and set alight to it in the sink.

'Are you sure you can handle this?' Alex wanted to know as Kathryn got ready to go to Laura's on Saturday morning. Her face was pale and he thought he had heard her retching in the bathroom.

'Positive. Stop fussing, Alex.' She turned to kiss him on the cheek to soften her words. She had not meant to snap.

He nodded slowly. Kathryn was hiding something from him, had been doing so for some time but now was not the moment to ask her what it was. He, too, had a secret – news which he intended breaking to her when she returned later. Despite his misgivings he had to accept that her tenacity had paid off. As much as he admired her, he had not believed that she would find Megan Morris. Maybe this alone had been enough to satisfy her driving ambition because she had made no more mention of the London-based jobs which she had been offered.

Laura had asked her guests for eleven-thirty. Only John had a journey of any length to make and it was simple enough, straight through from Cardiff Central to Reading then the branch line to Maidenhead. It did not entail a very early start.

Kathryn glanced nervously at her watch. It was time to set off.

She was the first to arrive, which pleased Laura who had been pacing up and down. She admitted her nervousness to Kathryn.

'It'll be all right,' Kathryn told her, although her own stomach was churning.

Drinks and nuts were set out on a sideboard. Laura poured wine for them both. 'I've only done a cold buffet,' she said. 'I didn't think I could cope with the full works. Besides, it's too warm for a hot meal.'

The day was only averagely warm and overcast but Kathryn knew Laura was chatting to hide her anxiety. A loud bang on the door made them both jump. Laura's hand shook and she spilled some wine as she placed her glass on a table. She straightened her spine, pushed back her hair and walked as steadily as she was able, out to the hall. 'Giles, come on in!' The relief in her voice was obvious. The first two people to arrive were the ones with whom she was in contact. It would be easier now to face the others.

Each with a drink they sat down to wait, keeping their thoughts to themselves. It was ten minutes before there was another knock – a quieter and rather tentative one. 'That'll be David,' Giles commented. They heard a muffled conversation then Laura and David entered the room.

Giles and Kathryn exchanged a quick glance. There was something very different about David, something that went deeper than his physical appearance. His hair had been professionally cut and he had abandoned his shapeless clothes for a casual cream shirt which complimented the moss-green trousers cut in the latest fashion. It was, Kathryn thought, his eyes which had altered. The hangdog expression was no longer there; he looked happy.

'It's a lovely room, Laura.' David studied it after nodding to Giles and Kathryn.

'Thank you.'

'No John yet? Still, he was never renowned for his punctuality.' David accepted a glass of wine and sat down. Conversation was made but there seemed to be a tacit agreement to leave important matters until they were all present. They were just beginning to think that John had changed his mind when he hammered at the door. It was ten past twelve. Laura got up to let him in.

'Damn trains,' they heard quite clearly from the hall. 'Anyway, you look marvellous, it's great to see you again.'

'In here,' Laura said rather coldly.

John's large frame filled the doorway. He arched one eyebrow and grinned. 'Well, well, if it isn't the old crowd. Oh, and the delicious Mrs Brooks. I should've guessed you'd be involved somehow.'

'Whisky, is it?' Laura walked over to the drinks tray. She guessed it would not be his first of the day.

'Thank you.' He was flattered that she still remembered what he drank. 'So, we are gathered together, as they say, but for what specific purpose, I wonder? No doubt young Kathryn, having gone thus far, now intends to prove one of us to be Sarah's killer.' His smile took the sting out of the words.

'I think it would be best if Kathryn explained.' Laura sat down, feeling weak and exhausted. It no longer mattered if it was one of them, it really no longer mattered who it was. Marcia was ill, very ill; she was dying, and Laura could cope with anything but that. She had almost cancelled this lunch when she heard, but had left it too late. Deep down, she knew things were coming to an end in every aspect of her life and she wanted to get it over with.

Kathryn sat on the edge of her seat with her glass clasped in both hands. Her mouth felt dry. 'Since I first met you all individually, several things have come to light, not least Laura admitting she is Megan Morris. I now know for certain that Jennifer Branagh was married to a man named Brian Morris,' she held up a hand as David was about to interrupt. 'That's another matter; it's not relevant today. Jenny is dead. She died of an overdose of heroin, accidental from all accounts. It still leaves the question of who killed Sarah and why. From what I've found out there seems no possible explanation for it to have been Jenny.' She stopped. Without making accusations there seemed little more to say.

'Very good, Kathryn, and very clever, but is that why we're here, for you to point the finger?' John asked.

It was Giles who answered before John became too belligerent. 'No. But another explanation has occurred to me.' Everyone turned to look at him. 'Jenny knew about the game, as we all did, but supposing, for whatever reason, Sarah planned to kill *her*, she might have had to kill Sarah in self-defence.'

There was silence whilst this possibility was digested. 'No,' John said emphatically. 'There was no reason for Sarah to wish to be Jenny. What do you think, David?' It was the first time John had spoken to him. There had been no shaking of hands, no acknowledgement at all between the two men. David no longer cared; he feared none of them.

'I expect you're right. I don't know why we're bothering to go over it all again. It's up to the police, surely?'

294

'Jenny was never questioned,' Kathryn stated quietly. 'There was no reason for her to have been. As far as the police were concerned, she did no more than serve in a café in Oxford.' She studied each of them in turn. Could one of them be so afraid of what she might find out that they were watching her? Although she thought John was the most likely candidate, she knew the practicalities made it unlikely, and still, at the back of her mind was one thing that was nagging at her but which she could not remember.

'Is this what I've travelled here for?' John went to the drinks tray and helped himself without asking. He was bitterly disappointed; he had had visions of a cosy reunion with Laura and a night in her bed. 'Look, if Jenny was responsible, then what does it matter? She's dead now. I think I may as well get the next train home.' Home, he thought. Yes, Cardiff really was home now.

'But ought we to go to the police now and tell them what we should have told them at the time?'

John's expression was incredulous. David was the last person he would have expected to suggest such a thing. 'Are you mad, man?'

'You seem quite adamant, John. Any particular reason?' Giles had uncrossed his legs and was leaning forward in his chair as he spoke.

'What are you implying?'

'I just wondered if you'd got anything to hide. You were the one in the know, you were the one who went back, and you were the one who fixed our alibis.'

'You've got a fucking nerve, Giles, do you know that? I did it for all of us. I thought Sarah had gone too far, that's all. You always were a pompous shit.' His outburst was followed by an embarrassed silence.

' "The courtiers who surround him have forgotten nothing and learnt nothing",' David quoted quietly. 'None of us can forget that night, or our version of it, but we haven't had the sense to see that because we were so wrapped up in ourselves and our own guilt, there are other possibilities.'

'Such as?' Laura asked.

David shook his head and took a sip of his wine. 'I have no idea, only that they exist.'

'I agree with David. It really is time we did the right thing, if it can be accomplished without harming any of our reputations.'

Kathryn, who did not know what to make of the various reactions, began to see Giles in a different light. She had decided not to say anything further, to allow them to needle each other and wait and see what it produced.

'Our reputations. How altruistic of you, Giles. Either you go to the police and do it properly or you don't bother. Could it be that you've succumbed to – what is it? "The moral flabbiness of the bitch-goddess success"?'

'For Christ's sake, stop playing your stupid games. You know where it got us last time.'

John turned to Kathryn and bowed from the waist. 'Accept my apologies, Mrs Brooks. I made a joke of your bringing us together to provoke a confession or at least a violent scene. We seem to be managing without your intervention. However, I think this little farce has continued long enough. If you'll all excuse me I shall go and find a suitable watering-hole in which to get stinking drunk and forget I've ever known you. You can cook up whatever you like when I've gone.' John headed angrily towards the door. He was sick of it, sick of the years he had spent carrying them all, protecting them from themselves and their fears. Whatever they might think, he had had no part in Sarah Milton's murder.

They waited until the front door had slammed before anyone spoke. 'She was carrying his child,' Laura said. Kathryn had told her, but she had already known. 'He had more of a motive than any of us.'

Except you, Kathryn thought. If you loved him so very much, how hurtful that knowledge must have been. And Laura had no children of her own. Another possibility sprang to mind.

It seemed then that no one wished to discuss it further. Laura poured more drinks and said there was food in the dining room. Kathryn had had more than enough. She wanted to be at home, with Alex. Her disappointment was crushing. None of them had shown themselves to be the likely murderer, or her own would-be assailant. John had a temper but it was an honest one. He had called Giles a pompous shit, which Kathryn suspected he was at times. Giles was possibly *too* bland; was his attitude a cover for deeper feelings? And Laura who had apparently been so honest with her, who had known who Kathryn was long before the reverse was true, who lived locally and who had loved John . . . had she killed Sarah out of jealousy then wanted to be rid of Kathryn to protect herself? Could she be sure it was a man in the hotel car park that night? David. She looked at him. What exactly had happened to bring about such an obvious change? It was no good. The only thing to do was leave, and see if anyone made an attempt to follow her. Then she realised that John had already left and could be lying in wait for her. I have to know, she thought. *I really have to know.*

'I must be going, Laura.' She offered no excuses.

'Won't you stay? I've done so much food.'

'I'm sorry, I can't.'

Laura came to the door with her. 'I'm sorry, too. It didn't work out, did it? And Kathryn, I can't help you any more.' She hesitated. 'You see, my mother's dying. I have to go to her.' She was still too numb to cry. 'I've never been closer to anyone than Marcia and I cannot imagine life without her. Do whatever you have to do. It really doesn't matter any more.'

'Oh, Laura.' Kathryn touched her shoulder gently then, knowing there was nothing she could say to take away the pain, walked over and got into her car without bothering to check if there was someone hiding in the back.

She almost jumped the lights when Laura's words fully registered. *I've never been closer to anyone than Marcia. Do whatever you have to do. It really doesn't matter any more.*

Outside the flats she parked the car and got out. There was no one in sight and nowhere for anyone to be hiding. She strode briskly across the tarmac, anxious to tell Alex everything. She took the stairs two at a time and unlocked her front door, calling his name as she did so. There was an empty silence.

297

On the kitchen table was a note asking her to meet Alex at the boat-yard as soon as she was free. She was intrigued. Desperate to see him, she picked up her car keys again and headed for the door. Before she could reach it there was a knock. At night the security lock downstairs was in operation but none of the residents bothered with it in daylight. Kathryn opened the door.

For several seconds she did not understand what was happening. This wasn't what she had expected, not what she had been steeling herself against. She was only conscious of the door of the flat being back-heeled closed as she was forced along the corridor.

Chapter 14

ohn walked rapidly along the tow-path towards Maiden-
ead town centre. He was furious at having been tricked
nd at the idea that Laura, Giles and David thought him
guilty. He amended the thought. David had shown little
nterest in the proceedings and had not expressed an
pinion either way. He did not really intend to get drunk,
ot today, and perhaps not so often in the future. He by-
assed the town and made a left and a right turning which
ook him past the football ground and which, he knew,
ust lead him to the station because he could see the
mbankment of the line on his left.

On the platform he sat with his head in his hands feeling
othing but disgust. It was apparent that none of them liked
im and they had wished to use him as their scapegoat. If
nly he knew what had really happened that night. He had
een rude to Kathryn Brooks but now he hoped that his
ssessment of her was correct, that she would continue with
what she had started and prove his innocence. Maybe then
e would have peace of mind.

'Bloody ironical,' he muttered when an announcement
tated that the next train on platform 4 was for Oxford. It
alled at Twyford and Reading but he did not listen to the
ther stops. At Reading he had coffee and a sandwich. He
ared not drink when he was so angry.

On the Cardiff train he handed his ticket to the con-
uctor. 'You should've got a day return, mate,' he said as
e clipped it. 'It would've been cheaper.'

'Indeed I should,' John replied then leaned back, folded his arms and closed his eyes.

He lasted the journey without going to the buffet and at Cardiff Central got straight into a taxi. Back at the house he threw his overnight bag into a corner of the kitchen and went to the cupboard. 'Sod the lot of them.' He poured a drink and swallowed it in one gulp before refilling his glass. The second whisky he sipped more slowly, walking from room to room and letting the peaceful atmosphere of the house do its work. He walked up the wide staircase, running his hands over the carved wood of the bannister, knowing that whoever had lived here before him had been happy. If he stayed there alone for ever it would be no hardship, but it would be better if he could find some female companionship, someone who would understand him, someone who could make him whole.

Aware that self-pity was a dangerous thing he pulled on a jacket and went out into the streets. He would walk along the river by Sophia Gardens and back on the other side, then he would buy himself a decent meal. It was time to forget Oxford; it was even time to forget Angela. He would do the proper thing and write her a long letter explaining it was best if they no longer had any contact with one another. She, too, would be free to get on with her life.

His visit, he realised later as he slowly ate a large steak, had been a catalyst. Whatever his student friends decided to do, he would face the consequences. He smiled at the pretty waitress. Suddenly he was no longer afraid.

David ate several platefuls of the food Laura and Peggy had prepared. His appetite had not been diminished by the emotional scene. At half-past two he thanked Laura and said he must be off. He had to get back to the shop to lock up. Polly had gone in for the day and would be having the Monday off in lieu. And later he was meeting Vicky. He had told her about Laura the day after the television appearance and she had hardly been able to take it in. 'What with the family mansion and all these glamorous people, what chance have I got?' she had said, but she was smiling, conscious that none of those things meant anything to David. He was kind and gentle and considerate, and quite different from her first husband, for whom she had hardly grieved.

'What will you do, Laura?' he asked when she saw him to the door.

She shook her head. There was pain in her eyes and dark smudges beneath them, and the vitality she had always exuded was lacking. 'I don't know. I don't think it matters any more. I always hoped . . . well, it's not important.' She couldn't tell him she had always hoped it was John who had killed Sarah, nor her reasons for wishing it so.

'I think you're right. It's best to let things lie.'

'Goodbye, David. It was lovely seeing you again. I just wish the circumstances could have been different.' She stood on tiptoe and kissed him on the cheek. David touched his face. It could have been the same kiss he had once given her. Not knowing how to react, he pushed his glasses firmly into place, nodded several times and crossed the road, where he waved to Laura who still stood in the doorway.

He wasn't sure what to make of the strange lunch-party, but as his train neared Paddington he found himself wondering what the takings had been and how Polly had coped.

There had been no problems and he told Polly she could leave at four-thirty as she was going out with friends. An hour later he locked up and took a deep breath. He had the whole evening with Vicky to look forward to.

'Laura, what's bothering you?' Giles was the last to leave and was helping to carry the plates and dishes of uneaten food out to the kitchen. 'It's more than what happened today, isn't it?'

'Yes.' She bit her lip. 'It's Marcia. Giles, I don't know what to do.'

'In what way?'

'She's ill. Very ill.'

'Oh, Laura.' He pulled her to him and smelled her perfume and felt the softness of her flesh, and he felt like crying. 'Look,' he continued decisively, 'go and pack a bag and I'll drive you up there. I'll just give Ingrid a ring – she'll understand.'

'No. Please, Giles, there's no need. I've packed already, I'm going first thing in the morning. I shall stay to – oh, God.' She slumped into one of the kitchen chairs and buried her face in her hands as the tears finally fell. *I shall stay to the end* is what she had been about to say. The reality had only just hit her. 'I need to be alone,' she finally said. 'I need to be strong for Marcia. Would you go, Giles? Please.'

'Of course.' He stroked her hair, feeling helpless in the face of so much misery, but he respected her wishes. 'Telephone me, Laura, at any time of the day and night, and if there's anything I can do . . .'

She did not answer and he let himself out, not liking to ask if he might ring for a taxi.

Harriet Milton had been told about the reunion. Kathryn had not wanted to build her hopes up, but simply said it was another step in the right direction. She spent several hours on Saturday afternoon attending to the pots and tubs outside the converted barn. Most of the plants were now in flower but as they were in the shade she could feed and water them. All the time she was half-listening for the telephone, for Kathryn to let her know what had transpired.

At four o'clock she swept the cobbled courtyard then made a cup of tea, taking it out to drink seated on a low stone wall above which was a small patch of lawn. The sun warmed her. She lit a cigarette and blew a cloud of smoke into the fresh, clean air. Sarah would not have been happy here, she realised; she was always more at ease in suburban surroundings. She had come to understand that there was a restlessness about her daughter, as if there was some part of her which could never be satisfied. All her achievements had meant nothing once she had attained them; she simply went on to find another goal to aim for. 'Did Jim and I go wrong somewhere?' she said aloud. She felt ashamed for not having been strictly honest with Kathryn Brooks. She had failed to mention the cruel streak in Sarah, which she tried not to think about because she was never sure whether it was intentional or whether it stemmed from a lack of sensitivity to other people's feelings. Once or twice she wondered if this was the reason why Sarah had been killed.

She flung the cigarette stub into one of the raised flower-beds and went towards the house. If Kathryn had not rung by five she would ring her.

Alex sat at his desk unable to believe that the lunch had gone on for so long. He did not have Laura's telephone number and when he looked, he discovered it wasn't listed. Of course it isn't, he thought, remembering her whole life had been a secret. In front of him was an architect's drawing and several letters. He had spent the morning discussing business with Jack Deacon, a man he had considered making his partner. He had not made the offer because deep down he prefered having total control. Now he was doubly glad he hadn't done so. If Kathryn agreed, life was going to be very different.

Alex was excited and enthusiastic about the future, but it would be Kathryn's decision by which he would abide. Her happiness came before everything.

'Goddammit she must be home by now.' He had left the note on the kitchen table, clearly visible for when she walked in. He picked up the telephone and dialled his home number.

Michael Jarvis had not meant it to be like this, but events had overtaken him. Once or twice he had rung the news-paper office where Kathryn worked and asked for her by name, but he had not been able to bring himself to speak to her. To ask her what he wanted to know would have been to incriminate himself. Then he decided he might manage better face to face. Finally he knew that his intentions were pointless, that whatever he said would make no difference, that there was only one way out of it. But things were not as simple as they appeared on television. He had followed her, but even that was not easy, not with traffic lights and overtaking cars. It had taken longer than he had imagined to find out where she lived, and he thought she might have noticed the van.

Watching the flat was easier but there was no pattern to her or her husband's existence and the man was big, bigger than himself. He didn't think he'd stand a chance if there was a confrontation.

On that Saturday morning he had received a call to deliver some urgent documents to a firm in Marlow. Having accomplished the task and received the requisite signature, he had driven to Burnham which was not very much out of his way. A man passed in front of the window of the flat he knew was Kathryn's. He had previously checked the names by the row of bells outside. A few minutes later the same man left the building and drove off in a car.

Michael went to the entrance. Before he rang the bell he pushed the glass doors. They were open. He went upstairs but there was no answer from flat number 3. It was worth a chance. He waited in the van which he had parked where it would not be too conspicuous. He had his mobile phone. If another job came up they would ring that number.

Just after two a car pulled up, driven by Kathryn. As always she seemed to be in a hurry because she almost ran to the flats. Slowly he got out of the van and followed her.

He was taken by surprise when she opened the door so quickly. His surprise was replaced by rage. How dare she live such a life and be so beautiful when he had nothing! How dare she hide Jenny's whereabouts from him! All of them, all that group who had corrupted Jenny, had carefree magic lives whereas he had a dead-end job and a snivelling girlfriend who was forever nagging him about getting married. Didn't she know he'd never marry anyone but Jenny? And Jenny was still out there somewhere, although he had not been able to find her.

Those students were responsible for that and now Kathryn Brooks was trying to keep Jenny from him. They had taken away the only thing he had ever cared about.

'What do you want?'

Michael grinned. Seeing him had wiped the smile from her face. She'd gone white and staggered a few steps backwards.

'I think you know that.'

'I don't, Michael. I've no idea. Is it more money?' Kathryn flinched as he spat in her face. She had known from the interview that he had never forgiven Jenny's friends for what he believed they had done to her. Myriad thoughts flashed through her mind. John didn't kill Sarah, John hadn't been following her. Nor was it David or Giles. She had not ruled out Laura, but during the drive home another thought had occurred to her. Marcia – Laura's mother. The one person in whom Laura had confided totally, the one who would probably do anything for her, the one person Kathryn would not be able to recognise. If her thoughts were accurate she had nothing to fear from Michael Jarvis. But as she looked up and met his eyes, she saw that she was wrong.

He took one pace forward and grabbed her arm, twisting it painfully. She recoiled in disgust as she smelled his foul breath.

Michael misinterpreted her expression. His fury increased. He swung his arm back and punched her in the face. She ought to be afraid, not looking at him in that way, in the way the students did all those years ago. 'Where is he? Where's Jenny?' His grip tightened and Kathryn wanted to scream. She bit her lip hard and tasted the blood from Michael's blow.

'She's dead, Michael. Jenny's dead. She died from a drug overdose in 1985.'

'Liar!' This girl had found out about Megan Morris, she had to know where Jenny was. The telephone rang, startling them both, breaking through the building tension. 'Leave it. Let it ring,' Michael growled. 'I'm not going until you tell me.'

'I swear to you she's dead.'

'Sarah's dead, you stupid bitch. *Sarah*, not Jenny.'

Kathryn tried to steady her breath. It was coming in rapid gasps. Michael was mixing things up. He was mad; there were eight years between the deaths of the two girls. No, he isn't mad, some rational part of her brain told her. Jenny went away, he thinks she's still alive. With blinding clarity she knew why he was so certain that Sarah was dead. Not because he'd read it in the paper but because he had killed her.

The sudden silence when the telephone finally stopped ringing was welcome. It wasn't switched onto the answering

machine. She was the one who always remembered, Alex
rarely did. For once she was grateful. If he was trying to
contact her, surely he'd realise something was wrong – if it
was Alex. How long before he would start to worry and
come home? How grateful she was that he wasn't like her
who might well have thought sod it and forgotten all about
it. But perhaps after the way in which she had neglected
him it might not be for hours. This is my punishment, she
thought. As Michael Jarvis lunged towards her she saw that
he meant to kill her.

She had not taken any notice of the cars parked outside
and could not, therefore, say which of her neighbours was
in. She had to take the chance. She opened her mouth to
scream but his hands were already around her throat. The
telephone started ringing again.

Alex picked up the plans and folded them neatly, then
added the various bits of correspondence which he secured
together with a large elastic band. His annoyance was
growing. Here was yet another weekend which Kathryn had
chosen to spend with someone other than himself. It was
starting to happen again. He had learned his lesson, there
would be no more women, but Kathryn did not seem to
have learned hers. As he placed the documents in his briefcase he realised it was a wicked thought. He had not started
seeing Rebecca to teach his wife a lesson; it had just happened at a time when he was at his lowest ebb. Kathryn
refused to discuss anything with him and seemed unaware
that he had a life of his own which did not automatically
dovetail around hers.

An idea occurred to him. He had to pass the end of Ray
Mead Road on his way home. He could see if Kathryn's car
was still there. Perhaps he was maligning her; perhaps she
had stopped to get some shopping or she might be in the
bath and had not heard the phone.

There was no sign of her car anywhere near where she
had told him Laura lived and there was only one car in the
drive. The lunch was obviously over. Feeling slightly
happier, Alex drove home.

When he placed his key in the lock of their front door

it wouldn't turn. He took it out and looked at it, thinking he had inserted the wrong one from the bunch on his ring. When it failed to turn a second time he knocked on the door. 'Kathryn?' He listened. There were no sounds from within. Perhaps the lock had broken. He called again. This time he thought he heard a noise, just a small movement, not a voice. Instinctively he knew something was wrong. The hair stood up on the back of his neck and his scalp tickled. He called louder and hammered on the door with his fists. There was someone inside, he was sure of that.

'God, no. Please don't let anything have happened to her.' His breath came fast as he pictured a burglary which had gone wrong. Someone had come to the flat imagining it to be empty. Then he thought about the Oxford students, about Laura and Megan Morris and Giles and knew he had been right, that Kathryn had led herself into danger.

Without stopping to think what he might encounter, Alex took a run at the door. There was a creak but it didn't give. Rage filled him and he kicked at the lock, oblivious to the sounds from inside the flat. Each time he kicked it a jolt of pain shot up his leg. Terrified for Kathryn's safety, he took one more run at the door and felt something give in his shoulder as it flew open, the wood of the jamb splintering.

He steadied himself and stood, motionless, trying to accept the scene before him. Kathryn lay on the floor, her eyes closed, her face as white as alabaster. Staring up at him, crouched over papers scattered all over the floor, was a total stranger. The man stood, flung an arm in Alex's direction which unbalanced him and fled before Alex had a chance to realise what had happened.

'Kathryn, oh, Kathryn.' He bent over her, tears forming behind his eyes. To think he had been annoyed with her, had believed she was avoiding him again. He felt nothing when he put his ear against her mouth. A lump formed in his throat. He must not panic. He tried to find a pulse but wasn't sure if it was a faint movement or his own blood coursing swiftly through his veins which he could feel. He grabbed for the telephone and rang for an ambulance. Only when he had done so did he notice the red marks around her throat.

Kathryn did not know where she was, nor could she recall what had happened. There wasn't much light and there was something over her face. Someone was holding her hand. She seemed to be lying down but her body was being jogged.

'It's all right,' said a voice she did not recognise. 'You're on the way to hospital.'

'Thank God.'

Alex's voice this time. Kathryn closed her eyes. It was too confusing to think about.

When she opened them again she was in bright sunlight, on a stretcher, being carried into Wexham Park Hospital. At least she recognised that much. Alex was beside her, smiling, but not with his usual grin. He looked odd. 'The baby?' she asked.

'What?' Alex bent over her as he tried to keep up with the ambulance crew. She was delirious but it didn't matter, she was alive.

He had to wait while she was examined but a doctor came to tell him there was no permanent damage. 'Do you need to keep her in?'

'Not strictly, no, but if she feels she wants to stay overnight, I've no objections. We've a bed at the moment.'

'I'd rather take her home.'

'All right. But if you're in any doubt, get your GP out.'

Alex listened to the doctor's instructions and the signs to look for if there was any delayed shock. An hour later, having been thoroughly examined and given a cup of tea, Alex helped Kathryn out to the reception area and placed her in a chair while he organised a taxi. He did not let go of her hand until they were outside their broken front door.

John Pearce from number 4 was waiting for them. 'I saw this when I came home, and someone said there had been an ambulance. I hope I did the right thing, but I called the police. I think they've gone to the hospital to find you. I hope you don't think I've acted out of turn, but I've also arranged for an emergency carpenter to come and fix the door. I told him to wait until he hears from you, I didn't know if the police would want to take fingerprints.' John Pearce blushed at his forwardness.

'It was very kind of you. Would you ring him again and say he can come immediately? There won't be any fingerprints on the door – I myself broke it open.'

John Pearce did not know what to make of that, but went to do as he had been asked.

Alex led Kathryn to the settee. 'Would you rather be in bed?'

She shook her head then wished she hadn't. 'I'm fine.' Her voice was a croak. 'Alex, I know.'

'Shh. Don't try to talk.' Before he could say any more the telephone rang. 'Hello? Oh, Mrs Milton, no, I'm afraid she can't speak to you at the moment. Can I get her to ring you back?' But before he could say any more Kathryn had dragged herself off the settee and taken the phone from his hand.

'Harriet, it's me. I know.' And then she collapsed onto the floor again.

'Ring back later,' Alex said and slammed down the receiver. He carried Kathryn through to the bedroom and put her under the duvet, fully clothed. He felt her head and did everything the doctor had told him to do and, satisfied that she was only sleeping, went to pour himself a drink. Half an hour later the police arrived.

'I'm afraid we do need to speak to her,' Alex was told. 'Both your neighbour and the staff at the hospital said there had been an attack of some description.'

Alex gave his version of events although he did not mention what Kathryn had told Harriet Milton. Reluctantly, he woke her up and asked if she felt able to talk to the police. Two of them, a man and a woman, came into the bedroom and Alex listened, fascinated, as Kathryn told her story.

'Inspector Forbes, at Oxford,' she concluded. 'I think he'd like to know.'

'Stay there,' Alex said when they had gone. 'There's a man coming to fix the door. And then there's something I want to ask you.'

The repairs were completed but were only temporary. The carpenter said he would return on Monday and fit a new frame. Alex thanked him and made out a cheque. When he had gone Kathryn came from the bedroom, wearing a nightdress and a robe. The marks around her neck were no longer red but beginning to bruise.

'Kathryn—'

'Alex—' They both began speaking at once.

'You first,' Alex said.

'I was going to tell you tonight anyway. I'd planned for us to go out somewhere, but it doesn't matter. Look, do you think it would hurt if I had a drink? They haven't given me any tablets.' She was nervous of his reaction to her news.

'Wine?'

'Yes.'

When the glass was in her hand she could think of no other way to say it than to blurt it out. 'I'm going to have a baby.' There was a stunned silence. 'Alex?'

She had never seen such a mixture of emotions in one person's face. He ran both hands through his hair and shook his head as if he could not believe what he was hearing. Then he put his arms around her very gently. 'I'm so happy,' he whispered. 'You've no idea what this means to me.' When he looked up he saw that she was crying.

For most of the evening they discussed the events of the day and their future. Kathryn explained about Michael Jarvis and how she had been followed. She left out the part about the incident at the hotel car park. Alex had enough to contend with. He was unable to believe that she was prepared to give up her job, that she intended using her copious notes as the basis of a novel and that Giles had agreed to publish it if it was any good. He did see that she might be about to achieve another ambition, but it would be safer than the Megan Morris thing.

When the telephone rang they ignored it. Kathryn had re-set the answering machine and Harriet Milton left a message to say she would try again in the morning.

Later Alex told her about his own plans. He had been offered the chance of a large boat-yard in Devon. Its owner was retiring. Alex had worked out the finances and knew it was a viable proposition, a chance too good to miss, if Kathryn agreed. His main worry had been that she would want to accept a job with one of the nationals but now, with

310

the baby on the way and the novel to be written, he saw that it would work out perfectly. Kathryn seemed equally enthusiastic. 'It'll be better there for bringing up a child,' she said. She did not mention that it would also be a relief to be away from the people with whom she had become involved.

'I must see you, Kathryn. I really don't know what to say.' Harriet Milton was almost stuttering as she spoke through her tears. 'Jim came home the minute I told him. It's unbelievable and it's all down to you. Inspector Forbes let me know. When can I come down?'

'Any time this week. I shan't be going to work.'

'Forgive me, how thoughtless of me. Are you all right?'

Kathryn smiled. Harriet had every reason to be thoughtless now that she knew her daughter's murderer had been caught after all these years. 'Of course I am.'

They agreed to meet on Tuesday. Harriet was to come to the flat. By that time Kathryn hoped she would be able to make it to the shops. She had not expected to feel so weak.

During the morning Inspector Forbes had contacted her and although his tone was severe and he had chided her for being foolhardy, there was no doubting his pleasure that the case that had puzzled him for so long was finally closed.

He did not go into great detail because all evidence was *sub judice* until after the trial, but he hinted that Michael Jarvis, who had more or less confessed, had killed Sarah, believing her to be Jenny. This would all be explained in court. He promised he would contact her again when it was over.

On Monday morning Kathryn started writing. The book was to be entitled *The Game* but no one who had been involved in that original game would realise what it was based upon. She knew how very careful she had to be but, like Laura Tennyson, she believed she had enough imagination and talent to conceal the origins of the story.

When Harriet Milton arrived half an hour earlier than the arranged time, Kathryn opened the new door to her but did not have a chance to speak because she was hugged so tightly she could hardly breathe. There was none of the awkwardness Kathryn had feared and Harriet, although as thin as ever, seemed changed. There was a peacefulness about her and a calmness about her movements. She refused a drink and said she would prefer coffee. 'I'll never be able to thank you enough. I can't even find the words to tell you what I feel. All those years there were lingering doubts about whether it really was Sarah. It was the baby, you see. I felt so sure she would have confided.'

Hearing the word, Kathryn unconsciously touched her own stomach. Harriet did not miss the movement. She smiled in delight. 'You're not pregnant?'

Kathryn nodded. 'Everything seems to be happening at once. I haven't told my parents yet.' Or Helena, she added silently. There would be time enough for that. This was Harriet's moment.

'Do the others know – Giles and Laura and David – about Michael?'

Kathryn had not given it a thought. 'I haven't told them, and I don't suppose the police will have either. Of course, they might have read about it in the press.'

'Good heavens, you'll be famous again.'

Kathryn had not considered that aspect. So far only brief details had been given about an arrest having been made. Soon, she supposed, her part in it would come to light. 'Do you think I ought to tell them?'

'I do. It's only fair, especially if they've been worried about it.'

A real understatement, Kathryn thought. Harriet had no idea how it had affected them all.

'I want to do something for you, to repay you for what you've done for me. Is there anything you'd like? Anything at all? I'm not short of money and—'

Kathryn reached out and touched her hand. 'Harriet, seeing you happy is enough and you might not believe it, but I'm one of the few people who can say I've got everything I want.'

'I'll never forget you, Kathryn Brooks. Never.' Harriet stood and brushed the tears from her eyes. 'I hope you always have everything you want. You deserve it.'

She left then and Kathryn promised she would send her a copy of the book if and when it was published. 'Unless you think it would bring back too many memories?'

'No. I shall have only good memories now.'

When she had gone Alex arrived home unexpectedly. He said he was taking her out to lunch. 'I'm not an invalid, you know.' But she went to get a jacket anyway. It was a double celebration as Alex had agreed to purchase the boat-yard in Devon.

The following day Kathryn wrote a letter to John, Giles, David and Laura. In each she simply stated that Sarah's murderer had been arrested and that the trial would take place at some point in the future. She did not include her home address or telephone number and she did not hear from any of them, not even through the office.

On the Monday she went back to work, still a little weak but regaining her fitness. She gave a month's notice, explaining only to her immediate boss her reasons for doing so. Keith treated her with more respect than previously and she was able to tease him about what he had thought would be a wasted afternoon in the Thames Riviera Hotel. It was beyond belief how much that had led to.

Alex and Kathryn put their flat on the market and waited for a suitable buyer. There was no immediate hurry. The proprietor of the boat-yard was prepared to stay on until they were ready, and Jack had agreed to purchase the business Alex was leaving.

In December, two weeks before Christmas, Kathryn and Alex moved into their cottage in Devon. From most of the windows they could see the bay with its pale sands stretching around the headland. They were made welcome by their neighbours who, once their curiosity was satisfied, began to treat them as locals.

The cottage was nothing like the flat. It had more rooms, one of which had been converted into a study for Kathryn, another decorated in readiness as a nursery. As the number of pages Kathryn typed swelled, so did her stomach. By January the first draft of her novel was complete. There had still been no word from the Oxford set.

In mid-February, two days after she had posted the revised draft to Giles, Kathryn went into labour. She soon forgot all her doubts about whether he intended keeping his word that he would read it.

On a bitter afternoon as sleet battered the window panes, Daniel James was born in the nearby cottage hospital with Alex in attendance. Kathryn held him in her arms. A new life, and a new start for them all. For the first time in ages she thought about Laura and wondered if Daniel had come to take Marcia's place.

'Go on,' Kathryn said. 'Go and ring my parents. And Helena.' Helena had been thrilled when she heard Kathryn was pregnant, and had made her swear she could be god-mother to the child. She and Gerald had come down to the cottage for a long weekend, leaving the children with Joanna because Helena felt it would be too much for Kathryn to cope with. Soon they would be down again for the christening.

Kathryn was discharged after twenty-four hours but a midwife would be visiting. A week after her return home, just as she was beginning to settle into some sort of a routine, she received a letter from Laura. Hardly a letter, she thought, as she read it for the second time, still unsure what it meant. Laura had been unable to reach her at the old address, but Giles had said he knew where to find her and had promised to forward it. Kathryn smiled. The same old Giles, protecting his writers from the outside world. The smile changed to a frown. Would *she* ever be one of his writers? She placed Daniel in his cradle and sat down at her word-processor. If the first novel failed she would not give up. She was already plotting a second, completely different one.

'Everything seems extraordinarily quiet,' Alex commented when he came in from work. 'Is the son and heir asleep?'

'Yes. Here, read this.' She handed him Laura's letter. Alex frowned. He had hoped there would be no further contact with the people who had put Kathryn in so much danger.

'What does it mean?'

314

'You tell me.'

'You'll have to listen.'

'I know.' The discussion ended as a thin wail came from the nursery.

A week later Kathryn stopped working and went to the kitchen to switch on the radio. She had already tuned it in to the correct station. Daniel had been fed and was sleeping. In her letter Laura had said there was a programme on in which Kathryn might be interested, and she would consider it a personal favour if she listened to it.

The news came to an end and she heard the female presenter say, 'Our programme this afternoon centres on the effects of bereavement on writers and their work. My guests this afternoon are Devi Choudhry and Laura Tennyson who writes under the pseudonym of Megan Morris.' There were some biographical introductory remarks which Kathryn ignored. Devi Choudhry was interviewed first and admitted that most of what she wrote was based on her own experience, including the death of her parents whom she had not much liked. None of her statements seemed relevant to Laura's note.

'Laura,' the presenter continued, 'your mother's death was particularly painful for you. Just how close were you?'

'We were more like friends. I expect it was because I never knew my father. She was, I realise, the only constant in my life. You hear of people saying they were devoted to one or both parents, but our relationship went a great deal deeper than that.' There was a little laugh. 'For an author I'm not being very articulate. I think, perhaps, there aren't the words to describe how close we were.'

'And when she was dying you went to live with her?'

'Yes. I'd always wanted her to live with me but we felt it might be harmful. I think we'd have become too dependent upon each other and Marcia – my mother – felt I would not be able to cope when the inevitable happened. I nursed her at home. Not only did I owe her that, I loved every minute of it. I would do it again if I had to. You see, there was nothing she wouldn't do for me. Nothing. And there was a time when I believed she had done more than any human being could ask.'

Kathryn gasped. So that was it.

'Even when I was at Oxford we spoke every day on the telephone. I told her absolutely everything; she was my friend and confidante, far more than any of the other students.'

Kathryn knew what was happening. This interview was being conducted for her benefit alone. Laura was using it to explain things she had previously found incomprehensible.

'In common with Devi,' the presenter went on, 'your marriage also failed. Was this in any way to do with parental influence, do you think?'

'No. The man I loved had let me down. He had been seeing a friend of mine and she became pregnant. My marriage was doomed to failure because I could not love my husband as much as he deserved. Also, I couldn't have children and I didn't think it was fair to him. I had known that since I was a teenager and made no secret of it. I don't know, I just wanted him to find someone who would make him happier than I could.'

The interview came to an end. Kathryn went to check on Daniel then made a jug of coffee. Laura couldn't have children. Laura spoke to Marcia every day, told her everything that happened. Marcia would have known that John had let her down, and worse, Sarah was carrying his child, a child Laura would never be able to have. Poor Laura, she thought. She lived all that time believing Marcia might have killed Sarah to leave the path clear for her daughter. No wonder she had been scared, more scared than if she had been guilty herself, and it explained her secrecy. She was trying to protect Marcia. Kathryn hoped that they had had a chance to put things straight between them before she died. It was possible Marcia had also believed her daughter to be guilty. The outcome of Michael Jarvis's trial must have prompted this belated confession.

Kathryn was right. It seemed that Sarah had intended frightening her friends – had, as John suggested, taken things a stage too far. She had hidden in Jenny's place, intending to return to her college in a few days' time. She was reported as missing.

Michael knew that they met in the woods because he had

followed Jenny once or twice and then Jenny had stopped seeing him. Desperate to get her back, he had gone to her bed-sit to try to plead with her but she had refused to speak to him. One night he had followed her, or a person he had believed to be her, identifying the girl who came out of the door only by the long blonde hair and the scruffy Afghan jacket she wore. Walking behind her through the deserted, dreary street where she lived he had called out. She had hastened her footsteps then started running. Hurt and humiliated, he had run after her and caught her from behind. She had screamed and he had shouted back and when she tried to get away he had pulled out the knife he always carried in those days and stabbed her. Only then, as the body had twisted and slumped towards him did he realise it was that bitch Sarah, who must have been hiding at Jenny's place. So very relieved it wasn't Jenny he had stabbed her again then dragged her into an alley as he decided what to do. Coldbloodedly he had shoved her body behind some dustbins and gone back for his car. He had been living with his parents then but parked it in its usual spot in the street.

The following day he heard that the police had been searching the woods. They were aware that some sort of orgies took place there and that students went out there to take drugs. He had admitted he thought it was the perfect plan. He would dump Sarah's body there. It was unlikely they would search again, and if she was found it wouldn't matter – one of those toffee-nosed Oxford bastards would get the blame. He knew the sort of games they got up to, now he'd played one of his own. And Jenny was still alive, out there waiting for him.

But the body wasn't found for years and by then he considered himself safe. But when he had gone to see Jenny she told him she was leaving for London. Neither of them mentioned Sarah. Michael was devastated. He could not admit he knew she had been hiding with Jenny, and Jenny assumed that Sarah had decided not to go back to university. She knew about the search but did not believe anything had really happened. Later, she, too, assumed it was her friends who had been involved.

Michael had contained his rage when he learned of Jenny's plans. She wouldn't go, he was sure of that. Now that Sarah was missing she would lose interest in that crowd and come back to him. Then, without warning, she, too, had disappeared.

If Kathryn Brooks had not come on the scene he would have been home and dry. His confession had come when he was finally convinced that Jenny had been dead for ten years.

Alex had read the details of the case with as much interest as Kathryn. So much passion and so much misery for all those people. Could he, he wondered, kill for his wife? Remembering how he had felt when he had burst open the door of the flat, he suspected it was not beyond the bounds of possibility. Nothing and no one would be allowed to harm his family if he could prevent it.

When he arrived home he found Kathryn sitting in a chintz-covered armchair, Daniel in her arms, staring out of the window at the lights of the small harbour and those of craft moored in the bay. 'Kathryn?'

'Hello. I was thinking. So much seems to have happened.' She told him about the radio programme. 'She did it for me, you know. And this came today.' From beside her she picked up a thick white envelope which contained a printed card. 'Shall we go?'

Alex studied her, knowing she wanted him to make the decision, but it had to be her own. 'Do you want to?'

'I'm not sure. What about Daniel?'

'You could always ask Helena to have him for the day. Witney's no distance. We could stay somewhere on Friday night and drop him off in the morning.'

Kathryn kissed the top of Daniel's head as he stirred. Alex had removed the only real obstacle. Helena kept begging to be allowed to look after the baby and Clara could not keep her hands off him when they were together. 'Yes. I think I would like to go. It seems a fitting ending somehow.'

David's wedding had been arranged at short notice because a cancellation had cropped up and he and Vicky had decided they couldn't wait. At the bottom of the invitation he had scribbled a note to the effect that the others would be there. It was a thoughtful gesture, allowing her the chance to think up an excuse if she did not want to face them again.

On the following Friday night they drove up to Oxford and booked into the Randolph where Alex had made a reservation. In the morning, wearing a new outfit purchased for the occasion, Kathryn delivered Daniel to Helena who would undoubtedly spoil him. 'Have a good time,' she said. 'And don't hurry back.'

'Can I hold him?' Clara stepped forward.

Kathryn grinned and went out to where Alex was waiting in the car. 'They'll ruin him,' she told him.

The wedding was a success. Vicky looked stunning and was much more attractive once she had overcome her initial nervousness. After the ceremony they went to a restaurant. Kathryn was surprised to see that the only guests were themselves, the Oxford group and one or two members of Vicky's family, but David had wanted it that way. 'You see,' he said, when he stood up to make a speech once the meal was over, 'if you hadn't come along, Kathryn, none of us would be as happy as we are today. You have freed us all from fear. Therefore,' he looked around at the others, 'I propose a toast to Kathryn Brooks, journalist extraordinaire.' Everyone rose, including Alex who smiled at her proudly.

'Thank you,' she said, and reached over to touch Laura's hand. Fatigue still showed in her face but she had told Kathryn that she had begun writing again. Kathryn was aware that she must be comparing this ceremony with the one she had attended not so many months ago.

John was jovial and remained sober, and Giles and Ingrid were entertaining company. Once or twice Kathryn felt him watching her, but she made no mention of the manuscript she had sent him. It was not appropriate; the day belonged to David and Vicky.

'I toyed with the idea of asking Harriet Milton,' David said as they prepared to leave the restaurant, 'but I thought it might be too painful.'

'I think you made the right decision. It's better that she

has no more reminders. We must be off now. Thank you for inviting us, it was a lovely day.'

Kisses and handshakes exchanged, Alex put his arm across Kathryn's shoulders and led her to the car. 'It went well.'

'Yes, I'm glad. Alex, that is the end of it now. I don't want to see any of them again.'

'I know. But you did right by coming. Can't you see how grateful they are to you? Almost as much as Harriet, I'd imagine.'

She nodded. 'Maybe. Come on, I want to see our son.'

They stayed overnight with Helena and Gerald and drove back to Devon after breakfast. Kathryn was relieved to be home and couldn't wait to round the corner and see the bay spread out before them.

When she had put Daniel to bed Kathryn picked up the tuatara whose new home was on the window-sill and took it to the kitchen. 'What's that doing here?' Alex asked.

'I was thinking about getting rid of it. I was going to check with you first though.'

'What's brought this on?'

'I'm not sure. Seeing them all again, and thinking about what they've all been through. It reminds me every time I look at it.'

'I thought it was your talisman.'

'I don't know if I need one any more.'

'Sleep on it. I don't mind what you decide.'

Alex did not see the tuatara for several days but he did not question Kathryn. Then, on Thursday evening, he went upstairs to say goodnight to Daniel who was already in his cot by the time he came home and saw that Kathryn's study door was open. The Anglepoise lamp on her desk had been left on. He grinned. The tuatara was there, its leathery skin gleaming in the circle of light. As he approached it to switch off the lamp he saw that the reptile was propping something against the word-processor. It had plainly been left there for him to see. He picked up several sheets of paper which were stapled together. 'Kathryn! My God, Kathryn!' He ran down the stairs to where she was in the kitchen, standing by the sink already smiling. 'Kathryn, this is absolutely

320

wonderful!' He hugged her, lifting her off her feet as he did so. 'I am so very proud of you. You don't know *how* proud!'

In his hand was the signed contract for *The Game*.

Kathryn laughed. Now she understood Helena better. A career *could* be combined with a family and she had been wrong, she had gained, rather than lost by having Daniel although she was still not sure whether he had been conceived by accident or whether, subconsciously, during the time she and Alex were settling their differences, she had come to a decision. Either way, it did not matter now. She struggled out of Alex's grasp. 'Champagne,' she said. 'I bought some today. We'll drink to my next novel.'

Alex nodded, grinning. There would be no stopping her now.

now available in paperback . . .

STANDING ALONE
Anne Melville

One moment of motorway madness is about to alter the lives of four women for ever.

Helen is bored in her marriage and plans little "adventures" to spice up her life. Madge longs to assert her independence and escape her husband's anxious kindness. Penny, though passionately in love with her partner, misses the bustle of the advertising agency where she used to work. And Candida, recently graduated from Oxford, ambitious and with a baby son to support, has important decisions to make about her future.

None of these women has ever met Jarvis Elliott. But his sudden illness triggers a train of events which brings Helen, Madge, Penny and Candida together even while each is forced to build an entirely new life.

0 7499 3041 1   £5.99

HER MOTHER'S SINS

Emma Quincey

A haunting novel of romance and suspense...

"What have I done?" Catherine cried. "How have I sinned? Tell me what I have done that was so wicked it made my father hate me? Why have I been kept a prisoner in this house?"

Catherine Benedict is brought up with every material comfort she could wish for but it is cold comfort when her father appears to blame her for her mother's tragic early death. Only when Catherine openly defies him by refusing to marry his partner's son, Hal Cartwright, does Samuel, in his rage, let slip something of the truth: that it was not love he felt for his wife, but hatred.

Catherine has always sensed her mother's presence in the gloomy house. Now she knows she must escape her father's control for the sake of her sanity, perhaps her life. And the only one who can help her is Hal Cartwright...

Emma Quincey weaves a web of jealousy, lies and betrayal that will hold you in its spell...

0 7499 3032 3 £5.99

now available in paperback . . .

PROMISES TO KEEP
Anne Griffiths

War drove them apart, but love would reunite them

Misha Martin is half-English, half-French and madly in love with Philippe Constantin. He sees the sixteen-year-old as a little sister, not a lover, and her heartbreak is complete when Philippe agrees with her parents that Paris in 1939 is no longer a safe place for Misha. Packed off to stay with her English cousins, Misha feels exiled and alone.

Seizing her first opportunity to return to France, she finds her beloved city in a mood of defiant gaiety as the Germans advance towards Paris. Despite danger, hunger and fear Misha's heart lifts as she throws herself into the fight against the invaders: for she is home.

And she promises herself that Philippe will find a woman, not a child, waiting for his return . . .

Through occupation, resistance and retreat, **Promises to Keep** is a poignant story of separation, heartache and love.

0 7499 3025 X   £5.99

The very best of Piatkus fiction is now available in paperback as well as hardcover. Piatkus paperbacks, where *every* book is special.

The prices shown above were correct at the time of going to press. However, Piatkus Books reserve the right to show new retail prices on covers which may differ from those previously advertised in the text or elsewhere.

Piatkus Books will be available from your bookshop or newsagent, or can be ordered from the following address:

Piatkus Paperbacks, PO Box 11, Falmouth, TR10 9EN

Alternatively you can fax your order to this address on 01326 374 888 or e-mail us at books @barni.avel.co.uk.

Payments can be made as follows: Sterling cheque, Eurocheque, postal order (payable to Piatkus Books) or by credit cards, Visa/ Mastercard. Do not send cash or currency. UK and B.F.P.O. customers allow £1.00 postage and packing for the first book, 50p for the second and 30p for each additional book ordered to a maximum charge of £3.00 (7 books plus).

Overseas customers, including Eire, allow £2.00 for postage and packing for the first book, plus £1.00 for the second and 50p for each subsequent title ordered.

NAME (block letters) _____

ADDRESS _____

I enclose my remittance for £ _____

I wish to pay by Visa / Mastercard   Expiry Date: _____

| | | | | | | | | | | | | | | | | | |